I0831818

BRAINSTORM

by
Gordon A Kessler

Brainstorm

a thriller novel

by
Gordon A. Kessler

Gordon@GordonKessler.com

ISBN: 978-0-9831905-2-3

What New York Times Best Selling Authors are saying about *Brainstorm*:

James Rollins, NY Times bestselling author of *Black Order*, *Sandstorm* and *Map of Bones* as well as many others, says: "Gordon A. Kessler's *Brainstorm* is a wild ride into the reality of human consciousness, forcing us to question who we are and our place in the universe. It's also a kick-ass adventure story that will have you thrumming through the pages well into the night. Its blend of topical research, cutting-edge weaponry, and current political tension is handled with stunning effect."

Douglas Preston, NY Times bestselling author of *The Codex*, and co-author of *Relic* and *Book of the Dead* as well as many more says *Brainstorm*: "...is as exciting and fast-paced as a thrill ride on a dive bomber, a maelstrom of action, violence, murder and mayhem, way too much fun to put down once you're hooked. It is also frighteningly believable, based on an actual black CIA program known as Project Stargate. Kessler is a former US Marine parachutist, recon scout, and Super Squad team leader and he really knows his stuff. An outstanding novel."

Preface

The *Star Gate*, *Grille Flame*, *Bluebird* and *MK-ULTRA* projects, as well as devices like the "stemoceiver," mentioned in the following work of fiction are not in the least bit fictitious and do not refer to Hollywood movies or to popular cable TV series.

During the early days of the Cold War, the U.S. Government, through the newly formed CIA, actually experimented on its own unknowing citizens with mind altering drugs, radiation, "narco-hypnosis" and electroconvulsive therapy in order to keep up with the technology being developed by its Cold War nemeses. They endeavored to create unwitting assassins that would be infallible against interrogation—as revealed by the U.S. Congress's Church Committee and the Rockefeller Commission.

Then, beginning in the sixties and early seventies, a number of the major world powers shifted focus away from the *control* of the mind and began conducting mind-*power* studies. During the latter days of the Cold War, the U.S. Government furtively threw its hat into the paranormal ring. For the next twenty years, the Central Intelligence Agency, the Defense Intelligence Agency and the U.S. Army conducted experiments in remote viewing and other psychic phenomena through the *Star Gate* and *Grille Flame* projects as well as others under various code names. They reported moderate success, likely relying much more on the information gathered through their remote-viewing teams than is recorded.

Through these gifted, psychically trained voyeurs of space and time came the opportunity to look into the past, the present and even into the future. Originally considered only slightly better than a coin-flip, their accuracy improved dramatically over the life of the project. The remote viewers became valued consultants, giving strategic advice and foretelling the outcomes of conflicts in Grenada and Panama as well as Operation Desert Storm and many other actions, both made public and kept covert.

Much of the nonlethal weaponry you will read about also exists. A few of the devices and substances mentioned herein are in prototype, experimental or yet in concept, but most are in use in at least limited amounts today by the U.S. military and by select local law enforcement agencies.

As well, many of the defensive measures described are actually being used in the field today and, although active and reactive camouflage is primarily in concept or experimental, it is expected to be fully developed and in wide use by the military in the very near future.

According to Albert Einstein: "A human being is part of a whole, called by us the Universe, a part limited in time and space. He experiences himself, his thoughts and feelings, as something separated from the rest as a kind of optical delusion of his consciousness. This delusion is a kind of prison for us.... Our task must be to free ourselves from this prison...."

Prologue

"It's time," Major Lionel Jackson said and patted the back of Sunny McMaster's hand. In the red night lighting inside their armored vehicle, her slender ivory hand seemed to glow, appearing remarkably delicate in his dark palm. But he knew it wasn't fragile. "Ready?"

"God, yes," she said, her voice determined and confident.

Jackson released Sunny's hand, then turned to the forward viewfinder and pulled down the microphone attached to his helmet. "Lion Team, move out," he said evenly, and the driver in front of Jackson cocked his head back and repeated the order over his shoulder.

The mission to rescue Sunny's husband and several dozen other missing elite citizens thought to be held in Gold Rush, Colorado, began under presidential directive —regardless that the latest reconnaissance reports indicated it was a ghost town.

Their six Stryker vehicles set out quickly and without faltering like dark, single-minded ants on a sugar trail, churning down the gravel roadway leading to the small town ten miles away. A blue-white full moon hugged the ridge behind their boulder-littered staging area, its frosty radiance washing over the rocky cliff sides and the snaking passage before them.

Inside the leading personnel carrier, the man known to his military peers as the *Black Lion* once again turned in his seat toward Sunny. Major Jackson never dreamed he'd see this woman dressed in black fatigues and combat boots, her fiery-red hair pinned back and hidden under a helmet. What she'd worn the first time they met in Maui was quite different—a wedding dress. Jackson had been best man, and the ceremony was in his garden. That was fifteen years ago.

Sunny asked, "How 'bout you, Jax? You ready?"

He knew she meant emotionally, not militarily. As he pushed his small microphone out of the way, he returned a thin smile. "We're going to find Dan, Sunny," he said. "I'm sure of it. We're going to find him, and he's going to be . . ." He hesitated, knowing *okay* or even *alive* was a promise he couldn't keep. Instead, he simply repeated, "We're going to find him."

His words seemed to cause a tear to trickle from her eyes, and he grimaced, realizing she'd understood his indecisive pause.

Sunny looked away and wiped the moisture from her cheek. When she turned back with her jaw clenched, her eyes set hard on Jackson. Through the crimson glow inside the armored vehicle, she stared—face stone-like and expressionless—and Jackson did his best to hide his anxiety. She seemed to look through him, gazing at something just out of reach in the past. Her tears were gone, any redness in her eyes imperceptible in the red night lighting. In her face was a grittiness Jackson had seen in only a handful of men, the ones sure to become great soldiers. But the major wanted no part in making the beautiful redhead before him into a Kevlar-tough warrior. He wished he had another choice, but today Sunny could play an important role in bringing in her husband and saving dozens of lives.

People were disappearing. Scientists, surgeons and men and women of *special* abilities were vanishing from all over the world, particularly from the United States. Jackson hoped that at least one of those presumed abducted, Daniel McMaster, hadn't become a traitor—that he wouldn't have to kill his best friend.

Behind them in the cramped steel carrier, eight of Major Jackson's soldiers sat nearly motionless, breathing lightly through parted lips, their faces blank. Occasionally, the rough road jostled them—their shoulders meeting forcibly, helmets clacking together, assault rifles tapping. But they showed no sign of discomfort. They were ready—for hell, for death, for anything, and that was what they were to expect today.

After nearly twenty minutes of driving, the digital mission clock on the console in front of the major changed to 05:42 a.m., and he took an anxious breath. Once again, he leaned into the forward-looking periscope of the commander's cupola as an abandoned guard shack and barricade came into view several hundred yards ahead. After turning back to his men, he held up two fingers and called out only loud enough to be heard, "Two minutes."

The next one hundred and twenty seconds elapsed too slowly—and too quickly. Jackson had hoped he'd never have to see another of his men die—prayed this rescue operation would unfold quickly and without casualties. But he didn't expect his prayer to be answered.

At thirty seconds before zero hour, the sun crested a saddle in the butte. Its brilliant rays illuminated the numerous periscope viewfinders surrounding the driver and commander's cupolas, overpowering the red night lighting. When Jackson turned the lock above him and threw back the hatch, the inside of their vehicle brightened like an operating room.

After a sideways glance at Sunny, he stood up in the opening, brought his high-power Bushnell rangefinder binoculars up from his chest and placed his elbows on the steel roof of the moving vehicle. Nestled below a cobalt-blue ridge a half mile in front of them was Gold Rush.

Major Jackson's breathing and pulse quickened, and his eyes grew wide as he repositioned the microphone. While holding onto the hatchway coaming, he commanded, "Eagle and Lion, Eagle and Lion—Go, go, go!"

Dampened by thrumming helicopter rotors, the instant reply came over his headset. "Eagle Force 'Go!' Roger, Black Lion."

Again, the young sergeant driving Jackson's vehicle acknowledged over his shoulder, "Roger, 'Go,' Lion!"

The six armored vehicles accelerated, lunging from

cruising speed to an all-out sprint. They crashed through the barricade and crushed the vacant guard shack, leaving it as a pile of loose, splintered boards.

In the following seconds, Apache helicopter gunships rose above the spruce trees and jagged ridges surrounding the small town. They hovered there as vigilant sentries, buffeting the evergreen boughs and raising dust along the crags. The four gunships carried enough firepower to level the entire town; however, that wasn't an option with hundreds of innocents likely to be in the mix.

As the troop carriers sped closer, three much larger helicopters roared overhead, their beating rotors saturating the air like the war drums of a thousand angry warriors. Their bellies full of heavily armed and anxious young soldiers in black body armor, these Pave Low IV rotorcraft dashed toward the middle of the village, then paused abruptly fifty feet above the business district.

After rounding a slight curve, the major reached inside and tapped his driver's shoulder, indicating to Staff Sergeant Chambers to apply the brakes. The wheels of the five vehicles behind them screeched lightly, their engines quieting to a low hum as they pulled to the shoulder within clear sight of the mountainside town.

In the same instant that the debarkation ramps on the back of the armored vehicles fell open, the soldiers spilled out and scrambled for cover along the roadway. With paternal care, Major Jackson visually inspected each of his men's position as he climbed from the commander's hatch and dropped to the ground. Satisfied his soldiers had taken sufficient cover, he took up his binoculars and scanned the area before them.

They'd met no opposition thus far, which was surprising. The town appeared totally lifeless, seeming to confirm the earlier reconnaissance reports that Jackson had discounted as erroneous. Still, he held his breath as he watched the operation through swirling dust clouds whipped up by the big helicopters' rotor blades—the proverbial *all hell could erupt at any time* dominating his thoughts.

In the town, the major's airborne element fast-roped from the choppers and onto the roofs and streets, then rushed to safe vantage points. Jackson watched until the emptied helicopters banked in unison and sped back toward the safety of the ridge.

Anticipation electrified the air. Tension and angst seemed tangible. But as Major Jackson watched the insertion, time passed monotonously, uneventfully, and the minutes ticked by allowing dark despair to settle in, frustration laying heavily against him like some kind of medieval torture device.

Jackson swung his glasses in the direction of the homes spread along the wooded mountainside. But he saw no lights from the houses. He spied no armed adversaries, no curious citizens on the sidewalks, in any of the yards or even peeking from behind their doors while still in their bathrobes. No cars drove on the streets or were parked in the narrow, gravel driveways. No morning newspapers lay on the porches—not even a single dog barked at their intrusion.

The houses were old, saltbox style, the newest of which had most likely been built in the thirties and forties. Some were obviously dilapidated, gaping holes in their weathered and warped roofs, shutters hanging at odd angles from graying wood lap siding, windows busted. Tall, brown weeds had overgrown the small yards. Garages, many leaning awkwardly from years of wind abuse and snow load, rested wearily aside a few of the homes, but they were too narrow to accommodate anything more modern than Model Ts.

Jackson's breathing slowed and deepened with dread. If today's mission failed, there'd be little hope of finding Dan McMaster. Sunny would be devastated.

Less than ten minutes passed before a half-dozen of the hostage rescue squads returned to the center of town, trotting in from the deserted residential area. Meanwhile, Jackson watched through his binoculars as several of his men stepped from the buildings and shops along the main drag and into the open. One man slung his assault rifle over his shoulder and moved out from the rest. He looked toward Jackson and the column of Stryker armored vehicles on the road five hundred yards away and shrugged his shoulders.

A voice crackled in the major's radio headset that he recognized as Lieutenant Carpenter's. "Eagle Blue Team to Black Lion, come in."

Major Jackson acknowledged, "Black Lion. Go ahead, Eagle Blue."

"Sir, we've finished sweeping. No one's home. Thick dust on everything. Hasn't been anyone here in years."

The major watched as Carpenter glanced up the street at his returning comrades.

A different voice came over the headset. "Sergeant Dixon, sir. Eagle Red didn't have any luck, either."

"Roger," the major said into his microphone. "Wrap it up, Eagle." He turned with a frown as Sunny dropped from the short hood of their armored vehicle. She stepped next to him, and he handed her the binoculars. "Not one bastard soul in the whole damn town."

"How?" Sunny's voice now sounded desperate. "They *must* be here." She focused the binoculars, scanning the empty, dust-hazed streets. After a moment, she said, "It's like a ghost town, an old movie set. Where else can they be, Dan and the others—an entire town, hundreds of people? They couldn't have just vanished." She pulled the binoculars away from her face, turned to Jackson and raised her voice in frustration. "It's been *two years*, Jax. Where is he?"

Jax looked down at her and narrowed his eyes in consternation. "There is another possibility. However, it's nearly too incredible to believe."

"Wait a minute!" Sunny slammed the side of her fist against the thick steel fender. "This isn't going to be more of the Defense Intelligence Agency's hocus pocus, is it?"

"Easy, Sunny. Don't forget who your friends are." He gave her what he hoped was a reassuring and sympathetic smile, but he doubted it was. "There are some other aspects to this thing we were reluctant to believe. Now it looks as though we have to consider them. For the most part, our intel is probably correct. But there is, let's say . . . a twist."

"A *twist*?" Sunny threw her helmet to the ground, and it spun briefly at Jackson's feet. She shook her head, and her hair fell over her shoulders. "You'd better do some quick explaining, or it'll be *me* who does the twisting when I spill my guts to the media." Her hands went to her hips, and she continued, "And don't think I won't do it. How do I explain to my daughter that her daddy isn't coming home, that I still don't know where he is, that he's just up and disappeared? How do I convince her that wherever he is, he still loves her?" She shook her head again. "A *twist*! What caliber of remote viewers does the Department of Defense have working for them these days? 'High probability,' they said. They told you where to look, bragged about their accuracy. Bullshit! They were wrong."

Jackson nodded. "Maybe." He looked to Staff Sergeant Chambers, who watched the operation from the driver's hatch of their vehicle. "Chambers, hand me my case, please."

As the young sergeant ducked back inside, Sunny's eyes pooled, and she spoke through her gritted teeth. "What now? They're underground? They're invisible? They've been changed into cockroaches?"

Jackson placed his hand gently on the side of her shoulder. He tried to look her in the eyes, but she glared past him, instead seeming to focus on a point in the small town.

Finally, she took a deep breath and leaned back against the Stryker vehicle. Her voice had softened. "I know, Jax. We go back a long way." After a silent moment, she met his gaze and her voice elevated once again. "But you'd better understand this: I'm not going to believe any more crap—from the U.S. government *or* from you. Be straight with me. I want to know the truth—everything."

It was the stress talking, not Sunny, Jackson reminded himself. He'd known this woman and had been best friends with her husband for such a long time. Her mistrust cut like a serrated bayonet, but how could he blame her?

He spoke slowly, emphasizing his sincerity. "Sunny, our remote viewers gave us two scenarios. We'd hoped this venue was the correct one. The RVs' majority opinion, five of six, said this was the most likely locale. The minority opinion had a much more complicated and challenging scenario—a different Gold Rush. If that single RV is correct, the scope of this plot is incredible. Dozens of people we thought were dead for years, even decades, might still be alive. But for this new mission, the difficulty level will be daunting, and I'm sure the government won't be willing to risk it."

Sunny shook her head again. "You're saying it's hopeless?"

"No. I'm only a major, Sunny, but I've made a lot of contacts over the past twenty years. A whole bunch of people owe me. I've called in all my markers for this one. We have equipment already staged at the alternate objective and we will be ready to go as soon as we get there." He paused, knowing what he was about to say would give her a glint of hope. "Since we can't count on our own government footing the bill or authorizing our mission, Gunny Sampson is backing us with money and logistics."

Sunny's face only hinted a reminiscent smile. Jax knew that several years had passed since she'd seen their friend *The Gunny*.

Staff Sergeant Chambers reemerged arm first from the driver's hatchway, his hand gripping the handle of a thin, black attaché case. "Sir."

Jackson took it and glanced into the redhead's vibrant green eyes. "Dan's like a brother to me, Sunny, you know that. And I owe him—I owe him my life. I'll search in every corner of this Earth for him, if that's what it takes—spend each hour of every waking day. I promise you that I *will* find Daniel, or I'll die trying."

He supported the case against the sloped front of the armored vehicle and opened it. As he took out an inch-thick file folder and handed it to her, he said, "I have some satellite photos I'd like you to see."

Chapter 1—*Gold Rush, Three Days Later*

I had no idea I would begin a killing spree on such a lovely morning. I felt animosity for no one. I willed no one dead.

My name is Robert Weller. I'm the type of guy who will trap a spider in the shower, take it out to the bushes in the middle of the night and bid it farewell and happy hunting. But early on this Monday morning a change seemed to come over my life as subtle and lethal as a glass of Chardonnay laced with arsenic.

I was dreaming. I saw myself sitting in a large room, white and cold. It smelled of antiseptic. In the middle of the room was a table with a large brown envelope propped up on it. I sat to one side in a hard oak chair. On the opposite side of the room, behind a small, gray-metal desk, sat a woman in a U.S. Army uniform. Her name was Lieutenant Vanzandtz, and she appeared to be in her early thirties. Her mismatched chair was thick and upholstered in burgundy leather or more likely cheap Naugahyde.

In this dream, I was shirtless and covered in goose bumps. I didn't know what the cathode-ray tube beside me monitored, nor did I care. That was their business. I was getting three hundred bucks. The jumping green lines and the constant blips from the machine *were* becoming annoying, however. The monitor's leads were stuck to my temples and to well-shaven areas on the base of my head and on my chest.

I closed my eyes but didn't concentrate on the envelope as the lieutenant had just instructed. Instead, I thought of her. She had yet to smile. I guessed she'd have a pleasant smile if she'd ever try. But she just sat behind her desk, her face stern, mouth small and tight. I considered how a broad smile on her narrow face would've nicely balanced out her large-framed glasses and the bun of walnut hair on top of her head.

My focus changed to the contents of the envelope. Somewhere behind my eyes a three-dimensional image formed. I saw blue-green water, deep but calm, near a beach with sand as white and fine as table salt. In the water, a white sailing yacht, probably eighty feet, floated peacefully with three large sails billowing in a light breeze. The name *Chairman* was scrolled in blue across the leisure vessel's stern. To the left of the boat, the sun posed like a huge tangerine ball drifting in the ocean, and above, the clouds were wispy ghosts painted coral by the sun's last rays.

With eyes still closed, I turned my attention to a thick file folder in front of the lieutenant. Another vision came clear, the file's jacket. Project: *Grill Flame*, it said in large, stamped-on letters. On its index tab was a name I didn't recognize—*Daniel McMaster*. I focused on the heading of the first page. *Remote Viewer Evaluation*, it said. A list followed with all of the boxes farthest to the left checked under the *Excellent* column. Under *Notes* was written: *Top candidate. Subject excels in all measured areas*. Someone's entire life put down in letters and numbers, I thought, and I got the distinct impression that this man's file, this Daniel McMaster, was being used for comparison—some sort of watermark, the bar everyone else should strive to reach.

I told the lieutenant what I saw in the thin package on which she had requested my attention, but I said nothing of what I'd discovered in the file folder, and I opened my eyes.

She stood and walked leisurely toward the monitoring equipment next to me. As she stepped past the table, she plucked the envelope from it. After taking a moment to check the equipment, she turned to me and pulled out a line drawing on a standard, letter-size sheet of paper.

Drawn in minimalistic pencil sketch was a scene

exactly as I'd described, sans color and detail, except the sun was setting to the *right* of the boat.

"Are you dyslexic?" the lieutenant asked, and she finally smiled. Her teeth were crooked.

"No," I said, "you had the drawing turned around."

* * *

Seeming more like a distant memory than a dream, the vision faded as the scent of fruity lotion and perfumed powder roused me to consciousness.

I didn't open my eyes, yet I knew what I'd find when I did—my wife Michelle sitting naked at her make-up table across the room.

It brought a smile to my face, and I reached for my glasses on the night table. When I looked, it was as I'd envisioned—Michelle sitting on her snow-white bathrobe like a Matisse painting I'd seen. I couldn't remember where. There sat my childhood and high school sweetheart, the girl of my dreams, the mother of my son—the sweetest, most generous woman I knew.

I must be strong for her today—be positive, *for her*. She had been through so much. This could be the day that would turn our lives around—that might bring Michelle out of the terrible slump of depression she'd succumbed to since the accident. Late this afternoon, we would find out whether or not our five-year-old son would ever be able to walk again—and we would finally be able to bring him home from the hospital after over six months of surgery and analysis.

While inhaling the sweet potpourri of aromas, I sat up to enjoy the pleasantness for a long moment, and I smiled at my thoughts and the image before me. I inspected Michelle's backside: the gentle curves, the soft and subtle beads of her spine—and I noticed the droplets of water her bath towel hadn't reached in the small of her back. In a nearly entranced state, I observed the faint motion of her back and shoulder muscles as she pulled an ivory brush through her coal-black hair. Then I watched her massage peach-scented body oil into the silky, cinnamon skin of her shoulders, arms, breasts, stomach and legs. My little China doll, I thought, and my smile grew into a grin.

Then, at precisely 6:42 a.m., according to the Sony digital alarm clock on the nightstand nearby, I slipped out of bed wearing nothing but a pair of silk boxers. A slight dizziness came over me, forcing me to hang onto the bedpost for balance.

Easy, Superman, a voice told me.

I paused while considering the voice and then quickly glanced around the room. Seeing only Michelle, I was momentarily perplexed. Slowly, I realized the voice wasn't totally unfamiliar—that it must have been my own thoughts. But I couldn't remember my thoughts coming so audibly, so distinctly. I immediately shrugged it off, supposing everyone heard voices at some time or another—the good spirit, bad spirit sort of thing. Perhaps mine was more of an alter ego, safely buried deep in my subconscious but there to give caution and warning whether I needed it or not.

With the light-headedness easing some, I felt stiffness in the side of my neck and rubbed it while recalling the fall I'd taken on Friday morning in the shower. I remembered the day and night long stay I'd been forced to make in the same hospital as my son. I thought of the intense, throbbing headache I'd had and the lump low on the back of my head, which I now touched gingerly. It was still tender.

My muscles were weak and tight, more so than I thought three days of recuperative rest should have caused. While doing a few tentative and simple stretches to limber up, I discovered something else a little odd—my underwear: purple silk boxers covered in pink hearts—*hmmm*.

My alter-ego voice surprised me again. Jeez, Superman! Where the hell did you get those sissy-assed things?

I made a cursory scan of the room for a second time with the same result—no one standing behind the curtain, nobody lurking beneath the bed. The voice definitely seemed to originate inside my skull as if George Lucas himself had wired Dolby® Surround Sound® to tiny speakers and bolted them to the inside of my cranium.

Deciding it was better than conversing with *Harvey*, the imaginary talking rabbit from that old Jimmy Stewart movie, I gazed at my shorts to answer my ostensible entity within. But I couldn't remember where I'd gotten the suspect sleepwear. A Valentine's Day present, I surmised. Probably stuffed into one of those *I [Heart] You* coffee mugs with a clutch of colorful balloons tied to the handle.

Yeah, uh-huh, sure.

I let the briefs fall to my ankles and then kicked them into an open clothes hamper in the corner next to the bathroom doorway.

Michelle glanced over her shoulder with an ever-so-slight smile. I answered it with a wink. Then I went to her and, as I did, her large dark eyes followed me through the mirror. She looked me over, and it did my heart good to find the almost imperceptible smile remaining on her lips indicating pleasure in what she saw. When I reached her, I pressed my nude body against hers and ran my hand gently up and down the full length of her backbone. Her eyelids heavy and nostrils flaring, she responded by baring the side of her neck, giving me all the room I needed to kiss it, and I lingered there.

God, I love this woman, these words coming to my thoughts so naturally as if whispered into my ear. A collage of memories from before the accident swam in my head: of Michelle, her brilliant smile, her laughing Asian eyes, her beautiful lips, the first time we kissed when we were still preteen, the night of the prom when she came ambling down the steps wearing a beautiful light-blue dress, the evening we went skinny dipping—her naked and shivering in a cold mountain pool—and then we made love for the first time.

That had been nearly twenty years ago, now. She'd always been so beautiful, so perfect. I couldn't stop kissing her tender skin.

She stroked my face with her slim fingers. "Rob-bert!" She giggled softly. Her voice was as tiny, yet as lively as she was. "Didn't you get enough last night?"

I knew her levity would be brief—it seemed she would only allow short asides from the guilt that haunted her daily—so I took advantage of the moment. My arousal grew as I gave her my best Boris Karloff, Frankenstein-monster groan and mouthed her flesh like a man insane with passion.

"Silly!" she squeaked with laughter. "You'll be late." She raised her shoulder and squirmed away, and her humor stole back into the place guilt kept it prisoner. "How's the head?"

I figured I wasn't getting anywhere—that I had opened the door to her old self for as long and as wide as it would go, and it had slammed back shut. Besides, she was right. I didn't have the luxury of idle time this morning. So I readjusted my eyeglasses and left a parting love peck on the hollow of her neck.

After clearing the sleep from my throat, I kept my lips close together to hold in the morning breath and said hoarsely, "Not bad, really." My throat was dry and scratchy. It felt as though I hadn't spoken in days.

"Good. Now use the handholds in the shower, okay, Robert?"

I frowned at her. She was treating me like a klutz.

"And you're not going to overdo it today, right?"

I grunted. What little sexual stimulation that had blossomed, diminished quickly.

"Need help?"

I shook my head.

"Your breakfast will be ready by the time you're dressed."

I grunted again and found myself staring at her shoulder.

My Harvey wannabe said, *Something's different. Something's changed*.

Having such a vocal inner voice wasn't normal—now, I was sure. However, the voice was correct.

I asked, "Didn't you use to have a mole there, Mish?"

"Where?"

I pointed to the top of Michelle's right shoulder. "I always thought it was sexy. Did you have it removed or something?"

She looked up at me, and the modest smile returned briefly. "No, dear. You must be thinking of one of your *other* girls." She rapped me on the fingers with the back of her brush, and the surprise stung.

"Ouch!" I said. I took her by the jaw tenderly, as if embracing a rare and delicate moth, and I gave her a long kiss.

I'm tellin' ya, there's something different here.

When we parted, we gazed into each other's eyes, and I said, "You're the only one for me, darling."

As I departed, she replied, "Of course I am."

Mush-shee!

In the bathroom, I placed my eyewear on the vanity. After relieving myself of a night's build-up of fluids, I turned on the shower and adjusted the water to a comfortable warmth. I stepped through the new tempered-glass enclosure and shut it, then found a bar of Dial soap in the caddy.

Look closer, Superman.

Still not used to the strangeness of having this inner voice, my eyes searched even the shower stall for its source. But then I took the soap bar from the caddy and briefly inspected it. Edges sharp, it was dry—brand new, fresh out of the wrapper. And glancing around me, I noticed the shower door had no water on it, no droplets, no little streams. But Michelle had just taken a shower. Her back was still wet.

I noted the small squeegee stuck to a suction-cup hook on the wall and then frowned, thinking of the new, paranoid personality inside my skull. Ease up a little, I told my alter ego. She'd obviously finished the old bar of soap and replaced it with a new one. And she'd squeegeed the stall after showering to keep down the lime and scum buildup.

My uninvited persona was becoming irritating. And what was this *Superman* thing? I didn't care for the nickname and certainly didn't plan to live up to it. I mentally pictured a switch on a man-sized, white rabbit and turned *my* version of Harvey off. Yet, I was sure he'd be back.

As I replaced the soap, I spotted a small piece of tissue paper lying in the holder, and it appeared to have writing on it. It had been under the soap bar, possibly stuck to it when Michelle put it there. I grinned. Perhaps it was a little love note.

When I picked up the tissue and held it close to read without my glasses, I discovered it *was* a note, but I didn't recognize the printing as Michelle's. The letters were irregular, almost scribbled. The paper was torn in several places as if the writer had been in a great hurry. It said, *Everything you know is lies. Trust not in what you hear or see, but solely in your emotions—within them is the only real truth. Be ready. They will come for you soon. Destroy this immediately.*

As I stepped back in amazement, the shower spray hit the tissue paper in my hand. The note melted instantly into a small mass, and I dropped it, disappointed I hadn't gotten a chance to examine the message further.

Some sort of a hoax? Who could've left it? When? Was it meant for Michelle? But she should have seen it. I could rationalize nothing else except that there was an intruder hiding inside our house.

Chapter 2

In wooded seclusion, Major Jackson, Staff Sergeant Chambers and Lieutenant Carpenter knelt next to two dune-buggy-like desert patrol vehicles. The *DPV*s were heavily armed, both with fifty-caliber machineguns in back and with modified grenade launchers in front of the passenger's seats. Eavesdropping on all of the town's communications, the lieutenant wore headphones attached by a long lead to a notebook computer and a small satellite dish—the SatCom unit. Fifty feet in front of the men stood the protective barrier surrounding Gold Rush—a twelve-foot, electrified, chain-link fence topped with razor-sharp concertina wire.

"Jet lag, sir?" Lieutenant Carpenter asked.

Jax looked to the lieutenant and then followed his gaze. Sunny McMaster sat in the farthest vehicle, her head against the headrest on the passenger's side, her eyes closed. This time she wore a green sweat suit and running shoes, which were more suited to her new mission than the military attire she'd worn three days earlier.

But something was wrong. Sunny's head shook violently, still against the headrest.

Jax sensed a problem more serious than jet lag, but he didn't know what. He stood, and the lieutenant took off his headphones. Both men hustled to her.

Jax gently held Sunny's head still, but her closed eyes raced from side to side as if in REM sleep.

"Convulsions, sir?" Carpenter asked. "Some kind of

epilepsy?"

Jax frowned. He touched the side of Sunny's face. It was cool and clammy. "I don't know." He patted her cheek gently. "Sunny. Sunny, wake up." He slapped her a little harder. "Wake up, Sunny!"

Her eyelids opened, but her eyes rolled back in her head. Her body lurched, muscles and limbs stiff and tense.

Jax shook her shoulders. "Jesus, Sunny, what's wrong?"

Her eyes finally centered and her body relaxed. She blinked and shook her head, then leaned forward and placed her hand on her forehead.

"You okay, Sunny?"

She cleared her throat. "Yeah—yeah. Okay."

"Here. Drink some water," Jax said and motioned to Lieutenant Carpenter.

The lieutenant placed a full canteen into Jax's proffered hand, and Jax opened it, then tried to steady the plastic flask for Sunny. She grabbed it ravenously, taking too much, and it ran from the sides of her mouth. She coughed.

"What's going on, Sunny?" He wondered briefly if she *was* an epileptic and somehow had kept it secret from him all the years he'd known her. "You up for this?"

She blinked again and frowned. "Of course I'm up for this. Just a damn headache."

Briefly, he examined her face. In fifteen years she hadn't changed much, hadn't seemed to age. Jax certainly could see what his best friend had found so inviting about this woman. She was always so cool and laid back, yet with a slap-on-the-back sense of humor and a real down-to-earth sort of intelligence. Now, her large green eyes looked tired, and the humor was gone from her face leaving only a pressure building inside as sure and as strong as Mt. Kilauea's—and she needed to be one hundred percent for what she was about to do today. Otherwise, not only was the mission at risk, but also her life and the lives of hundreds.

"But Sunny—"

"I felt his presence, Jax. I know he's here."

She must have been dreaming, hallucinating. "You . . . *felt* him?"

"Yes. I know it sounds strange, but I'm sure he's here, Jax. He's really here, this time."

A long moment passed as Jax considered her words. What Sunny and Dan had between them was truly special—but telepathic?

His list of options short, he told her, "Okay, we'll proceed if you're sure you can handle it. You realize radio communication is out?"

"I can handle it. I won't need a radio. I'll find this guy who's supposed to be so important, and I'll bring him back before you can say aloha. Let's quit wasting time, and let me get going."

Jax didn't like the chance for success of any of their other options, but he hoped using Sunny wasn't a mistake.

"Sunny, I'm going to be very honest with you. I wouldn't have brought you along if it wasn't for one of the remote viewers insisting that, for this mission to work, *you* must be the one to make contact with Robert Weller."

She narrowed her eyes at him but said nothing.

"Some will say what we're doing is treasonous even if we do succeed—our success will likely come at a very burdensome price. I've cut you in on nearly everything I know . . . because I felt I had to if I was going to ask you to risk your life. You've been let in on a lot of top secret information—now you know nearly as much about this project as I do . . . and a lot of dirty little secrets that we must never divulge."

Jax waited for a reply, an indication she understood.

Sunny finally gave a solemn nod.

Jax brought out a small black box from his field-jacket pocket and opened it. He plucked out a ring, a simple gold band with a tiny, red-rubber plug attached. Opposite the plug, the ring was wrapped with a small piece of black cloth tape. After pulling off the rubber plug, he inspected the half-inch-long hypodermic needle point sticking from the ring. He then replaced the protective piece of rubber, ensuring its receptive groove meshed with the corresponding land on the ring so that it would not come off accidentally, and he handed the band to Sunny.

"Put this on," he said. "It contains a tracking chip so we can keep tabs on your location—but it doesn't work well if there are too many obstructions. Unfortunately GPS doesn't work around here because of some sort of interference they've created—a smoke screen filled with some kind of magnetic particles. Oh, and, be careful of the needle."

Sunny slid it onto her middle finger.

Jax said, "Keep the point in toward your palm, and pull that little plug off when you're ready. Inside the ring is a tiny reservoir containing a couple of drops of sulfuric acid. The subject has an implant much like the *stemoceiver* they experimented with back in the days of the MK-ULTRA project. Of course that was fifty years ago, so this one is bound to be much smaller and more powerful. Be sure you stick the needle point as close to the center of that implant as possible."

"Where is it?"

"Just below the external occipital protuberance," Jax answered and gave a sideways smile when Sunny frowned at him. "Sorry. The lump where your neck meets the base of your skull. I hadn't heard of it either until yesterday."

Sunny felt the back of her head. She put her hand flat against her skull and seemed to be getting an idea of where on the subject the needle should impact.

"The center of the implant should be about an inch below that little bump," Jax instructed. "You need to slap it hard to ensure it works. If you feel you've missed the first time, try it again—a third time if you have to. Even a very small amount of the acid will short out the circuitry and make his receiver inoperable. Our remote viewer tells us we must do this in order to release Biotronics' control over the guy."

Sunny thumbed the ring while scrutinizing it. "Acid? Transponder-tracking, acid-needle ring? Where'd you get this, *Best Buy*?"

"The transponder was an add on—it's under the tape. I borrowed the ring itself from Gunny Sampson. You knew he collected war memorabilia of all sorts. This particular piece of jewelry came from his collection of antique spy weapons. I told him about the implant and this is what he came up with. It originally contained a very deadly concentration of blowfish poison. The OSS found it on the body of a Nazi spy during the closing days of World War II. They think he was on a mission to assassinate Eisenhower."

Sunny seemed shocked. "Jax, what are you asking me to do?"

"Don't worry, Sunny. It's not poison this time. The acid is a diluted solution. At the most, it'll cause a minor burn."

"And what do I say when I whack him—'How 'bout those Yankees?' It's going to sting like hell."

"Tell him there was a wasp or a spider. Maybe better, a bee."

Sunny shook her head. "God, I hope this works."

"I can't lie to you, Sunny. This is the most complex mission I've ever attempted—by a long shot. That's why we had to go rogue. I knew our own government wouldn't back us. Hope of success is small, but whether or not we will succeed isn't the question. We must."

Jax reached over Sunny to a plastic file folder between the seats. He pulled out a smudged report of around twenty pages. It was stapled in one corner, the other corners curled up and creased as if it had been handled on a number of occasions, and not many of those times from behind a desk. In the middle of the top sheet was typed *Project Brainstorm* in what might have been a size twelve, Courier font. Below that was *Robert Weller*. In each of the four corners, *TOP SECRET* was stamped in large, red letters.

Jax placed one foot next to Sunny's on the floor of the DPV and laid the report on his thigh in easy view. He began, "His name is *Robert Weller*, and he is the key to Biotronics' entire, incredible undertaking."

The major turned the top sheet. This page contained a poor quality, black-and-white photo in the upper left corner with the name Robert Weller underneath.

Sunny squinted at the picture. Her gaze seemed to shift reluctantly from the photo to Jax. "I was hoping, somehow . . . it would be a picture of Dan."

"*Robert Weller*, Sunny."

She nodded. "What's he got to do with this?"

"At this point, the only information we have to go on is from our remote viewers, and they are unsure."

"Why doesn't that surprise me?"

"I'm sorry, Sunny. All other intel sources are cold. And the information the RVs are receiving is unusually sketchy, even for remote viewers. None agree. One says a *clone*, another is calling him a *replica*. The others seem undecided and are only calling him *the key*."

"Mystery man, huh?" Sunny said, and stroked the face in the photo with her index finger.

Personal information filled the rest of the page; birth date, birthplace, parents' names and backgrounds, address, where he went to school, occupation, social security number, wife's name, child's name, blood type and general health.

She shook her head and sighed. "Your remote viewers came up with this?"

"No. It was smuggled out. CIA picked it up yesterday afternoon along with a note saying we 'must rescue him immediately.' We have an asset—a friend—on the inside. We just don't know who it is."

"What about Dan?"

"We think our most direct route to success is through Weller. All of the RVs do agree on this point: we get this guy Weller, and we'll be able to save nearly everyone, including Dan."

Jax turned the page. This sheet had even more personal info on it. It included Robert Weller's likes and dislikes, his favorite sports teams, best friend's name, his parents' names and how they died, wife's parents' names and backgrounds, more detailed information on his son, including the boy's injuries from an automobile accident, and how it had affected Robert and his wife Michelle. The following pages were more detailed and read like some sort of short story.

Sunny looked up at Jax. "It's all here. His entire life. All that's missing is what the hell he has to do with this thing."

"Hopefully, we'll discover that very soon," he told her.

Sunny took a deep breath. "What's the plan?"

"Find him and make contact. But don't push any of this project or the rescue operation on him. He won't find it credible. Don't go too fast. Convince him you know him from someplace. Maybe you'll say some things he'll somehow connect with, and you can work on those. One of our RVs has recommended that you tell him you knew him from college, that he and your husband were friends, and—"

"Do you think it's wise to deceive him? I mean, I'm not a good liar. I don't know if I can pull it off."

"Just remember, in order to save Dan, you'll have to get this Weller character back to safety so we can find out what he knows. It's the only way we can find Dan since the remote viewers are unclear on his location."

Sunny seemed convinced, nodding slowly.

"The RV also suggested you tell him that you were once lovers."

Sunny faced him with a scowl.

"Think about it, Sunny. Certainly, the best way to pull him in is for you to gain his trust. But if that doesn't happen, you need to at least make him curious enough to go along with you. It might work."

She looked back at the report and said nothing.

"If you can bring him back here, we'll have time to question him in safety. But, if for some reason you can't, you'll need to take him to a safe, isolated location so we can grab him. But as soon as we break the ridge with our helicopters—even with our jamming and counter-sensor devices—it'll stir up the biggest hornet's nest you ever saw. Then we'll have to interrogate him on the run. At that point, we'll be forced to pull out all the stops and make a full assault against the Biotronics facility. In that scenario, many lives on both sides will be lost. It is a last resort."

"So, you're counting on me."

"At some point, we must raid their facility, anyway, and attempt to rescue as many hostages we can. It's just that the element of surprise will save many lives. That place is sure to be like a fortress, so whatever help this key Weller can give us will be crucial."

"You really think this is going to work?"

"Like I said, we have no choice." Jax laid the papers on Sunny's lap. "I'll give you a few minutes to study the report. And there's a time constraint. Our remote viewers did a future view and agreed unanimously on a second point. If we're not successful and out of here by sunrise tomorrow, we'll *all* be dead. That includes Dan, this guy Weller and all the hostages."

Jax stepped away leaving Sunny gaping momentarily. She recovered quickly and began leafing through the twenty-some pages.

Chapter 3

I opened the shower door and poked my head through to look about the bathroom. An intruder couldn't have slipped past Michelle through the bedroom without being seen. The crank-out casement window above our Jacuzzi tub was the only other access into the master bath. Even without my glasses, the window was close enough for me to see that its locks and inside screen were in place. No possible hiding places existed, except . . . the small towel closet across from the shower. There would be just enough room inside for someone to stand between the shelves and the door.

As my pulse accelerated, I snatched the back brush hanging from another suctioned hook on the tile wall of the shower and cautiously stepped out.

Harvey came back. *Nice, Superman. Whata weapon. No gunman or knife-brandishing maniac'll mess with you. Not and risk getting whacked with that mean back brush you're wielding. Uh-huh, boy. They'll be shakin' in their boots for sure—*

"Shut up," I whispered. I was a little surprised when Harvey did as told.

I quickly seized my glasses from the vanity countertop and put them in place. Feeling vulnerable in my nakedness, I covered my manhood and tiptoed to the closet with water running down my back and legs and dripping onto the floor. Then, holding my breath, I placed my ear against the closet door. No suspicious noises. No breathing. No sound. After not hearing a thing for several seconds, I began to feel totally stupid. What if Michelle came in and saw me standing there, naked, back brush raised offensively, dripping water, with my head against the towel-closet door?

Still, I should check the closet quickly to satisfy my own curiosity and then get back into the shower where I was supposed to be. But as I grasped the doorknob, I *did* hear a noise, although faint. Could it have been a raspy gasp, the intruder on the other side taking a chance breath—or my own imagination, perhaps Harvey shifting around in his rabbit costume while nibbling on a carrot somewhere in the recesses of my mind? I couldn't tell for sure.

Now my heart hammered inside my chest, sending adrenaline-laced blood throughout my body, pumping it past my eardrums, its visceral pounding drowning out any sound from inside the closet.

Ready to quickly shoulder-slam the door back into place if the need arose, I yanked it open.

Inside were towels, washcloths, extra soap and shampoo—and a small, odd-looking rodent.

Mickey Mouse, Harvey said.

From atop a stack of folded bath towels, it gazed at me with large, black eyes while sitting back on its haunches. Its hind feet were large in comparison to the rest of the thing and its tail disproportionately long. It watched me without alarm, as if we were old roommates. The more I gazed at it the better I recognized what this small beast was—some sort of gerbil, much like the ones I'd seen in pet stores. I couldn't remember that our son Will had ever owned a gerbil, and Colorado certainly wasn't their natural habitat. Someone's escaped pet, perhaps—on the lam, scavenging for handouts.

My glasses had steamed over. I swiped my finger across the lenses. "Where'd you come from?" I asked the rodent as if expecting it to strike up a conversation with me—maybe answer, *Well, my ancestral heritage is Africa and the Far East; however, presently, I've taken up residence in this small homestead you call your towel closet.*

The little creature watched me curiously, sniffing the air, and then glanced up at my raised back brush. I wasn't about to use the thing on the innocent-looking rat. I could try throwing a towel on it and, if successful, contain it in a trashcan until I got dressed. But the little fellow would probably get away and terrorize Michelle. I should leave this job to professionals.

"You won't poop on the towels, will you, Mickey?" I asked as I hid the brush behind me.

It gazed back, still sniffing.

I blew out an extended breath, but before I closed the door, I took a fresh towel from the shelf above the rat, remembering I hadn't gotten one earlier for after my shower. I closed the door hoping the gerbil would stay put. Later this morning, I would call the exterminator and request he use a live trap to capture our houseguest so he could be released somewhere more suitable.

Great, I thought as I tiptoed back over the wet floor to the shower. Now I had Harvey the imaginary rabbit inhabiting my head and Mickey Mouse living in my closet. What next? Would Donald Duck be my chauffeur?

I hung the fresh towel on the outside of the shower door, hooked my glasses over it, and stepped inside. While placing the brush back onto its hook, I glanced around for the remains of the tissue note. Evidently, it had disappeared down the drain. Now, I remembered something my doctor had said. Trauma from my Friday morning fall had caused some brain swelling. It wasn't unusual for someone who'd had such an injury to be confused and for their mind to play tricks on them. My increasingly vocal alter ego might be proof of that. The note could have been imagined—hell, who knows, even the closet rat.

"Nuts," I said aloud, "I'm going nuts."

* * *

Jax checked their perimeter carefully as he waited for Sunny to peruse the report. His team had found an excellent spot for concealment: a small clearing nestled in the scrubs with groundcover spotty and sparse, mostly low-growing weeds in the rocky soil between tall evergreens.

He glanced back at the dry creek bed running along one side that facilitated the DPVs. The vehicles were snugged in nicely. He'd had Lieutenant Carpenter switch on their reactive camouflage, making them appear as only shimmering mirages, like transparent mounds of bent light. Sunny and the weapons affixed to the DPVs were the only things that could be clearly seen.

Jax nodded as he scanned the rest of the area. It was a fine place to operate from—now they needed a lot of luck.

Only six hours earlier, Major Jackson had spoken with his Commander-in-Chief. United States President Francis Allen Mason admitted he didn't completely comprehend the situation, nor did his cabinet. The many Presidential advisors offered little help. They only recognized something diabolical was happening, something far beyond normal reason. Still, these irresolute advisors had convinced the President to wait—that *another* rescue mission, like the last stab in the dark three days ago, was not in the country's best interest.

The Director of the Central Intelligence Agency seemed confident his organization had a better handle on this state of affairs than the rest of the world. Through information gained from the Defense Intelligence Agency's team of five remote viewers of the *Thousand Eyes* project, the CIA found concern for much more than the disappearances of three dozen *special* citizens and the safety of a couple hundred hostages. Without tangible intelligence to go on, they were left to rely solely on the remote viewers' findings—and it was obvious no one completely trusted the RVs.

The last thing President Mason told the major was to stand down until more hard intelligence became available.

Major Jackson's refusal to tell President Mason where this most recent operation was taking place seemed to be the thing that burned the President's butt the most. However, Jackson did not regret his disobedience. President Mason's concern for the *big picture* was misguided as was his distrust of the *soft* intelligence the

RVs were giving him. The President was forgetting that he was not just a politician, and this thing was much deadlier than political polls.

Jackson tried to clear his head of the who and the why, attempting to focus only on the tactics of the awesome task before him. But he found little success—his involvement too personal.

As he knelt next to Staff Sergeant Chambers, Jax wondered how many men he would lose today. He allowed himself this distraction, agonizing over what would happen if they were unsuccessful—if they were found out and caught. Would all of his men take the little red pill? Would they be tortured—or just executed? Would Sunny? He wished, if only for this moment, *he* could remote view and look into the near future to see what might be. He shook his head.

Chambers glanced at him. "Sir?" There was no hint of fear on the young sergeant's face—only a sort of faithful determination and trust.

Jax knew that this man and the three dozen other warriors who had accompanied him this far would follow his orders to the letter, without hesitation, without questioning him even for a second. Where did such men come from? How did he gain and control their unquestioning trust? He could not explain it. And perhaps it was better he wasn't able to foresee the outcome of this mission—it could be tragic, and there was no turning back now.

Jax wouldn't allow these doubts to seep into his thoughts again.

He finally answered Chambers, "Nothing, sergeant." He gave the young man a slight smile and patted his shoulder.

Five minutes passed before Jax returned to Sunny's side with a topographical map.

As he approached the DPV, the lieutenant with the SatCom unit called to him, "Sir, I think you should see this."

"Bring it," Jax said pointing to the driver's seat next to Sunny.

"Jax," Sunny said, frowning as she flipped back through the pages, "this is too much, unbelievable. It's like a nightmare." Sunny stared at the top page, and Jax could see her emotions building. He had a good idea of what she would say next.

Her eyes didn't leave the report on her lap. "Let's talk about Dan a minute, Jax. Tell me the truth. They think he's a traitor, don't they? They think Dan's responsible for this mess—in charge, even?"

The lieutenant slipped behind the steering wheel and turned the laptop's screen so that both Jax and Sunny could see it. "It's an image from Doctor Ultar. He says this drawing is typical of what he's getting now from his remote viewers."

Relieved by Lieutenant Carpenter's interruption, still Jax knew he would have to answer Sunny soon. He studied the jpeg image before him—a simple pencil drawing. It seemed to depict a small town, rectangles representing buildings. Above it was a large mass that could have been either a nuclear cloud or perhaps a huge brain. Lines had been drawn attaching the thing to the buildings. Within the brain-like cloud were the words *Daniel McMaster* and *Chairman*. *Gold Rush* was printed below the town.

Sunny frowned at the image, obviously confused. "What's this telling us?"

"Dr. Ultar says the people at *Thousand Eyes* believe it means Mr. McMaster is in control of the town," the lieutenant said. "Or at least—"

Jax filled in Lieutenant Carpenter's pause. "Or his brain is."

It took a long moment of astonishment before Jax reined in his thoughts—picturing his best friend's brain being enlarged to the size of the Goodyear Blimp and hardwired to an entire small city. He brought focus back to the mission, the more reasonable facts they knew to be true. He reached over Sunny and turned the laptop's screen away from her frozen stare.

"That will be enough, lieutenant," Jax said and gently took Sunny by the chin to look her face to face. Her eyes were bloodshot, confusion obvious, worry lines enhanced by the miles of dust from their journey. "It's only a drawing, Sunny. You know how these second protocol RVs work. They draw pictures after viewing, then they're interviewed and their thoughts are interpreted. Those drawings are only symbols."

She pulled his hand away from her face. "You mean, we're not going to find Dan's disembodied brain tethered and pumped up to the size of Snoopy at Macy's parade? Or do you mean that Dan isn't the one behind all this—the *chairman*?"

"That speculation is obvious," Jax said and nodded toward the laptop. "Some of the RVs have been relating Dan to the term *chairman* all along, as if he were somehow the leader, perhaps in control of these Biotronics people. I'm not going along with it, though. I won't—I can't. If Dan is somehow involved, I'm sure it's against his will."

Sunny shook her head. "This is ridiculous—the *chairman* thing. Dan was chairman of the board of McMaster's Nonlethal Solutions. That's what these RVs of theirs are hitting on."

"Maybe."

Sunny sighed. "And if we can't rescue Dan and the hostages, they're going to be killed, aren't they?"

"Sunny, all of us are expendable. We must understand that. Prior to embarking last night, I spoke to President Mason again. He was . . . let's say, pissed. If we're not successful, the danger will be too great—immediate. I can't believe that our own President would order a strike against us. But as soon as Biotronics finds out we're here, I'd guess they'll destroy their facility as well as the town. That is unless we can gain the President's support and he sends in help. And the only way we can get his support is if it appears we're going to be successful. We can't fail. And I'll promise you this—*I* won't leave here without Dan."

Sunny stared at Jax. "We're in agreement, then." She gently pushed Jax away in order to get out of the DPV. "Let's get this party started."

Jax handed her the map. "The RV who's batting a thousand so far says Weller will be here at 07:45," he said, his finger near an intersection on the chart. "You've got less than an hour, and it's about three miles up this gulley." He nodded toward the ravine before them. "I can't go with you—the RV insisted that you be alone. But I will send the counter-sensor, laser team out behind you to knock out some of the cameras."

Jax pulled what looked like a ragged camouflage blanket roll from the back of the DPV, untied it and let it fall loose. He handed the thing to Sunny. "Wear this ghillie suit until you get close. It's adaptive camouflage. Somewhat like the patrol vehicle you're sitting in, it has dozens of tiny, camera-like optical sensors placed in various spots around the outside of the suit. They see the color on one side of you and change the colors of thousands of organic, non-light-emitting diode crystals on the opposite side. That way it actively adapts the ghillie's appearance by mimicking its surroundings. Anyone who looks your way, from any distance, effectively sees right through you to what is in view of the optical sensors on your other side."

"Yeah," Sunny said, inspecting the suit with an analytical frown. "Smart fabrics—electronic textiles, wearable computers. Dan and I had our own version on the drawing board when he disappeared." She slipped the poncho-like camouflage over her head and ensured that it covered herself completely. "Not bad."

Jax said, "With about a hundred thousand of those tiny diode crystals; two hundred, miniature optical sensors; a whole bunch of small, dry-cell batteries; and miles of ultra-thin fiber optics and stainless-steel-covered conductive yarns woven throughout the suit, it's about thirty pounds heavier than even the normal ghillie. You'll find a small switch to activate the camo below the face opening."

Sunny didn't seem to mind the extra weight. She was obviously fascinated. From inside the ghillie, she reached up and flipped on the camouflage, then glanced around the suit in amazement as it transformed into a translucent blur before their eyes.

Sunny let out an amazed gasp. "This is near nanotechnology," She said, then gaped at him. "Where did you come up with all of this cool stuff, Jax?"

"Like I told you, a lot of people owe me. Many of those people are on staff at either private or governmental labs. Some of our new equipment is experimental and was loaned out freely. And some of it is top secret—thought only to be in the concept stage—and was, well . . . borrowed. These ghillies I spirited out of the Objective Force Warrior Program at Natick Soldier Center in Massachusetts. The director is an old friend. He looked the other way for fifteen minutes while Lt. Carpenter and I went on a mad shopping spree."

With the camouflage on, Sunny's face seemed to light up and float in the air like a beautiful, white Kabuki mask. She was regaining her confidence.

He put his hand on her arm and caught her gaze. "Don't let anyone see you and don't rush our *Mr. Robert Weller*, Sunny. It's the one time you must be patient. You can't be more than a *passive* catalyst to guide him. Use your humor, your wit. He must come with you of his own free will, or you'll lose whatever trust you've gained with him. If that happens and we have to snatch him, it'll make extracting the information we need from him very difficult."

He went to a toolbox in the back of the DPV, took out a buttoned medallion on a chrome-beaded chain and slipped it over Sunny's head. "If anything doesn't set right, you activate this locator beacon. It has a much stronger signal than the ring, and it'll warn us that you're in trouble."

She tucked the thing under her shirt and pulled the ghillie's hood back over her head.

"Robert Weller *is* the 'key.' We have little hope of getting Dan back unless Weller trusts you."

When Sunny stared out at nothing, still without speaking, Jax realized her hesitation and wished he had a backup plan. With no obvious alternate strategy to rely on, he knew he must prepare his men for an all-out assault should Sunny fail.

As Sunny ducked under the chain-link barrier through a large, freshly dug-out hole in the fence line, Jax said quietly, "Sergeant Chambers, take DPV 2 back to the choppers. Return with Corporals Tippin and Dorsey on the double and have each bring a set of civvies. They'll need to look like civilians for what I have planned for them."

He watched Sunny leave. Her suit activated, it appeared like light bending heat waves, reflecting the green and brown colors from the other side of her—a sort of scintillating, five and a half foot tall pyramid.

Speaking louder this time, he said, "Sunny, he needs to trust you—did you hear me?"

She turned to Jax, only a small part of her face truly visible. "He'll trust me."

Chapter 4

Closing the shower door, I dismissed further thoughts of the note or an intruder. I let the hot water rinse the confusion from my mind and tried to think of the day ahead.

Our little town of Gold Rush was small, but even small towns need hardware stores, and I had the only nuts-and-bolts shop within seventy-five miles. There'd be folks coming in to find out how I was doing. I'd have to be courteous to them, even though there'd be plenty of work to catch up on.

While washing my hair, I carefully avoided the large, tender lump at the base of my skull, caused by the nasty fall I'd taken three days earlier in this very shower. A victim of a silly, nevertheless potentially deadly, home accident, I'd become one of those *statistics* by slipping on the slick tub floor and crashing backward through the shower curtain. The back of my head hit the rim of the toilet, resulting in a mean little goose egg and a concussion. Had I remembered to put down the commode's cushioned seat and lid after using it, as Michelle religiously reminded me, I probably would've walked away with little or no injury. Instead, I made an ambulance trip and had a night's stay in the hospital.

Along with the concussion came the loss of a seemingly unimportant portion of my memory. It was mostly small things. I couldn't remember the accident. When our family physician tested me in the hospital emergency room, I easily remembered my own name, my son William's, and Michelle's. But I couldn't remember Michelle's birthday or the pastor's wife's name at church. Doc Xiang wasn't alarmed, telling me with a warm smile that I was doing as good as most men.

Now, a skid-proof mat covered the tub floor and, courtesy of my best friend Mike Wu, a tempered-glass enclosure and two handholds were securely in place. Mike, brother-in-law and handyman extraordinaire, had come over the day after my fall and taken care of our shower. A better friend there could not be, and with Mike being Michelle's brother, it was a double bonus.

As I rinsed my hair, my mind went back to the day's schedule. At three-thirty, I'd close shop early to slip away with Michelle for a four o'clock appointment at the children's ward inside Mount Rainy Biotronics. By then Doc Xiang assured us he would know the test results and our five-year-old son's prognosis.

I took the back brush from the hook on the wall, applied soap to it and began scrubbing my shoulders. Again, while using caution near the lump on my neck, I thought of my good fortune. Keeping my optimism would be important today. Why not? It could have been much worse. Only a few inconsequential memories were lost. I was fortunate to have a prosperous business. I was fortunate to have such a wonderful wife. I was fortunate my boy hadn't died in the car accident that nearly claimed his and Michelle's lives.

It had happened on an icy bridge six months back. Michelle and Will were returning from visiting relatives in Summitview. She'd lost control of the car and crashed into the railing. A ruptured spleen nearly killed Mish, but she recovered quickly from her physical injuries. Recovering from the emotional ones—the guilt for what had happened to Will—was a different story. Our son had broken his neck, but he was alive. We were fortunate. And there could be good news today.

My optimism spilled over into song as I scrubbed my arms and chest.

"Up every morning in the drizzlin' rain," I sang in a

spontaneous eruption—a deep loud bellow. "I grab my chute, and I board the plane. C-130 rollin' down the strip." I turned my singing volume down a notch, but continued while wondering from where this cadence-like song had come. I sang it more slowly and considered the words that came out so naturally that it was as if I'd sung it a hundred times. "Airborne daddy gonna take a little trip. Stand up, hook up, shuffle to the door. Jump right out and count to four. If my chute don't open wide, I got another one by my side. If that one don't open, too, I'll hit the ground before you do. If I die on the Russian rear, bury me with a Russian queer. And if I die on the Russian front, bury me with a Russian . . ."

Where had I gotten such a song? My memory failed me once again. I was never in the military, but maybe I'd heard it in one of those war movies like *Full Metal Jacket* or *Platoon*.

I finished my shower and stepped out, quickly going to the doorway to see if Michelle was within earshot, which I hoped she wasn't. She might not care for my choice of stimulating morning shower tunes. Mish wasn't in the bedroom, and seeing once again I'd forgotten to put the seat down on the toilet, I was glad. I set the lid in place.

From the towel rod on the shower door, I reclaimed my glasses and pulled off the towel I'd just hung there. Even though it smelled fresh and still had a new stiffness in its fibers, I inspected it carefully for gerbil droppings, just in case. When satisfied the towel hadn't been desecrated, I dried off briskly and wrapped it around my waist.

At the vanity, I picked up my Norelco Advantage electric razor with the shaving lotion inside and began work on the stubble on my chin. I loved gadgets, and this little number applied the soothing lotion to my skin with the push of a button and without missing a stroke—ah, the wonders of modern man.

A whiff of frying bacon caused me to hasten my morning preparations. My stomach growled. I finished my shave, snatched up an unblemished tube of Dentisol toothpaste and pushed the first dent into its side. While applying it to a spotless toothbrush, I recalled the

Dentisol toothpaste slogan from their television commercial: *Nothing's fresher than a Dentisol-fresh mouth*.

Upon reentering the bedroom, I saw Michelle had already made the king-size bed and neatly laid out my clothes for the day. Light brown, argyle socks; a tan, heavy-knit T-shirt—I didn't like ties—and a chocolate-colored, Arnold Palmer sport coat with matching pants. All were neat and pressed as if they'd come straight from the store. I quickly dressed and stepped into a pair of unscuffed brown Rockports. Immediately I noticed the shoes were a bit stiff. They appeared to be a recent purchase, as was evident by the rigid leather. I shrugged off trying to remember where I'd gotten them—simply another of those lost memories.

In the breakfast nook, the morning's *Denver Post* waited beside my place at the table. Michelle turned away from the small TV on the counter and flashed me one of her award-winning morning smiles. It was a wonderful thing that I had not seen in over half a year, and it caught me by surprise—she was finally starting to cheer up some. Perhaps my optimism was becoming contagious. I only hoped that today's doctor's report would be a good one. Otherwise, I was sure the tremendous guilt that weighed on her delicate frame so mercilessly would set in once more and suffocate her beautiful, naturally cheerful spirit, never to be resurrected again.

She brought me a plate of eggs over easy, crisp bacon and toast, and I sat down and watched as she placed it before me. She poured my coffee and then prepared herself a plate before sitting at the other side of our small, round breakfast table.

I recalled the day we met in grade school. I was in second grade and she was in first. She'd been wearing a pretty blue windbreaker and a smile, sans eye teeth. I'd never seen a girl so cute, and I fell in love immediately. Now, she was still the cutest girl I'd ever known, and she looked really good in the dark-blue blouse and blue jeans that she wore this morning. An old proverb came to mind—something about those who wear blue are always true. I remembered *true blue, trust them, do*.

Huh? Harvey asked.

I answered him in my thoughts that you can always trust a person who wears blue.

Are you for real?

The voice inside my head—an *imaginary* persona—was asking if *I* was real. I ignored him. To Michelle I said, "Navy's your color." I nodded and gave her a wink.

She glanced at me. "Last week you said it was green."

I didn't remember, but I made a quick recovery. "On you, they're all your color."

She pursed her lips at me.

"By the way," I said, "don't open the linen closet door in the bathroom."

She raised her eyebrows while placing a napkin on her lap.

I told her, "We have a gerbil."

She stared at me.

I elaborated. "*Big gerbil* with *big* feet and Mickey Mouse ears."

Now her eyes crinkled, and she gave me a dubious smile—but even the skeptical upturn of her lips warmed my heart and gave me hope that her spirits were slowly lifting from the bog.

"I'm serious. There's a gerbil in our closet." I wasn't about to tell her about Harvey.

"Okay," she said, nodding slowly, "I'll go along with you. And I'll call the exterminator when they open."

"I can call them from work," I said, wanting to ensure the little fellow wouldn't be harmed. "I want to make sure they use a live trap."

"Robert, I will defend your little friend with my very life," she said, her eyebrows raising again as she smoothed out her napkin. She wasn't really smiling anymore. She had one of those *you-really-have-gone-whacko-on-me* sort of expressions on her face. "I'll call first thing, and—"

"Remember," I said, "live traps. No reason to kill our houseguest."

She nodded again.

Enough about Mickey, I thought and dug into my eggs.

Michelle seemed in agreement. "I called the children's ward while you were showering," she said and bit into a slice of toast.

"I was going to ask you if you had."

"Will's sleeping in." Her eyes lowered, and her voice was somber. "I think we stayed too late last night."

I recalled the night before when we'd sat at William's bedside and talked to him about the coming test results. His hopes were high. My son had given me a big grin and said, "I want to play catch again, Daddy. And ride my bike." Michelle had broken into tears then and had to leave William's hospital room.

I reached across the table and took her hand. "Mish, don't worry. Good news today. Gotta think positive."

She looked up at me, her eyes sad and teary. "You won't forget our appointment?"

She was referring to my little memory problem of late, and I couldn't blame her. "How could I forget it?" I smiled at her. "Thought we might bring Will a present. You know, maybe something that'll cheer him up a little . . . give him something to shoot for."

Michelle didn't ask what. I released her hand, and she wiped her eyes with her napkin.

I slurped my coffee and used a slice of toast to sop up some egg yolk. "What do you think about snow skis?"

She frowned, an incredulous look in her eyes. "Robert, he's paralyzed. What if Dr. Xiang has bad news?"

"He won't. Look, winter's coming. Maybe Will'll be walking before it's over." I frowned realizing how ridiculous that was. Even if Will qualified for the experimental surgery he needed, it would be weeks or even months before we could get him in and, after that, there would be months of therapy ahead. I recanted, "If not this year, maybe next. If we give him the skis, he'll know for sure he's going to get better—he'll be encouraged, it'll lift his spirits. I had a pair of kid's skis and snow boots his size delivered to the store last week. We can wait until after Doc Xiang tells us the test results, then we'll go to Will's room and break the good news to him with the skis. Good plan?"

One corner of Michelle's mouth curled up again, and I realized why I loved her. She smiled that same way last year when William had made her a mud birthday cake on the breakfast-nook table. "Wonderful plan," she said softly.

I took two chomps from a piece of bacon and said, "Doc Xiang's a big man with a big heart. We're lucky to have such a caring doctor, don't you think?" I suddenly had one of those *déjà vu* moments that makes a person pause. It was as if I'd heard or perhaps even said those exact words before, not long ago.

This is weird, my Harvey voice told me.

I pictured the white rabbit again, its switch off. In my mind, I plucked out its batteries. But I knew what Michelle was going to say, and I couldn't help chewing vacuously as I watched and waited for her response.

"Very lucky," she said in an almost rehearsed, mechanical manner. "Dr. Xiang is a good man and—"

In my mind, I finished the sentence with her, *and a good friend*.

I was right, word for word. It made me shiver. I felt the hair on the back of my neck prickle, and I had a sudden feeling—a premonition of sorts—of impending trouble. I whispered, "Very weird."

"What?" she asked, but then turned her attention to the weather report on the TV.

Jerry Denton, the local weatherman for more years than I could remember, told of a beautiful morning ahead, highs in the low seventies and marred only by haze from a forest fire now under control in Estes Park, a hundred miles away. By late afternoon, however, temperatures were to drop, and scattered rain in the early evening would quickly turn to snow. There could be an accumulation of up to fifteen inches in northwestern Colorado.

"Brrr," I said.

"Mmm," Michelle agreed.

She pushed back from the table, pointed the remote

control at the TV, and switched it to her favorite morning news program, *Breakfast with America*.

Hosts Sid Keats and Charlotte Dunn welcomed their guest, Senator Avery Lawrence, to the show. They began talking about the senator's presidential aspirations in the next year. He didn't say he would run. Nevertheless, he was obviously leaving the door wide open.

Michelle asked me to pass the grape jelly.

Host Sid Keats queried the senator on his position concerning China. Avery replied, saying he would stand tenaciously against giving a Presidential waiver allowing *Normal Trade Relations*—formally known as *Most Favored-Nation Status*—to a government so deaf to human rights.

"What do you think, hon'—our next President?" Michelle asked between bites. She frowned as she chewed.

I grunted. I wasn't too excited about the possible candidates—actually, at that moment I couldn't remember any of them.

Michelle said, "He's pushing that big bill he sponsored in the Senate to lower taxes with across-the-board cuts. That means no more government funding for stem cell and spinal cord regeneration research. He's also pretty heavy handed with insurance companies. I heard a news story last week that said if he got elected, insurance companies are likely to disallow any kind of payment toward operations that seem in the least bit experimental." Michelle's brow was drawn, face full of concern.

I hadn't heard about either of those things. Just last week, Dr. Xiang had given us hope—telling us that we'd received the acceptance letter from Bethesda Hospital in Washington, DC. All Will needed now was to pass some tests—the results of which we were to discover at our appointment this afternoon. The mending of Will's severely damaged spinal cord depended on the yet experimental regeneration procedure done in the U.S. only at Bethesda. It was likely to cost hundreds of thousands of dollars that we didn't have. I gritted my teeth. A powerful rush surged through my body, and my fork dropped from my hand and clattered onto the plate.

The thought of Senator Avery standing in the way of William being able to walk again seemed to trigger a stabbing pain in my temple and the base of my skull tingled. I glared up at the TV as a gush of what seemed like fire rushed up my backbone.

The back of the television exploded with a flash. It flared twice. Sparks showered out in a fiery fountain. The tube went blank as the light above the sink popped, and its fragments chimed into the stainless-steel basin below.

Chapter 5

U.S. President Francis Allen Mason gazed into the dim light from the tinted, bulletproof picture window of his study in Upstate New York. Three years ago, at the age of forty-five, he was elected as the youngest U.S. President aside from Theodore Roosevelt and John F. Kennedy. During the election, his athletic nature, charm and youthful looks had elicited a comparison to Kennedy, and the media coined him "the Republican's JFK." Such visual ties to one of America's most honored statesmen and heroes opened the door to connotations of strong leadership, good judgment and political savvy. Mason had tried hard to live up to these high marks. He now stood rigidly, his hands clasped behind his back as he waited.

The window of the President's ranch-style summer home faced the rolling foothills that quickly grew into the Adirondacks. Three Secret Service agents had taken position within easy view from that window, and the President knew at least a dozen more were within a stone's toss.

Surrounded by six hundred acres of wooded hills, the home was the quietest place he knew, making it his favorite locale for a little *R and R*. Modestly decorated with cornflower-blue country curtains, family heirlooms and antiques, it was as comfortable as the worn out pair of Adidas sneakers and *Go Navy* sweatshirt he now wore. The hardwood floors and built-in oak cabinets and bookshelves were original—an important part of the home's design when a rich mink farmer built it back in the early thirties.

The "Double R" was also President Mason's favorite place during any sort of crisis—international, domestic or personal. The past three years had been turbulent, and he had been here almost as much as he had been in the White House.

Secretary of State James Coates sat to the left of the President's desk, his hand patting the chair arm impatiently as he watched his Commander-in-Chief. Seated next to him, Defense Secretary Jacob Banks leafed through an intelligence report that had been handed to him by his attaché fifteen minutes earlier as he'd entered the room. Chief of Staff Edward Thurman had found his usual seat, symbolically, as far to the right as possible. He sat slumped in his chair, flicking his nails. An unoccupied spot between Banks and Thurman was reserved for Central Intelligence Agency Director Carl Winston.

Paramount decisions would be made today, and Mason wanted no distractions from any of his other advisors. He wanted no bleeding heart opinions, no humanitarian whining.

The four were deep in their own thoughts and silent, Mason studying the window's reflection of three of his most trusted advisors. Sweat beaded on Coates' upper lip, which had sported a broad mustache during his prior assignment as Secretary of the Navy. With the more politically scrutinized station of Secretary of State that Coates now held he'd decided with great reluctance that his facial hair go, and Mason was sure his friend of thirty years still missed it every morning when he shaved. He knew Coates also missed the mustache at times like these when he would have normally pulled at it while considering such an important dilemma. Although Coates was a warm and passionate man, he had yet to let his emotions get in the way of his job.

Defense Secretary Jacob Banks was also personable. When he spoke, it was important and honest. A third generation military man, Jacob Banks came through the ranks as a former U.S. Air Force pilot and Vietnam War Veteran, and most recently was the first African-American governor of Kansas. The air of a simple man, under this thin layer of restraint was a complex strategist.

Chief of Staff Edward Thurman was a different story. The closely cropped, gray hair added to his cool and hard character. He seldom showed any sort of emotion, was always curt to the press and as aloof as a hermit. Considered as one of Mason's political coffin nails by most Republican Party leaders, Thurman had been a close friend since college days, and the President would have no one else for his Chief of Staff. Over the past thirty-two months, Thurman had pegged every foreign crisis before it arose. He'd given advice that helped stave off many tense situations that could have blown quickly out of proportion and would have required U.S. troop involvement on foreign soil. He was a needed and trusted confidante, no matter that the man lacked any sort of personality trait that could be mistaken as the slightest bit mammalian. And the cigars he insisted on smoking were detestable. The air still stank of the one he'd put out directly after arriving.

When CIA Director Winston joined them, the room would become as electrically charged as a summer thunderstorm. Winston was always Mister Cool—expressive, yet reserved and normally soft-spoken. Although at all times courteous, he acted as though he thought himself slightly better, knowing more, smarter than everyone else—including Mason. Hell, he probably was correct, President Mason thought and nodded to himself.

While waiting for Director Winston, Mason decided he would not rein in the passions of his four advisors, but let their feelings come out. In a situation such as this, there was no place for holding back.

Coates looked at his watch for the second time in less than a minute.

"He'll be here, Jimmy," Mason said, causing the Secretary of State to look up in amazement. He gave the President a slight and knowing smile, seeming to realize

Mason had been watching him in the reflection of the window.

Mason had kept them waiting long enough. They could rehash what they needed after Winston arrived—probably wouldn't have to update the CIA chief on much anyway. Mason turned to face the three men and leaned over his desk. "So, what are the facts? What do we know for sure?"

Chief of Staff Thurman's voice was even. "Major Jackson's last communication with us was over an hour ago. It had been bounced from satellite to satellite like his phone call to you earlier. We've got our best Com people working on pinpointing his location. So far, no luck. But they've assured me they're narrowing the search and should find Jackson in a matter of hours, perhaps minutes. What we do know is that the so-called 'Black Lion,' with his band of mutineers, has proceeded with this rescue mission more in the manner of a *blind kitten*—against your orders, sir. We think he is now in position, and we should have word of the outcome—success or, more likely, failure—within hours."

Mason shook his head. "To this point, what's our best guess on his location?"

Thurman said, "He couldn't have gone far, Mr. President. He doesn't have the resources. I believe he's in the Rockies. Probably still somewhere in Colorado. Wyoming or Montana are possibilities, but somewhat less likely."

Secretary of Defense Banks raised his brow. "He *did* have access to some very sophisticated radar jamming and electromagnetic pulse devices, Mr. President. And he *did* have help. How else could he bounce his communication signals as he did? We believe former Marine Master Gunnery Sergeant Bernard Sampson assisted him with logistics and support."

"Gunny Sampson?" the President asked. "*The* Gunny Sampson?"

Secretary of State Coates reached up to pull at a mustache that wasn't there. "That's correct, sir." He brought his hand down and continued. "Sampson retired from the Marines about ten years ago. Good man. I became acquainted with him when I was SecNav. Since he retired, he's had a number of windfalls, invested wisely, and now owns several airlines including three of the largest, privately held and profitable ones in the world; Canadian Skies, U.S. Wings and Thai Eastern. He's a billionaire."

"Okay," President Mason said. "Why?"

Coates sat forward in his chair. "You've already been told of Major Jackson and Daniel McMaster's acquaintance—well, it runs deeper than that, sir. McMaster saved Jackson and Sampson from certain death during a clandestine mission into Iran a number of years back."

"Iran?" the President asked, thinking he'd misheard.

"Yes, sir. Black ops," Coates said. "During the early Clinton years. Jackson was with a pararescue group that went in to rescue McMaster's four-man recon team in southern Iran. McMaster's group was mapping an invasion route in the event the U.S. would be called on to help topple Ali Khamenei, the successor to Ayatollah Khomeini. They got cut off from their beach egress. Jackson's group went in to SPIE rig them out." He paused, then explained, "On a rope. Jackson's helo took fire and crashed. He was copilot, a young lieutenant back then. Pilot and the rest of his crew were killed. Jackson suffered severe internal injuries. Sampson was a gunnery sergeant—McMaster's team leader. Was wounded in the leg and couldn't walk. The other two men in McMaster's team were dead. Daniel McMaster, a young sergeant at the time, pulled Jackson from the burning wreckage and, under heavy fire, carried him out of the trees on his shoulders to the beach. He went back for Sampson. A team of SEALs picked them all up. The rest is history. The Gunny and Jackson most likely feel indebted—wish to repay McMaster for saving their asses."

"I'm sure they do," the President said. "And McMaster *is* a one of a kind. His Nonlethal Solutions company is ingenious. Their research and development of nonlethal weapons is undoubtedly responsible for saving hundreds of lives, thousands will be saved in the future. But these men have to know this is a sensitive issue. If we act before knowing who's behind this—who's responsible and why they're doing it—a messy rescue mission could be very costly."

"They, no doubt, know that, sir," Defense Secretary Banks said. "But they seem to be getting intel and direction from what might be regarded as a less than conventional source. It appears they believe they have no choice but to act now. They've been in constant contact with our Thousand Eyes—"

Thurman interrupted, "Mr. President, I suggest we stick with the facts and not rely on crystal balls."

Banks said, "The facts are; we have dozens of scientists and surgeons missing. And then there's the death of Spain's President last Monday. As you know, sir, Thousand Eyes thinks it's related. Garnica had just turned sixty-five, but his doctors were flabbergasted by his heart attack. Said he was in excellent health."

"Black magic and mumbo jumbo," Thurman said. "I suppose if he'd slaughtered a couple of chickens and hanged them on his bedposts he'd still be alive today."

Banks stared at his own hands, seeming stifled.

Coates placed his index finger across his top lip, looking almost as if he was hiding it. He fixed his eyes on the front of President Mason's desk without comment.

Mason swiveled his chair to face the window again. He gazed out for a moment, thinking he would let their emotions simmer, give them time to consider what they were all really in for. Nearly a minute of silence passed before he turned back and asked, "What are our options?"

Thurman raised his eyebrows. It was the most emotion he would ever show, and even that was rare. "You're correct about a 'messy rescue mission,' Mr. President. Whoever is behind this is obviously well organized. If a rescue effort fails, it could end up costly not only by way of human life and financially, but politically unpopular, as well. You don't need that, right now. Election's coming up. The necessary course of action is obvious. Not only are our bombers prepared, but we have nuclear subs within striking distance of any location on this continent, as well as any other continent, for that matter. They're armed with cruise missiles that—"

This time it was Coates who interrupted. "Jesus, Mr. President. We'll be killing our own people."

Thurman didn't look at Coates. He continued to gaze directly at Mason. "They knew the risk. It was their choice to become rogues—not let the President, the U.S. Government in on their intel. As I was saying, Mr. President, as soon as we determine where they are, we could surgically remove the facility and the town in question—if need be, with small nukes. The missiles can fly *map of the earth*, under radar. Nobody would see them coming, couldn't prove where they came from. It worked last year at the North Korean nuclear plant. It'll work again, now."

Mason wasn't one hundred percent pleased with his own decision to destroy North Korea's nuclear arms plant the year before. Disguised as a nuclear power plant, to intelligence sources it was an obvious façade. The bombing had worked out well for the U.S., however. The North Koreans had no proof that it had been American bombs that destroyed their facility, and they weren't about to let UN inspectors in to look over the mess. The swift action had set back the North Koreans' nuclear program at least ten years and diverted what was building to be a costly confrontation between the North and the South that would draw the major world powers into the fray. The swift and decisive action had come at the cost of several hundred innocent lives, however. And those skeletons would not easily be buried away in the President's subconscious.

"But we're talking about on our own soil," Banks protested.

Thurman continued, "Like I said, 'if *need be*, small nukes.' Depends on the scope of this thing. We have bunker busters, fuel-air bombs that would pack nearly as big a wallop without the radiation. Whether we determine nukes are warranted and use them or not, we'd cordon off the area and send in our cleanup teams to tidy up a bit. Collateral damage could be kept to a minimum resulting in negligible long term environmental effects."

"Theoretically," Banks said, "but highly debatable, Secretary Thurman."

"What about the civilians?" Coates asked, horror filling his face.

"If these swamis of Banks' are correct," Thurman went on, "the death toll will rise exponentially if we don't do something decisive and immediate. And if they're wrong, Mr. President, this craziness could be your political knell. That's what we should be concerned with. We have no proof any *innocent* civilians are even there.

"I personally believe something much less paranormal is skulking about in the dark—no less dangerous, politically. These scientists and surgeons—the people who seem to be missing—none are essential personnel, that is to security, defense, secret projects in the works. These people who have them—we've seen their workings before, the so-called militia movements of the Aryan Nations, Branch Davidians, *Posse Comitatus*, other paramilitary crazies within our own borders. They've set up shop somewhere discrete, and they're up to no good—God knows what . . . plotting assassinations and delving into the paranormal, mind power studies, things we don't understand and they don't either. Admittedly, what's happening on the world scene is unnerving, perhaps they've linked with another paramilitary group—possibly even *Al Qaeda*, *Hezbollah*, *Hamas*, Islamic *Jihad* or one of the other terrorists organizations around the globe.

"Find them, wipe them out in one fell swoop, and I'm confident the entire thing can be swept under the rug as an unfortunate accident—a denial-of-knowledge sort of thing—and your office could be kept out of the ensuing controversy almost completely. We could head off this mess—if there really is some sort of smoke-and-mirrors plot going on. Hell, we could easily blame it on Al Qaeda. It could be over in a matter of twenty-four hours, and we could all be sleeping, safe and secure, in our own soft featherbeds by tomorrow night."

Coates gripped the arms of his leather-upholstered chair. "Mr. President, I'd suggest we give Major Jackson some time. That when we discover his location, we offer support for his rescue mission—national guard troops, ATF, FBI SWAT—and do this right, take care of our people. We're not Russia and this isn't Chechen rebels."

Thurman said. "Talk about controversy—it could be Waco and Ruby Ridge times a thousand. Whatever this *isn't*, we do know some of what it *is*—a well-organized operation being carried out by a large group. A small band like Jackson's doesn't stand a chance. We'll be caught up in having to rescue the rescuers—end up worse than Mogadishu and the *Mayaguez*. The prudent thing to do is destroy all evidence and sweep it clean."

Coates blurted, "You're an *idiot*!"

Coates' outburst caught Mason off guard, and he stared at his trusted, normally reserved cabinet member as the door opened without a knock or introduction. CIA boss Carl Winston stepped in, briskly went to the empty seat in the middle of the room and sat down. He brought his briefcase to his lap, turned the small tumblers on both of its latch locks and opened it smartly.

"Mr. President. Gentlemen," Winston said. "I see we've already started the bonding session."

Chapter 6

Michelle gaped at me wide-eyed almost as if the television explosion had been something I'd caused.

Awesome, Superman, Harvey said, but I didn't take the time to scold him away.

I jumped up from the table and hurried to the counter. After snatching the TV cord from the wall outlet, I turned off the sink light.

Michelle sat still, her back to me. Her head and shoulders trembled.

"Mish, you okay?"

When I placed my hand on her arm, she cleared her throat and glanced over her shoulder. She chuckled nervously and patted my hand. "I'm fine. Just startled me."

I looked at the microwave and saw its LED was out and then realized my eye glasses had cracked slightly. When I went to the refrigerator and opened the door, the light didn't come on. "Power surge, I guess. Electricity's out."

"I'll call the electric company," she said, her voice quavering.

"I hope it didn't ruin any of the other appliances. I can stay home, wait until they've checked it out, and they have the electricity back on."

"Don't be silly," Michelle said. She seemed to have recovered and found her normal voice. "I'll be fine. Your customers are expecting the store to be open. Besides, I know how much you want to get back to work."

"You're sure?"

"I mean it. You go. I'll take care of the electric company. Don't you think I can handle that either?"

"I think you can handle about anything." I smiled at her. "But I'll need to check with our homeowner's insurance about claim forms for the damages, and—"

Michelle nodded. "I'll call the insurance company, too. And the exterminator about taking care of your little friend with Mickey Mouse ears."

Then she frowned at me, and I realized she had noticed my broken glasses. I pulled them off and inspected them. "They're not that bad. Just small cracks." I looked at her, my memory failing. "Do I have another pair?"

Her eyes shifted. A long moment passed before she answered, and it was as if she had a revelation. "At work. You always keep a pair at work."

"I can wear these until I get there," I said and glanced at the clock above the refrigerator. It had stopped at seven thirty. I checked my watch. It showed the same time, and the second hand wasn't moving. I held it to my ear. Old habit as it was battery powered, and I could hear nothing.

"Odd," I said. "Watch stopped, too. Almost like some kind of sonic thing—a sonic boom or something, but I didn't hear anything."

Michelle shook her head absently. She wasn't wearing a watch. She reacted to my gaze with a kind of shrinking look, her eyes lowering again. I didn't know what to make of it.

"Don't worry," I said. "Battery's probably dead. I'll get one at the store. And if it's the watch, I have a new shipment of Seiko's. I'll just pick out one for myself."

Even with his batteries removed, Harvey popped into my head again. *Pretty day. Supposed to snow. How about a walk?*

I glanced out the window of the nook. Harvey was right. The houses across the street were silhouetted by a gorgeous orange and purple sky—like a painter's canvas, all the colors in between blended smoothly at the hand of a master. "I'll bet it's seven thirty-five by now," I told Michelle. "I'm going to be late."

"Late? You still have ten minutes."

I pointed outside. "Look how beautiful a day it is. It might do me some good if I walk to work. You can pick me up from the store on the way to the hospital, say—three thirty. How's that sound?"

She said nothing for a moment as if considering my suggestion. She finally said, "Another good plan. But don't forget our lunch date."

"Lunch?" I tried to look questioning. Maybe I'd get a genuine smile from her if I joked a little. "I'm sorry, I've already made a date with one of my 'other girls.'"

She raised her eyebrows again. "If you're not at the Gold Mine Grill by twelve fifteen, I just might find another boy."

The diner she referred to was only two blocks from the store. I tucked the newspaper under my arm. "Yeah, but would he be as good a lover?"

She gathered up the dishes and went to the sink. "You are always so sure of yourself."

"Yep." I looked at her backside while she stood at the counter. I'd heard of some study claiming men have a sexual thought every couple minutes. I was having mine. "By the way, did we make love last night?"

She turned and frowned. "You're joking."

I thought about it, unsure if the concussion was a good enough excuse for spacing it out. "I mean, you asked earlier if I ever got enough. So I guess we . . . I don't remember. Last night. Did we?"

"You mean after seven years of marriage, it's gotten that bad?" She flung the dishtowel at me, but I caught it before it covered my face.

Looking at her petite but nicely rounded body, those feminine curves, the way the morning light shone softly on her tan face and black hair, I would have felt very cheated of such a sweet memory if we *had* made love. I had to know. "Sorry, sweetheart. Did we?"

Her frowning eyes widened. "Poor darling," she said and hurried to me with her arms out. "Of course we did.

Don't you remember? I drove us home from seeing Will. I helped you into bed even though *Mr. Macho Man* insisted he didn't need me to. And I found out you really *didn't* need any help—any help at all." She gazed at me coyly. "I didn't want to because of your head. But I gave in pretty quickly, Casanova."

I wasn't pleased at being robbed of the reminiscence, but now, Casanova was a nickname I could live with. "I'll make up for it tonight with a lovin' neither of us will ever forget." I lifted her off her feet and twirled her light body around one full swing.

"Careful," she said, "you'll get dizzy."

I set her down, and we kissed.

"See you at noon." I handed back her dishtowel and started toward the front door in the living room.

She patted me on the butt as I walked away.

"And don't forget—" I began, and when I reached the door, I turned back to see her watching me with her hands on her hips.

"There's nothing wrong with *my* memory," she said. She paused and then added, "Oh, by the way, Mike phoned while you were in the shower."

"Ah-hah! Your own brother. You almost forgot he called, didn't you?"

"*Almost* doesn't count. Anyway, he said you won the football pool. Ninety dollars. Said he'd be by later this morning to settle up."

"Cool." I nodded. "And I already thought I was the luckiest man in the world."

"Yeah, right." She rolled her eyes. "So whatcha gonna buy me?"

"How 'bout a large Coke for lunch."

"Cheapskate."

I wriggled my fingers and smiled as I went through the doorway.

But suddenly, when I stepped over the threshold and closed the door behind me, it was as if I'd entered another universe.

I leaned back against our front door, staring out at the yard and the neighborhood, not understanding what was happening to me. My heart fluttered inside my chest, and a dizziness came over me like vertigo. What I saw was not the issue, it was how I saw it. The yard was my yard; the street, sidewalk, trees, neighboring houses—my neighborhood. But it seemed so open, so different. I felt the need to clutch the doorknob behind me for fear of falling into what suddenly appeared like a broad expanse of openness. Agoraphobia, I thought—fear of open spaces. Could that be it?

I slowed my shallow, quick breaths, closed my eyes and breathed deeply. When I slowly looked again, nothing had changed, but I seemed to be adjusting. The concussion, I remembered—that was obviously my problem. But how bad of a problem was it? Should I wuss out, go back inside and tell Mish that I couldn't go into work today? No, there was too much to be done. I'd be okay. I just needed to get past this.

I slowly released the doorknob and took a tentative step, then another and stood on the edge of our front stoop. I gazed around me at the trees and houses that lined our lovely street, and I breathed in deeply once again. It was so calm. No birds, no breeze, not even a car passing in the street—a sort of quiet before the storm, I thought. But why should I think of something like that? What brought on that idea? What storm?

The voice came again. *Hey, Superman*, it said. But this time, the voice was different—somewhat clandestine, a gruff whisper. *Where are you?* it continued.

I knew the question came from my own mind, still I queried myself in my thoughts *What do you mean, where am I?* I imagined the Harvey character again. But this time, I couldn't see him. Gazing out at the brightening day, I imagined him somehow in the shadows, hooded, only his eyes apparent, glowing from the dark. And they were yellow, reptilian slits for pupils.

Whe-air-r-r are-r yo-ou? he sung.

I frowned at my surroundings. *I am going mad,* I thought. I wanted to yell out, *You're not Harvey! You're something evil. Leave me alone!* How ridiculous my thoughts had become.

Still, I considered what the voice was asking. As I looked out through the trees and behind the houses on the other side of the street, I could see the nearby mountains. This was my home. I had gazed upon those mountains—that same ridgeline—for thirty-five years.

But as I gazed my point of view seemed to travel past the mountains, and I felt my body follow, as if suddenly being yanked, slingshot at supersonic speed through the air. With the sound of rushing air, pressure built inside my skull and the agoraphobic feeling spun my thoughts again. The din increased, like white noise on a radio, it blared louder and louder, a tremendous cacophony. Soon I saw stars, but not the kind you see when you're whacked on the head and about to pass out—these were real stars, the ones you don't see on bright, sunny days.

Now the disruptive clamor that had blasted in my ears slowly decreased and, for a moment, sounded like some kind of ethereal choir. The harmonic noise finally calmed to a light hiss as the dark universe lit up with billions of pinpoints of light. It was like what I'd seen when I'd been camping, way up in the mountains, and there were no city lights in any direction on the horizon to interfere. But I was closer to these stars, I realized, and the world became completely silent again. The silence became loud, indescribable. The stars grew larger and I sped by them, now, not at supersonic speed but at light speed—Star Trek warp speed. I zoomed past the celestial bodies, and they appeared all around me like bright streaks of intense light.

As quickly as if a hypnotist had snapped his fingers, I suddenly was back on my front stoop, standing in the advancing morning light once again. The agoraphobic sensation had evaporated. I blinked several times and noticed a squirrel on a low tree branch in our front yard staring at me. Below the grey, tree-dwelling rodent, a walnut lay on the sidewalk. He had dropped it—the hypnotist's finger snap. The squirrel's tail flipped in the air as he chewed—or was he only chewing?

I wasn't sure, but I thought I heard a whisper, *Get ready! Here they come!*

I scanned around me, fearfully, as my heart hammered. But I saw nothing to be alarmed about.

This was not normal. What was wrong with me?

"Good lord," I said, shaking my head. Again, I knew the words I'd heard only came from my own thoughts, but that knowledge did little to settle my nerves. I hustled out to the sidewalk, kicked the walnut up close to the tree trunk and walked on briskly without looking back.

* * *

Located four miles up the snaking blacktop from Gold Rush, Mount Rainy Biotronics was built into the south face of Rainy Mountain. With the mountain's rocky bosom at its back and its arms of granite on both sides, the front of the building was the only portion visible from the wide expanse of parking lot. On a busy day like today, the lot was filled to near capacity, as many as a thousand vehicles. Without windows, the only exterior glass on the building was in the main entry doors, a carousel wide enough for three people to push around, shoulder to shoulder. No fire escapes or fancy fascia marring its smooth, five-story-high, stark-white walls, it was neither an architectural wonder nor a gaudy blunder. It was purely functional.

Doctor Xiang Gao had joked during its construction that if the building inspector and fire marshal of Summit County, Colorado, ever saw the facility, they would just *shit*. Certainly, he would welcome both onto the premises—open the wide front gate, raise the steel barricade arm personally. He would show them around while they jotted down notes, made out citations for the many building codes and public safety rules broken. He would show them the dark secrets, tell them the many things going on here that the world should never know. And then he'd take them to dinner in the hospital wing's cafeteria, treat them to a fine vintage of Burgundy, maybe a little pâté or caviar, and perhaps have Maurice, his personal chef, whip up some beef Wellington or lamb chops with mint sauce. When they'd finished and had a nice cherries jubilee or perhaps some tiramisu dessert, he would wrap his large hands around each of their throats and choke them both to death at the same time. That was, if they would ever show. Odds were against that—a pity.

In the west wing of the facility was Mount Rainy Medical Center with over twelve hundred beds. In the east wing, Mount Rainy Biotronics Research Center bustled with activity, most of the scientists and technicians thinking their research would help heal mankind's many wounds. They did not need to know the truth.

Now, in the restricted control room, center of the structure on the second floor, Dr. Xiang put his hands in the pockets of his dark-blue lab coat, and with dark, deep-set eyes scanned the bank of eighteen video monitors. At six-foot five, he was taller than most men of Chinese heritage, his biological Russian father a contributing factor. In his long silver hair, only an occasional black streak was a noticeable remnant of the past. Still he wore it pulled back in a ponytail that reached the middle of his back. The band holding his hair behind his head was an odd feature to most who observed it long enough to realize what it wasn't—an elastic fabric strip. Dark and shriveled, no one except Xiang knew what the thing really was; two curled and connected human fingers—those of his long dead but never forgotten foster parents.

Things were not going according to plan. Three screens were burnt out. Fourteen of the remaining fifteen displayed a number of street and intersection scenes from all over town and around the Biotronics facility. In the middle, the fifteenth monitor showed the inside of the Gold Rush hardware store. All camera angles were from an elevated point of view.

On the screen immediately right of center, a man walked down a sidewalk. The tall Oriental doctor bent over the technician seated in front of him and, with one large hand on the tech's shoulder, he used the other to push forward on a small lever on the control panel. The technician flinched with Xiang's contact while the camera zoomed in on the walking man—Robert Weller.

"Damn it. He is walking," Dr. Xiang said.

An Oriental woman, also in a dark-blue smock, stepped into the room and stood just behind and to the side of Xiang. She inspected the monitors apprehensively. "On schedule, Dr. Xiang?"

Xiang smiled slightly. He appreciated his assistant. She was conscientious, obedient and not all that bad looking for a forty-year-old neurologist.

Xiang spoke over his shoulder, "Yes, Dr. Yumi. A minor complication, however, yes. It appears he has exceeded even *our* hopes." He scowled as he turned to a dark screen near the middle. "He projected earlier than planned. I believe he not only burned out the television, but the three cameras inside the house as well. All of the microphones, the power supply and even the telephone are out. And now, for some reason, he is walking. However, Chief Dailey has arrived at the house. I will have him provide physical surveillance as a precaution."

He pressed the *Radio Speak* button on the console and leaned to the microphone.

Before he had a chance to talk, the screen he'd been observing went blank. It no longer showed the section of sidewalk it had a moment earlier. He could no longer watch Robert Weller.

He turned to the technician. "What . . . ?"

Next, a screen to the left went out, and they looked to it in surprise. Another sidewalk scene was gone.

Xiang grimaced. A short, a breakdown, a rat had gotten into the circuitry again? "What is happening?"

"I don't know, Doctor Xiang." The tech flipped several switches, then stood up and pushed reset buttons on both monitors. Nothing happened.

Yet another screen dimmed to dark gray.

Xiang rubbed his white goatee and narrowed his eyes. Perhaps the equipment malfunctions were caused by something less obvious. He scanned the bank of monitors for a moment. The others remained on. He glanced down at one of the gauges on the console labeled *Subject #374* Signal. Its needle pointed to the green range, and Xiang was thankful for that. They could not afford another failure—especially considering a subject this promising.

"At least we have not lost control," he said.

But when he glanced at a small screen in the middle of the control console, he was stunned. The tiny arrow that indicated Robert Weller's path along a street in a computer-generated town was not there. "Damn it. Tracking has been affected, also." He looked over his shoulder again at Yumi. "Perhaps it was not him who destroyed the cameras and microphones. Something may be amiss. Get a support team in here without delay. I want this resolved, now. And dispatch troubleshooters in boom trucks to make repairs to the surveillance equipment."

"Yes, sir," Dr. Yumi said. She scurried to the doorway, but paused briefly before leaving. "Oh, and, Dr. Xiang, the Consul General is here from the New York City Consulate."

Xiang's eyes widened. This particular consul was in charge of the entire northeastern United States, including Washington, DC. He would be overseeing the operation in that area. "Damn them! Why cannot they leave me alone and let me work? This is not Disneyland. I am not a tour guide."

"I believe the Honorable Mr. Meng Juhong wishes to see the facility today and to accompany the subject to his placement tomorrow, sir. He is waiting in your private office."

"You will delay him, Yumi," Xiang snapped. "I must have fifteen minutes to assure complete control here before Consul Meng is allowed to view our facility."

"Yes, Doctor," Yumi said and slipped out.

Xiang leaned back to the microphone, glancing again at all of the monitors. Dignitaries and politicians were the worst lot. Aloud, but to himself, he said, "That is all I need, a fat-assed diplomat to snoop around where he does not belong and into what he does not understand!"

His distaste for diplomats ran deep. His mother had been a Shanghai prostitute and his father a Soviet dignitary—their consul general to Shanghai. When the second Sino-Japanese war erupted, his Russian father had fled China, abandoning Xiang's mother—then pregnant with Xiang. The Russian returned to his own Mother Russia, his legal wife and safety. But the atrocities Xiang's mother was left to endure were incredible during that tumultuous time in China's history. She'd sought safety in nearby Nangjing with her younger sister and newborn Xiang. But there, over three hundred thousand civilians were slaughtered by the Japanese, and Xiang's mother was raped and killed. His adolescent aunt had managed to escape death with little Xiang, until she was senselessly slaughtered—literally butchered, in a Japanese prison camp—while Xiang watched helplessly at the age of five.

Xiang's parents had made him what he was, and he hated them for it. And he especially hated diplomats.

Xiang pushed the *Radio Speak* button once more. "Chief Dailey, we now have a total of six blank monitors here—and Robert Weller is walking. You must keep surveillance from the house and all the way to the store. Find our subject quickly, and tell me where he is. I do not want him making contact with other citizens, yet."

"Yes, Doctor," the chief replied.

"First, let me speak to Michelle," Xiang said shortly. Disobedience was far worse than equipment failure, and Xiang would not tolerate it. People were more responsive to the threat of death than were machines.

Michelle's voice trembled as it came over the speaker. "I am here, Doctor Xiang."

Xiang made his voice stern, scolding. "What have you done?"

"I—I did what I thought best. His glasses broke. I told him he had more at the store."

She was stammering. Good. She should be worried. It made Xiang smile, but not for long. "I will ensure a new set of glasses are placed in the desk drawer at the store. Now, back to my question. What have you done?"

"I thought it was best that . . . "

"You thought deviating from the plan was best? He was to drive to work. Now we must make other arrangements."

"But it was not going according to plan, sir. There was nothing in the plan about the television exploding. It was his idea to walk. I thought I should not try to persuade him otherwise."

Xiang hated excuses. He grew impatient. "That is what you are there for, to lead him according to the plan."

"Forgive me, Doctor. I was surprised, frightened. I had not imagined the power. I thought it better if he left right away."

Xiang slammed his palm onto the control panel. He raised his voice a notch. "You were afraid for yourself. You had no worry for the project, only for yourself."

"I have failed."

"You have!" Xiang snapped, then paused a long moment. He didn't like to lose control. But he had measured his anger precisely to ensure Michelle understood his disappointment, that she understood her failure, that she understood the possible consequences. "You know I would have protected you at the first sign of danger. I maintain control here and would have turned the device off. It is not in the plan to sacrifice you. Nevertheless, you did not trust me."

Michelle's voice was argumentative and approaching shrill. "I have just checked the inside cameras and microphones—they are all burnt out, as well. Without the cameras and the microphones, how could you have known to protect me?"

Xiang glared at his mike. He said nothing. A moment of silence passed as he gripped the microphone in front of him. Enough banter with this underling. He wanted to tell Dailey to shoot her dead on the spot. But she might still be useful. Without her, this time could end up in miserable failure, as had many others. The project could easily proceed without Robert Weller—still, it would be a letdown. He had extraordinary promise. They had gone so far with him, and optimism was high. Weller had exceeded all of their hopes in the lab. It would be a terrific waste for him not to be included in the upcoming operation, besides the adjustments that would have to be made and targets changed.

The interlude seemed to have given Michelle time to consider her mistake and the consequences of it. Her voice was calmer and more apologetic as she said hesitantly, "I-I am sorry, Dr. Xiang. I beg for another chance. I will prove valuable."

Good. She had reminded herself of the severity of her mistake and the importance of her mission. Xiang surveyed the other monitors as three men in the same type of dark-blue lab coats came in and immediately began working on the computer system around him.

"One last chance, then," he said.

"Thank you, sir."

"No more. If you fail again, you will no longer be of value. You will become a liability I cannot afford."

"Yes, sir. I will not disappoint you again."

"No. You will not."

Chapter 7

Five minutes earlier, Staff Sergeant Chambers had returned from the helicopters that were stationed at a small discrete clearing a few miles away. Immediately, Corporals Tippin and Dorsey proceeded with their new mission and slipped through the perimeter fence.

Chambers now joined Jax, who waited impatiently nearby. Twenty-five feet behind them at the DPVs, Lieutenant Carpenter continued to monitor the town's radio and telephone conversations with the sophisticated listening device attached to the team's satellite communication unit.

The waiting allowed Jax's mind to slip into the past. He looked at the colorfully beaded bracelet on his wrist and toyed with its tiny arrowhead pendant as he considered what an odd team of friends they had been. Lionel Jackson, his mother Hawaiian and father black, had married a beautiful Cherokee Indian named Moonfeather. Jax's parents made him what he was, and he was thankful for it. His African-American father had given him courage to overcome adversity, and his Polynesian-American mother contributed a free spirit and live-and-let-live attitude. Factoring in the influence of Moonfeather's spirituality, Jax found comfort in knowing who and what he was.

Then there was Sunny O'Donnell, one hundred percent Irish Catholic, married to his best friend Dan McMaster, a California surfer boy and the best Marine to ever hit a beach. Sunny and Moonfeather had hit it off from the start, regardless of the night-and-day differences in appearance that their names implied. Both possessed a unique beauty that proved to be much more than skin-deep. Whenever he looked at Sunny now, Jackson was reminded of Moonfeather. The memory of his dead wife caused an empty ache to return to the middle of his chest, awakening familiar longing from the deepest pit of his heart.

Again, the suppressed doubts crept into Jax's mind. If something should happen to Sunny, he would never forgive himself. Perhaps there had been another way he hadn't considered in their haste. Perhaps the plot could have been stopped without a rescue mission or the terrible alternative of a nuclear strike that he was sure the boys in Washington were now considering. Perhaps there was a way they could have pulled this thing off without involving Sunny.

When three men wearing active-camo ghillies came trotting up on the other side of the fence, Jax refocused on the mission. Chambers ran out to meet them—the counter-sensor laser team. The patrol ducked under the chain-link barrier through the large gap. On hands and knees, they pushed their heavy equipment through. Once each man had made passage, Chambers kept guard at the fence while the men jogged into the tree-lined ravine where Jax waited. The first soldier, Senior Airman Winestat, held a long, black, rifle-like device. The counter-sensor laser weapon was about the size and shape of an M-16 assault rifle, except its barrel was tapered and much thicker. The next two soldiers carried burdensome black cases in each hand, and thick power cords hung from their shoulders. The group gathered around a topographical map spread out on the ground in front of Jax.

"Mission accomplished, sir," Winestat said. "Took three of the cameras out. They were mounted on streetlights." He smiled. "Fried 'em like eggs."

As the other two men chuckled, the major clenched his jaw. This was not the time for humor or cockiness. "You weren't seen?"

Winestat's smile left quickly at the stern tone of Jax's voice. "No, sir. We did pass Tippin and Dorsey."

The major nodded. "What's the charge on the laser?"

One of the other men checked the small meters on each of the black cases. "Looks like about fifty percent, sir. Should have enough for two, maybe three more heavy pulses."

"Good work, men. Winestat, take your team back to the helicopters. Load up six more covers for the infrared and motion detectors along this fence line and stand by. We may need an alternate penetration point, and I want to be ready." Jax narrowed his eyes at the young soldier. "If Mrs. McMaster or Corporal Tippin push their panic buttons, we're going all out. You get back here and follow us up the ravine. At that point, we'll grab our people, rendezvous with the choppers and assault the facility."

Winestat nodded. He and his two men carefully set their equipment next to a clump of nearby bushes, climbed into the closest DPV and strapped in. The small all-terrain vehicle's engine came to life; however, only a low hum emitted from its five-foot-long, extra quiet muffler.

As the team drove away, Lieutenant Carpenter's voice came over Jax's headset. "Chatter on their com lines, sir."

Jax hoped they were not found out. He looked to Carpenter and spoke low into the small, voice-activated microphone attached to his helmet. "What's up?"

"Seems they'd had some other power failures even before we hit them. Don't know what happened. They're talking about *someone* having more power than they thought."

The major raised an eyebrow. He wondered if they were talking about Dan, or perhaps this new guy he hoped to snatch and question—Robert Weller. In the past, Jax hadn't been one to believe in things he couldn't touch or see, or what couldn't be explained by scientific formula—even though he'd been married to one of the world's most renowned remote viewers whose only equal was his best friend. That was their realm—he would rely on what he saw in the tangible, real world. But with the happenings of late, he was inclined to consider a more objective way of thinking about the paranormal. After all, the American government itself had toyed with paranormal projects for over three decades.

But if these Biotronics lunatics somehow had been successful with what they were trying to do, the potential was incredible and horrific—making a human weapon without bounds.

* * *

I was soon able to put the agoraphobic episode behind me. But, with the premonition of impending doom, what was to be a pleasant stroll to my store had become a lively stride. Still, I could not deny the lovely morning, my senses seeming more open, more sensitive than I could ever remember. I took a deep breath. Except for a hint of the smoke the weatherman had reported, the air smelled fresh. The light haze on an otherwise bright morning was not uncommon. Numerous national parks and half-a-dozen national forests lay within a couple hundred miles of Gold Rush, and the dry summer had contributed to a larger than usual number of forest fires. The smoke traveled a long way, tending to gather in the valleys and around the mountains.

As I took in the lovely morning at the brisk pace, I thought of what it would be like for Will to be out of the hospital and able to use his legs again—the ballgames, the fishing trips, the hiking and the ski trips we'd enjoy together.

A pleasant morning breeze flowed down from the Rocky Mountains, and the chirping birds added to my optimism. Somewhere in an American elm across the street, a cardinal sang a cheerful jingle. The tree's fine branches swayed gently in the soft wind like waving hands. A good omen, I thought, even though I didn't consider myself superstitious.

In the next block I strode by my childhood home, now owned by a couple who had recently moved to Gold Rush from Virginia. They'd fixed it up nicely, repainted and hung new insulated windows and doors. It still looked like home. I remembered passing the football in the front yard with my father, my mother coming to the screen door and calling us in for supper. The remembrance made me smile. My mother's cancer and father's bad heart had saw to it the memories of my parents did not extend past my twenty-second birthday. They had both died that year.

Two houses down, I would walk past Michelle and Mike's childhood home. My wife and brother-in-law's parent's, Sam and Suzan Wu, still lived in the house but were away now on a Caribbean cruise to celebrate their fortieth anniversary.

With my eyes on the Wu house up ahead, I walked by a clump of late-blooming honeysuckle and mountain wild flowers, and the sweet scent drew my attention. Not one to normally be attracted to such things, still I couldn't help but be pulled in by the colorful flowers enclosed with a white picket fence, next to the sidewalk.

An elderly black gentleman busied himself in the same shallow yard dabbing paint onto the porch railing. George Washington Banks had been my childhood neighbor when my family lived in the house next door. I'd known him all my life. A picture like a family photo came to mind. It was of this man, an elderly Oriental woman, their daughter and her husband—both of them in their early thirties—and a granddaughter around ten.

When Mr. Banks noticed me about to walk past, he laid his brush on top of the paint can and then took long, slow strides in my direction. His mustache and hair were so white that they seemed fluorescent against his coffee-brown skin. The Denver Broncos cap he wore protected his shiny, bald crown.

I waited by the short ornamental gate leading to his front door and smiled at the elderly man as he approached. He didn't return the gesture, and for a reason I couldn't explain, I became slightly unnerved.

"You look like a nice young man," the old gentleman said, his eyes dark and clear. "Brown Suit. That'd make you Mr. Weller, wouldn't it?"

"Good morning, Mr. Banks," I said and held out my

hand, remembering that his Alzheimer's had allowed him fewer clear-minded days of late. I hadn't a clue of what my brown coat and pants had to do with my name and figured the terrible disease that gnawed away at his memory had confused him. "Please call me Robert," I said—he had called me Bobby since I could remember, but at least calling me Robert would be better than Mr. Weller.

We shook hands while Mr. Banks studied me.

"That's right, Robert," he said and nodded. He pulled his head back and studied me. "They'll be wanting to get you some new spectacles, that's for sure."

"My glasses just suddenly broke this morning," I said, but didn't wish to explain more.

He grunted as if it didn't matter, then said, "Name's George Washington Banks. Corporal, United States Marine Corps, serial number five-five, six-one, two-four, seven-seven. Korea, nineteen hundred and fifty-two."

The Alzheimer's seemed to have a firm grip on his mind this morning. I couldn't help but feel for the poor old guy. I raised my eyebrows trying to look very impressed. "Retired military?"

He chuckled. "I guess that's one way to put it."

"Painting, huh?" I asked, nodding toward his porch.

"Yeah," he said as the faint ringing of a telephone came from inside the house. He turned toward his home. "Winter's coming on. Want it to look nice before the weather sets in." He glanced back at me. "Got that paint at your hardware store two weeks ago from the last guy."

I smiled again. I liked Mr. Banks and always had, no matter now that he seemed to be rapidly growing senile. I'd purchased my store from old man Whitaker over twelve years ago. Except for an occasional high school student helping me part-time, I'd been the only one behind the register.

Banks continued, "This is my crib." He jabbed his thumb over his shoulder at the house. "They give it to me. But it ain't home. Closest I could get, though." He looked down at his feet. "Whole hell of a lot better than laying naked in a muddy pit, I'll tell ya that." He shook his head and looked at me again. "Yeah, boy. Got a wife here, purdy daughter, grandbaby. I love 'em all like they was life itself. That's why I do it. That's why I keep on."

I nodded politely, again not understanding exactly what he meant. "Yes, Mr. Banks, I know them. Lovely family."

"Robert . . . ," the old man said with a sudden frown. He glanced around us as if he was making sure no one else could hear. His voice lowered. ". . . it ain't too late for *you*. You got to get outa' here. Go home where your family be—where they love ya."

I stared at him in puzzlement as his daughter came out the front door. Jolene Berry was a pretty, slender woman with her father's height and her mother's lovely Asian eyes. She was two years behind me in school. She came to us with one of those *is-he-bothering-you?* sort of grins on her face.

"Good morning, Robert," she said.

I nodded to her. "Jolene. Good to see you on such a beautiful morning."

She glanced around at the lightly smoked sky. "Yes, it is a pretty morning. Not supposed to last long, though."

I nodded. "We better enjoy it while it's nice."

She smiled putting her hand on her father's shoulder, and he cowered slightly. "Daddy, better come in, now. Mama's got breakfast ready. And little Rachael wants to see you before she goes to school."

Without protest, the old man turned away and walked toward the front door of his house, but he paused midway. Not looking back, he said, "Maybe they'll let me buy some more paint today. Maybe we can talk more, then." He stepped up on the porch and opened the screen door.

Jolene gave me a half smile. "I'm sorry if Daddy bothered you."

"He's a wonderful man," I said. "He'll never be a bother to me."

Jolene nodded.

"He did say something that made me a bit curious—something about 'laying naked in a muddy pit.'"

Jolene frowned momentarily, then seemed to understand. "He was a POW during the Korean War. Still has nightmares. And that Alzheimer's is getting worse every day. Don't take him too seriously." Jolene smiled. "Nice talking with you." She turned away and followed her father inside the house as I watched.

I paused in front of the flora, gazing down at the honeysuckle. What a shame Mr. Banks had Alzheimer's—such an awful memory-stealing disease. With my concussion and seemingly minor memory problem, I could relate, only slightly.

Seconds after I turned and proceeded toward the store, a woman appeared from nowhere about fifty feet down the sidewalk. Perhaps she'd stepped out from the end of some tall hedge bushes edging a short section of the footway. She wore sunglasses, a green sweat suit and tennis shoes. For this woman, I had no mental photo, no words coming from a memory filed away but within easy reach.

The woman stepped toward me, the red hair covering her shoulders thick and full of bounce. I couldn't help but watch her. Such an attractive figure. Fifteen feet away, she raised her glasses revealing her large green eyes and gazed at me as she drew nearer. For a moment, I became entranced, finding something familiar in those lovely eyes. I slowed my pace cautiously as we were about to pass. When she stepped up to me, a big smile came across her face like she'd bumped into an old friend she hadn't seen in a while. Her full lips parted as if she was going to speak to me.

But then, her expression changed. She glanced down the street, frowned and tapped her sunglasses back over her eyes.

She stepped past, and the next thing I knew she slapped me on the back of the neck.

I saw stars and cringed. "Damn!" It felt like I'd been stung.

"Bee," she confirmed. She didn't say it like *Watch out, bee!*—only, matter-of-factly, *Bee*.

I winced, not knowing whether I should slug her back

or thank her. "What the hell, lady?" I said, but when I looked around, the bushes rustled and she was gone.

Feeling the fresh wound, I realized the thing had stung the lump—the remnant of my fall in the shower. But I found no bee, no insect of any kind. Inspecting the ground around me, I discovered no small perpetrator there, only what looked like the eraser end of a pencil. What kind of madness was this? I was careful to check under my collar and shirt to ensure the little bastard hadn't fallen inside where it could cause more trouble. Still nothing. Had it flown away after such a solid smack? Had it somehow stuck to the woman's hand or fallen onto her clothing somewhere?

Suddenly, something seemed to click inside my brain. As if the proverbial dam had broken, a rush of incredible images came at me from behind my eyes. I saw helicopters, guns spitting fire, ripping up the ground around me; fierce explosions in the air and on the ground; soldiers bloodied and dying; then a huge conflagration—a nuclear blast, sweeping away all of the town's buildings and houses in a terrific tsunami of flames—the shock slamming into me, making me stagger, rattling my lungs.

I grabbed onto the spirea branches next to me to keep from losing my balance. I sucked in a deep breath as the horrific images dissipated as quickly as they had come. What did it mean? Was it something from the past—memories that suddenly were flung to the forefront of my mind, repressed by my concussion? Or could it be some kind of a premonition—a view of what was about to happen?

I shook my head in confusion as I heard a car pulling up beside me.

* * *

Sunny almost had this Robert Weller guy. Two minutes—that's all she would have needed, and somehow, she would have gotten Weller to go with her. She would have done anything, tried *anything*. But the police car pulling up just when she'd made contact spoiled it all. She'd failed—and doing so, she'd failed Dan. In a town of five thousand people controlled by a hostile force, how could they possibly find Dan now? Jax had said, if she failed, they'd have to attack blindly, a full-fledged assault against an enemy with unknown numbers and capabilities.

"Damn it," she hissed, trying to hold back her emotions as she crouched behind the bushes only long enough to slip the bulky camouflage ghillie back over her head. She eased out of the shrubbery on the opposite side of Weller and then sprinted toward the narrow band of evergreens separating Gold Rush from the rocky slope. Toward the east edge of the city limits, the tree line spread wide as it slipped down a three-mile incline. A small ravine ran the middle, widening also by the time it reached the base of the hill where Jax waited next to the dry riverbed. During spring thaw, the gully was probably a mighty torrent of water. For now, it lay impotent and worked well as a pathway.

Sunny only made the nearest tree before stumbling against it. A strong rush shocked her entire body, quickly followed by dizziness and tingling like fingers lightly massaging her temples. She rested against the old pine's trunk where no low boughs grew.

Cursing, she threw the gold ring to the pine-needle-covered ground. With both hands against the evergreen, she panted heavily and shook her head. So close. Only a few seconds longer, and . . . .

Her head spun as she closed her eyes, then she staggered behind the wide tree trunk, stumbled backward, and sat down hard. The tingling fingers massaged deeper, firmer into the sides of her head, into her brain. Her thoughts tumbled, fragmented, as confusion set in.

From her mind's eye, she saw herself and Dan, and their daughter Lilly. They were chasing crabs and laughing on a beach near San Onofre, California. On a sunny day, they were hiking at the Sequoia National Forest while whistling theme songs from kids' shows and Disney movies. Then Lilly was on Dan's lap as they played a board game on a stormy afternoon in their summer cabin north of San Francisco.

She longed to be home, for them all to be safe and happy as they were only two years ago.

The kneading in her brain intensified, and Sunny realized she'd had this same sensation several times before—the strongest episode earlier while seated in the DPV waiting for Jax's briefing. The odd feeling was not painful, but neither was it soothing. It interrupted her thoughts, pleasant memories of the past—stole away her reminiscence of a happier time. The stirring inside her skull was an invasion, the feeling as if someone—some sort of burglar of thoughts—had entered the most secret places of her personal domain, was sifting through the private recesses of her mind, her soul.

But she could not stop this intruder. There were no alarms, no thought cops to come to her rescue. Her mind opened submissively, as if laid bare with legs splayed, completely at the mercy of this mysterious entity.

Sitting with her hands pressed against her head, within a few seconds, she felt overwhelmed, knew she was going to faint. Finally, she fell back, sprawled out onto the dry evergreen needles—and then she felt Dan's presence, saw him before her like a misty apparition.

She opened her mouth. "Danny!" she said, her lips unmoving, her jaw locked as if it was paralyzed. The REM started again, her eyes racing in their sockets. Unable to stop the probing digits earlier—now, with Dan's face before her, she no longer wished to stop them.

Within a few seconds, control slipped from her grasp, and she succumbed to the invisible thief groping inside her head.

With a final conscious breath, she whispered, "Dan-nee—"

Chapter 8

"Carl," President Mason said, "glad you could make it so quickly from Miami."

CIA Director Winston didn't look up at his boss. The compact, sinewy man seemed out of breath. "Sorry if I've delayed things, Mr. President. The balmy Florida weather was tough to leave." His apology was flat and insincere as he passed a file folder to each of the other men, Commander-in-Chief first. "We have updates on our intel," Director Winston continued as the others studied the folders they had been given. "We received the fax on top only minutes ago from one of our field ops in Paris. It seems it went the long way around to get to us."

President Mason opened the file before him. The top sheet had come across at least two facsimile machines and only God knew how many copiers to get to his desk. In the upper left-hand corner of the fax was a small picture, a mere ghostlike draft of a man captioned *Robert Weller*. The poor quality made the photo unidentifiable—the subject could have been twenty years old or sixty, had brown hair or blond. Mason shook his head and scoffed. "Paris? I should guess so—it came a *very* long way around!"

Still winded, Winston spoke rapid fire, "Regardless, sir, the information is crucial. It seems we have an asset on site, an informant working undercover. We don't know who it is."

Chief of Staff Thurman closed the file folder on his lap.

His voice was stern and direct. "I have no trust in this."

"Please," Winston said, "we must at least give it due consideration."

"Who is this Robert Weller?" Secretary of State Coates asked. "And what does he have to do with anything?"

"Seems this man is somehow a key to these maniacs' plan," Winston said. "A note was included in the fax saying we 'must rescue Weller immediately.' He appears to be an innocent man being groomed as some kind of assassin."

Thurman's emotionless tone and face didn't indicate the incredible skepticism of his words. "Oh, brother."

"What do we know of him?" President Mason asked.

"Absolutely nothing, sir," Winston said. Still short of breath, he continued, "There are dozens of Robert Wellers in this country and over the world. We're searching for any possible matches in age and basic appearance. Our remote viewers are calling Weller a clone or some sort of replica—of Daniel McMaster."

The President couldn't help frowning incredulously as he looked at the poor photocopy likeness of Robert Weller. "Does he even look like McMaster?"

"Just speculation anyway, sir," Winston said. "But a clone wouldn't necessarily look exactly like its original cell donor—a twin so to speak, but not necessarily identical. And theoretically, the DNA could be manipulated to change hair and eye color, etcetera—give the clone different characteristics. Still, they'd have to overcome the issue of age—perhaps they've discovered some sort of accelerated aging process."

"I don't believe this," Thurman said. "Science fiction. The technology just doesn't exist."

"I'm not endorsing it," Winston said. "Actually, Secretary Thurman, I tend to agree with you on that one point. But I'm just laying out the RVs' report."

Mason didn't go along with it either, but he wanted to be as objective as possible until they found something concrete. "Why would they clone McMaster?"

"It might have something to do with his physical and mental abilities. He's a genius, very athletic—perhaps even having something to do with his psychic abilities," Winston said. "McMaster's been documented as very adept in both remote viewing and telepathy."

"Recommendations?" Mason asked.

Director Winston took a deep breath and slowed his speech. "That we either attempt to rescue Weller, Daniel McMaster and anyone else being held captive, or . . ."

"Yes?" Mason asked.

"Kill them," Chief of Staff Thurman finished aloud what President Mason was thinking. "A preemptive strike."

"Last report," Banks said, "we had no idea where they were."

"Only a matter of time," Winston said. "Should know within a couple of hours."

Coates grimaced. "Mr. President, surely giving them the balance of your twenty-four hour deadline would be prudent. Give them that much of a chance. What if somehow they're successful, and this big fiasco we're all afraid of doesn't happen?"

Thurman picked a piece of lint from the forearm of his suit jacket. He brushed it from his fingers as he glanced at Coates. "Strike now, Mr. President, as soon as we pinpoint them—before this thing gets out of hand."

Secretary of Defense Banks frowned and said hesitantly, "Our remote viewers have given us more information, sir."

Thurman asked, "More smoke and mirrors?"

"You were holding back information?" Mason asked Banks.

"I'm sorry, Mr. President," Banks said. "I felt that after comments like Secretary Thurman's here coming from this administration of late, there wouldn't be much interest in what our Thousand Eyes project had to say." He glanced at Winston, who returned a nod.

Thurman shifted in his chair. "Your little group of warlocks did miss the mark by a mile or two on the last rescue mission."

As Mason glared at each man alternately, Banks ignored Thurman and said, "They're telling us hundreds of innocent people are caught up in the middle of it, sir."

The President scoffed. "How could there be? Hundreds?"

"Perhaps even more than hundreds," Banks said.

Mason asked Coates, "Have that many people been reported missing?"

Coates shook his head. "Not that I'm aware of, Mr. President."

"Just more BS, Mr. President," Thurman said. "I don't care what kind of mumbo jumbo this is, there's no way in hell we've got hundreds—or thousands, if that's what Secretary Banks is trying to say—of people who've been spirited away."

Banks said, "But maybe this is going on in or near a populated area."

The room was silent briefly, the others seeming to mull over Secretary Banks' comment.

"What about Daniel McMaster," the President asked Winston. "I'm hearing speculation that he's gone over—been paid off somehow and become a traitor—in some manner involved deeply in this mess."

Winston shook his head. "For that, I have little information, Mr. President. Our remote viewers have associated his name with chairman indicating to them that he is in charge of this plot—some sort of *chairman of the board*, they're guessing."

"Chairman of the board?" Mason asked. "What *board*?"

"Don't know, sir," Winston answered as a soft tap came from the office door. Winston raised his eyebrows at the President questioningly.

Annoyed but curious, Mason nodded back to the CIA director who then went to the door, opened it six inches and spoke in hushed tones to one of the secret service agents.

Meanwhile, Banks seemed to have an epiphany, and said, "McMaster a traitor?" He drew a deep breath and appeared to be considering it. "I was reluctant to believe it before, but it's very possible. He has a great deal of the knowledge they would've needed for such an undertaking—he'd be a valuable resource, has demonstrated strong leadership ability with his company

McMaster's Nonlethal Solutions as well as during his hitch in the Marines. He *could* be in charge."

The President scowled at the idea. "But why would . . ."

Winston closed the door and turned back to Mason. "Sir, I'm afraid we have another incident to consider. Senator Avery Lawrence has suffered a heart attack and is en route to the ICU at Bethesda."

No matter that Lawrence was his chief rival among the Democrats for next year's Presidential election, Mason certainly didn't wish the man harm. "What? Good God!"

Winston said, "They had to defibrillate him, but he's conscious, now. Still has arrhythmia and complaining of shortness of breath."

Mason stepped backward again and dropped into the high-backed leather chair behind his desk. He glanced at each of the four advisors. "Another coincidence?"

Winston was the only one to speculate. "Mr. President, are you familiar with MK-ULTRA and the similar projects undertaken by our adversaries?"

"Vaguely. But MK-ULTRA was closed down in the early seventies, wasn't it?"

"Yes, sir. But that was *our* project. Our enemies weren't concerned about human rights, like we were back then or even now. They're still very active in their research and actual development of some very interesting concepts." He narrowed his eyes, emphasizing the need to consider carefully what he was about to say. "There are those who say that certain American and ally assassins had been cultivated by those enemies, and were responsible for some very high-profile murders—JFK, RFK, Israeli Prime Minister Itzchak Rabin."

The room fell silent again for several seconds until the intercom on the President's desk buzzed.

Mason glowered at the blinking indicator button but didn't press it. "I need to know more about this remote viewing thing. The first I'd heard of it was when I took office three years ago. Until this week, I was under the impression that project had been officially closed, also."

"Essentially correct, sir," Banks said. "Phased back

considerably—went deep back in 1995—is now working out of the pockets of Major General Gregory Santos, once again at the Army's Intelligence and Security Command. Years back, it was in INSCOM's hands under the code name of *Center Lane*—actually originating in 1969 with the CIA's *SCANATE* program, an offshoot of research done at Stanford Research Institute. And I anticipated your need to understand it better, Mr. President. I've prepared a video link with the project director, Dr. Charles Ultar. He's just outside of Fort Mead, Maryland. We can have it hooked up in a matter of minutes."

Again, the intercom buzzed insistently.

Restraining his annoyance, Mason pushed the intercom button. What could it be now—to bother him at a time like this? A second intrusion could only mean his personal secretary considered something of utmost importance had come up. "Ye-es, Carmen. What is it?"

His secretary said, "Vice President Andres is on line one, Mr. President. She says she needs to speak with you urgently on a secure line."

Mason frowned. "All my lines are secure here, Carmen. You know that."

"I reminded her of that, sir. She told me to 'just get the damn President.'"

Vice President Geraldine Andres was in Hamburg, Germany taking Mason's place at the World Peace Accords. Wondering what would be so important for his VP to interrupt this meeting, and what could have gotten her so worked up, Mason hit the speakerphone button.

"Go ahead, Geri. You're on the speakerphone, but the line is secure. Coates, Banks, Thurman and Winston are here, too. No one else."

"Mr. President," Vice President Andres said, an edge in her voice unfamiliar to Mason. The first woman to become the nation's second in command was normally unshakable—her nerves were one-hundred-percent steel when it came to crises.

"What is it, Geri?" he coaxed.

"Mr. President, I'm sorry, but I have bad news. Prime Minister Kyoto has just died of a heart attack."

President Mason's jaw went slack. Senator Lawrence, one of the most physically fit politicians in the country had just had a heart attack and was in intensive care. Last week the Spanish president, an important Free World leader and close ally, fell dead while addressing his nation. And now this—the leading advocate of Mason's *World Human-Rights Agreement*, the *young* Prime Minister of Japan, had died.

Mason's gaze darted to each of the four astonished faces before him, then rested on Winston, recalling what he'd just been told about the very infamous assassinations. He gave an anxious sigh and shook his head. "My God! It's begun."

* * *

The redheaded woman who slapped the bee on the back of my neck had disappeared. When I looked to the curb, Tom Dailey, the local chief of police, was leaning over the passenger seat of his patrol car, a large wad of the usual Hard Day's Work chewing tobacco in his cheek.

He yelled out the open window, "Hey, Robert! Good to see you up and around. Great day, isn't it?"

I rubbed my neck, but avoided the fresh wound. "Beautiful, Chief." No reason to bother Chief Dailey about a little sting. "What're you up to?"

I glanced to where the mysterious woman had been. Either she had slipped into the hedge bushes, or she vanished back to where she had come—nowhere. My mind playing tricks again? Voices, notes, gerbils, bee stings and beautiful redheads?

The chief answered, "Same ol' same ol'. But hey, how's about that boy of yours? Any progress?"

I noticed a pair of binoculars on the seat beside him, and I didn't answer his question at first, wondering what he was doing with them. For some reason, I got the feeling Dailey had been watching me.

"Robert?"

I looked at him. "Huh? Oh, we'll find out today. Michelle and I are pretty optimistic. He's a tough kid."

"He is at that. The wife and I are wishing you folks the best."

"I know, Chief. We appreciate it."

"What happened . . . ?" Dailey asked motioning to his eyes.

I guessed he was talking about my glasses. "They just broke during that power failure. I've got another pair at work. What was that—some kind of electric anomaly? Sounded like a sonic boom."

"Haven't heard for sure, but it affected this whole neighborhood. Power company said electricity should be back on within the hour."

Pleased with his assurance, I nodded as the chief's radios squawked—both the one bolted to his console and the one holstered to his duty belt. "Dispatch to Chief Dailey."

He frowned as he reached to his walkie-talkie and turned it off. Then he picked up the mike from beside the steering column. "Yeah. Dailey here."

"Code three, Chief. Please respond immediately."

He glanced at me with one of those sideways smirks that told me Barney Fife could as easily handle the call.

"Gotta go, Robert," he said, rolled his eyes and shifted the plug of tobacco to his other cheek. "Big meeting at the donut shop. Let us know if there's anything we can do."

He turned away, preparing to leave, but I stopped him. "Chief, there is one thing you can do."

He turned back, concern on his face. "Sure, what's that?"

I don't know why I asked, but I did, "Can I trust you, Chief?"

He smiled back at me. "Sure," he said smiling, his hands open, "I'm wearing blue."

Blue. After my earlier internal dialogue with Harvey, the idea of him speaking this fact and associating it with trust briefly shocked me. But I forged ahead, somewhat unsure of how to voice an additional concern. "Could you check in on Michelle every once in a while today?"

He frowned at me questioningly.

I tried to explain. "It's just that . . . well, with the power outage, and . . ." I didn't want to mention the note and have him thinking I was going crazy, too. "I don't know. Something feels different today. Something . . . I can't describe it—something feels wrong."

It surprised me when he narrowed his eyes and nodded as if he understood. "Sure, Robert. Don't you worry." He glanced around us as if ensuring that no one else was within earshot, then he lowered his voice nearly to a whisper. "No matter what happens today, I want you to remember that I'm on your side."

I nodded even though what he was saying wasn't soaking in, and the chief pulled away.

As I walked on, I considered the chief's words, but couldn't make sense of it—"*No matter what happens today, I want you to remember that I'm on your side*"—what did that mean? Surely he was referring to Will's prognosis.

For now, I was preoccupied by the sting. It burned. I gently touched it, and it was moist. The tiny puncture wound was about dead center on the bump.

I hadn't had a chance to miss Harvey.

Don't sweat the small stuff, Superman.

I remembered Doc Xiang saying that if the lump was aggravated, it could cause "serious complications," and I wondered what kind of "serious complications" could be caused by messing with a little bump. Brain damage?

You're a real optimist, huh, Superman?

Grudgingly, I knew Harvey was right. I was being ridiculous and optimism was very important today.

I shook my head and continued my walk. I didn't care to have an imaginary cheerleader, and I didn't want to admit I was starting to get used to his presence inside my skull. I pictured the white rabbit with his switch off and battery compartment empty as I'd left him after his last appearance. In my mind I stapled his lips shut.

When I got to the store, I'd put a Band-Aid on my wound. This afternoon, when we went to see Doc Xiang, I'd ask him to look at the sting. He'd probably give me some salve to put on it. No big deal.

Down a side street, I noticed one of those boom trucks the utility companies use. A worker in dark-blue coveralls manned the cherry-picker bucket, busily installing a new lamp in one of the streetlights. Power surge, I remembered. As Chief Dailey had said, the entire neighborhood had been affected.

Otherwise, the morning's activities were ordinary. Already older folks were in their yards, doing the usual fall chores. It was as if I were strolling through a Norman Rockwell print—white picket fences surrounding nicely trimmed fescue lawns, saltbox houses with white lap siding and shutters every color of the rainbow. I smiled at the scenery's quaintness.

Gold Rush was an interesting place. Typical small town, and yet not. It sat at the base of the south slope of Rainy Mountain. Its heyday population of thirty-five thousand dwindled to nearly a ghost town after the mines played out back in the thirties. Mount Rainy Biotronics moved in over twenty years ago bringing back jobs and prosperity.

Since then, Gold Rush had grown into a *We Are the World* sort of town of five thousand with a blend of diverse races and cultures, an attribute of a worldwide research corporation. Nearly half of the population, maybe more, was Oriental folks, many the descendants of railroad laborers from back in the mid-eighteen hundreds. The big railroads hired thousands of Chinese back then to help lay rail through the Rockies and on west to California. They called them the *coolies*, a hardworking people who would labor long hours and for little pay, almost like slaves. Their descendants were good folks, and I was proud to claim many of them as friends. And I was certainly proud of Michelle, the lovely mother of my handsome young son.

Gold Rush was isolated. The only manmade construction between town and Mount Rainy Biotronics' five-story facility, tucked into the south face of the mountain, was a winding, four-mile stretch of asphalt. In the other direction, the same blacktop slowly meandered down seventy-five miles to the nearest town of Summitview. It was only twenty-five miles if you were an eagle; however, over two hours away by car. Besides the two years away at Summit County Community College, this little town was the only bit of the world I'd really experienced or even wanted to. After all, I'd built up a respectable hardware business, and I was enjoying this nice little nugget of prosperity, also.

Thinking of my business, my wife, and my son brought back my optimism.

And just before two smiling body-builder types stepped in front of me from out of nowhere, I had assured myself that the rest of my day would go my way.

Where are these people coming from?

* * *

Dr. Xiang sat behind the control console in the restricted area at Mount Rainy Biotronics. He glared at *the Subject #374* Signal gauge. The needle pointed to the left side, in the red. The technician stood behind him, near the wall.

The service team had left several minutes earlier, finding nothing wrong with any of the computer monitoring equipment in the control room. They suspected the trouble with the surveillance equipment was in either the communication lines or the individual cameras and microphones. They speculated that the *subject* might somehow be responsible for not only that, but also, for the loss of signal to the implanted enhancement device. But Xiang didn't go along with them. The receiving switch on the back of the subject's neck was electromagnetically protected, encased in a thin copper shell.

Xiang tapped the signal gauge—the needle stayed in the red. "Dailey, you are sure you saw no one else with or near him?" Xiang asked into the mike. "A camera technician reported he saw a strange woman in green while he was repairing the camera on the light pole at position seven. That same technician said he thought he saw movement toward the tree line after you arrived—'an odd sort of blur' he said."

The chief's voice came back over the speaker, "Just Banks, Doctor."

Xiang was skeptical. He had known Dailey nearly thirty years, had been inside his head, through every synapse and brain cell of his mind in one way or another, and he noted a slight hesitation, a sort of hitch, in his voice. For the time being, he had no reason not to believe him, however.

Sometimes a little pressure helped bring out the truth. Xiang said, "After you radioed, I called Banks' daughter and told her their neighbors had been complaining about her father's irrational talk again." Xiang drummed his long fingers and focused on the mike in front of him, pausing only long enough to give Dailey a chance to realize to what he was leading up. "That old man has long outlived his usefulness. From the beginning, he was the most difficult to influence. Has always been troublesome, prideful." He paused again as if to consider a solution. "He's become a liability."

"Come on, Doctor Xiang," Dailey said. "He's harmless."

Xiang smiled. The mediocre minds of his subjects made them like puppets. It was hardly a challenge to direct them where he wished. "The older Banks gets, the looser his tongue becomes. He has forgotten our agreement, and his family may get suspicious from his *senile* talk." Dr. Xiang sighed heavily, theatrically. "He will have a heart attack tonight and die in his sleep."

"But Doctor Xiang, be reasonable. He didn't—"

"Would you rather his entire family have a very unfortunate auto accident—perhaps a house fire?"

Chief Dailey sounded frustrated and pleading. "I don't think that will be necessary—"

"Enough, Chief Dailey. Banks no longer concerns you. Now, I want you to stay clear of our subject for a while. I fear his device is still on, and we have lost the control signal to turn it off. You have yet to outlive *your* usefulness, and you should be glad of that. In the meantime, go to the hardware store and meet a runner there. He will give you new eyeglasses with an implanted transponder chip for the subject, and you are to place them in the desk drawer. Use the back door so you will not be seen."

Xiang released the *Radio Speak* button and punched a key on a small keypad labeled *Intercom*. He selected a three-digit number and pressed *Intercom Speak*.

"Vanzandtz," came a quick reply.

"Captain Vanzandtz, you must replace the stemoceiver implant's antenna microchip on Subject 374."

"I'll have an operating room prepared and assign a surgeon, Doctor. When should we expect him?"

"No, Captain. You don't understand. It has stopped working." Again, he looked at the meter on the console labeled *Subject #374 Signal*. He tapped it once more. Still, it didn't move from the left side of the gauge, pointing in the red to zero. "We have lost control. He is in town, on foot, and I believe his device is still armed." He looked at the tracking screen. Still there was no arrow indicating the subject's location. Xiang hoped the new eyeglasses would remedy that. "Several of the surveillance cameras are down and we've lost tracking. However, we believe he is on his way to the hardware store."

"We have *no* control? And you want *me* to replace the receiver antenna, Doctor Xiang?"

"You heard me correctly. The antenna microchip must be placed within three inches of the device for it to be effective. That means you will have to stick it on the middle of the back of his collar so he will not notice it. It will require approximately ten seconds to connect with the device and work. Once it links, we can shut the enhancement device down. We do not need to test his abilities any further. I am satisfied. With the device disabled, he will be able to continue his practical memory phase. This way we do not risk the schedule, harm to Subject 374 or the loss of any of our personnel. We will operate on the plane tomorrow and make the necessary adjustments."

"Can't we isolate him, doctor? Put him down and bring him in to do it right?"

Xiang's jaw tightened involuntarily, but he did not raise his voice. "Do not question *me*, Captain. We do not have the luxury of time. We are keeping a schedule here. He must be through his practical phase, ready and on his way to placement by early morning tomorrow."

"But Doctor, can't we send someone better suited—"

"No. You have the greatest knowledge of the subject and the situation."

"And that's why—"

Xiang finally raised his voice sharply. "No, Captain Vanzandtz, you are not indispensable! No one is. Do not forget that!" He disliked losing even the smallest strand of the controlling cable he held over the project and its people.

He looked at the digital clock on the console and shook his head. The time was seven forty-five. After a deep breath, he regained his grip with what he felt was a reasonable consolation. "You may take your pistol armed only with sedative darts. But use it solely for emergency. Now, enough delay. You must go now. A van is on its way to pick you up. The driver has the stemoceiver antenna. Good luck, Captain."

As Xiang quickly released the *Intercom Speak* button, Yumi's voice came over the speaker. "Forgive me, Dr. Xiang, but Consul General Meng grows impatient."

Xiang's lip curled. He wondered what his superiors would do if he were to murder a diplomat.

Chapter 9

"Mr. Weller?" the first smiling man asked as we met on the sidewalk. He was the taller of the two men stepping toward me, blocking my path.

They were both younger guys—probably early twenties—well-built and with thick necks. Both had short, military-style haircuts. They wore Polo shirts, the taller one light green and the other a medium grey. Their tan slacks were nicely pleated and they had on black athletic shoes. I had no reason to fear them, still I was very apprehensive—they wore no *blue*.

"Yes," I answered, not returning their smiles.

"Could we speak with you for a moment, sir?" the other man said, politely. He was stockier than the taller guy, his arms like thick tree limbs.

"What? What's this about?"

"I'm sorry, Mr. Weller," the taller man said. "Please don't be alarmed." He glanced around us. Seeming satisfied no one was within a hundred yards, he produced a five by seven photo from his back pocket. "Do you recognize this man?"

They both kept their smiles, but behind their pleasant faces I recognized a seriousness that was a bit frightening. I wondered if they were detectives, FBI or possibly with the IRS. But, if they were, they should have identified themselves. It made me leery. Then I noticed a smudge of dark green on the tall guy's ear—it reminded me of camo paint, the kind you see soldiers wearing in the movies to camouflage their faces in order to blend in with the vegetation of their surroundings. Evidently GI Joe missed a spot before getting dressed up in his civilian attire. Focusing on that ear, I saw something else odd—some kind of tiny earpiece or hearing aid.

The guy must have noticed, because he angled his head so I couldn't see. I shot a glance at the other one's ears and saw that he had one, too.

Hesitantly, I averted my gaze away from them and frowned at the picture proffered in front of me. I took it and studied it briefly. "What's his name?" I asked finding the face vaguely familiar, but I couldn't place him.

"Daniel McMaster," the tall guy said.

At first, the name didn't register. Then Harvey came back—with his more excited but cordial voice this time. *Geez, Superman! That's the guy's name from your dream*.

I quickly realized he was correct. I flashed back to this morning's dream. That was the name on the tab of the file that laid open on the Air Force Lieutenant's desk. I wasn't about to tell these two that the only time I'd ever heard the name was in a dream. But how was I going to explain the surprised look I was giving them, now?

"Uh," I said dumbly, trying to buy some time for thought. What was this all about? I'd heard of déjà vu, but this was ridiculous. How could I have dreamed up a name while sleeping that two men would ask me about a couple of hours later? "What was the name again?"

My two interrogators glanced at each other as if to say, *Uh-huh, we got a winner!*

The stocky man repeated, "Daniel McMaster."

"What's this about?" I asked. "Has he done something?"

"No, Mr. Weller, nothing like that. We think he might be in some kind of trouble and need our help."

"Why are you asking me? Who told you that I might know him?"

Now the looks on their faces were more like *we're losing him* when they glanced at each other.

"Please, Mr. Weller. Daniel McMaster needs our help.

Could you just tell us where he is?"

I looked at them skeptically, growing tired of their evasive friendliness. "The name is vaguely familiar, but I can't place where I've heard it. And I don't have a clue as to where he is. Why don't you ask Tom Dailey," I said, shoving the photo back to the shorter man.

"Tom Dailey?" he asked.

"The chief of police," I said. "He should be driving by again any minute."

I began walking around the two men who were still blocking my way. But the short stocky one grabbed for my arm, and I didn't like it. I felt heat, an ache building in my temples and the tingling at the base of my head again, like before the television blew up.

My reaction was quicker and more offensive than even I expected. I blocked his right hand with my own left, brought my arm over his and locked his forearm behind my back. With pressure on his elbow, I bent it in a direction it wasn't intended to bend. With a quick jerk, I could have easily broken his arm.

My right arm cocked, the V of my hand was aimed at his throat. I didn't know where I'd come up with such a move—TV, movies, a demonstration I'd once seen—but I did know that in less than a second, I could crush the man's trachea, quickly causing him to either suffocate or drown in his own blood. By the surprised looks on both men's faces, they knew it, also.

The ache intensified in my temples and the men's faces contorted. The tall man stumbled back behind the guy I had a hold of, holding the sides of his head. I saw the look of incredible pain on the shorter man's face and it shocked me. I didn't wish to hurt anyone. I released him.

Immediately, the ache subsided and both guys tried to shake it off, their eyes wide.

"Go away," I said. "Go away and leave me alone."

They did as I had ordered, turning quickly and then sprinting between the two houses we had been standing in front of. I watched them disappear. But they didn't disappear into the distance or run behind a house. They seemed to reach for something next to one of the homes, and then they . . . just simply vanished—leaving my sight in a blur, blending in with scenery. Did they just evaporate? It made me wonder if I had hallucinated the entire thing or at least their departure. It could only have something to do with my concussion, I was sure.

Getting over my astonishment, I became angry, but not at the disappearing men—more so at myself. Had I overreacted? Had they really planned to attack me? I could have seriously hurt—even killed—one of them. And what was happening inside my head, physically—the intense pain and pressure that built so suddenly.

I hurried on, mulling over all this, and decided that the first thing I should do when I got to my store was to call Mish—hoping the phones were working by then—and tell her to be watchful for the two men, should they come by the house. They knew my name, so they were sure to know where I lived—and where I worked if they wanted to pursue this matter further. I'd also call Tom Dailey and report the incident to him—make sure he kept an eye on the house, too.

But what about this McMaster guy? Was he in some kind of danger? I thought my unconscious had created him in the dream. But was it only a dream? Maybe it was some sort of remembrance, reality obviously distorted by my mind's subconscious wanderings—I had never taken part in any sort of experiment or studies conducted by the military . . . had I?

Within two minutes, I came to the first stoplight on the east side of town and paused at the red light. The gentle breeze had calmed, and the birds became quiet. Anxiously, I watched the light traffic, waiting for the signal to change. I noticed the man and two women waiting on the other side of the street, but I didn't concern myself with them—they weren't the thick-necked military type. Instead, I gazed absently through the smoky haze at Rainy Mountain hulking protectively over the town, and I tried to make some sense of the earlier encounter. I couldn't.

When I glanced back at the light, it had already changed to green, and I stepped into the street. I exchanged good-mornings with the man and one of the women. The other lady lagged behind, digging through her purse. From her salt-and-pepper hair, I guessed she was in her mid-fifties. She acted nervous, her eyes shifting about but never meeting mine.

As we passed, a horn blared. A van came to a screeching halt next to us, barely short of the crosswalk, and we both stepped aside and bumped into one another. She let go of her purse, dumping its contents into the street. Little tubes of lipstick rolled everywhere. Gum, a compact, her wallet, a pack of tissues, keys on a ring with a big K on it, all lay in a loose pile.

I glared at the man behind the wheel of the Ford van who had caused the disturbance.

What a jerk! Give him a piece of our mind, Superman. Go on. He deserves it.

"Leave me alone, Harvey," I said under my breath, and the woman took a questioning glance at me. I curled the corner of my mouth and shook my head slightly. Obviously, I had no power over my imaginary yet unwanted companion, so I figured I'd simply have to ignore him.

The big, chubby-faced van driver just sat behind the wheel in an expressionless stare. I thought better of Harvey's advice and helped the lady round up her belongings. It didn't matter that the light had changed. The big bruiser in the van would just have to wait.

The woman said nothing and gathered her things quickly. I handed her several items, and she stuffed them into her bag. When we had finally collected most of it, she stood over me as I picked up one last lipstick case.

She reached toward the back of my shoulder, I'm guessing to pat me on the back, and she said, "Thank you so much."

At the same time, I pulled away defensively, and her hand only brushed against my collar. I hadn't intended to be standoffish. It was a subconscious reaction, considering my earlier meeting with the two inquisitive men.

Her face was as blank as that of the driver in the van,

who had since backed up and now drove around us.

I dropped the lipstick into her open handbag, and she scurried on her way, and I went on mine. However, as I reached the curb I thought I heard her say something, and I glanced back.

"Did you hear me?" she said in a low voice. "I couldn't get it close enough. It won't work. I'll have to put him out." Her purse strap was on her shoulder now, and she was holding one hand to her ear. The other hand was under her jacket as if she was getting something from an inside pocket.

Who the hell is she talking to? Harvey asked.

I scanned the intersection. There was no one else within fifty feet of her.

"I have no choice," she complained. "He's too dangerous."

At that moment, I felt the familiar pressure and buildup of heat in my forehead and then that shooting pain across my temples. The base of my skull tingled. I leaned against the traffic-signal pole and rubbed my forehead. The concussion's aftereffects were lingering much too long. I probably should have stayed in bed, I thought.

Then a new but smaller crack snapped across one lens of my spectacles, and I realized this had nothing to do with my concussion. As the odd feeling wore off, I glanced back across the street. The woman I'd bumped into only a moment earlier was lying sprawled out and face down on the sidewalk.

Disregarding the red light, I sprinted back to her side, knelt down and gently rolled her onto her back. Her eyelids were half-open. Her pupils were dilated. I touched her neck to get a pulse, but felt nothing. I saw no rise or fall from her chest.

By now, several people had gathered, and I called out, "Does anyone have a cell phone?"

"I do," a man on a bicycle said. He pulled it out of a blue fanny pack that matched his blue shirt and biker pants and then punched the keypad four times with his finger.

A man in a small Volvo parked at the curb and came trotting up just as I pulled the lady's chin down and checked her airway, preparing to give her rescue breaths and chest compressions. Her teeth were crooked. Her thin face was somehow familiar.

It's the woman in the dream, Superman. Lieutenant Iron Pants, remember?

"My god," I said aloud. It *was* her, Lieutenant Vanzandtz, but she'd aged a good fifteen years since this morning's dream.

The man from the Volvo interrupted my thoughts. "Kindly let me through, please. I am a doctor." His skin was dark as a Hershey bar, and his accent sounded Pakistani or Indian. He wedged his rotund body through the bystanders. "May I be assisting you?"

"No breathing or pulse," I said, as a faint siren blared in the distance.

Damn fast, wasn't it? Harvey said. *Too fast*.

The doctor said, "Everyone kindly stand back, please."

As I moved away to give him room, the woman's coat fell open, exposing a handgun. It was tucked into a webbed holster and neatly harnessed to her side. The holster's flap was unsnapped.

Nine-millimeter Makarov? Harvey asked.

I thought he was correct. But how in hell did I know? I couldn't remember ever caring about guns or ever actually firing one, let alone knowing one brand from another. And more puzzling, how did this Harvey persona inside my mind know?

Then I noticed that the pistol barrel had an extension on it.

Silencer!

I looked at her face and saw that she wore an earpiece—like the GI Joes.

She was going to kill you, Superman!

Again, Harvey was being ridiculous. That didn't make sense. Why would the woman want to kill me? She was probably a cop, or some sort of special agent in town on business. Maybe that earpiece was only a hearing aid. Her holster flap had come open when she fell. All that made sense—except for the silencer.

The dark-skinned doctor began giving the woman chest compressions with clasped hands. He then moved back to her head, more agile than I would have expected a man of his bulk might be. He held her nose and, with his mouth covering hers, gave her two breaths.

The ambulance came around the corner, its lights strobing, and its siren fell silent as it stopped in the street.

I backed away and watched along with a small crowd of seven or eight people while the EMTs took over the CPR from the doctor.

"She's not responding," one of them said.

"Load her up," another one said, and they swiftly, yet skillfully gathered her, placed her on the gurney and took her to the ambulance.

Within thirty seconds, the small crowd and I were left to watch the back of the emergency vehicle driving away.

The doctor stepped up to me. "Poor woman. Did she speak to you of having problems?"

"No," I answered. "Except when I passed her in the street, some idiot blasted his horn at us, and we bumped into each other. It scared her so much she spilled her purse all over the street. We got it picked up and then went in opposite directions. She did seem to be talking to herself for a moment. The next thing I knew she'd collapsed."

"It may be found to be a heart attack. One never knows when their heart might simply stop beating. They are more delicate machines than we wish to think." He looked up at me. "My name is Rajiv Shekhar."

"Glad to meet you, Dr. Shekhar. I'm Robert Weller."

"It is truly an honor. Not everyone on the street would react as you did. But please, you must call me Rajiv."

"Rajiv," I repeated and shook the man's small, pudgy hand.

"Well, I must go. It has been a long night—working at Mount Rainy Biotronics, you know. I hope we will meet again under more pleasant circumstances."

I nodded as serious doubt crept into my mind as to

whether or not I would ever again be a part of "more pleasant circumstances."

* * *

Major Jackson sat with Sunny in the DPV while the lieutenant and sergeant kept guard nearby. He scanned their small encampment. Things were peaceful now—the wind still, no sounds, human or animal. Jax wondered how long the calm would last.

Sunny was rubbing her temples. It had been a couple of minutes since she stumbled through from the hole in the fence, tossed off her ghillie and collapsed in the DPV. Her expression made it evident she had not been successful. Her mouth was drawn, her eyes low and her cheeks were flush. She appeared distraught and in pain.

Corporals Tippin and Dorsey had returned directly behind Sunny. As they threw their camouflage ghillies to the side, they'd apologized to Jax about their failure. They didn't understand how they'd been thwarted. Weller seemed to be armed with some kind of self-defense weapon that created intense pain to whoever accosted him—"Like some kind of electric eel," Dorsey had said.

Frustrated, Jax had instructed them to get back into their black military fatigues.

Jax allowed Sunny a moment to catch her breath and gather her thoughts before he asked, "How's the head, Sunny?" He touched her shoulder.

"Better. I've had these killer headaches for the past two years—since Dan disappeared. Lately, the pain's had company, a kind of tingling." She moved her hands to her face and stroked her closed eyes with her fingertips for a moment, then looked at Jax, a kind of ironic smile on her face, tears pooling in her eyes. "I almost had Weller, Jax. If it wasn't for that damn patrol car."

Jax nodded sympathetically. "We'll have to rethink snatching Weller. He seems to be able to thwart any unwanted contact. Tippin and Dorsey didn't have a chance. You may be the only one who will be able to get him. Do you feel up to trying again?"

Sunny nodded. "I'm sure I can coax him to come with me, but I don't think we'll be able to make it all the way back here without stopping. I need a midway point. Set up some sort of safe haven. I'll need a little time to do some considerable convincing."

Jax pulled out the plastic pouch from beside his seat. He opened it, took out several satellite photos and held them on his knee where Sunny could study them also. The two browsed through the photos.

"First of all, we need to find out where Weller is now." He placed his index finger at specific points on the pictures as he spoke. "Our most accurate remote viewer has identified several places in the town, but I haven't had contact with her lately. Weller could be at this hardware store or even several miles farther out at the Biotronics facility. That might make things difficult."

"If he's in the town, I'll find him," Sunny said and pointed at a small rectangle on one of the photos. "What's this?"

"Let me look." Jax brought out a piece of paper that had been under the pictures, and he unfolded it. On the paper was a list of locations in reference to the photos.

Sunny was studying him. "Jax, I thought the Defense Department's remote viewing team was made up of only five RVs—you've mentioned six. This one remote viewer who's been correct on everything so far—the one you just called 'her'. . . who is it?"

Jax stared at the paper in his hand without an answer. How could he keep credibility with her if he told her the truth?

"Jax?"

Perhaps she would understand. After all, Sunny seemed to have some sort of paranormal connection with Dan, and she obviously believed in his abilities. Jax glanced to a bracelet made of colorful beads on his wrist, and then thumbed the small arrowhead laced to it. He glanced up at Sunny, realizing the sadness in his own eyes but unable to wipe away the emotion.

"Your warrior's bracelet?" Sunny asked. "Moonfeather?" She put her hand on his. "Your wife? Jax, she's been gone for more than four years."

Jax turned back to the bracelet, and he spoke slower

than he intended, knowing she was staring at him still astounded. "It started over three weeks ago. Her words just appeared on the laptop monitor—seemed to come from nowhere, untraceable. Had nearly two dozen messages pop up since then. I know it's her." This was no place for emotions that wouldn't do any good—sentiment that wasted time. He cleared his throat, and his attention went back to the list accompanying the photos. "The building might be a motel."

A long moment passed before Sunny said, "A motel?"

He was thankful he'd been able to redirect her. "Appearances, Sunny. Most mountain towns this size have at least one motel for the tourists and visitors. They probably use it for their guests, visiting dignitaries and scientists, perhaps."

She smiled at Jax. "Maybe I can find a vacancy."

Chapter 10

The crowd dispersed, and I hastened on my way, becoming more concerned and anxious about all of the morning's odd happenings by the minute. The simultaneous cracking of my glasses, recurring pain in my head and the woman falling dead could have been coincidental—still I was befuddled by it all. Without being able to make a logical connection, I shoved it to the back of my mind with the already mountainous pile of befuddlements I'd tossed there.

I thought about what Rajiv had said, that the human heart was more fragile than most people think. Seeing the lady die like that reminded me of how quickly a life can terminate. I should be thankful for every minute my wife, son and I had, no matter what fate awaited us. Regardless of Dr. Xiang's prognosis this afternoon, I would be thankful for our time together.

I bid cautious hellos to several more people on the street, a number of them fellow merchants. Some of them I knew, but I was a little surprised I didn't recognize more—a strange thing, memory. Doc Xiang told me that in order to retain experiences in memory, specific connections had to be made in the brain. If those connections weren't made, neither were the memories. Or if they were somehow jostled loose, those memories would be lost. Many of mine had been jostled considerably and, according to the doctor, there'd be little chance of retrieving most of them. "Do not worry," Doc

Xiang had said. "Go out and make new and happier ones." I was trying to take my doctor's advice, but even since the accident on Friday morning, I'd had experiences I couldn't remember. The doctor told me that would be temporary. I hoped he was correct.

When I reached my hardware store, I noticed the front display windows could use a good washing. I couldn't recall the last time I'd cleaned them. Fumbling for my keys, I looked up at the traffic in the street. It was still sparse, but one of the drivers happened to catch my eye as he drove past. He looked at me with an emotionless stare. Again, the shooting pain struck my temples, and the base of my skull tingled. It was less severe as if I had become more tolerant of the pain, and I shrugged it off.

As I pushed open the door, again the sound of screeching tires came from the street, this time accompanied by a crash. When I stepped back outside, several cars had stopped. Then, across the street and about four shops down, I saw the back end of the vehicle that'd passed a moment earlier hanging out of Calamity's Café. It was a dark-blue Ford van. The guy who had honked at us before the woman died—his van was dark blue, also.

It's the same guy.

Unlikely, I told Harvey as I jogged across the street. Two men were pulling the driver out of the van. A navy-blue suit coat fell out of the door as they laid him on the tile floor of the café. It *was* the same man. Body limp. Eyes half-open. No obvious injuries. The van's windshield had not been broken. Clipped to his collar was a wire, an earpiece hanging from the end, just like the one the woman, Lieutenant Vanzandtz and the two GI Joes was wearing.

A waitress behind the counter picked up a telephone and punched three numbers. The two men worked on the driver, attempting to revive him. Within a minute, sirens blared once again, and I realized I could do nothing except get in the way. I walked away stunned, dodging the traffic as the ambulance pulled up.

Back at my store, I tried to bury myself in my work,

but I couldn't concentrate, a heavy fog seeming to settle over any sort of normal thought. Remembering Michelle had told me I kept an extra pair of glasses in the desk drawer, I checked. They were there in a cushioned case next to a new box of pencils. I took off the cracked pair I was wearing, put on the replacements and slipped the broken ones back into the protective pouch.

I tried to call Michelle, but the line was busy. Then, I called Chief Dailey's office and left a message with the desk sergeant, asking for the Chief to call me back. He did right away. I told him that I had been near the woman who had fallen dead earlier, and I sensed that he understood my stress. He told me that he and his two officers on duty had been delayed on the other side of town at a minor traffic accident. He tried to calm me—assuring that he would keep tabs on Michelle and our house. I also told him about the GI Joes. He said that he saw two men fitting their description leaving town a few minutes earlier and not to worry—he reiterated that he would check in on Michelle—would stop by our house right away. I was relieved.

Again, I tried to involve my mind into the busy work on my desktop. Next to the desk, I found the packages Mike Wu had left for me, collected from Frank's Barbershop on Saturday. Then I reviewed the UPS bills of lading a number of times to ensure the orders were correct. At eight thirty, I replaced the battery in my old watch but it did no good. The second hand still didn't move. I tossed the watch in the trash and picked out a new, moderately priced Seiko from the display case, set the correct time, and stuck an IOU in my register so I wouldn't *forget* when I did the daily books.

Having a new watch didn't keep time from dragging. I called Paul's Pest Control and got the machine. I left a message about our little houseguest, and within ten minutes a woman called back. She said Paul had a cancellation and would go right out. "Live traps," I told her and "Release him in a nice field somewhere." She said that would not be a problem.

The line was still busy when I tried to call Michelle

again. I figured she was talking to Colorado Power and Light about our power surge and outage problem, to the insurance company or maybe to one of her friends. I followed up with a call to the electric company's main office in Summitview, just in case. I found it odd when, once again, I got voice mail. Sure, they were probably busy with the power outage, but what was the world coming to? Soon, there would be no more two-way human phone conversations. Only human/machine messages. Or perhaps machines calling machines.

Yeah, have your voice mail call my voice mail, and we'll do a conference-call lunch, Harvey said.

Again, after I left a message with the utility company, a woman called back. She said she did have a record of a Michelle Weller calling only a few minutes before. She promised to send a service order immediately with the hopes a technician might respond soon. However, the outage seemed to cover a good part of the east edge of town, which included over a hundred homes, and she could not give any promises. I asked her to do the best she could, as if that would do any good, and I also asked her to have the service person bring a claim form for the television and any other appliances we found had been damaged. She said she would, but our homeowners insurance would probably have to take care of it.

Sure, pass the buck, Harvey said.

Then, I realized the possibility that our home phone could have been affected by the power surge, also. I hadn't checked it before leaving for work. Perhaps that was why the line had been busy. But I remembered hearing the Banks' telephone ringing, and he lived only a couple of blocks from our place. Still, I called the phone company, and I was surprised actually to be connected to a human. The guy in customer service said what I'd expected. He checked our line and found it not working. There'd been no other complaints from my area, so the power surge seemed to have only affected our home phone. Neither Michelle or I had cell phones—she must have called the utility company from the neighbors. The service rep told me they had someone in the Gold Rush area, and our service should be restored soon.

I briefly considered closing the shop and walking home to check on Michelle. She'd be upset if I did. So much required my attention here at the store. She was a big girl. She would surely go to the neighbors and call or drive the eight blocks to the store if she needed anything. The phone would be working again soon, anyway. Besides, Chief Dailey was watching over her. I had nothing to fear.

A number of customers stopped in, but they mostly wanted to talk about the van accident, so mainly I listened. One man had been there when they took the driver away, dead at the scene. The EMTs had told him the victim was probably dead before the crash—heart attack.

When the store was empty and I had time to myself again, I looked down at my hands as I stood at the register. They trembled.

Don't wor-ry, ba-by, Harvey seemed to sing in a whisper.

My heart began to pound as if I'd just ran a hundred-yard dash.

Everything'll turn out all right.

I wasn't sure that I liked Harvey, anymore, if I ever had—or his choice of oldie's lyrics. And, I certainly didn't like these little coincidences in which I seemed involved. *What is happening?* I asked Harvey in my thoughts. *Am I going insane?*

No, it's the rest of your world.

I looked forward to Mike Wu's promised visit. At least then I could speak my thoughts to a real person.

* * *

Sitting at the control console, Doctor Xiang studied the figure in one of his few working monitors. It displayed a view of the inside of Gold Rush Hardware, the temporary proprietor watching as three customers left and then standing at the cash register and staring at his hands. Xiang wished he knew Subject 374's thoughts. He would like to be inside that complicated head now. Was he frightened about what was going on around him? Did he understand any of it? How much did he know that was really happening? Xiang suspected he still knew very little, and soon he would ensure even those concerns would be wiped from Subject 374's memory.

Xiang pressed another set of three buttons and pushed *Intercom Speak.* Things were getting complicated with this subject. He was well worth the extra trouble, however. Xiang would ensure they regained his control, now. Subject 374 did have an equal, and his equal's loyalty was not in question.

After a few seconds a voice responded, "This is Wu, Dr. Xiang."

"We have lost yet another man. The Czech Jaworsky was only to watch our subject. He died while driving by the hardware store."

"I would like to help," Wu said.

"You were scheduled to meet with the subject yet this morning, anyway. I need you to go now and to complete the task Captain Vanzandtz could not," Xiang told him, still staring at his motionless subject on the monitor.

"Yes, Doctor," Wu said. "I am ready. I will easily overpower him."

"No, you will not," the doctor said quickly. "You are to only place a new antenna microchip on his collar as Vanzandtz failed to do. I do not want him dead—yet. We have too much invested to give up so easily. Your *overpowering* him could end up fatal, for one or both of you."

"I have the focusing plate. I am the strongest, sir. You said that yourself."

"Must all of my subordinates argue with me today?" Xiang had conceived and started this project over three decades ago—he thought *he* was the one in charge. Yet today, Xiang's underlings had questioned him more often than in the entire past thirty-five years put together. "I said, *no*. You are only to place the microchip. Besides, his abilities seem more advanced than we realized. Do as I say and do it quickly."

Xiang pressed a different set of three buttons and then *Intercom Speak*, again.

"Yes, Doctor," came a feminine voice.

"Yumi, have security send two of the Caucasians to watch our subject—perhaps the two young Russians."

With so many of Xiang's monitors and microphones out, his people were not able to keep adequate surveillance, and he did not wish to put Chief Dailey in jeopardy. And to him, any Russian was expendable—countrymen of his father, the man who made him a bastard by screwing a young Shanghai whore and leaving her for the Japanese to torture and kill.

Xiang said, "Instruct them to keep their distance, but ensure they understand that they cannot lose him—or there will be consequences."

"Yes, Doctor," Yumi said.

Xiang released the intercom button and watched the monitor as the subject sat down at a desk and covered his face with his hands. Xiang nodded understanding Subject 374's confusion. He swiveled his chair away from the console feeling assured the project would soon be back in his complete control. He trusted Yumi and Wu. They had never failed him, only questioned his orders when their enthusiasm to please him spilled over.

He thought of Yumi and smiled. How lovely she could be, how sweet her scent, the air of her presence. Xiang had many women before but hadn't any sort of affection for any of them. He'd never wed—marriage was for lazy men and not for leaders. He'd saved Yumi for a special occasion, savoring the idea of their first sexual tryst, and he knew she would be as eager to please him in the bedroom as she was in the laboratory. Soon, he would have her in celebration, but more importantly, he would soon have all the power he could imagine. With no desire to *rule* the world, only to milk it for anything and everything he desired, he would leave that to the politicians and diplomats. But out of sight, above the world's stage, he would be the one working the leaders' puppet strings. And if any of them got in the way, caused him the least bit of problem, he would sever their strings.

The door opened slowly interrupting Xiang's reverie. A rotund Oriental man with hat in hand and cue ball head stepped in—Consul General Meng Juhong.

Xiang felt his lip curl uncontrollably.

* * *

Still in his den at the Double R, President Mason gazed out blankly, overwhelmed by the thought *of psychic assassins* killing off heads of state of allying countries—perhaps he was next. He had been discussing the situation with his four most trusted cabinet members for over two hours and, during that time, little new information came in from any of their intelligence sources.

A moment of silence had passed when Mason finally turned to Chief of Staff Thurman. "Eddie, I want *Marine One* warmed up. We're going back to Washington."

"Good, Mr. President," Thurman said as he stood up. "We can provide better protection in the White House's Presidential Emergency Operations Center. Going to "Site R" at Raven Rock or staying aloft in Night Watch would be even better, though, sir."

"Protection, hell. Things are about to hit the fan. I want to be able to talk to the people. I'm not going to cowl underground in the PEOC bunker or fly around in the National Airborne Ops Center wasting taxpayer's money like some kind of chicken shit."

"As you wish, sir. I'll be prepared to implement Enduring Constitutional Government measures should you decide, Mr. President."

As Thurman left for the spare bedroom converted to a communications center down the hall, Mason asked, "Where's Greta?"

CIA Director Winston checked his watch. "Mrs. Mason should be in the air about now, just out of LAX. I believe her next stop is Dallas for the start of her children's hospital tour in the Midwest."

"Cancel that," Mason said. "I want her with me. And get a hold of Secretary Zimmerman. Homeland Security needs brought up to speed on this, as well as the rest of the cabinet. Instruct Zimmerman to put the country in Condition Orange and prepare to move it to Red at my order."

"Yes, Mr. President," Winston said as he departed for the Com room.

In the doorway, Defense Secretary Jacob Banks moved aside to let Winston past and then stepped back into the room. He'd been outside the President's study, speaking on the phone with Dr. Ultar about the video hookup.

"Jake, while we're waiting on this video feed from Ultar, fill me in on the players.

"Good timing, Mr. President," Banks said. "That's exactly what I was about to do. I've referenced the names I just got from Dr. Ultar with our intelligence database."

The President asked, "First of all, who's behind this? It must be sanctioned by a foreign government or political concern."

"We have several possibilities, sir," Banks said. "They're the usual suspects—Arabs, possibly Al Qaeda or Taliban, Iranians. Could even be Chinese or North Koreans. We're looking at other possibilities, even domestic, but still nothing more than speculation, yet."

"Brief me on the names, then—everyone your RVs have come up with in this mess, both ally and enemy."

Banks said, "You already know as much as we do about Daniel McMaster, Major Lionel Jackson, Master Gunnery Sergeant Bernard Sampson and our mysterious Mr. Robert Weller." He opened a notebook he'd been carrying and began scanning the information. "The name Dr. Xiang Gao comes up quite often. He came to the U.S. in 1958 at the age of nineteen. A Chinese child prodigy, he attended Peking University and Shanghai Medical University, earning a PhD in psychiatry. It's thought that his rich foster parents then secretly helped him defect and sent him on to Stanford to broaden his education. He was there for ten years prior to the start of U.S. government studies in the paranormal. He's thought to have had some involvement in MK-ULTRA, although we can't find corroborating documentation."

The President's eyes grew wide. "He worked with narco-hypnosis—the mind-control experiments?"

"We believe so, sir. Studying the effects on

unsuspecting students after they'd been administered mind altering drugs like LSD, mescaline, scopolamine, BZ and sodium pentothal, as well as radiation, electric shock—electroconvulsive therapy. He may have been involved in the latter experiments with the *stemoceiver* remote-control, electronic implant."

"Judas Priest," the President said, shaking his head in disbelief.

"Then, he headed up Stanford's research in psychic phenomena and specialized in brain-wave projection. Our predecessors actually considered hiring him to help manage our studies there when we started them in 1969. After he originally defected, the background check we did on him didn't throw up any *red* flags, so to speak. But, in 1970, after a second thorough background check, it was discovered he'd been implicated in the 1958 murder of his foster parents back in China, and there was some concern that he might have had ties still with his homeland—that he was a Chi-Com here as a spy. He must have been tipped off because he disappeared with ten million dollars of donated and grant-derived project funds before he could be either tried and imprisoned or extradited back to his homeland.

"Our best guess is that he's now hiding out in a remote area of the Rockies and has somehow perfected his experimentation. And now he's using some form of brain-wave projection to psychically assassinate special targets. Our greatest fear at this point should be that Daniel McMaster has aligned with Xiang, and together they've contrived a very frightening scenario."

Mason clasped his hands against his chin and said nothing, soaking in the information. He still couldn't believe all this paranormal crap. It was fiction.

"Dr. Yumi No is a former Stanford alumna and was also a faculty member in the early nineties after she completed her PhD in neurophysiology. She is believed to be Xiang's right hand woman. Nothing on record of it and a bit contrary to this information, our RVs are linking her name with Falon Gong, an ancient Chinese discipline that has become a voice for their human rights movement. It's been banned in their home country.

"Captain Vanzandtz was a U.S. Army lieutenant in charge of *talent discovery* also at Stanford in the early eighties until her psychic research project was terminated in 1986. She was promoted to Captain and transferred to personnel in DC. A month later she resigned her commission and disappeared. Funny thing is, now our remote viewers are saying she's either no longer involved in the scenario, or will be out of the picture soon. Regardless, she'd built up a database of hundreds over her four years at Stanford—those who had psychic potential. And with her personnel job, she had access to a good number of the names of those involved in the Army's research in psychic phenomena through the years. Some from the Stanford study were recruited into the *Grille Flame* project—a precursor to *Star Gate* and what we now know as *Thousand Eyes*.

"Daniel McMaster was one of those taken into *Grille Flame* from Stanford. That's also where McMaster met his wife Sunny. From what our *Thousand Eyes* RVs are saying, Robert Weller is suspected of going through the talent discovery phase at about the same time, but we've been unable to find any record of it, nothing with his name on it. He could have been using an alias, or is now. Or perhaps our RVs are barking up the wrong paranormal fruit tree.

"Daniel McMaster's wife Sunny took part in the study briefly, but she didn't seem to offer much promise psychically and dropped out. She has an MS in Physics. Her expertise is holographics. We believe she is accompanying Major Jackson and Gunny Sampson, now.

"Most of the other names the RVs are coming up with—we're unsure of. Might just be combinations of letters that mean nothing. Wu, Shekhar, Mish. We find no connection to these names with any other aspects we're investigating except an obscure possibility with a Dr. Rajiv Shekhar who's been missing for about two months. He's a Pakistani immigrant—former head of neurosurgery at Mayo Clinic. He and his family seemed to have just disappeared one night."

Mason laid his hands flat on his desk. The remote viewers had come up with much more than their intelligence agency siblings, still it wasn't nearly enough to put together this conundrum—and their guessing was just too incredible.

Banks continued, "I'm leaving the most curious for last. The remote viewers have come up with the name Meng Juhong several times. He just happens to be the Chinese Consul General of New York."

"New York?" Mason repeated and turned to the large window behind him. He stared out at the silent woods, not pleased with the implications.

Chapter 11

It was about eleven a.m. when Mike Wu stopped in the store. Taller than the average Oriental man, my brother-in-law wore a big grin, blue jeans and a dark-blue T-shirt. I was happy to see him.

"Hey, Mr. Lucky!" He slammed an open, greenback-stuffed envelope onto the counter in front of me.

I couldn't help but smile. "Ninety bucks, huh? Finally, something good this morning. I hoped my luck would change before Michelle and I go to see Will this afternoon."

Mike frowned back. "What's wrong, brutha, bad day?"

"Yeah. You know, the two deaths. You've heard?"

"Sure, I have. But what's that got to do with you?"

"I was there both times. It's like I'm a jinx or something."

Wu frowned sympathetically. "That's a shame, man. But you know that's gotta be a coincidence. They were both heart attacks, right?"

"Yeah, right."

"There you go then. Hey, you and Mish up for another football game in two weeks? The Broncos and the Chiefs. It ought to be a good one. Lucy and I'll get the tickets *and* drive."

"Sounds great, Mike. But can we get back to you on that? I mean with things up in the air with Will and all. And the concussion, well . . . how about if we let you know by this Sunday?"

"Sure, Rob. You know I'm pulling for Will and you guys."

I was reminded of how good of a friend Mike had been. "Yeah, Mike. By the way, thanks again for redoing our shower. Nice job. And for bringing over the UPS packages."

"Hey, no prob, bud," he said. "What're brother-in-law, slash, friends for?"

He shook my hand and at the same time reached across the narrow counter with his other hand to pat my shoulder.

I don't know what got into me, but I drew back like before with the woman in the street. Maybe it was something about the way he had his hand cupped. When I looked into his eyes, I saw alarm, maybe concern about something, as if he didn't know what to do next. His expression startled me, and I let go of his hand and stepped back.

"You okay?" I asked.

"Yeah," he blurted and recoiled two steps. It looked like he placed something in his pocket from that cupped hand. His other hand was now behind his back. "It's just that . . . I've got to go. I just remembered I have an appointment at the *Gazette*."

I got that tingling in the base of my neck again. My ears began ringing. My temples ached.

Mike frowned at me, his eyes growing intense.

I became dizzy. The tingling on my neck amplified.

Mike stumbled back. He seemed as confused as I was.

From all around us came a sort of harmonic hum. The resonance slowly increased to a roaring reverberation. In front of the store, the three large picture windows cracked one at a time. The front door glass fractured. Six feet to my left, the Seiko watch display case shattered. My skull vibrated. My lungs became heavy and my breathing burdened. My heart hammered in a sudden arrhythmia. Fiery heat enveloped me. I felt as though I was spinning, and my vision blurred making only the center of my focus clear.

Mike kept his forceful stare on me until my eyeglasses

not only cracked, but burst out, fortunately sending the shards away from my face. His eyes went wide. He gasped as if it were the first breath he'd taken after surfacing from a long dive to the ocean's depths. His hands now to his throat and chest as if he also was having trouble breathing, he bolted and rushed toward the door. His shirt was above his belt in back, and something stuck out that looked like the handle of yet another pistol.

Everyone's got guns, Harvey said. *It's like Dodge City!*

Wu swung the door open wide and rebounded off the doorframe as he went through as if he'd been body checked into it. In a staggering trot, he left.

A bit off balance myself, I hurried to the doorway to see if he was all right. He was gone. A late-model, blue Ford pulled away from the corner, but he hadn't had time to get into the driver's side and start it. Someone, maybe his wife Lucy, had been waiting for him. But I didn't recognize it as their car—I couldn't even remember what kind of car they drove.

The pain inside my head subsided quickly. The hum diminished like a jet engine shutting down, and the ringing in my ears went away. I went back to my chair at the desk behind the counter, collapsed into it and considered the strange morning. What was wrong with me, with my head? Could the humming and ringing really be caused by a concussion? But what about my glasses breaking, the windows and display case? And what was with everybody else? Why were people carrying handguns, especially Mike? In what kind of world had I awakened?

I tossed the empty eyeglass frames to the side, took out my old pair of cracked spectacles and put them on. Reaching for the phone, I thought about calling Mike at the *Gold Rush Gazette* newspaper, where he was editor, to make sure he was okay—or maybe try calling him at his home. But I began questioning Mike's friendship. I didn't know why. He was my best friend, had been since grade school. He was best man at my wedding and me at his. He was Michelle's brother, my brother-in-law. He had fixed my shower so I wouldn't fall and hurt myself again, and he'd given me ninety dollars and invited me to a football game. Why would I doubt his friendship?

I couldn't put my finger on it, then Harvey did. *He was afraid of you, Superman. And he was packing heat.*

I told Harvey he'd been reading too many Raymond Chandler novels, as if imaginary talking rabbits could read. At the same time, I was becoming more and more confused by it all. And my abundant disarray had spilled over into something much more unnerving—terror. I began to tremble again, a shiver at first and then uncontrollably.

Should I go next door and call Chief Dailey?

No, Harvey said.

Was I going mad? Did I have some sort of disease? Should I call Dr. Xiang, or the emergency room?

No.

What then?

Hang on. Help is coming. You'll know soon.

My eyes shifted around my store. There were no customers. Harvey's voice was still crystal clear. Where was it coming from? It couldn't be my own thoughts. Yes, it was inside my head, but there was more to it—more to all of this. I began worrying for my own safety. For Michelle's. For Will's. Something very strange was happening in Gold Rush, and I seemed to be the focal point.

I stood up and quickly went to the door, locked it and flipped over the door sign to say *Closed*. After backing away from the entrance, I shrank to the floor behind the counter, and sat in the broken glass of the display case. I prayed whatever was happening would be temporary, caused by my concussion, and it would soon dissipate . . . and I tried to hang on, afraid of what I was hanging on for.

* * *

Defense Secretary Banks opened the large wall cabinet opposite the President's desk and turned on a wide-screen TV. President Mason came around and sat on the desktop, and the rest of his advisors turned their chairs to better view the demonstration. Banks pressed the remote control several times. He stepped back as the screen lit and several figures quickly materialized.

"Dr. Ultar, Jake Banks here with the President and some of his staff. Can you hear me okay?"

On the TV, a balding, dark-skinned man in his early sixties turned to look up into the camera. He adjusted his thick glasses. His voice came over the speaker sounding as if he were talking into a can. "Fine, Mr. Banks. Mr. President, it's truly an honor to be able to give you a little video tour of our project."

President Mason went fishing. "Dr. Ultar, I'm pleased to meet you. I've been wanting to learn more about your work. I understand there's no one else with your kind of experience and expertise in the field of remote viewing in the world."

"Thank you, Mr. President. I wish I could say that's so. Since Dan McMaster left our project seven years ago, I try to get by."

Mason frowned at Banks then looked back to the TV. "So what about this demonstration? Are you ready to give us a show?"

"Yes, sir." Ultar stepped away and the camera pulled back showing more of the white-walled room. Five large containers filled with water were arranged like wheel spokes in a five-point star at the center of the room. Inside each of the clear aquarium-like boxes was a floating human body, clad only in bathing suit, electronic leads fixed to various points of the cranium, neck and torso.

The camera zoomed in on Ultar as he approached the tanks. "These are our sensory deprivation tanks." He rested his hand on the side of one. "We've tried about everything over the years—hard wooden chairs, big, plush recliners. It seems with our RVs inside the SDTs they are distracted the least and find better focus." He motioned across the room with his hand. "Even the white walls are relatively new. For the longest time, we thought complete darkness would be more conducive to concentration. We found the white walls stimulate brain function and alertness without disrupting attention."

"Are your RVs awake?" Mason asked. "From here it looks as if their eyes are closed."

Ultar smiled looking over his aquatic team of three men and two women. "In literal terms, awake yes. However, they are all in a self-induced, altered state of conscious. Notice the thin covers over their ears. They're unable to hear us—a soft electronic noise is being piped to them. It is neither rhythmic nor tonal. Note the microphones near their mouths. You'll see their lips move slightly on occasion. They quietly speak what their subconscious mind sees, and that information is recorded for their debriefing. That's where they draw out what they've seen onto paper, and we help them interpret it. It is not a science, more of an art at this point, really." Ultar smiled at the five RVs. "They are completely involved in their assignment."

"And that is?"

"They've been instructed to remote view Gold Rush and to find Daniel McMaster."

Mason was confused. "Of course you know we've determined McMaster isn't in Gold Rush, Colorado."

"Yes, Mr. President. We're well aware of your physical findings; however, all five of our remote viewers are unbudging about the locale—perhaps there is another Gold Rush or a place with a similar sounding name. Anywhere, Montana . . . far south in the Andes . . . Asia, Europe, or even in our own backyard—the Appalachians, the Adirondacks."

"Ridiculous," Chief of Staff Thurman said under his breath.

Remembering that the RVs had conjured up the name of the New York Consul General from China as a part of this assassination scheme, Mason glanced at Defense Secretary Banks for assurance and got a skeptical head shake in return. Even the thought of the possibility such a plot was being carried out a stone throw from the nation's capital or the nation's largest city caused a shiver.

Ultar continued, "Regardless, I've decided not to tell our RVs any different as they seem to be finding a considerable amount of other information."

"Considerable?" Mason asked.

"Well, Mr. President, it is considerable for us as remote viewers. You see, this process cannot be rushed. The information we glean from a remote viewing session comes in precious small quantities. It materializes in images, shapes and forms that must be further analyzed before its true meaning can be learned and attested to. And the sessions themselves are exhausting. We've determined that any more than two, at the most three, fifteen minute sessions over a twelve-hour work day is as much as a human body can stand without serious physical health risk."

"Is it that taxing on all remote viewers? Do they all go through this process?"

"Well, no, sir. There are those rare and gifted few—like McMaster for instance—who actually see and seem to experience their target assignments in a realistic, three-dimensional view. They seem to move through the ether with relative ease. McMaster compared to one of our current RVs would be like pitting a marathon runner to a Sumo wrestler in a footrace around the DC beltway. There are only a handful of those special remote viewers in the world. Many are considered shaman, prophets, conjurers or witchdoctors in their cultures. McMaster was second to none as far as I know."

"Tell me more about McMaster."

"Daniel was special—he was an RV of the third protocol. He could transcend into the universal matrix and connect to it upon a whim, travel through space and time freely."

"Do you expect me to really believe that, Dr. Ultar?"

Ultar smiled again into the camera. "That makes no difference to me, Mr. President. I know it is true, and I speak only the truth. What you do with that truth is up to you. I would suggest, however, that you keep an open mind. I'll only ask you if just because you don't see something in your everyday life, does it mean that it doesn't exist?"

"Okay, say I believe you. Why did he quit if he was so

good?"

"Perhaps I've made it sound too simple—too easy. Daniel's trips into the ether were not without cost. Although the physical effects to him were relatively minor, the emotional and psychological ones were very exhausting. To see the true past, to experience it as if you are there, to learn the lies, is an incredible shock. To see the suffering that has happened, see the faces of the tortured dying. To hear their pleas for only one thing—to live, and to realize that their words are futile, that you can do nothing about it, and their suffering will be long and hard until they die. To see the future, have knowledge of it and learn what is to come is no less stunning. And with this knowledge, what do you do? Change the present so that this or that does not occur in the future? Then what? How have you affected the future? Have you made it worse? Who are you to say what should and shouldn't happen, who should and should not live? The responsibility was overwhelming."

Mason saw his point, but couldn't understand it fully. He assumed it would not be all candy and ice cream to be able to see the future—to use the knowledge to make the world better—but how could any sane man turn away from such power? This fact added to his skepticism.

He asked Ultar, "Your present staff—what are their capabilities and limitations? What, exactly, can we learn from these RVs of yours?"

"These fine viewers are of the second protocol. Highly trained. Skilled, their minds well-developed, psychic instruments. They see shapes, colors, sometimes even clear images and interpret them. Connecting what they see with what they have been assigned to see, we are able to translate that into useful information."

Chief of Staff Edward Thurman turned away and went to the window where Mason had stood earlier. "Bunk!" he said. "I've heard enough. Pure bullshit."

A knock came from the door, and Banks opened it slightly and looked out. When he turned back to the President, he said, "*Marine One* is ready and waiting, but we've got some bad weather coming in, Mr. President.

The pilots are concerned that if we don't get you on the way now, we'll get socked in."

Mason punched the power button on the television screen. "I've heard enough. Let's get going."

* * *

Sitting on the floor behind the counter in my hardware store, it took a while for me to gather my thoughts and mold them into a halfway functional form. When I checked my new Seiko, it still showed only a couple of minutes past eleven. Its hands were motionless, its crystal cracked and smoky. I'd been damn hard on watches lately.

If I rose only a couple of inches from behind my busted display counter, I could see a large clock in the print shop across the street. Occasionally, I checked it but time seemed to creep around the big clock's dial. Finally, when it read a quarter till noon, I could take being alone in the store no longer. If I wasn't insane now, I would soon drive myself crazy—with Harvey's help. I had to get out and find some sort of distraction from the madness.

I tried calling Michelle again, but now the store's phone was out, too—no dial tone. I hoped she had already left for the restaurant. It was a little early for lunch, but getting away to see Michelle's cheerful face was sure to be therapeutic.

I locked the cash register and grabbed my sport coat. At the cracked front door window, I set the hands on the closed sign for one p.m., and I hoped somehow the world around me would quit tumbling by then. I wasn't in the mood to deal with all of the broken glass and windows right now. It would have to wait. I would call the glass shop in Summitview when I returned from lunch. I didn't have any idea what my insurance company would say about the damage and couldn't remember what my deductible was.

As I stepped outside and locked the door behind me, I noticed two men looking in my direction from across the street.

Harvey was as curious as I was. *What're they looking at?*

I tried to pay them no attention, but after all that had happened earlier, a chill shot through me. On the second glance, as I walked away, they still watched me. One threw his cigarette to the sidewalk and smashed it out with his toe. They both stepped from the curb and started toward me. I expected them to say something, I didn't know what, but they didn't utter a word.

Then, I considered the color of their suits.

Navy blue, Superman, like the woman's.

Navy blue like the guy in the van—the dark-blue van. Like the car that had pulled away from the curb after Mike Wu ran out. True blue, I thought. That means trust.

Wake up! Get real. Where'd you get this conditioned response?

I turned up the street and walked briskly, wondering about that—a conditioned response. It was just something I'd been taught by my parents, grade school teachers—I didn't know. Then I thought about the first two men who'd waylaid me. At least they hadn't died—they just vaporized. But they wore no blue.

I looked back to see the two men jog around the corner, so I sped up. After a few feet, I checked over my shoulder. Now, they were running. Still they said nothing, only ran, so I sprinted all out but soon found I was obviously out of shape. I gasped with every breath I took. My legs were like concrete columns. The men were closing in on me. I didn't dare look back as it would slow me down, but I could hear their footfalls.

I made it to the next corner in front of Prospector's Bank and had another one of those shooting pains, and I staggered. I turned up Sluice Drive toward the police station. The pain worsened, and I finally had to stop and use one hand to steady myself against the limestone wall of the bank. Whatever was going on wasn't normal. Two people had died this morning for no apparent reason. I'd driven two men away who had just simply vanished. The meeting with Mike Wu and the breaking glass was far too weird. Now two more men were chasing me, and most of these strangers and Mike wore the same color clothes. And these headaches. It was too *Twilight Zone.*

The pain diminished quickly, and I was about to resume my run when I realized I couldn't hear their footsteps anymore. The way those guys were sprinting, they should've been within a few feet. I took the chance to look over my shoulder again, but saw no one on the street behind me.

Maybe it had been some sort of bizarre coincidence. Those men were trying to catch up to a friend or something. How crazy to think they were after me. When I was back at the store, my concussion must have somehow distorted my perception of Mike's visit and a sonic disturbance had cracked my windows and broken my glasses and the display case. That was as good of an explanation as any—a lot to happen in this sort of coincidence and compounded by the earlier happenings of the morning, but it took me out of the *Twilight Zone* and back to an explainable realism.

Still panting, I chuckled to myself and bent over, my hands on my knees, trying to catch my breath. For a while, I had been wondering if I might run smack into the extended belly of Alfred Hitchcock or the grim face of Rod Serling. After all, I had convinced myself I'd been plucked from reality and dropped into the middle of one of their films. I was being far too paranoid, and neither the concussion nor Harvey was helping.

Then came the scream. Several people from across the street ran toward the front of the bank. I cautiously walked in that direction. In spite of my breathlessness, when a man's voice called out, "Get a doctor!" I trotted to the corner.

Careful, Superman, it could be a trap.

I slowed up at the intersection and edged to the corner of the bank. Carefully, I peeked around it.

I couldn't believe what I saw. Just past the corner, two groups of a half dozen or more people had gathered about twenty feet apart. Someone lay in the middle of the closest group.

I shoved my way through the crowd. There before me was one of the men, the cigarette smoker, his body still, eyes parted slightly, lifeless. At the center of the other group was the second man. He also lay motionless.

It was too much to bear. Something terrible was happening, and I sat unwarily in the eye of it. For some reason people were dying because of me. Who else might die? Would others in the crowd drop dead if I didn't get away from them? Would more people in blue chase me? Should I go to the police, a doctor, a priest? If I were to go to Michelle, would she also be in jeopardy?

I could think of nothing else to do but run.

And I ran aimlessly. Hiding behind trash dumpsters, in alleys, in corners and behind delivery trucks. But all along I felt I was being watched. When I came to the Gold Rush Memorial Park, I ran into it and finally collapsed under the protective boughs of an old blue spruce tree surrounded by spirea bushes.

Exhaustion and bewilderment took over. I curled into a fetal ball, as a montage of memories came to me in images like pictures on playing cards shuffling through my mind. My head ached again, this time a steady and throbbing stab that debilitated me. The card-like images tossed, fluttering in all directions inside my head. From around the neighborhood, came explosions of various magnitudes—the pops of streetlights to dynamite-like blasts of electrical power transformers. It would be absolutely crazy to think they were somehow related to my dilemma, but I was sure they were.

I soon passed out in pain and confusion.

Chapter 12

Major Jackson had been speaking with Sergeant Chambers at the fence when they were interrupted by odd popping noises. He frowned curiously at the distant sound of explosions. Something unusual was happening in Gold Rush. Was it hand grenades, gunfire or fireworks? He hoped whatever was taking place wouldn't interfere with their mission.

When Lieutenant Carpenter called out frantically for Jax, he turned to see his young officer standing over Sunny who was sprawled on the ground.

Jax rushed from the fence line and knelt beside her. As he lifted her limp head and shoulders, Carpenter said, "She passed out, sir. Fell out of the DPV right here in front of me."

"Sunny," Major Jax said lightly, noting her skin was pale, almost blue. "Come on, Sunny, wake up."

He shook her, but got no response, her eyes closed. He laid her down gently and felt for her pulse. It was rapid and weak. He carefully pealed back her eyelids. Relieved to see her pupils were responsive, he placed his hand on her forehead. Her skin was cool and clammy.

"Damn it," Jax said. "Give me a canteen." he instructed, and as soon as he did, he found one next to his hand. He poured a handful of water and splashed it on her face, then patted her with his wet palm. "She seems in shock—nearly comatose." He nodded toward the back of the DPV. "Get me a thermal blanket."

Jax lifted Sunny, took her to the passenger's side of

the vehicle, and sat down with her in his lap. The lieutenant shook out the thin reflective blanket and placed it over the both of them, camouflaged side up.

The major held Sunny—her legs up and head down to keep sufficient blood flow to her brain—and kept her warm, while the other two men watched the small camp's perimeter. If Sunny was down for the count, their only hope to save Dan and the others would be an all-out blitz on the Biotronics Facility. But, right now, his concern was that she might be out for good.

* * *

From the corners of his eyes, Xiang watched Consul General Meng and drew close to the microphone on the control counter. Meng stood inside the control room door, his head bowed respectfully. He had seen the whole thing. Meng had witnessed Wu's encounter with Subject 374, the ensuing glass shattering and finally the monitor blacking out. Of course, Meng had no idea of what was happening, that Xiang had lost control, did not have control even now, of their most promising subject—but then, why did it matter what Meng knew?

The first thing Xiang had noticed about Meng was that he was a fingernail chewer. The squat little man wore a navy blue suit—some sort of expensive silk, probably—and his shoes seemed reptilian. Xiang had no idea of brands or styles, he did not care for those kinds of snotty amenities.

"Find him," Xiang yelled into the mike. "Now!"

"Yes, sir," Chief Dailey's voice answered over the speaker. "It won't be easy without the cameras. Power's out at a number of locations—some of our radios aren't working. Might be why we've lost contact with Yudin and Kozlov—the Russians we had tailing him. Hopefully, they still have him in sight. If they've lost him, though—"

Xiang said lower, but still agitated, "No excuses! The project itself is at stake. I want everyone on this. All available security, going door to door, looking under every rock. Do you understand?"

"Yes, Doctor," Dailey said. "We'll find him, sir. You can bet your life."

"It will be your life, Dailey. No one seems to realize the ramifications. This matter has not been taken seriously. Tranquilize him if need be, but allowing his escape is unacceptable. I do not care who else dies, just get him, alive. You know, like in your westerns, dead or alive. Except, if you do not get him alive, you are the one who will be dead!"

Xiang turned back to the Consul General.

Meng's eyes widened, his small mouth tight. He spoke his apologies anxiously to Xiang in Mandarin.

Xiang glared. "We speak English here. You are not inside your New York Consulate or at one of your big government parties in Beijing."

"Very sorry, Doctor Xiang," the rotund man said, his anxious bow of respect past the point of balance. He stumbled forward, his arms out, groping for stability, and Xiang caught him by the hand. The doctor's large hand constricted around Meng's meaty palm, Xiang's half-inch-long manicured nails digging into the skin on the back of Meng's hand.

Meng gave a reluctant and submissive smile, and his lips trembled. "So very good to meet you, Doctor Xiang." He tried to shake hands with the doctor, but Xiang wouldn't budge. Meng's smile left briefly, returning to be even broader and more patronizing. "I have heard so much about you and your work. So very sorry if I have intruded upon--. "

"Silence!" Xiang said, still holding Meng's fat little hand. He began squeezing.

Meng's eyes bugged. "Ah, Doctor Xiang," he said trying to pull away from the doctor's grasp. His face reddened. "You hurt Meng."

Xiang kept the pressure, steadily increasing his grip when the intercom buzzed. It was Wu's voice. "Doctor Xiang?"

"Yes, Wu. Go ahead," Xiang said, still compressing harder. With concern for Wu but oblivious of the Consul, he asked, "How do you feel?"

Meng frowned. His mouth twisted, and his face contorted in pain.

Wu said, "I am recovered, sir. Please forgive me for my weakness. But there is news. Senator Avery Lawrence has had a heart attack. He is in serious condition."

Xiang was puzzled. He frowned at the report.

"Also, we just received the call from Germany. Kyoto is dead."

Xiang smiled. "Thank you, Wu."

"Yes, Doctor," his assistant returned, and the speaker went silent.

Even with the good news, Xiang did not let up. He could feel Meng's hand bones through the thick layers of flesh, pressed them hard knuckle to knuckle. The veins obtruded on Meng's temples.

The death of Japan's Prime Minister Kyoto was no surprise, nor was that of Spanish President Garnica the week before. Xiang's telepathic assassins had gotten within range of their targets, close enough for eye contact, and done their jobs well. But this news about the senator was perplexing. Senator Lawrence was to be Subject 374's initial target, that was correct. However, the morning television interview the subject had watched was taped—months ago. And the purpose of its showing was to only familiarize the subject with the target. Yet the TV did explode unexpectedly. There had been an incredible amount of power released—unlike Xiang had seen before. But was it only a coincidence, a fluke? Still, he smiled when he realized what Lawrence's disability meant, coincidental stroke of luck or not—now, Subject 374 could go on to his primary target, President Mason.

"Over such a long distance," Xiang said aloud but to himself as he turned his glare to Meng, "and to a person without actual eye contact, how could that be?"

Tears came to Meng's eyes, squeezed tight in agony. His voice eeked out, "Ple-ease, Doc-tor."

Xiang clutched fully, his teeth set. More pressure still, constricting tighter. His thoughts were not on the Consul General. Subject 374, Robert Weller occupied his mind now. Perhaps Xiang had finally perfected his device to such degree that it surpassed all his hopes. If this was true, Subject 374 had somehow transcended space and time.

The cracking of Meng's hand bones brought back Xiang's thoughts. Finally snapping under the pressure, the sound, the feeling caused Xiang's eyes to widen with pleasure. Meng shrieked. He moaned and whimpered under the torturous mashing, but the doctor would not let up until he felt the metacarpal and phalanx bones crush into fragments. He worked his strong fingers against Meng's appendage, wringing it until blood streamed to the floor, and the Consul General's hand seemed like a boneless fillet.

"Open your eyes, Meng!" Xiang said, his voice strong, but no longer containing anger. He released his grip slowly, could feel Meng's pulse throbbing into the broken vessels, swelling the tissue, darkening his fleshy extremity into a solid red bruise.

Meng's eyes fluttered, his face now pale in misery.

"Open them," Xiang said somewhat softer, encouraging.

They opened, at first still grimacing in pain, but soon his face slackened, his look empty.

Direct eye contact made, Xiang entered Meng's thoughts. He soothed the screaming receptors, calmed the throbbing nerves, banished the pain reporting to Meng's brain. "You feel no pain?"

Meng's lips moved slowly, without emotion. "No, Doctor Xiang." He stared blankly into Xiang's eyes.

"You will go to the nurse's station. Have them bandage your hand. Tell them Doctor Xiang says you only need it dressed—that it will be okay, and they are not to be concerned. Then go to the plane, find a comfortable place to sit, and wait. We will leave in the morning."

"Yes, Doctor," Meng said, and turned toward the doorway. As Xiang got up and opened the door for him, Meng held his own right arm by the wrist, fingers flopped over like those of an empty, bleeding glove.

"Thank you, Doctor Xiang," Meng said smiling, his voice as natural and pleasant as if he were bidding hello's at a Sunday social, and he stepped through into the hallway.

As the Consul General left, Xiang wiped the blood from his hand onto the shoulder and back of Meng's silk coat.

The injured man stumbled away toward the nurse's station, and Xiang watched with an air of satisfaction. Augmented by the wonderful report from Wu, his meeting with Meng had been nearly orgasmic. But Doctor Yumi's appearance, stepping up slowly from the opposite direction, was a surprise.

At first Xiang found an unfamiliar feeling—at least unfamiliar over the last fifty or more years. Shame. He felt as if he were the naughty little boy whose mama had just caught him setting fire to the cat. The feeling didn't last long—after all, he never knew his mother—and it quickly turned to pride.

Yumi approached cautiously, awe on her face. She watched Meng, then gaped back at Xiang. "Doctor, what . . . ?"

Xiang held the door wider. "Please, come in, Yumi." He felt his smile quiver as he gazed down into her lovely, frightened eyes, the limpid russet ponds. Through their visual connection, he entered for the first time a place he had kept sacred just for such an occasion—her thoughts—and he found an incredible fear. It pleased him greatly.

She stepped into the room, her countenance blank.

His smile became a grin. Perhaps the good turn of events and his adrenaline-surging meeting with Meng was cause to celebrate.

The intercom buzzed. It was Wu again. "Dr. Xiang, the Russians are dead. Subject 374 is loose!"

* * *

Over three hours had passed since Sunny had fallen unconscious. After holding her for more than an hour, her color had slowly come back, and Major Jax had gently wrapped her in the reflective Mylar blanket rated for Artic weather. In the low sixties now, it was still important to keep Sunny warm to help stave off shock. Soon the temperature would drop rapidly, and tonight there was to be a hard freeze.

Now, while Sunny dipped from motionless calm to the depths of REM sleep, Jax watched over her from the driver's side of the DPV. Without taking his gaze from his best friend's wife for longer than ten seconds at a time, he consulted their SatCom laptop computer. After bringing the laptop out of standby, a new message appeared without sender name or location trail. Again, it seemed to materialize from nowhere, from the ether. The message consisted of only six numbers followed by four words—*THE KEY—before sunset*. Any military man would recognize the numbers as 100-meter map grid coordinates. Jax did not know how, but he was sure the message came from his dead wife, Moonfeather. He briefly smiled, and in his thoughts he thanked his long departed companion.

Jax dreaded their next step. They would have to go in without Sunny and with guns blazing. They would use the grid coordinates to hunt down Robert Weller, snatch him and interrogate him on the run, while avoiding a heavily armed defending force. Then, they would attack the Biotronics facility with their helicopters, attempt to find and rescue Dan McMaster and as many hostages as they could. They would use their nonlethals as much as possible, but still inflict, and have inflicted upon them, heavy casualties—likely including civilians. And if they were lucky, at least one of the choppers would make it out, rescuing a handful of the captive innocents at the cost of dozens of their rescue force. This was the scenario Jax feared would be the most to hope for.

Jax softly called out to Lieutenant Carpenter, and the young officer immediately returned to the major's side.

"Yessir," the lieutenant said, concern on his face.

"I'm afraid we'll have to proceed without Mrs. McMaster. I want you to take her back. Chambers and I will keep watch here until you return. Come back with both DPVs, Senior Airmen Craig, Jagger and Chang, and bring the dynamic hologram illumination devices. Tell Gunny Sampson and the pilots we'll go live thirty minutes after sunset. I'll radio them instructions. Keep radio silence until then."

The lieutenant only stared at him.

"I don't know how we're going to find him, but we have

no other choice, Lieutenant."

"I understand, sir."

"And we'll need to make room for as many of the other captives as we can snatch."

The lieutenant nodded and got into the driver's seat as Jax fastened the shoulder harness around Sunny.

Sunny's eyes fluttered. They opened. She groaned as her hands went to her head and squeezed. "God, my head," she said, frowning. "What happened? What time is it?"

Jax checked his watch. "Four thirty. We're taking you back to the choppers. You're in no shape to go on."

Sunny sat up abruptly. "What? Are you nuts? You won't be able to find Weller and bring him in without attracting a whole bunch of attention—not without me. I'm okay. Just a damn headache, that's all."

"Sunny, it's more than a headache," Jax said, as he unwrapped an energy bar and handed it to her. "I thought we'd lost you." He placed an open canteen next to her.

"All right, it's more than a headache," she said, taking a bite of the chocolate covered, high sugar treat, then gulped down some water. "I don't know what it is, but I do know you need me."

The lieutenant butted in. He'd put on the earphones attached to the SatCom unit and opened the eavesdropper program again. "Sir, more talk on their com lines. Their telephone circuits are really buzzing. A half dozen electrical transformers seemed to have just blown up all over the town."

"Those were the popping noises we heard earlier," Jax said.

"Sounds like more than fifty percent of the village is without power," the lieutenant added. "Also, civilians are saying there've been four heart attacks in town today. Lots of speculation. Viral heart disease, maybe."

Lieutenant Carpenter punched a couple of keys on the laptop. He listened intently as the major and Sunny waited. Soon, the young officer turned to them. "And sir, it sounds as though Robert Weller is on the run. From their command radio, orders are being put out to capture Robert Weller at all cost."

"He might be a little harder to find, this time," Sunny said, finished with her energy snack. She unsnapped the shoulder belt.

Jax stepped back so she could stand up, but he kept his arms out protectively. "Sunny, no."

"Jax, yes," she said, and went to the back of the DPV. She took out a pack. "I don't have much time. I've got a lot to do before sunset. A girl has to look her best, you know."

Jax gave in. "You still have the panic button?"

Sunny nodded, pulling it out from her shirt only long enough for him to see it.

"You activate it at the first sign your attempt is busted," he said, and Sunny nodded again. "And you still have the map?"

She pulled it from the back of her waistband and presented it to him.

"The dynamic hologram is your baby," he said unfolding the map before her. "Where do you propose putting the illumination devices in the event we need them?"

She pulled a grease marker from Jax's shirt pocket and narrowed her eyes at the map. After studying it briefly, she placed an "X" at three ridgelines about two miles apart.

Jax eyed each mark, then looked out in the physical direction indicated by each.

Sunny said, "My instructions are in the devices. Easy to understand—a first grader could set them up in fifteen minutes. And the DHIDs are self-calibrating. They use a radio signal to find each other. But don't forget that even with a full charge, they will only work at hundred-percent capacity for about thirty seconds and won't be convincing in full daylight."

Jax nodded. "And for you, I have Weller's location coordinates." Sensing Sunny was staring at him, questioningly, he added, "Yes, I got them from the laptop. No signature." He took the grease pen back from her and placed an "X" at the coordinates he'd received. "He should be there for another hour or so."

Sunny snatched the map from him. "Moonfeather," Sunny said sympathetically, a knowing smile on her face as she refolded the map.

Jax wondered if she was thinking he'd gone mad and joined the paranormal party train to netherworld.

She stepped over to her camouflage ghillie, slipped it over her head, turned away and trudged toward the hill in front of them.

"Our backs are against the wall, now," the major said. "We get your signal, and all our covert plans are busted. We'll go all out, rush in immediately, salvage what we can and pray to God we can get you and as many others as possible out. Do you understand, Sunny?"

She didn't allow the sergeant who watched the fence line to help her. After slipping through the hole under the fence, Sunny turned her face slightly toward the major.

"Yes, sir," she said, giving a weak salute and then pulled the ghillie's hood over her head as she started up the wooded ravine.

Jax watched her leave. Over his shoulder to the lieutenant, he said, "Go ahead with my instructions, minus Sunny. But tell the helo pilots to wait for my word. Get back here as quickly as you can."

"Yessir," the lieutenant said.

As Carpenter departed, Jax called over his shoulder, "Sergeant Chambers, bring my ammo can full of firecrackers—I have a job for you. We'll just mix our high tech stuff with a little old-fashioned fun."

* * *

As Sunny plodded up the hill, she considered how she would befriend Robert Weller enough to gain his trust and get him to come back with her. Now on the run from his subjugators, he might be open to at least some half-truths that sound semi-believable. She'd have to feel him out a bit and play on what he knew. And if he *was* some sort of a clone or copy of Dan, perhaps he'd have some of Dan's traits and idiosyncrasies that she could work with.

Actually, Weller did look a little like Dan. About the

same height and build—perhaps a few pounds lighter. And although he wore glasses and Dan did not, their eyes were the same shape. Weller's nose was smaller—Dan's was a masculine, prominent one that had been broken twice. Dan had a sexy cleft in his chin but always covered it up with a beard and mustache, whereas Weller's chin was smooth and clean shaven as was his top lip. Weller looked a bit younger, had walnut brown hair with no gray, and Dan's blond hair had been graying at the temples.

Lastly, Dan's eyes were blue. Still, there was something familiar in Robert Weller's brown eyes. She couldn't help but think that somewhere, at some time in the past, she had met this man.

* * *

Upset over loss of contact with Subject 374 because of the bungling Russians, Xiang had put the disappointment of doing without celebratory coitus with Dr. Yumi to the back of his mind. She had rushed from the control room when Wu's report disrupted their psychic connection. There would be time to make up for it later.

Now, after searching for the fugitive for several hours, the search teams finally were closing in on Subject 374—one of Wu's men had reported movement in the park that he thought was the subject.

Pleased things seemed to be going his way again, Dr. Xiang went to his office to make preparations for the coming days.

He sat behind his large wood desk, made from the best Arkansas black walnut, and ran his long fingers over its smooth, high-gloss finish. Except for a matching credenza against the near wall, the rest of the windowless room was simple, bleak. He could have had any kind of desk he wanted—he chose this one because he just loved the rich, dark grain. It was the color of his aunt's hair as he remembered it as a child. She had been the only one Xiang had truly known, the only one who had really cared for him. But while they were in a Japanese prison camp only months before the end of WWII, she had been killed—pulled from his grasp, tortured sadistically and then gutted before his five-year-old eyes. His aunt had been only thirteen.

Xiang slammed his fist against the hard wood of the desktop. He did not cry when she had been murdered, would never shed a tear for her or anyone else. But he would get even. And with his plans going better now, he would soon be able to realize his revenge.

The next step would be to place Subject 374 in Washington D.C. From there he would assassinate the U.S. President and a number of other political and military leaders who did not fit in with the plan. Meanwhile, hundreds of assassins would finish their programming and join those already in place. They would enter the civilian population benignly. After being programmed specific reasons for disliking their targets, they would be placed in positions strategic to the use of their telepathic powers. Then, they would carry out their individual missions. Without cause or any sort of evidence that they could have possibly had a hand in the natural deaths of their targets, and without knowledge of it themselves, they would not be detained long, if at all. Then, they would be free to be reprogrammed for their next targets. The authorities would get wise or at least suspect the assassins involvement eventually, and many of Xiang's psychic killers would be captured and taken out of play. With hundreds to do his bidding; however, it would be much too late. Even Xiang's superiors did not understand the extent at which the doctor's influence would soon reach.

Xiang pushed his thumb against a fingerprint scanner embedded in the front of his desk, and a snap came from the inside indicating the drawers were unlocked and could be opened for the next five seconds. He slid open a side drawer and pulled out a daily planner notebook. After opening it to a blank page, he began to reorganized his thoughts with a *to-do* list.

Before sunrise, he would send Subject 374 along with injured Consul General Meng on Xiang's private jet to Washington, D.C. Within hours after landing, the subject's support team would have him completely programmed and awaiting the first opportunity to kill President Mason.

This president loved public speeches, was always in front of the people. Opportunity should be quickly at hand.

Xiang was having trouble concentrating, disturbed by the many mistakes his people had made. He kept his list simple. As the first item, Xiang wrote *Assassinate U.S. President*.

Before that, however, after they caught up with Subject 374 and things calmed down some, he would find time to coerce Dr. Yumi into a *compromising position.* Second on his list, but with an arrow that pointed above the first item, he wrote *Screw Yumi.*

Xiang smiled. For the third item, he printed in all capital letters *CONTROL THE WORLD.* He chuckled as he tore the list from his planner, wadded it up and threw it into a nearby trashcan.

From the speaker at the side of Xiang's desk came Wu's voice. "Dr. Xiang! There is a disturbance on the west side of town. Dailey has reported automatic weapons' fire. He's requested help, and I've pulled the search teams in for assistance."

Xiang didn't know who was responsible, but his gut feeling was that this reported disturbance was a trick. "You fools!" he yelled into the microphone. "It is a diversion! Get your search teams back in place, now!"

Chapter 13

At sunset she came back to me, her fiery-red hair bounding around her shoulders like a horse's mane on fire. She had entered the park from the east, about a hundred yards away. Except for her, I hadn't seen anyone in probably fifteen minutes.

I was sure I'd been on the run for nearly six hours now according to the setting sun. The majority of that time I'd spent in the park, hiding in the middle of a clump of spirea bushes under an old blue spruce. It was here that I'd passed out. I sighed, realizing I'd missed the appointment with Doc Xiang. I wondered about my son, his prognosis, when and if I'd ever be able to see him again. I thought of Michelle.

I had come to consciousness with the worst hangover I could remember, but oddly enough, I couldn't recall any specific instances when I'd actually been hung over. The pain and most of the fog inside my skull had dissipated over the last half hour, and now I was deciding on my next cautious step. Darkness would play a large role in my escape, and I waited for its protective shroud.

Only minutes earlier, there had been men positioned at each of the four corners, watching the streets. Of course, they were wearing blue suits. Once, a man in SWAT gear, armed with what I thought was an M-16, had actually pushed through my hiding place in search of me. I'd been lucky, avoiding him by crawling and weaving through the bushes. He finally left. A few times I spotted a head bobbing behind the cornice of a three-story building about a hundred yards away. I had no idea what that guy might be up to, but I couldn't help thinking it wasn't something I would be pleased with. After the faint sound of what might have been fireworks came from the west side of town about fifteen minutes ago, it seemed everyone who had been searching for me had left.

The air had become chilly. In my inactivity, I felt the cold deeply and knew I must do something soon. My plan was so simple it was not really a plan at all. As soon as it became dark enough for me to pass unseen, I'd go to the public telephone two blocks away, punch 911 and explain my situation.

Harvey didn't like my plan. He'd been cautioning me to sit tight, that I would be okay if I stayed out of sight. *Something will happen. An opportunity will arise, and you'll recognize it as such. Then you'll be able to get to safety and straighten everything out.*

I wished he'd leave me alone.

Then she came again, the beautiful redhead I'd seen that morning on my way to work. She still wore her green sweats, and it appeared she was on a late afternoon run. I drew my head back into the bushes as she jogged by. Her image was only a dark silhouette, and her hair blended in with the bright orange of the western sky. She stopped a few feet past me and started shaking her arms and walking in circles. My first thought was that she was going into some kind of pre-death convulsions.

"God, no!" I said, stepping from my leafy sanctuary, fearing I'd killed her, too.

She turned with a start, her hand to her chest. Her big eyes were wide in surprise and as clear as the iridescent-green water of a calm Okinawan cove that I must have seen on a calendar somewhere. And they seemed that deep, too. I couldn't describe it exactly, but from that first moment I saw those eyes on my morning walk to work, I had the feeling I was falling into them, naked and entranced. They were the kind of eyes that explore souls, looking past any kind of guise, that draw you deep inside them while eliciting an overwhelming feeling of euphoria.

I felt some sort of connection between us, not that I wanted one—Michelle was a wonderful wife. Still, I felt it as tangibly as a lover's reaching arms. It could've been chemical, electrical, psychic, mystical, I didn't know.

I saw quickly she wasn't in her death throes and stepped back to my concealment.

"I'm sorry." With a half smile, I shook my head and then scanned the corners of the block and that three-story building on the other side of the park. My pursuers seemed to have given up. None were in sight. When I looked to her again, she was staring back. I told her, "I thought, well . . . that you were having an attack or something."

She gave me the cutest frown I'd ever seen, her face glowing. She shook her arms again. "I was shaking it off. I've been jogging, you know. Five miles."

Something about her I couldn't describe temporarily disarmed me, brought down my defenses and even the common sense fear for my own safety and hers.

I said, "Jeez, five miles. I get winded just looking at running shoes."

She snickered. "Aren't we just all kinds of witty?" She held out her hand. "They call me Sunny."

I gave her hand a cordial shake. "How 'bout that, Sunny and Funny. We could have our own variety show."

Her hand was soft and warm, but it made me shiver. I quickly released her, afraid I might be putting her life in danger, too. I stepped back. Mostly shielded by the spruce tree, I took another scan of the area and decided I was safe from view, at least momentarily. Still, I hunkered down.

The woman stepped closer to me, and she also bent over slightly.

Apparently, the only way to get rid of her would be to run. Hell, she might run after me. She obviously could keep up. I had to be firm, yet not too loud. But I found being firm with her was difficult. Everything that had happened and was happening now told me I should shove this woman away as hard as I could. However, everything inside of me, emotions I couldn't understand, told me I needed her.

For the first time since my morning shower, I thought of the mysterious note. Whether real or imagined, besides the warning it had contained words of wisdom. *Everything you know is lies. Trust not in what you hear or see, but solely in your emotions—for within them is the only real truth.* What I'd been seeing over the past several hours had been crazy. What I'd heard had been insane. My emotions—what I had felt—had been incredible fear for my life. And now this, an emotional connection, a need for this woman. I was thankful Harvey hadn't popped up with more advice to add to my confusion. Still, I was endangering the woman's life.

"Look, miss, you've got to get out of here," I told her. "Something really bad might happen."

"Oh, are you a rapist or something?"

I felt stupid, unable to explain, not even wanting to.

"Cause if you are, I know Ca-rotch-ee." She took another step toward me and placed a snap kick two inches from my groin. Her full lips thinned into a broad smile.

I tried to shield myself, but way too late. This woman seemed a little nuts, and I really didn't need her to complicate my life any more than it already was. "No, it's not that—"

"Hey. I know you."

"Yeah, this morning on the sidewalk, we passed and you slapped the hell out of—"

"Oh, yeah, the bee. If you're thanking me, you're welcome. But I meant College. Stanford, right?"

I'd never been to California, nor ever wanted to go, and I certainly never attended a school like Stanford. My college experience was limited to a two-year degree from Summit County Community College nearly twenty years ago. However, she did seem familiar. Surely though, as stunning as she was, I would have remembered her, that is if we'd been close enough acquaintances for her to recognize me.

"Yeah," she said, answering her own question, and she came at me.

I backed away, but before I knew it, she was hugging me. Her body was warm and damp and her soft hair smelled like lilacs in the rain. I couldn't help but nuzzle into it briefly.

"Robert. Robert Weller!" She pushed back to look into my face. "Come on, Robert, Sunny, remember? It's been more than fifteen years, but surely, you remember me. Sunny O'Donnell. I wore glasses, and I was a little frumpy."

"Sunny? Uh, well, you look, maybe, a little familiar. And you've got my name correct, but I've never—"

"Robert, I am surprised at you. After all we went through." She put her hand to her mouth and whispered, "After all we di-id!"

God, I thought, seeing past her unzipped sweatshirt to her filled-out Adidas T-shirt, noticing her trim waist and slender legs, *I wish I could remember*. "Listen, I'm sorry but you need to get out of here. There've been people dying."

"Robbie! Quit it. Be nice or you're going to hurt my . . . " She stopped and a pall came across her face. "You're not joking. How awful. Are you okay?" She took a second to look me over.

"Yeah, I'm fine, for now, I guess." I was about to insist I didn't remember her, but I thought, why bother.

"You . . . look fine." She grinned wide again and nodded. "Except for those broken lenses."

I touched my glasses, about to explain, but decided it would do no good.

"Well, it doesn't matter," she said. "It doesn't matter a bit whether you remember or not. Come on. Let's go someplace more comfortable, have some coffee or something. We've got a lot of catching up to do." She started pulling me by the arm. "What are you doing hiding in the bushes anyway?" She glanced back at me. "No, don't tell me, you really have become a rapist."

I couldn't find the words to answer her.

She sang out, "Who cares, I'll take you to my room anyhow." She tugged on my arm again. "I'm staying at the Mother Lode Inn, just down the street."

I kept my feet planted, and she put her hands on her hips.

"Uh, Sunny," I said, trying to be firm, "My wife wouldn't like it."

"Rob, I'm only kidding. There's a restaurant nearby." She glanced at her watch. "It's nearly six o'clock. You look hungry. Let me guess—cheeseburger with the cheese on the bottom, right?" She gazed at me seeming to study my reaction.

But how could she have known that? Such a small detail. Maybe she'd been in the Gold Mine Grill when I'd ordered one. It was a little quirk of mine. Cheese on the bottom of a burger made it different from the fast-food variety. It made it homemade. I was suddenly convinced that somehow this strange woman did know me. She'd simply gotten the place she knew me from wrong. I wanted so much to remember her.

"No, I can't," I told her. "Really. You don't understand. It'd be dangerous."

"Robert. You're scared. This isn't a joke, is it?"

I shook my head.

"Tell me. What's wrong?"

"I can't."

"Come on, Robert. After all we've been through. You can tell me anything."

I wondered all *what* she thought we'd been through. It didn't matter. "You wouldn't believe me."

"Try me, Rob. We used to be close. You used to tell me all of your secrets."

I exhaled with a puff and shook my head again. "This one, I don't even believe."

"Come on. If I laugh, you can quit."

I felt the need to tell someone, to talk it over and try to figure it out, even if that someone was a stranger. What could it hurt? Whatever I had was probably killing me, too. She'd been exposed to me longer than anyone else over the last ten hours, so she might drop dead, also. She must have had a stronger resistance than some of the others, that's all. How my customers in the store earlier in the day weren't affected, I didn't know. Maybe it was their clothes. No blue suits. And of course, Sunny's jogging outfit was green, not navy blue, if that made any crazy difference.

"First of all, I've never been to Stanford or California for that matter. Either you have me mistaken for someone else, or we met at some other place. You're vaguely familiar to me, too."

"All right, Robert," she said skeptically, "I'm not laughing. Now, what's going on with you?"

"Okay, you want to know? I'll tell you." I looked around for some soft grass. "Sit down." I pulled her toward a large patch of blue grass by the spirea bushes.

We sat cross-legged, our knees touching. She looked at me intensely, those eyes of hers, the deep pools opening up and drawing me inside. They made it difficult for me to concentrate.

I said, "People are dying because of me."

"What? Don't be ridiculous."

"I'm serious. I don't know how. But there have been at least four people I've been around today who just keeled over. There could be more I didn't see. I don't know. And I'm concerned about my wife."

"Yeah," she said, and her eyes went wide again. "All the deaths. It's the big topic all over town. They think it might be some kind of epidemic or something. Some sort of new viral heart disease, maybe. You mean you think you're like a carrier or something?"

"Or something. I don't know."

"That's crazy. It's only a coincidence. No virus works that fast."

"Maybe not. Maybe nothing they've discovered yet. Maybe it isn't a virus. Maybe it's a kind of charge or something I emit. Some poisons act real fast, and all it takes is less than a drop to kill somebody. Maybe I'm putting off some kind of fast-acting, toxic chemical. I don't know. I can't explain it. It's just happening."

I hoped this would be enough to scare her off, but instead, she tilted her head and her eyes narrowed with concern.

"Robbie," she said and reached out to me. Her long

bangs had fallen down around her eyes and her lips were moist and inviting. She stroked the side of my head, running her fingers through my hair. It felt good, and I relaxed a little. I gave up on convincing her I didn't know her. I didn't care. Her voice came out as soft as her hand. "We're going to find out what's going on, I promise. You'll be okay."

Looking at her, I couldn't think of what to say, as if my mind was stuck in neutral. She gazed back at me, taking all of me in, looking at my hands—touching them, my wrists, my face. I felt as though I was being examined—not by any sort of medical professional, more like by a lover.

Her eyes grew misty, and her lip trembled. "Whatever happened to us?"

An odd question to ask at the time, but still a good one. I certainly wished I could remember, even if the memory was stolen from whoever she had me confused with. Evidently, at one time, she'd had strong feelings for me or whoever she thought I was.

She dropped her hand to my knee and blinked the tears away before they could form. "I'm sorry. Go ahead. Tell me more."

I took a moment to think. "It started this morning with a note I found in my shower that said for me not to trust anyone."

"A . . . note in your shower?"

"Yeah, then my TV blew up. Then, after I bumped into you, and I got that little bee sting . . ." She grimaced in sympathy as I gently patted the back of my neck. I continued. ". . . I was accosted by a couple of goons—military types—looking for somebody. They tried to grab me, but I pushed them away . . . and they just disappeared." I didn't elaborate about them vanishing into thin air. "About three blocks down the street, I noticed that the air had calmed, and the birds had quit chirping. It was like something was going to happen, something bad. You know, like in the eye of a storm, and you're just there waiting for it to hit you again."

"Again?"

"Yeah, I'll get to that later." I carefully recounted to her the incident I'd had with the woman in the street.

"The car horn, Rob, the excitement killed her. She probably had a bad heart, anyway." Her face looked so kind and smooth. Faint freckles were splashed across her nose.

I told her, "I'm not nearly finished."

She took my hand.

I drew a deep breath and went on. I told her about the van driver.

"There you go. Another heart attack. A little odd, but nothing more than a coincidence. Don't be so silly. You're okay. Quit worrying."

"Silly? Huh. I wish I were. There's more to this little 'coincidence.'"

She patted my hand, but said nothing. I could tell she was being cautious not to be too patronizing.

"The van. It was a dark-blue Ford van. Then I remembered the guy who honked before the lady died. He was driving a dark-blue Ford van, too. It was the same guy."

We stared at each other for a moment.

I looked at the ground. "Then before lunch, while I was walking over to the Gold Mine Grill, I noticed a couple more goons—guys I hadn't seen before—were watching me from across the street. These two were wearing suits. Navy-blue suits." My words came out faster. I couldn't slow down. "Then I realized both the guy in the van and the lady wore blue *fricking* suits. Next thing I know, the two guys start chasing me."

Sunny was looking at me as if I'd told her aliens had kidnapped her grandmother.

"I know," I told her, "you're still thinking I'm paranoid or something. Maybe what happened next will change your mind."

"I believe you, Rob. It's just kind of difficult for me to take in all of this. Go ahead. What happened then?"

"I couldn't hear them behind me anymore so I turned around. They weren't there."

"You were getting too close to the police station. They

were afraid they'd get caught for whatever they were up to."

"No."

"What, then?"

"They were lying in the middle of the sidewalk, both of them, dead."

Finally, the skepticism left her face and she appeared convinced I was in trouble. "My god, Robert, this is terrible. What are you into? Who are these people?"

"I have no idea. I didn't ask any questions, I just ran. I ran and ran and ran. And everywhere I ran, I saw people in blue suits. I didn't know if they were after me or not. A lot of people wear blue suits. And you're supposed to trust people in blue suits, right?"

"What do you mean?"

"You know, you always hear, 'true blue, trust them, do.'"

"I've never heard that. Sounds ridiculous. Where'd you get such a thing?

"I don't know, everywhere. My mother, father, teacher, I don't remember. I just know it's supposed to be true. Right?"

"No," she said simply. "Don't believe it. How could the color of someone's clothes make them trustworthy?"

I stared at her, and it finally sunk in. It *was* ridiculous. Still, somewhere from the back of my mind, a whisper came—not from Harvey—and I heard *true blue, trust them, do.*

Sunny looked sympathetically at me. "Now settle down a little. Let me see that sting on your neck."

I obliged her and began to lean forward.

Before my head had moved six inches, I heard a snap, and I felt something like another bee buzz behind me.

"Damn," I said, "am I wearing a bull's eye back there?"

We frowned at each other. She gently pulled my head down, and I wondered if the sting had something to do with this disease or whatever it was I had. This time, as she brought my head forward, I heard a solid thud, and splintered bark seemed to jump from the spruce tree beside us.

Our eyes met, wide in amazement. I remembered the silencer on Vanzandtz's gun, and it took only a second for me to realize we were being shot at.

Chapter 14

I bolted to my feet, at the same time pulling Sunny to hers.

"Run," Sunny shouted.

"The police station!" I said leading her by the hand. We ran a hundred feet to the street and leapt from the curb onto Sluice Drive, the main artery joining the east side of Gold Rush to Summit County Road 539. That blacktop was the only way out of town to the south, and it dead ended at Mount Rainy Biotronics to the north. As we ran across, I briefly considered going in that direction. I'd already missed our appointment with Dr. Xiang. I wondered if Michelle was okay, if she had gone without me. I wondered what Will's prognosis was, if he would walk again. I wondered what they both thought, if they knew the truth of what was going on, and if that truth was that I was somehow deadly to them.

As we made the opposite sidewalk, the stop sign at the intersection danced to the unmistakable whine of a ricochet.

Two seconds later, a small chunk of limestone popped off the side of the building we rounded. Both occasions were absent sound of an initial gunshot.

We ducked and cut the corner to head back up Prospector Lane toward the police station and flung ourselves against the side of the wall, gasping for air as we savored our brief safety. With our arms entangled protectively, we only had a second to give each other a questioning look of incredible terror.

From the angle the shots came from, I guessed the corner of the building kept us safe from the sniper, at least temporarily. He was probably the guy I'd seen earlier behind the roof parapet of the building on the other side of the park. I scanned the street and sidewalk around us to ensure our momentary safety. No one in view.

Sunny glanced at my shoulder and reached beside my neck. I felt her messing with something below my collar.

"God, Sunny. This is no time to pick off lady bugs."

But she persisted even at this deadly time. She looked puzzled as she pulled back the sport coat. One hell of a time for fussing with a loose hair. She took only a second to inspect whatever it was she found, and as she yanked the thing off, I remembered Mike Wu and Lieutenant Vanzandtz also having a fixation with my collar. I thought of the bump, the bee sting, and everyone wanting to touch me back there. I wished they could all keep their hands and stingers to themselves.

She held her discovery in front of me, and I took it. Roughly the size and shape of a dime, it was sticky on one side and covered in black latex about the thickness of a condom.

"What the hell?" I threw it on the sidewalk and scuffed it with the toe of my shoe. The thin latex cover peeled back and underneath was a copper foil with a tiny gold-plated circuit board like some sort of a computer chip. I had no idea what it could be. Sunny stared at it also, and I began to wonder if she didn't know more than she seemed to about the quagmire we'd stepped in.

I lifted her chin with my index finger to make her look at me. "Let's go!" I said and took her hand.

* * *

At the wooded staging area, Jax heard the DPVs approaching and walked to where they would park. Shortly, Senior Airmen Craig, Jagger and Chang pulled up in the first DPV. Lieutenant Carpenter whipped the second vehicle in beside it, a German shepherd sitting at his side.

"We're ready, sir," the lieutenant reported. "And we brought the infrared and motion-sensor covers you requested."

The dog leapt out and ran to Jax. He wagged his tail and licked the major's hand.

The lieutenant explained, "Sorry, sir. I know you didn't tell me to bring him, but I thought he might come in handy.

"Good thinking, lieutenant," Jax said. "That's why he's on the team, to help."

The major knelt and pet the dog, and the canine whined enthusiastically in response.

"That's right, Sarge. We might need you and that wonderful nose of yours. Whadaya say, boy, you up for it?"

The dog stomped his feet eagerly, and it made the major smile.

"Good, boy." Major Jax looked to Carpenter and said, "Put on your ears, lieutenant." To the three newcomers, he said, "Let's get those covers in place on the detectors to our west."

Carpenter put his headphones on. The other men went to the back of the DPV.

"Set the counter-sensor laser on low for their sensors," Jax instructed. "We only want them temporarily disrupted while we put on the covers. Don't burn them out, or they'll be all over us." The next step would be to send his men out to place the hologram illumination devices. That might take a couple of hours.

Jax looked up the ravine Sunny had followed. To himself he said, "And then, we wait."

* * *

Xiang got out of his limousine and headed for the back entrance of the police station. Bungling idiots—he was in charge of a bunch of bungling idiots. His men had fallen for a diversion of fireworks, sending all of the search teams to the opposite side of town to find a burning tool shed and the fragments of about a thousand Black Cat firecrackers.

Chief Dailey came through the doorway slowly and down the steps to meet him.

Xiang growled, "Firecrackers!" and shook his head.

Bailey looked at the ground.

"I understand our sniper spotted the subject and a woman hiding in the park," Xiang said. "But he missed them."

Dailey nodded. "He couldn't get close enough. Those tranquilizer darts aren't very accurate at much of a range."

"Who is this woman? Who?"

"We don't know, Doctor. We're checking."

"I've been told she isn't one of ours."

"We—"

Dr. Xiang exclaimed, "Who the hell is she, then? Where did she come from?"

"We don't know yet, but we'll get 'em." Dailey held his hands out in a calming gesture that only pissed Xiang off more. "We're right on their trail, now."

"We will see," Xiang said as he shoved Dailey to the side and stomped to the back steps. As Dailey followed, Xiang turned to his driver waiting outside the car. "Get me some supper. I will be coordinating the search from here."

"No need for that, Doctor," Dailey said. "I've done everything you instructed. All my men except the desk sergeant are out looking for him. We've alerted all the merchants whose stores are open late, put the word out to as many citizens we could contact. They're watching for him as if he had the plague. As a matter of fact, that's what we're saying, that he has some sort of contagious disease. I'm sure we're going to get the both of them within the next few minutes."

Dailey's patronizing words set Xiang off as the limo drove away. Xiang had controlled his anger, measured and doled out only what was necessary until now, but he felt that grasp on civility slipping. His arms waved emphasizing his frustration. "That is what you keep telling me. Yet I do not see them. Do you?"

* * *

Sunny and I sprinted all out, both of us panting heavily as we ran. From as out-of-shape as I'd felt earlier, I knew I was drawing my energy from pure adrenaline. However, the nearer we got to the police station, the more I was sure we'd soon be safe. Gold Rush had only ten full-time lawmen, the chief and his nine officers. I knew them all to be good men.

When we made it to within a block of the city building where the jail was housed, I saw Chief Dailey standing outside with Dr. Xiang. How could we have been more fortunate?

Sunny held back, pulling my arm like an anchor. "I'm not sure . . . ," she said in between breaths, " . . . this is such a good idea."

"Come on," I panted out. "Why back out on me . . . now?"

"It was on the way . . . to my motel room," she gasped, her words coming out in short bursts. "Let's forget about the police . . . and go to my room. We can hide out there for a while. Figure this thing out."

"No, look," I said. "It's Doc Xiang . . . and Chief Dailey. They're my friends."

Until they saw Sunny and me stampeding toward them, the doctor and chief seemed in a heated discussion. Doc Xiang's long arms flailed in the air as if he were describing King Kong loping through New York. The chief was giving the doctor a come-on, settle-down wave. I couldn't tell what they were discussing, but conflicting opinions were obvious.

Then Dailey turned toward us and quickly became moon-eyed as if the grim reaper himself were coming for his soul. Xiang, in the middle of his arm waving, glanced to see what the chief found so frightening. He gave a double take and stared. The look in Xiang's eyes could not be mistaken—pure anger—and it was being directed toward me.

I was in utter surprise. For a moment, I felt the hair actually raise on the back of my neck as we gazed at one another. I expected him to do something, yell something, and I was sure he was going to as his lips curled, and at the same time, the pains started in the back of my head again. But Doc Xiang seemed to reconsider, and within a second he did an about face. His once flailing arms reached for the handrails along the five concrete steps leading to the back door of the jail.

By the time we were within a hundred feet of them, the doctor had slipped inside, and my head pain subsided quickly. Chief Dailey watched the door close then gawked at us as he took three steps back with his hand on his sidearm.

"Don't come any closer," he called out. "I have nothing against you, boy. I wish you no harm." He released the grip of his pistol and raised his hands to chest level. "Just stay back. Take my advice. Get out of here."

Sunny and I slowed to a jog, and she stayed behind me.

"Chief," I begged, "what's going on? We need your help."

My words had no effect. Dailey shuffled backward a couple more steps. He turned so hastily he stumbled but caught himself and ran into the woods behind the building.

We stopped in the middle of the sidewalk and stared at the back door of the cop shop.

The sun had disappeared now. Only its pink glow remained, framing the wooded tree line behind the city building. A couple of seconds passed before common sense and a police cruiser two blocks away told me we had to keep moving.

"I don't understand what's going on," I said, "but I don't think the police are going to help."

"Doctor either. Some friends."

The patrol car sped toward us with its red light flashing and its siren blaring.

Sunny tugged on my hand, leading me on a trot to the alley, and I was pretty sure of where she was taking me.

Five blocks ahead was the Mother Lode Inn. With these blue-suited morons chasing me, a sniper after my ass, and now the police somehow involved, I couldn't go home or to my store. I hoped the sheet-rocked walls of Sunny's motel room would contain my deadly problem, keep me from killing anyone else, and be a haven until we could sort things out.

Chapter 15

We found a commotion of some sort at every street we came to on the way to Sunny's motel room. People scurried everywhere. As I'd done earlier in the day, we hid behind trash dumpsters and refrigerator boxes along the alley. We watched as police and emergency vehicles, and dark blue Ford vans, roared past.

A block from the motel, we stepped into what appeared to be an empty street. However, as we did, an elderly Oriental couple came out of a bakery half a block away and spotted us as they hurried to a little red Volkswagen. The man pointed in our direction, barked something to the old woman with him and then shoved her into the passenger seat. He scampered around the car like Grandpa McCoy on speed, slipped inside, and they raced away.

* * *

When Dailey came through the back door into the police station, Xiang greeted him with a backhand across the nose. Dailey fell back against the closed door, a shocked look on his face.

Twenty feet down the hall, a police sergeant gaped from his desk.

"You, fool!" Xiang said to Dailey. "You had him. You could have coaxed him to you and caught him then and there."

"But Doctor, I had no protection," Dailey said, pushing slowly from the door. "And when I saw you hurry inside, I thought . . . I didn't know what to do."

Xiang got in his face. "Do not give me shit, Dailey. He had no reason to harm you. If I had confronted him, and he had become unmanageable, I would have had to kill him." Dailey backed up to the door as Xiang continued. "Are you becoming soft? Are you becoming an ingrate? After all I have done for you, all I have given you, and you defy me like this?"

Xiang came at Dailey again. The tall thin man shoved the much heavier police chief against the door once more. Again, he backhanded him. Slapped him a third time. And again. Inflicting true physical pain was so much more satisfying to Xiang than the psychic kind. If he wished, he could look into Dailey's eyes, and do as he wanted—lead him around like a pup, make the police chief feel incredible pain that wasn't really there. He could make him feel as though his body were completely engulfed in flames—burning, Dailey would even have the sensation of smelling his own charring flesh. Or he could make him feel as though he had just been ran over by a pavement roller. He could give him any sensation he desired, and it would seem so real to Dailey, that if it were sustained long enough, his body would forfeit life, he would have a heart attack and die. But this would not be real pain, and there was no substitute for that kind of pleasure—more physical and stimulating—the kind that got Xiang's own knuckles bloody.

Dailey's lip bled. He held one eye closed. "Doctor," he said, "I'm sorry. I won't fail you again."

"Of course you will not," Xiang said. He reached to the hefty man's side and pulled out the chief's revolver without protest. "You will not fail me again because I am going to kill you now." He pushed the barrel of the .357 against Dailey's cheek.

Xiang glanced up at the quiet desk sergeant. The man's eyes couldn't have been wider.

"Please," the chief pled, his voice quavering. "Give me one more chance. We'll get him, I promise. No more misses. Please, Doctor."

Xiang pulled back the gun's hammer. Only light pressure would put a bullet through Dailey's cheekbone, into his brain and splash the chief's grey matter all over the wall behind him. Instead, in a seamless move, Xiang safely eased the hammer into place while bringing the gun back and giving it a broad, hard sweep against the chief's temple.

Blood splattered from Dailey's mouth and nose as he collapsed to his hands and knees, and the doctor glared down on him.

Xiang said, "A citizen called in while you were cowering in the woods. Said they were headed farther east. The last thing on this end of town is the motel."

Dailey spat blood onto the floor. He lifted his head toward the astonished policeman twenty feet away. "Sergeant Qian," he yelled out. "Call the security people at the facility. Tell 'em to bring their helicopters and have 'em run blocker at the perimeter fence in sectors Alpha, Bravo and Charlie. Then, get yourself and four men in SWAT gear down to the motel. Use infrared and night vision. Search the woods and every house down there, including the motel. Now!"

The doctor grinned. "That is more like it." He looked toward Qian. "Wear the copper-lined helmets, Sergeant Qian. They are the only protection against this man."

Xiang gritted his teeth as he looked over Chief Dailey. Someone was trying to rescue Subject 374. All could be lost if the subject got away—but how could he escape? Xiang did not like the idea of killing his latest and most promising assassin, but Wu had an even later version of implant. Surely Wu would be able to duplicate what Subject 374 had. And now that the device seemed more successful than Xiang had ever dreamed, he could produce them—stamp them out—implant them in a handful of warriors and easily manipulate the invisible strings of world power.

As Sergeant Qian left, Xiang called to him, "Try to restrain them first. But do not hesitate to kill either or both of them to prevent their escape."

* * *

At the motel, Sunny ushered me up an outside stairway and along an exposed balcony. We stopped at room two twenty-three and stood outside the door, while she dug into an inside pocket of her sweat pants.

"Watch," she said. "Make sure we weren't followed."

I scanned the street along the front of the motel waiting for her to pull out the key and open the door. No cars, nobody walking, the town suddenly seemed empty. The air grew chillier, a cold breeze creeping down the side of Mt. Rainy, its icy fingers slowing wrapping around the town. I looked out as the community's few remaining streetlights and home lights glowed to life. Darkness laid the mask of serenity softly upon Gold Rush, and a numbness unlike any I could remember surged through my mind and body.

When I turned back to Sunny, I saw she held a small toolset instead of the key. From it, she pulled out two thin metal instruments barely larger than toothpicks.

"What the hell?" I said.

"Couldn't pay for a room. Left home without my American Express."

She jimmied the lock and opened the door.

Within a minute, we were sitting at the foot of one of two queen-size beds, Sunny holding a warm, damp washcloth to the back of my head while I leaned forward. I didn't know if it was the tension or the bee sting on the back of my skull, but my brain throbbed. I glanced around the room as much as I could with my new, old friend making sure I didn't move my head. There was no luggage in sight. No clothes hanging up. Maybe she'd put her bags in the bathroom—or left them at home with her American Express card.

"You're lucky there isn't a bullet hole there, too," she said, peeking under the cloth.

"Yeah, today's been my lucky day."

"At least we got away," she said, placing it back gently. "I think we lost 'em."

"We can only hope. We should call someone."

"Who? You got more friends? If they're like the last two, you'd better forget it."

I couldn't think of an answer. Whom could I trust besides my wife Michelle? Getting her involved would surely put her in danger. Right now, it was only Sunny. However, our meeting was a little too convenient, staged, maybe.

"If no one saw us come up here," she said, "we should be safe for a while, until we can sort things out. When it's good and dark, we can slip away to my car."

"I need to call Michelle, make sure she's okay. At least try to. They should have fixed our phone by now."

"Michelle?"

"My wife."

"Yeah, right. You can do that in a minute. I'm sure she's fine. Let's tend to the bee sting, first."

I nodded and asked, "So, what have you been up to all of these years?" Maybe there was a clue to this chaos hidden behind her lovely façade. "I mean, you married? Have any kids? What do you do?"

Sunny pulled the washcloth back and dabbed a couple of times at my injury.

It burned, and I flinched.

"You need to keep your head just like that for a bit longer," she said. "Hold this on it lightly." She let go of the wet rag and leaned back on both hands. "Yeah, I was married. He simply up and left me two years ago."

"I'm sorry," I said, but her response was only a sort of thoughtful pause.

Out of the corners of my eyes, I could see her face crack with a broad smile, and the tone of her voice elevated. "I have a beautiful daughter, she's seven. She wants to be an Olympic dancer, like I was going to be. I made the Olympic team in high school, but I broke my ankle and didn't go. I'm betting she'll make it, though. She's stubborn and determined like her daddy." After another pause, she lost the giddiness in her voice and took a serious tone. "Ever since I got out of college, I've been in sales mostly, even though I have an MS in physics. But then, my husband Dan and I started a business five years ago called McMaster Nonlethal Solutions, in Sacramento. Have you heard of it?"

I thought for a moment, but the company didn't sound familiar. I shrugged lightly as I found a hint of memory about the name McMaster. I couldn't place it until I added Sunny's husband's first name to it. Dan McMaster. The name hit me hard like a slap upside the head. Daniel McMaster was the name on the file folder in my dream—the name of the person I was seemingly being compared to—and the guy the two GI Joes had questioned me about. I held back saying anything.

Sunny went on, "Not surprising you haven't heard of it. We design nonlethal weapons for military and law enforcement. I've been able to use my physics degree some, helping develop a few of the devices. But now I'm VP and marketing manager again—in the area on business visiting all of the local police and sheriff's offices."

She hadn't indicated she knew Chief Dailey—of course maybe she hadn't been to see him yet before we met in the park. I frowned, not finding much credence in what she said.

She must have noticed. "I could never catch your local yokel at his office."

"Nonlethal weapons for a *quiet* little village like Gold Rush?" I said with a half-smile.

She smirked at my small attempt at levity. "Hey, even small town cops run into situations they can't get out of without force. If they have a choice, they can use nonlethal instead of deadly force, and they can save lives—sometimes innocent ones."

"That's great. But you don't look like a marketing manager or a physicist." I realized I might be insulting her feminine lib side, so I added, "I mean, no briefcase or dark-gray suitcases, and you're too pretty to be someone's manager."

I glanced at her to see if I was in trouble. She straightened up and folded her arms.

"It was meant as a compliment. You're very attractive. And you seem very smart. You could probably be anything you wanted."

She kept it simple. "Thanks."

Neither of us said anything for a moment, but before long I felt her fingers searching through the hair on the back of my neck.

"This thing . . . ," she said and lightly touched the tender lump on the base of my skull. " . . . it isn't a mere bee sting."

"Ouch, easy. It's a bump."

"It's huge," she said. "Have you seen it?"

"Yeah, like I have eyes in the back of my head. Don't mess with it. The doctor said I shouldn't disturb it."

"What happened?"

"It's from a fall I had last Friday. I had a concussion. It'll just take some time for it to go away. He said it could cause complications if I messed with it."

"That's preposterous."

"Maybe, but that's what the doc said. It's a little tender because of that bee sting this morning right before my world turned to shit."

Sunny sprang up, went to the far side of the other bed and pulled a backpack out from underneath it.

"A backpack toting sales rep?" I asked.

She said nothing as she opened it and pawed inside. I wondered what this woman really was—what she was actually after. Did she have anything to do with the people who chased me—or with the deaths? Would she try to kill me next?

I squirmed on the edge of the bed. "What's wrong, lose your burglar tools?"

She pulled something like a ball out of the pack and threw it at me. I dropped the washcloth and caught the fruit projectile in the center of my chest—an apple. Next thing I knew, a banana came sailing by, and I grabbed it, too.

"Is this some of your nonlethal weaponry? Are you trying to fruit me into submission?"

"Eat," she said, as she started on her own red delicious. "We've had quite a workout. You need energy food—sugar, potassium for your muscles."

I'd missed lunch and felt weak. I bit into the apple. It was sweet, good. I'd never been through an apple so fast. I peeled the banana. "You know, a thick rib-eye steak would be nice," I said. "Medium rare. You don't have a Black Angus in there, do you?"

She didn't answer my foolishness but returned with a small first aid kit and laid it on the bed between us. In a few seconds, she had cotton swabs, a small bottle of alcohol, a penknife and some tweezers placed on another washcloth by the kit as if she were preparing for an operation.

"Now, what are you going to do? Look, it's only swollen up like that because of the bee sting. Leave it alone."

"I don't think it's a bee sting or a bump from hitting your head. There's something under your skin. It's manmade."

"You're the one who hit the bee, right?" I said but she seemed preoccupied. I reached back and felt the lump gingerly. "You're a marketing manager, not a surgeon."

"Move your fingers and eat your banana," she ordered. "Think about it, Robert. All these crazy things happening. And I'm telling you, somebody's put something under your skin."

This *was* crazy. But I needed to trust someone. She was the only one who hadn't run or pulled a gun on me . . . yet.

With its peel, I recovered the banana. I laid it on the bed and gripped my knees. "Easy."

"Don't you worry. It's for your own good," she said, her voice as cool as the wet swab she wiped across my skin. The strong scent of rubbing alcohol struck my nose and burned my sinuses.

"I'm tellin' ya, the doctor said there could be complications if that thing was messed with."

"You mean the doctor who ran inside when he saw you?"

"Yeah, so? That doesn't mean he was wrong."

"Superman, the way things are going," she said as I felt the sting of the tiny knife slicing the tissue around the bump, "you ain't gonna see sunrise, let alone have time to worry about any other complications."

Her term of endearment for me was a surprise.

I grimaced with pain but didn't verbally protest, gritting my teeth instead. The alcohol burn was the worst, and I was able to get past it by considering what she was saying.

She had a good point. Besides, for some strange reason, I found myself trusting everything she was doing was for me. Something deep within, and not Harvey this time, told me to have faith in her judgment. Again, I recalled the TP note that said, *trust . . . solely in your emotions—for within them is the only real truth*. Somehow this woman, with a soothing touch and pleasing scent, was familiar to me. I had a definite feeling we were, or at least had been, very close.

"Why'd you call me that?"

"What?"

"*Superman*. Harvey calls me that."

"It's the nickname I gave you back in college." She giggled. "You used to call me Wonder Woman. So, who's Harvey?"

I frowned. "A voice in my head."

"You have a voice in your head named Harvey?" She shook her head slowly. "You really are in trouble."

I shrugged.

"What about you, Robert? Any kids?"

I stared out, searching for some sort of emotion, deep feelings, for what I was about to tell her. Oddly, I couldn't find any. "That's the other part of the hurricane. You know, when I said I had this feeling like I was in the eye of a storm, and I was just waiting for it to hit me again? There was an accident last winter." As I spoke, something like a home movie played in my mind. A beautiful Oriental woman, Michelle, with short hair, pregnant and cooking at the stove; her laughing as she hit me with a pillow; her changing a baby's diapers; her with longer hair, carrying a bag of groceries into the house and calling out, "I'm home, honey," a young boy smiling big as he caught a ball I'd just thrown; my arm pushing the boy in a swing; my arm helping the boy ride a bicycle with training wheels.

My tone was unintentionally flat. "My five-year-old son was paralyzed when the car my wife was driving slid off an icy bridge. He's in the children's hospital ward at

Mount Rainy Biotronics' medical center. Michelle almost didn't make it. Not so much from her ruptured spleen. The guilt nearly killed her. She's okay now—mostly. But things haven't been the same since."

"Hmmm," Sunny said, not offering any condolences as she picked up the tweezers.

I found her indifference strange and cold—but not unlike my own memories, I reasoned. Maybe she was concentrating on my little operation. My own lack of emotions, of real, heart-felt sentiments for my wife and child, puzzled me even more.

I mumbled the words from the note as if it were a chant. "*Everything you know is lies. Trust not in what you hear or see, but solely in your emotions—for within them is the only real truth.*"

"What's that? Are you getting philosophical on me?" She asked and tugged at something under my skin.

I remembered the rest of the note: *Get ready. They will come for you soon. Destroy this immediately.* "Do you write notes on toilet paper?" I asked as I felt something slip out from my lump like the head of a ripe boil.

"No, but I like origami." She said.

"That note in my shower, besides telling me not to trust anyone, it said for me to 'get ready', and that '*they* will come for me soon.'"

"Hmm," she said sounding a bit disinterested as she brought a small, black object on the end of her tweezers around to my face. "There ya go."

I took it, and she dabbed more alcohol on my wound. I gritted my teeth while rolling the small disk over in my hand. It was the same kind of black disk as the one she'd pulled from my shirt collar earlier. This one had a tiny puncture hole in it. I pressed my thumbnail into the thing and tore open its protective latex covering. It was also contained in thin copper foil, another tiny gold circuit board inside. This one was corroded as if it'd been exposed to moisture or some sort of acid.

"Where else you hidin' those things?" she asked.

"My God," I said under my breath.

From behind, Sunny put her chin on my shoulder.

"Mine, too," she whispered next to my ear. "What's next? What are we going to do?"

I turned, put my arm around her and drew my face close to hers. I had no idea what she was up to, but asking nicely didn't work with this one. "First, we aren't going to do anything. I think it's better if you stay clear of me from here on out."

"Are you kidding? I love mysteries, and this is the best one I've found in years."

"It's no joke, Sunny. Haven't you seen enough? You could get killed. They might be after only me, but any minute a couple of guys could bust into this room and shoot us both dead."

"Robert, think about it. They've seen me with you. I'm in it now, too. Let's quit quibbling over the small stuff and try to figure this all out."

I looked away. "I am thinking. And the only thing I can come up with is that, somehow, you're involved." Facing her again, I narrowed my eyes. "You're too cool about all of this. And this accidental meeting all of a sudden in the middle of a shit storm. All this bullshit you're pumping me with—that we were friends or whatever it is we used to be. I think you know more than you're telling me, and . . ." I quickly reached up and placed my hand across her throat. I was gentle but firm. I didn't like two-stepping to a tune I didn't know, and this one I couldn't even tap my toe to. " . . . and you'd better start spilling it, or I'm going to have to hurt you. I don't like getting screwed without getting kissed."

She placed her hand gently on my wrist. "Don't be ridiculous, Robert. I'm here to help you." She moved my hand away as if it were a helium balloon. She looked at me longingly. Her eyes were like those nonlethal weapons she was talking about, and she knew how to use them. I quickly felt disarmed.

She leaned to me and planted a lingering kiss on my lips. Although I didn't give her one in return, tendrils of warmth spread through my body tickling my nerve endings and leaving me weak with passion. I pushed her away without really wanting to. I was married, and anyway, I should keep up my tough guy act in order to find out more. And I was sure she knew much more.

"It must have to do with something you've done or seen," she said, still gazing at me.

I nearly shouted, "There's nothing. Nothing." I stared at the floor.

She pulled my chin up and gazed at me again. This time she took off my glasses. "Do you really need these? The lenses are all cracked up, anyway."

I glanced around the room actually considering her question. "I'm blind without them," I said but almost felt as if it was some sort of conditioned response. I seemed to see everything in the room just fine. I could actually read the In *Case of Fire* sign next to the door, all the way down to the fine print, even though it was a good ten feet away. I could see her face clearly although it was mere inches from my eyes. I didn't need the glasses. I wasn't blind without them.

"I don't understand it," I told her. "I can see fine without the glasses."

"You have beautiful eyes," she said. "I like you better without the specs." Then she seemed to examine the eyeglasses. She rubbed over a burned spot on the bridge. "Hmm," she said, and then snapped them in two.

As I began to protest, she raised the broken frames up for me to look at. Another even smaller computer chip stuck out from one of the broken pieces, as if I hadn't seen enough computer chips today. It appeared burnt.

"I'll bet this is some kind of tracking chip," she said. "I think they call them transponders."

I didn't understand how she could possibly know that. But she seemed to know a lot more about all this than I did. She discarded the glasses, tossing them into a small wastebasket in the corner of the room, and then placed her hand on my cheek.

I frowned at her and shook my head. "I don't get it. It's like I'm in a tunnel with no light."

As if on cue, at the same time the words slipped from my lips, bright lights blared through the drape-covered windows.

Chapter 16

Sunny went for her backpack on the other bed in the motel room. She flung open the pack's flap and reached inside as I stood up and started toward the curtains.

"Don't!" she said, and when I turned to her, she pulled out a little .32 caliber, Beretta Tomcat pistol. I knew exactly what it was, but I didn't know how I knew, not remembering ever shooting a gun in my life.

"There's a window in the bathroom," she said and ran to it, taking her backpack with her.

When I followed, I saw the small window high on the wall between the sink and the shower. Maybe, just maybe, she could fit through it, that is if she were slicked up with Vaseline first.

"No way," I said, and as I did, something crashed through the window in the living room. I had the presence of mind to pull Sunny under me and protect our faces.

An incredible explosion and flash of light followed. My guts and lungs trembled violently. It felt like I'd been slapped on both sides of the head. We were both staggering. For a moment I thought Sunny was screaming but soon realized it was my own ears. Flash-bang grenade. I knew what they'd hit us with, but again, I didn't know how I knew. Luckily, our eyes hadn't been exposed to the blinding light.

This was only the start. The room lights went out, and I tried the wall switch to no avail. The only light we had was coming through the small window from a cloud-veiled full moon until Sunny pulled a flashlight out of her backpack.

They'd be crashing through the front door any second, and there was no other apparent way out of the tiny motel room except that same door.

Sunny seemed to realize it also. She searched in her backpack of tricks again and produced a smoke grenade. That confirmed it. Carrying a pistol, a smoke grenade and who knew what else—she wasn't at all what she appeared.

She stepped from the bathroom, pulled the pin out like a pro and tossed the smoke canister under the bed nearest the front door.

Thick yellow smoke began filling the room, and the bedcovers ignited like kindling. I pulled her back inside the bathroom, yanked the door closed behind us and pushed in the lock button on the knob. The dense smoke and fire might buy us an extra ten or fifteen seconds as our unidentified adversaries fumbled through it. The doorknob button lock wouldn't add any more than a couple of seconds to that.

"You won't fit!" Sunny yelled, looking at the tiny bathroom window. She'd screamed out the words, and I wasn't certain if it was to ensure I could hear her over the ringing in my ears or because of the ringing in hers. She turned toward the door and set the flashlight on the vanity, it's light beam on the doorknob. Keeping the small pistol at the ready in one hand, in the other she held what might have been some sort of medallion under her T-shirt. It was a little large for a Saint Christopher's.

I looked below the window at the bare wall between the tub and the toilet and instinctively went at it with my foot. Memories of building a house flashed like an old, black-and-white Charlie Chaplin movie through my mind—in and out, in and out. It was just another snippet from my past mostly lost to my concussion, I reasoned. If the construction was conventional and contemporary we might be in luck. Few people realize how easily even an outside wall can be busted through.

With the first kick, the sheet rock cracked. I stepped

back against Sunny in the small room and gave the drywall three quick snap kicks about waist high. The sheet rock gave way.

Sunny got the idea and turned the flashlight on the sink top, shining it toward the hole I'd made. She assaulted the wall directly under where I had. After she kicked it twice more, we both tore at the wallboard like starving coyotes after a prairie dog, yanking pieces of the wall out and pulling away large chucks of pink insulation. A section of sheathing over a foot wide and three feet tall was exposed between the wall studs. Again, we were fortunate. It wasn't plywood or wafer board, instead it was Celotex-like fiberboard as I'd hoped. Used for its insulation properties, it was much softer than wood and easier to break through.

Again, I attacked the wall, but as my sidekick made contact, I heard the front door slam against the inside of the front room and glass crunch under running feet. My foot went through the sheathing and the siding up to my ankle, and Sunny had to help me get free. I stepped back and kicked twice more, the wall finally giving in, and my leg busted through past my knee. I knew they would soon make it through the smoke, past the flaming bed and up to the bathroom door. Still they did not say, "Police! Open up," or "Don't' move! You're under arrest." They said nothing.

I put my weight against the door, hoping they would try to break through and not shoot through, and I shoved Sunny toward the hole.

Hurried footfalls came from the other side of the door.

Sunny didn't take time to snatch up the flashlight but did snag her pack and went at the opening as if she were chasing her own white rabbit. She punched the edges of the hole, making it a few inches larger, and wriggled her way mostly through. But the broken siding caught her left foot. She struggled briefly as I watched the doorknob turn slowly. Finally, her Nike slipped off, and her socked foot disappeared. A crash came from what sounded like trashcans below.

As I lunged for the hole, I swiped up the flashlight

along with Sunny's shoe and dove head first like my unwanted nickname, Superman. The bathroom door splintered behind me. My head, arms and shoulders made it out into the cool night, but I became lodged there, caught up by my belt buckle. I was writhing to get through when I felt hands clutching my legs.

Sunny stood ten feet below, reaching up, leaping and grabbing at me. I dropped her shoe but hung onto the flashlight. Our hands slapped at each other as my captors pulled me back inside.

But I was ready. I only saw two of them, helmeted, in body armor and dark-blue fatigues like SWAT team members. Somehow, I recognized the guns slung on their shoulders as silenced MP5 assault rifles—and they wore night-vision goggles. As they pulled me back and my extended arms cleared the hole, I yanked away more of the siding and sheathing from the opening with my free hand. I flopped back onto the floor, turned quickly, jabbed Sunny's flashlight at their faces and tossed the building material from my other hand at them, too.

They both took a step back with one hand shielding their night-vision goggles then flipped them up and out of the way. Still, they said nothing, and as they attempted to restrain me, I regained my feet.

I had that sharp pain inside my head again, but it didn't impede me. For a moment I had my balance and one arm free. It was time enough to place a roundhouse punch alongside the closest intruder's neck right below his helmet. My fist knocked his Kevlar pot off, and he fell against the vanity.

I ducked and rammed my shoulder into the midsection of the other guy. His feet left the floor as he went back through the door they'd recently smashed. I took no more time to fight, but did briefly shine my light into the faces of three more of his body-armor-covered companions who had caught him from behind in the smoke-filled room.

As I rushed back to the opening, my light found my first combatant, sitting against the bathroom vanity, his eyes staring back, blank and lifeless—his sewn-on nametag said Sgt. Qian.

This time, I dove through the hole without encumbrance like a jungle cat through a burning hoop. I cleared the trashcans Sunny had fallen into, but when I landed, the flashlight busted into pieces as I rolled on the grassy ground below the window.

The next thing I knew, rapid-fire snaps from the silenced assault rifles filled the air, and the motel's siding fell off in chunks. They'd decided if they couldn't catch me, they'd kill me.

A familiar smell came to my nose and even under the deadly circumstances, I felt the need to pause and consider it. Gunpowder, the unmistakable scent of burnt nitrites and sulfur—but not the kind in fireworks, the kind in bullets. Still I couldn't recall ever firing a gun.

Sunny's hand was on my shoulder as dirt and grass leapt from the ground around us. A crimson light beam shown from the hole in the wall we'd created. It made a pencil-thin line that searched through the gun smoke then ended up on the center of my chest. They were using laser sights in the darkness. A fraction of a second later, two more red lasers beamed out from the opening.

Chapter 17

"Come on!" Sunny said, yanking me out of danger.

A burst of shots whizzed by.

We broke for the trees and soon were running down the steep, wooded hill behind the motel. At first, I didn't ask where she was leading me and simply followed her blindly. So far, I figured, it had worked—I'd followed my emotions, ignored everything else as lies, and somehow, stayed alive.

Fog had set in, and the air became heavy and moist. It lay like a thick, wet blanket on the side of the hill, getting denser the farther down we ran. On top of the naturally composted ground were patches of crusted-over snow, making footing unsure. Nevertheless, even on the steep descent, it did little to slow us down.

After nearly a half mile of dodging pine trees and stumbling down the slope in the dark, I finally panted out, "Where?" as I grabbed her hand.

She squeezed mine back, still running all out with the little Beretta in her other hand. "My car," she said, breathing heavy. "About two more miles."

It wasn't a good time to ask more questions, but why would she park her car two and a half miles of rugged terrain from her motel—as if it really was her legally acquired motel room? I was sure to find out soon.

Seconds later, lights shot through the white mist from above us. The roar of helicopters drew nearer. Brilliantly glowing shafts of white descended the hill from behind us, giving life to the trees' shadows that capered in a surreal and dizzying waltz of light and dark.

"Shit," I said, losing hope we'd gotten away.

Sunny looked over her shoulder toward the lights. "No time for that now. They're not our choppers."

"We have choppers?" I said more to myself than to Sunny, then slid on the slick forest floor. As I regained my balance on the run, I asked, "How can you see where you're going?"

"Pure instinct," she said, and in the next second she also slipped on the loose ground cover.

I was able to catch her and quickly pull her back on her feet. We raced on, this time with me leading, and something like a flashback shot through my mind. I didn't know when or where, but I remembered running through the darkness, a helmet on my head and something heavy like a rifle in my hands. On my back, I'd had something much heavier, something like a large pack—no, a body.

The beating helicopter's rotor wash pounded down on us from the treetops, and a searchlight blazed through, snatching me away from my reminiscence. Seconds later, a second and then a third chopper joined in, but still none of the intrusive beams caught us for more than an instant as we ducked limbs and dodged the small trees.

When we came to a dried up ravine our antagonists seemed to have lost us temporarily, their searchlights wagging through the woods to our left. I hesitated. Sunny let go of my hand and started into the ditch, going farther down hill.

"This way," she said. "Only a little ways more."

Most likely, this ravine was the same one that ran about a hundred yards behind my house. I looked up the gully and considered going home. They'd probably leave my house alone, now. Whoever was after me had most likely been there already and gotten anything they wanted. Michelle, too. If they were the police, the good guys, I figured she'd be okay. I wasn't sure these guys were so good, though.

I had to go. I had to see if she was all right. However, it might be too late. If the bastards had hurt Michelle, I didn't know what I'd do.

They were surely searching for us downhill, where we now headed, not at my place. These people were organized and well armed. How much of a chance did we have if we went in the direction they were expecting? My car was in my garage. We could get Michelle and use my Buick instead of Sunny's car to make our getaway to the authorities in the next county. Besides, with what little I knew of Sunny, her car was probably hot—stolen. She was good with door locks, probably knew her way around a car ignition, too. At my house, I might find some clues as to what these people wanted. Maybe, if they'd left Michelle alone, she would know something.

"I'm going home," I said. "They won't expect us to do that. My house is about three miles up this creek bed."

"Robert," Sunny exclaimed, "are you crazy?"

"No, come on. It's not that far. They won't expect us to go that way. We can get my wife and car and drive to the sheriff's office in Summitview."

A dog barked wildly from below.

"Damn!" I said. "They have dogs. Let's go. Hurry." I held out my hand to her.

"No, Robert." She brought the little Beretta up and pointed it at me. "You've got to go with me. Don't make this ugly."

"Jeez, Sunny. Make it ugly? What the hell is this?"

"Come on, Robert. We're running out of time."

We stared at each other from about fifteen feet apart. I backed up several steps slowly.

"Robert! Please! I'm '*they*' from the note."

"You're '*they*'?"

"Yes, Robert. Me and a rescue team—at the foot of this hill."

"You left the note in my shower?"

"No, but whoever did knew we were coming. They were trying to get you prepared. We've come to rescue you and dozens of others."

"Rescue me—dozens of others?" I realized that she'd been deceiving me. She was probably lying to me now. How could I trust her? "Sorry, Sunny. I guess you'll have to kill me, instead."

I turned and began running up the gully, my head ducked in anticipation of a shot I hoped wouldn't come. I'd made it about a hundred feet when I heard running behind me and thought she'd changed her mind. I didn't know if that would be good or bad, now.

I turned back quickly. "Sunny . . . ?" I couldn't see anything through the milky mist until a figure appeared lower to the ground than I expected. It was a dog—a large German shepherd charging full bore.

"Sarge!" Sunny called out from far below, her voice faint and muffled by the distance and the fog. "Sarge, come here, boy."

The dog didn't respond to her so I quickly scanned the ground around me for a stick to defend myself. There was nothing but twigs.

At fifteen feet, I braced for his attack and yelled, "No! Stop!"

Suddenly, the dog stopped, almost rolling over from his momentum.

"Go back!" I ordered firmly.

The dog faltered and sat down. He was a magnificent animal, ears erect, eyes large and intelligent, and I couldn't help but admire him fearfully. Panting, he cocked his head and blinked as he watched me. For a moment, I thought he too might have been affected by my disease. If he was, it didn't last long or produce the same deadly results it had previously on the five humans. He whined a couple of times, stood up wagging his tail, turned and trotted back in the direction he'd come.

* * *

President Mason was in the third chopper in the flight of four Sea Kings. At least two other helicopters always accompanied the President's, with the Commander-in-Chief never flying in the same one twice in a row for security. Above them, four F-16s circled protectively, ready to swoop down to defend the President, even fly into an incoming missile if the need arose.

The President had boarded the U.S. Marine Corps helicopter, a VH-3D Sea King designated *Marine One* when he was on board, with his four cabinet members and had opted to ride the helo all the way back to the White House. They had gotten away ahead of a storm front bringing with it a heavier than usual snowfall for this early in the season. Now about five minutes away from landing on the White House lawn, Mason gazed out the port-side window at the glowing D.C. nightline on the horizon. It was always a relief to leave the Capitol, but he never failed to be eager to return. This time, as the lights grew brighter and snow streaked by the window, he wondered if these so-called "psychic assassins" were being trained somewhere nearby, perhaps even within a couple of hundred miles in the Appalachians. As he turned to look past his four cabinet members to the nearest starboard-side window, he considered the intel he'd just received. Still with no idea of where Major Jackson's rescue operation was taking place, it seemed the Major was finding moderate success and might be close to grabbing Robert Weller and being able to answer a whole bunch of questions.

* * *

Sunny ran back to the small wooded encampment where Major Jackson waited.

"Damn it, Jax," she said, nearly breathless. "I brought him within two hundred yards, but he ran off."

Jax trotted up to her, and four of the five other men came behind him from their small, advanced camp. "Where's he going?"

"Back to his house," Sunny said. "Come on, we can catch up to him."

Lieutenant Carpenter sat in the DPV with his headphones on and the notebook computer on his lap. He called out, "Major, I think you need to know about this."

"Come on, Jax," Sunny said, tugging on his arm.

The major turned away from her and hustled to the lieutenant. "One moment, Sunny. This could be important."

Lieutenant Carpenter said, "Got a message on the laptop again. Appears to be from the same source as before, it's not coded and there's no source signature. It says we need to get everybody out."

"What do you mean?" Jax turned the laptop to him and looked at the screen.

Must get all hostages out. No time left. There will not be another chance. Those left behind will be killed.

"That's impossible," Jax said facing the laptop's LCD screen. "We're up against a hostile defensive force of probably a thousand, and we only have three dozen men in two helos armed mostly with nonlethal weapons. We knew there was a time constraint, and we'd only get a couple dozen out at best. But there's no way we can get everyone out. Last information we got, there were nearly a hundred hostages."

Words appeared on the laptop again causing Jax and the young lieutenant to gape at the screen. *There are over four thousand*.

"That's ridiculous," Jax said. "How could that be?"

The lieutenant said, "The good news is the President is starting to soften up a little about our 'little rogue mission.' He and his advisors didn't think we'd get this far. But he's still upset at you putting this together under the guise you had Presidential authority. And he still insists to know where we are. Gunny Sampson's Com people are doing a good job bouncing our messages all over the place—keeping those DOD boys busy trying to track us down. The bad news is the Thousand Eyes RVs are still real insistent there's a nuclear element in the picture."

"Still sunrise?"

The lieutenant nodded.

"That corroborates what we're getting here," Jax said, pointing to the laptop. "Do they have any suggestions?"

"They're working on it, sir."

The major shook his head. "We're going to need help. A lot of help. We might have to give the President our coordinates. But we don't have any assurances that *they* won't be the ones who nuke us."

"Let's go, Jax," Sunny repeated. "We've got to get to Weller before he gets too close to that house."

Jax looked up as Sarge came trotting back to Sunny's

side. The dog turned quickly and growled.

"I see movement," Lieutenant Carpenter said. He pulled off his SatCom headset, laid the laptop to the side and motioned for the men to spread out as he put on his helmet.

"Down," Jax ordered in a whisper into his mike.

He hustled to Sunny and pulled her to the ground. The dog went prone beside her.

"Company on the right, too," came one of the other men's urgent and low voice over Jax's headset.

The rhythmic thumping of a helicopter rotor beat through the fog.

The major tapped the arm of the soldier next to him and said, "Chang, get on the fifty. If the chopper fires at us, we have no choice but to defend ourselves."

Airman Chang jumped to his feet and sprinted to the fifty-caliber machinegun mounted on the back of the DPV.

Into his mike, Jax said, "Sergeant Chambers, get the smoke pots out there. We need a screen." He glanced at Sunny. The dog was licking her face. Her eyes were closed, and she was unresponsive to his prodding. Had he pulled her to the ground too hard and caused her to hit her head? Or had she been struck by a sniper's silenced bullet?

Chapter 18

I struggled up the ravine, nearly breathless, every muscle now aching. With each step, I shoved off with a hand on the corresponding knee. I was definitely out of shape. If I lived through this night, I vowed to spend at least twenty minutes a day on the Stairmaster for the rest of my life.

Then Harvey paid me another visit. *Keep at it, Superman. Don't slow down.*

"Leave me alone, Harvey," I said aloud. Then my thoughts began tumbling like a sparrow in a tornado. Michelle—would she be okay? Had they left her alone? Sunny—friend or enemy? Why? Who was she working for? Who were these guys in the dark-blue, SWAT outfits? Were they police or military? And the other guys in blue—and what about the people dropping like cut tree limbs around me? There were now five lives I would account for when my day of reckoning came. It was a heavy burden to carry up the hill. My eyes watered with confusion and exhaustion as my breath puffed out in clouds of steam.

I glanced over my shoulder. Maybe I was making a mistake—I should turn around and go back to Sunny.

No! Harvey said. *It's not safe*.

But Harvey wasn't saying where it *was* safe.

I considered the day's many strange happenings. What was with the black disks, the bugs or whatever they were? Why didn't my pursuers say anything to identify themselves? What was up with Sunny, and why didn't my condition affect her? Why did my enigma affect only certain people, like the one SWAT guy I'd punched and not the others? Why my first victim, the lady? And had she planted the bug on my clothes?

I tried to think logically. It all started this morning—the note in the shower, the exploding TV. People were dying from something I had or was doing. Then the people in blue began stalking me, trying to catch me, and when that didn't work, they tried to kill me. Why not? People were dying because of me. They had to stop me, they had no choice. They were doing the right thing. I was doing the wrong thing, and if I kept evading them, more people would die. Maybe they could help me. Maybe they could cure whatever it was I had, if only I turned myself in.

Harvey said, *And maybe you'll be arrested for murder, tried, convicted and sentenced to death.*

I stopped, took a deep breath and scanned the misty gully and small trees surrounding me. Briefly, I thought of those trees as people, people who might approach me, and whom I might will dead. Or the disease I had would fell them. Or some sniper would shoot them with a dart gun with tiny darts, poisonous and deadly, that would somehow dissolve or disappear when they hit the skin. I shook my head. Hell, maybe the town had been taken over by aliens. That thought wasn't much more far-fetched than the others rattling inside my head. The possibilities were endless, but none of them made sense. All seemed to come out of B sci-fi movies and paperback spy novels.

The wind picked up, and the cold but gentle breeze thinned out the fog. A light mist touched my face, and raindrops beat the canopy of aspen above. By the time I made it home, I'd be soaked. I swallowed hard and decided on another simple plan. Since Michelle hadn't been affected by my problem when I left for work this morning, I would go home, kiss my precious wife, change into dry clothes, and then surrender to the authorities.

Let's not get too hasty with the "surrender to the authorities" plan, shall we? Harvey said. *How 'bout taking things one step at a time?*

I could care less what Harvey said—tried not consider his words that were forced into my head. I continued ascending the gully, and in another five minutes the rain turned into a fluffy snow. The moisture made what had been a dry and rocky creek bed as slick as a whale's belly, and I slipped several times. My brown trousers became coated with mud up past the knees, as were the sleeves of my sport coat past the elbows.

As I struggled along, Harvey attempted to distract my focus from the burden of worry. I envisioned him reaching deep into a dark corner of my memories and finding in the shadows there an old dust-covered box that contained another one of those cadence songs I'd forgotten about years ago. Quickly shaken dust-free, brought into the light of thought and to my lips was this jingle, "Saw an ol' lady runnin' down the street." Harvey sang in accompaniment. "She had tanks on her back, she had fins on her feet. I said, hey ol' lady, ain't you been told: better leave that divin' for the brave and the bold. She said, sonny, sonny, can't you see, I taught Recon U-D-T."

Once again, I was confused at where this ditty could have come. I knew what Recon UDT was—probably heard about it from a news story, the television, or in a movie. It stood for *Marine Reconnaissance Underwater Demolition Team.*

I paused at the remembrance, absentmindedly stepping on a spot of wet, loose soil and slipped face first into the mud.

My little mishap doesn't faze Harvey. I imagine him looking into that dust-laden box of hidden memories again, searching deeply. He whispers in a low, raspy voice, *It's not just from knowledge of the term—memory of the song—but from experience, Superman. And look, there's more.* In my vision, he tips the box for me to look inside, and what I see is terrifying—a swirling, dark storm, full of death and carnage, explosions and screaming, grotesque mutilation and frightful things. And when I look at Harvey again, he has fangs—long and dripping with blood.

* * *

I couldn't see and I gasped for air. Shook my head, feeling the mud on my face, covering my eyes. I'd fallen face first into the mud, must have blacked out momentarily. Harvey was gone, and I was glad. I gathered a handful of snow and used it to clean the mud from my face.

Ahead, I finally saw the clearing that was behind my house. I recalled taking solitary strolls there after Michelle had driven off the bridge, and our son William had been paralyzed. Still, this cool wet night had numbed my memories and my body of all but one emotion, now—incredible terror.

In another three hundred feet, I'd be at my back door. I proceeded watchfully up to the bank of the creek bed in case the house was under surveillance. Although I intended to turn myself in, I'd rather do so on my terms, in dry, clean clothes. Additionally, I didn't wish to surprise anyone and receive a lead-pill cure for my deadly condition before I had a chance to raise my hands in surrender.

An inch of snow covered the treeless area that was slightly smaller than a tennis court. The white blanket completely hid the narrow path leading from the ravine I stood in now to the back of my house. I climbed up and hurried across the opening unconcerned with the tracks I left. By the time anyone saw my footprints, I would already be in custody.

A hundred feet past the clearing, I heard voices. I slowed and left the path, taking to the woods once again. Instead of coming up directly behind my home, I made my way along a cedar fence between two houses about a half block down from my own. When I came to the front yard, I edged along some bushes beside a front porch and slipped next to a Toyota SUV parked in the driveway. Then I crept up to the rear bumper and peeked around the side.

I decided my little plan was hopeless. My place was three lots down. At least a dozen more of those SWAT-looking guys waited, spread out in a perimeter around the house. These men carried M-16s on their hips or hanging down at their sides. Some were smoking cigarettes, and all seemed at ease.

Next to a patrol car parked in the street, I thought I recognized Chief Dailey talking to one of his men. He too was wearing SWAT gear. His Southern twang was unmistakable, but I couldn't make out what he was saying due more to the sound-absorption quality of the snow than the volume of his normally boisterous voice. Eavesdropping on their conversation before giving up could be valuable. I figured I'd have to forget about the clean, dry clothes. At least I might hear a little more of what was going on before I allowed them to take me into custody.

Car lights came from down the street, and I flattened to the snowy ground next to the SUV to wait for the vehicle to pass. A dark-blue limousine drove by slowly, and I read Mount Rainy Biotronics on the side. They used this vehicle to chauffer their officials and visiting board of directors around.

After the limo passed, I brushed the snow from my clothes and carefully made my way along the vacant automobiles parked at the curb. Every now and then, someone would turn my direction forcing me to duck down beside a fender or behind a car trunk. Each time, I was able to slip a little closer after a few seconds of cautious pause. When I came to a deserted but idling ambulance parked across the street from the police cruiser, I hunkered down behind it. I wondered who the medical vehicle was for—was it a precaution or did they know who would be its next passenger? Was it for me?

I peered carefully from the back window glass through the front windshield of the ambulance. The limousine had stopped in the middle of the street only fifty feet away, and Dailey and another man also in the SWAT gear stepped to the back window. When the other man turned in my direction, I was surprised to see it was my best friend—my brother-in-law—Mike Wu.

* * *

I dropped low behind the ambulance, shocked at Wu's

appearance in the paramilitary outfit. I didn't remember Mike being a reserve police officer or in the National Guard. I would have known that. He'd never been in the military or associated with law enforcement. He was the *Gold Rush Gazette*'s editor, for Pete's sake.

I heard a hum that sounded like the limo's window motor, but I didn't risk peeking to see.

The voices were low, but the one I figured was from the limo sounded like Dr. Xiang's. After hearing his voice, the temptation became too much. I crab-walked to the side window of the ambulance and raised my head to get a good look. It was Xiang all right.

And yet another surprise came into view. Michelle hustled down the walk from the house toward the street. The snowflakes had become huge, and they drifted lazily in the still night. Michelle hugged herself, wearing a blue cable-knit sweater, and her breath came out in fog as the big flakes gently found her head and shoulders. Her face, always angelic even when sad, had lines of worry across it, and I wished I could reach out and assure her I was okay.

"They have them cornered along the outside of the perimeter," Xiang said. "Your helicopters have helped, Colonel Wu."

"This has been a nightmare," Michelle said as she stepped up to them.

I couldn't help but fall behind the ambulance again. Colonel Wu? How ridiculous. He was no colonel. In addition, he sure as hell had no helicopters. What kind of drug-induced trance had I been put into? Michelle's nightmare comment was right. Had I gone into a coma when I hit my head, and now my life had become only a dream from a hospital bed? I pinched myself on the hand so hard it bled and hurt like hell.

Nope, reality, Harvey said in a not-so-welcome return to my rattled brains.

Yeah, I told him in my thoughts, like the words of an imaginary rabbit would convince me I wasn't dreaming?

I don't know what possessed me, but I raised again and tried to get Michelle's attention with a weak wave. At first I thought she saw me when she glanced in my direction. Maybe she had but didn't want to alert the others around her.

I remembered this morning, before I left for work.

She had been in such a great mood while cleaning up the breakfast dishes before I left. She looked so cute, the straight black hair, the large dark eyes, the full lips and high cheeks—my little China doll, I'd thought, as she smiled at me and gave me a wink before I went out the door. I asked her then, "Did we make love last night?" She'd laughed and asked, "What? You don't remember? Is it that bad after seven years of marriage?" I'd persisted, and she threw the dishtowel at me. She'd giggled and called me her "big stud" and then kissed me.

That was before the world began spinning backwards.

Dailey cleared his throat. A large wad of chewing tobacco in his right cheek influenced his tone. "What're their orders?"

Colonel Wu asked Xiang, "Shoot to kill, sir?"

Dailey frowned. "If they have him surrounded, they can catch him, right? I mean, he can be reprocessed."

Hey, Mike, I thought, easy on that "shoot-to-kill" stuff. And reprocessed? What did that mean?

"We can take no chances," Xiang said without the compassion I was accustomed to hearing in his voice. "The chairman has ordered the situation be contained immediately or he has threatened to close the facility. Do you understand what I am saying, Dailey?"

"Is he insane? Close the facility? Damn it, he can't be serious. This is a ten-billion-dollar operation, thirty-five years of work, five thousand lives! He won't do that."

I tried to analyze what they said. What did the Chairman of the Board of Mount Rainy Biotronics have to do with this situation? Chief Dailey was understandably upset. Closing Mount Rainy Biotronics' research facility would make Gold Rush die within weeks. And what about William? We'd have to transfer him to another hospital.

"He can," Xiang said flatly. "And he will. He is very upset at the breach of security—that they were able to get this far. We have until morning. Your orders are simple. As Colonel Wu has said, if you see the subject, shoot to kill."

I shrank back with a gasp I hoped wasn't audible, but I kept watching. No one seemed to have heard; however, Michelle looked my way again. She was playing along with them, she must have been. She knew it was the only way to keep me safe from whatever they were up to, I was sure of it.

My giving up was certainly out of the question now. If these were the good guys, I would have hated to see the bad. I faced a triple dilemma. I not only had to escape from this mess myself, but I also had to rescue Michelle and then Will.

The doctor went on. "We have others. Granted, they are not the specimen he is, but even those with half the talent will serve the purpose, especially with our refined devises."

Again, I questioned their choice of words. Talent?

"What if we can take him alive?" the chief asked. "And the woman?"

At-a-boy, Chief, I thought.

But Mike Wu shook his head as Dr. Xiang answered, "Do not. Neither of them. And we will need their bodies for proof."

"All right," the chief said. "All right, but I don't like it."

"You do not have to."

The radio squawked on the police cruiser, and one of Dailey's deputies went to answer it.

"One Adam two, this is Prater. Do you copy, over?" Along with the cop's voice came the snaps of silenced weapons and several echoing pops from what could have been Sunny's pistol, perhaps from MP5s and M-16s.

"This is one Adam two, go ahead Corporal Prater."

"Yeah, Hank, we're about a quarter mile east of Checkpoint Alpha. I think we got 'em. He got Sergeant Qian, though. Just like the others."

The doctor said to Dailey, "Apparently you will not have to worry."

The chief spat his tobacco, and it splat in the snow on the street. "No," he said softly as if there might be remorse in his voice. "No, I guess I won't."

The window motor complained again, and the limousine drove away.

Chief Dailey reached over to Michelle and gave her a pat on the shoulder. "You did your part," he said, and as he did, Mike Wu scanned the area, making me duck. Dailey told Michelle, "Sorry it had to end up this way."

"It doesn't matter, chief," she said. "I'll have other opportunities." Her voice was cold and void of feeling.

That a girl, Michelle, I thought. She must have seen me. Good act. I didn't understand what she meant by other opportunities, though.

A rapid and sharp hammering echoed from the woods. It came from several miles away, but still, I recognized the sound. The snaps of the silenced bullets hadn't carried this far. Sunny's little .32 caliber couldn't do that, nor even the bad guys' MP5s in the snowfall. These were the unmistakable reports of a fifty-caliber machinegun.

More static squawked over the radio and Prater's yelling voice came on again. "We need the meat wagon down—" Confusion and yelling voices interrupted Prater, and he sounded distracted. He called out away from his keyed mike. "What? Did you get her? Is she dead? What about Weller?"

I took the chance of looking over the edge of the window again.

A dome of yellow light rose above the trees followed by a sudden slam like two train cars colliding.

Back into the microphone Prater's voice bellowed, "They've shot down a chopper, and we need reinforcements and medevacs!"

Mike Wu immediately called out to the men surrounding the house, "Go! Checkpoint Alpha. Now!"

Dailey yanked open his patrol car door. "Davis, you and Gomez come with me."

Wu said to Michelle, "You stay in the house in case he shows up." From his pocket, he pulled out an object about the size of a Bic lighter with a short wire attached. "Since all of our cameras and microphones in there are fried, you'll need this microphone so we can monitor you." He peeled off something from what was probably an adhesive backing and handed the thing to her.

Michelle took it and snaked it down the collar of her sweater, then briefly pressed her fingers over where she had placed it.

Wu ran toward the back of the house. He turned briefly and instructed Michelle further. "But don't let him get too close, and under no circumstances confront him. Leave that to me."

My house had been bugged. And now Mike Wu gave Michelle a wire to keep tabs on her.

Most of the officers were converging on the backyard of my home. Two EMTs came sprinting toward the front of the ambulance from where they'd been leaning on another patrol car down the street, so I edged around to the back. Dailey and his two officers were in his squad car. He turned on the lights and siren and sped away.

From the rear of the vehicle, I felt the ambulance rock as the EMTs got in, and it soon followed the cops. I made no attempt to hide after it took off. Michelle and I were the only ones left. It was like I didn't care anymore if I got caught, didn't care if they looked in their rearview mirrors as they drove away and saw me.

Harvey said, *Don't do it!*

I smiled, a little apprehensively now, still not listening to Harvey, and held out my hands as I hustled to where Michelle was standing on the sidewalk. Her back was to me. She watched the ambulance as it too switched on its lights and siren.

She's going to kill you!

I paid no attention. When I stepped onto the sidewalk, Michelle turned to me.

Run! I'm tellin' you, the bitch is going to shoot you!

"Shut up, stupid!" I said, my voice rising at the irritant inside my psyche.

Michelle appeared startled, her eyes nearly bugging out of her small round face.

"Michelle?" I said. "No, baby. Not you. I was talking to . . ." How could I explain it to her?

She backed away, screaming, "He's here! Come back,

he's right here!"

What did I tell ya? So, now who's a dumb bunny?

Now, I'd done it. I'd frightened her. With everything that'd been going on this evening, how could I blame her for being scared with me yelling out like that. *Jeez*—telling myself to shut up.

Then it happened quickly—so very quickly, it left me standing in a stupor. She reached under her sweater and pulled out a nine-millimeter Makarov pistol.

A flash of pain shot from the back of my head to my temple, and Michelle collapsed onto the front lawn like a *lifeless* China doll.

Chapter 19

"Sunny," Major Jackson yelled as he pulled her from the ground.

Her eyes fluttered open, and she staggered.

Jax yelled into her ear, "Snap to, Sunny. You've got to be one hundred percent now." He flung her toward the DPV. "Get back to the choppers. We'll try to hold them off. Fill Gunny Sampson in on what we know, and tell him if he hasn't heard from us in the next twenty minutes, it's his baby."

Sunny climbed into the DPV still stammering as if not yet in complete charge of her faculties. She fired up the vehicle as bullets sang through the smoke-filled air around her. One projectile hit the exhaust pipe, and the muffler fell to the ground. It hung on by only a thin piece of the pipe. The DPV's small but high-horsepower engine suddenly became loud and complaining.

The airman on the back, who'd been manning the machine gun, jumped to the ground and took loose an equipment bag strapped to the side. "Go!" he said as he stepped back.

Sunny spun out in the DPV, and the German shepherd leapt into the passenger's side as she drove past. They headed down a small trail, having to avoid burning debris from the helicopter the airman had shot down with the fifty-caliber machinegun.

"The smoke pots are about out," Lieutenant Carpenter said as Jax took the bulky equipment bag from the soldier. "They'll be all over us any second."

Jax flopped the large bag onto the ground, and the three men gathered around it. As he yanked down the zipper, he told them, "Remember, some of these people we're up against might be our own. Nonlethal weapons only, unless I direct you otherwise." He pulled out two satchel charges and passed them to his men. After taking one for himself, he zipped the still cumbersome bag up, swung it to his back and put his arms through the shoulder straps.

"Count down from six, pull the pins, and toss the Bucha charges. These are a helluva lot more powerful than the grenades you've trained with, so, for God's sake, make sure everyone has goggles on, eyes shielded and are down and clear."

Jax looked toward the fence, now in easy view as the smoke pots died out and their smoke screen dissipated. Muzzle flashes came from within thirty yards on the other side. They ducked as several rounds zipped over their heads. The optical Bucha charges would fix this group of adversaries. The strobing lights the charges produced flashed at human brainwave frequency, causing serious vertigo, disorientation and nausea.

Jax continued, "Rally two hundred feet to the west and go under the wire. We won't have to worry about this bunch, but there're surely more on the way." He made direct eye contact with both men. "Start now!"

The three soldiers split up and ran for cover near the other two men who were firing their M-16s well above their adversaries' heads. All pulled down their goggles.

In unison, they counted down to one, pulled the pins and tossed their satchels over the concertina wire edging the top of the fence and in the direction of the muzzle flashes. As they flattened to the ground, three loud pops came from the other side of the chain link and lightning-like bolts of electricity shot out, crackled down the fence line, into the trees and along the wet ground.

Even in the heavy snowfall, the smoky woods illuminated for a quarter-mile radius in a tremendous and eerie, strobing glow like the cosmic birthing of a galaxy.

* * *

I had just killed my wife.

She lay on her side on the snow-covered sidewalk before me, like a road-killed deer. I saw no sign of life. She did not breathe. I hoped I was wrong as I bent down to look over her precious body, and the world around me became fragile, brittle, as did my mind. I felt the delicateness of it inside my head as I scanned the houses lining the street, the cars in the driveways, the few streetlights haloed in a mist of crystalline snow so light it was hardly perceptible on my skin. If I breathed, I was sure my world would break. Already fractured, its paper-thin shell was about to collapse from its own weight.

However, I did breathe, ever so lightly. I touched Michelle's hand. It was soft and as delicate as skinned-over pudding, and at first, I was careful of bruising it.

The emotions struck me suddenly, pouring into my brain like scalding water. My eyes burned. Even in this crisp night, my temples and forehead began to sweat from the rush.

Going to her was the dumbest mistake I could have made. So careless, so terribly costly. Worried for my own survival, I had risked her life without carefully considering the consequences. I had to undo the harm.

As the woods behind the houses glowed from the fight taking place at the foot of the hill, I gathered Michelle up and hugged her. She did not respond. She was limp, her arms dangling. However, I felt her warmth and realized it was not too late. I was wasting time, her precious time, grieving prematurely.

Cradling her slight body in my arms, I rose and nearly tumbled in my haste. But I overcame my awkwardness enough to trot, guarded yet briskly on the snow-slickened walk, to the front door of our house.

I opened the door clumsily and laid Michelle's body on the living room floor. When I knelt over her, I found no pulse in her throat, no sign of respiration in her chest. Nor, did I feel her breath on my cheek as I put my face close and listened for it.

I couldn't break down now. I had to bring her back to

life, this special woman with whom I'd shared my life and dreams for the past seven years. She was the mother of my son, which placed her in an even more exalted position in my life. As I thought of this, I remembered Will, that he might also be in danger, and it reinforced my resolve. With the hint of hope, the cracked shell of my life healed over slightly for now, but it was still dreadfully flimsy. I had to revive my dear Michelle, find Will, and protect him from whatever was happening even if it meant protecting him against me—my disease, my deadly infectious being.

"Come on, Mish girl," I whispered urgently as I lifted her chin and opened her mouth. I held her nose closed as I blew into her airway. "Wake up," I said, and I repeated my attempt to resuscitate her. "Come on, baby." I moved to her midsection, my eyes becoming bleary.

I fished out the small microphone she'd placed under her sweater and tossed it to the side. At the end of her breastbone, I placed the heels of my hands on top of one another. "Please, Michelle," I said while pushing firmly upon her chest. I thrust every second four times, then went back to her mouth. I pressed my lips to hers, praying for a response.

Relentlessly I worked, giving chest compressions and rescue breathing on her small body. The minutes passed like hours. I became exhausted. Her skin and lips had cooled.

Finally, I gave up, wrenching my eyes to the ceiling as the tears flooded through. "I'm sorry," I whispered. "My, God, Michelle, I'm so sorry!"

I released her and tried to stand with no idea where I was going. Stumbling after only two steps, I collapsed into the nearest corner of the dark house, worn out and grief stricken. How could I have been so stupid?

I tried to remember how special Michelle had been to me. This morning we'd had our last invaluable moment together, and I was glad we had vowed our mutual love. That memory was the only clear and distinct vision of her I could conjure. The rest were like when I'd thought of her and my paralyzed son, earlier—like watching a home movie in a dark room, a white screen in front of me. Strange, the way memories come to a mind.

I recalled her on that screen laughing and dancing, and in a wedding gown, and cooking and doing laundry, and going on walks with me, and taking care of our son. Nevertheless, I didn't have enough memories for our seven years of life together, and I felt cheated, staring at her frail body ten feet away in the darkness. I was convinced the disease had a hold of me, this thing inside of my body that caused people to die. I shook my head trying to remember how we met, but couldn't. I couldn't remember her favorite food, color, or even her preferred sexual position. I couldn't remember her favorite author, movie or drink.

Outside, a car approached, its headlights shining through the curtains as it turned the corner and drove slowly by. I rose and glimpsed through the narrow parting in the drapes. It was another patrol car. It pulled up past my yard and parked. As I watched, I realized the Makarov pistol Michelle had pulled on me was still lying near the front walk, its small black frame clearly visible in the snow. I didn't know where she'd gotten it. I should've known if she'd owned a firearm. Regardless of whose it was, if the cop found it, he would surely come to the door looking for Michelle and probably call for backup.

I remembered the wire I'd taken from Michelle. The small microphone lay a few feet from me, appearing in the dim light only as a small dark lump on the carpet. Mike Wu had told Michelle they would monitor her. My house had been bugged, but somehow, those devices had been *fried*, he'd said. I recalled the power surge that blew out the TV and the light above the kitchen sink. But had I been too loud while near the microphone Michelle had been wearing, praying for her to come back to life? Had I made enough noise as I worked on her lifeless body for them to hear me? That was likely, if they had been listening—unless the skirmish they were currently involved in was keeping them too busy to notice.

I glanced around the dark living room. The clock on the stereo was blinking. At least power had been returned, but Michelle hadn't bothered to reset the time. I moved quietly to the CD case next to the entertainment center and searched through the albums in the light from the flashing LED. They were all best-of-type records of the sixties, seventies, eighties, and nineties—country and rock, a little jazz and some easy-listening stuff. I found one I remembered faintly, Eagles Live. After turning on the CD player, sliding the disk in, and pushing *Random* on the control panel, I turned the volume low and placed Michelle's microphone next to the speaker. *Desperado* played softly. I hoped they'd think Michelle was listening peacefully to some oldies, and the melodic voices of Don Henley, Glenn Frey and the rest of the band would mask any noise I might make.

I needed to get my thoughts together and figure this all out. Why did Michelle attempt to call back the very people who were trying to kill me? Because she was afraid for her own life and the others, of course. But her voice had seemed void of emotion when she spoke of me. I was more of a problem to her. The emotionless solution to her problem and to the others' was to kill me. Somehow, it was reasonable. However, selfishly, I wished she would've shed at least a couple of tears.

What happened to start my deadly spree? The answer was in when it started. This morning, the lady who bumped into me. Had she started it in motion? Or was it the bee sting? Sunny? When she slapped the "bee" this morning had she somehow caused the mess? And what about the bugs? Why had I been monitored, and what exactly did the little disks do? Were they some sort of tiny transmitters, listening or homing devices? Or did they do something more? And where did they come from? Dr. Xiang must have implanted the one on my neck. After all, he was the one who told me it was a bump from the fall I'd taken and instructed me not to mess with it. But when did he do it? When I was taken to the hospital after falling in the shower, of course. The only remembrance that came to mind was in one of those home-movie-like memories when the doctor had told me not to disturb the lump or there might be complications.

What about Xiang in the Biotronics limo, and what about the van that was the same dark-blue color as the limousine? Somehow, the Mount Rainy Biotronics company was involved, but how? Why? Was I some sort of an experiment? Were they trying something out on me? I surely didn't volunteer for it, did I? Were there others? If it was all an experiment, didn't they understand the incredible cost before they committed to it?

I stood up but stayed low. Maybe there would be something to jog my memory or some kind of clues in the house.

* * *

When Chief Dailey arrived on the small trail at checkpoint alpha in his squad car, he found one of Biotronics' helicopters lying in a smoldering pile and four of his remaining SWAT team members staggering in circles and vomiting.

The security force that had come down from the Weller residence had arrived and were scouring the area, and Colonel Wu stepped up to the chief as he got out of the car.

"You see anything?" Dailey asked

"No. No one came by us," Wu answered.

Prater wrenched hard one last time and spit into some bushes. "The lights," he said, still bent at the waist and struggling to speak, "they were so damn bright. Blinding. Made us dizzy, sick." He squinted toward Wu and Dailey.

"Take your men back," Wu told him. "Give them fluids and allow them thirty minutes rest. Then get them back on the job." He turned toward the crashed chopper and told Dailey, "That's helo three. The tail rotor was shot up—they lost control and hit a tree."

"Any survivors?" Dailey asked.

Prater spat on the ground again. The rest of his team was on their hands and knees. "When we got to them . . . ," he began, then gagged twice, ". . . all four were all laid out in a row, all breathing, but unconscious. They're on the other side of the wreckage. We couldn't do anything for them in the condition we're in."

Colonel Wu tossed his helmet on the ground. "They knock out our sensors and cameras, they tear through our security fence, they shoot down our helicopter—yet rescue the crew, and they carry illumination charges to incapacitate our people." He spun around and looked squarely at Dailey. "Who in the hell are they?"

"Don't bark at me." Dailey narrowed his eyes. "I'm only the police chief. You're the one who's supposed to be up on this shit. How should I know?"

Wu glared at him.

"And don't try any of your thought-projection crap on me," Dailey said. "You can bet Xiang will have your ass if you do." Dailey turned back to his patrol car. "What I do know is that it's only a matter of time, now. This thing's coming undone, and the good wave we've been ridin' is about to crash on the rocks."

* * *

I didn't dare turn on a light. Even though they might expect Michelle would be moving around in the house, I didn't want to take any unnecessary chances. I scanned the living room in the darkness. The streetlights' glow and the reflected light from the snow cover filtered through the curtains and weakly illuminated my surroundings. Nothing appeared out of place.

I moved toward the master bedroom, feeling my way along the walls in the dark. The doorway came sooner than I'd expected. When I stepped inside, I found an Indianapolis-racer-style bed illuminated by a nightlight and I realized I was in William's room. I should've remembered every step to take in this house, my house. But I couldn't, even though I'd lived here over seven years. Back in the hall again, I found the master bedroom doorway on the other side.

In the bedroom, I closed the door. The meager light from the street outlined the closed shades. When I pressed them against the windows to ensure as little light as possible would escape, I found myself in complete darkness. Using a flashlight seemed advisable, but I couldn't remember where we'd kept one. Surely, we had several, probably one in each of our nightstands. When I knocked over a small lamp on Michelle's side of the bed as I fumbled around, I realized my memory of this room in which I'd slept thousands of nights was inadequate. After reaching inside Michelle's bedside table drawer, rummaging around and not finding so much as a penlight or candle, I stood in the dark and considered my immediate situation. Undoubtedly, I would find a flashlight in the garage, in the least inside the glove compartment of our car. The thought of stumbling around in the garage made me shiver. The memory of it was absent from my mind. Besides, a flashlight could cause flashing bursts of light to be seen from the outside, should I mistakenly direct it toward a window or catch the wrong angle of a mirror. On thin shades, it would make telltale circles of illumination. Those on the outside searching for me, looking for something out of the ordinary, would think more of not seeing normal room lights than they would a simple lamplight. If Michelle were alone in the house she wouldn't be using a flashlight—she'd have the room lights on. Still, I shouldn't get carried away. Someone outside standing close to a window might catch a glimpse of me. I righted the small lamp by Michelle's side of the bed that I'd just knocked over and turned it on. I welcomed it's glow.

The first thing I noticed was that the bed was nicely made and everything seemed in perfect order. I gazed at the framed photos on the nightstands. Michelle's picture sat on my side of the bed and mine on hers. On the dresser was a photo of Michelle and our son. Nothing seemed unusual.

I opened the dresser drawers. Each one was filled with either her underwear or mine, neatly folded and stacked as if they were fresh from their packages. Oddly, none showed even the slightest wear, elastics like new. They all were creased where they were folded as if the undergarments had been pressed that way or folded for a very long time.

Michelle's purse lay beside the dresser. I picked it up and rummaged through. I found no car keys. Other than that, nothing was unusual or of any real interest. I took out her wallet and opened it. A Colorado driver's license with her picture on it was tucked inside. It was a typical DL photo—her eyes half shut, her hair slightly mussed. Surely, I'd seen it before—I should have remembered it, but I didn't. A VISA card and a MasterCard stuck out from one side. Both had her name on them.

Above the dresser was the key hook where I always hung my car keys, and they were there, where they were supposed to be. The key ring had a Buick symbol on it, just as I'd remembered. I plucked them off and slipped them into my pants pocket.

I went to the closet and opened the bi-fold doors. The first thing I noticed was the smell, the new smell of a clothing store, new fabric, shoe leather and polish. Added to that was the pleasant scent from the cedar-lined walls. On one side hung Michelle's dresses, pants and blouses, at least a dozen of each. On the other side were my sport coats, trousers, casual shirts, a few ties, and several belts. All hung perfectly as if in a clothier's. The shirts still showed the fold creases as if new and freshly out of the packages. Our shoes lined the floor, maybe a dozen women's and half-a-dozen men's in a neat row. I picked up several and inspected them. None showed scuffmarks or wear on their soles. Their leather seemed stiff as if they came right from their boxes. Nothing more to be seen in the closet, I stepped out and checked the clothes hamper in the corner. Except for my purple silk boxers, it was empty of dirty clothes.

In the master bath, the towels hung neatly folded, none frayed, the fibers firm and crisp, as if they'd never been through a wash cycle. Michelle had been meticulous. Even the soap bars, including the one on the vanity and the one in the shower, were nearly new as if they had only been used this morning. The shampoo bottle was full. The carpet was, for the most part, unworn, and I couldn't remember if it was relatively new or if it had been in the home over seven years ago when we'd bought it. The walls showed no nail holes or smudges. The tempered glass enclosure had but a few water spots on it probably from my shower this morning. But no signs of those nearly-impossible-to-get-rid-of buildups of soap or mineral deposits were evident on it, the tub, or the fixtures. The commode shined. No unsightly body hair. The toilet paper roll was brand new. At the double vanity, no toothpaste or soap splatters on the mirror. The toothpaste tube had only the slight dent I put in its side hours earlier and the toothbrushes had no toothpaste residue. I picked up my hairbrush. It had a solitary hair on it. I pulled it off and examined it close to my face. I wondered if a crime scene investigator were to inspect the place, would this single hair have been the only evidence I'd actually ever been here, let alone made it my abode for seven years?

I checked the linen closet. Neither Mickey nor his tracks were anywhere to be found. Once again, all of the bed linen and bath towels on the shelves were painstakingly pressed and folded.

I stood in the bathroom doorway and looked out at the bedroom while running my thumb over the bristles of the blue toothbrush I'd used earlier in the day. The brush was stiff, only used once, if I were to guess. I wondered if I would be questioning any of this if it wasn't for what had happened today. I doubted it. Now, despite my memories of this place, I also doubted it had been my home at any time, let alone the past seven years.

There was no obvious way of solving my mystery here. The answer must be with Chief Dailey, Doctor Xiang, *Colonel* Wu and Mount Rainy Biotronics. Sunny was also suspect, but she was probably long gone—or dead. I shook my head. What the hell happened there? At first she acted enraptured, risked her life for me. The next minute she threatened to shoot me. I hoped she was okay, somehow. But the reports over the police radio didn't sound positive.

These people would be watching the streets and searching the woods for me now. There would be roadblocks. I could try to sneak out of town. I'd never make it in my Buick. They'd certainly be looking for it—if it *was* still in the garage. They might have towed it off or made sure it wasn't drivable some way. It would be a hell of a long walk down fifty miles of winding roadway to Summitview.

The only plan I could come up with was probably suicidal: to someway make it to Mount Rainy Biotronics, get inside and rescue my son. Then, I would steal—or perhaps carjack if necessary—a getaway car. While I was there, perhaps I would find out what really went on inside that windowless, sterile-white facility.

After turning off the lamp, I went to the door and slowly opened it. The hallway leading to the living room was still dark. The only sound other than the ticking of the wall clock in the guest bath across the hall, was the Eagles softly singing *I Can't Tell You Why*.

I'd make a surer getaway if I left through the bedroom window to the side of the house instead of the front where the occupied patrol car was parked, or the back where the police had gone. But before I left, I couldn't help but go back into the living room where Michelle lay. I wondered if she was truly who she'd claimed to be. But how absurd of me to question that. Of course she was. She was my wife, mother of my child, companion, lover. I remembered that much in the twisting cyclone of my mind. But with the strange goings on, the lack of crucial memories, the odd flashes of reminiscences and how they presented themselves to me—perhaps I had been deceived. Perhaps she was somehow alive. Maybe she wouldn't be lying where I'd left her. Maybe I'd find her sitting in the recliner, listening to the Eagles and sipping a merlot while reading a Good Housekeeping magazine. I was being ridiculous again. She was dead, and she would be where I'd left her, and the way things were going, it could be the last chance I'd get to see her.

With my back against the hallway wall, I crept toward the living room. As I approached, I noticed my son's bedroom door ajar, the way I'd left it, and the faint light coming through the doorway. I stepped up to it and pushed the door open. A Buzz Lightyear nightlight glowed from the near wall. Will's Indy-racer-style bed sat in the middle of the far wall. In the poor light, I couldn't make out its color, but I remembered its bright, red and white, lacquered finish. I went to it and glided my hand over its smooth surface. I found no chips or scratches. At his dresser, I opened a drawer and removed several pairs of his jeans. All were the same dark shade. Holding them close to my eyes, I could see the knees weren't lighter than the rest of the fabric and didn't show any wear, but still felt stiff. I questioned whether they'd ever been washed. I put them away and picked up his Air Jordan basketball shoes from beside the bed and brought them up to my face—no grass stains or dirt or even rocks buried between the tread. The shoelaces weren't worn. Will was permanently paralyzed, the neurosurgeon said. He'd never have a need to wear the shoes again—if he'd ever worn them at all. I frowned at the shoes. Doc Xiang had given us hope. I was determined to turn the hope into reality, if I could live long enough. With Mish dead, that was all I had left.

From my peripheral vision, I thought I saw a shadow pass by the door, and I put the shoes down. I watched the doorway for a moment and finally decided it was nothing. Perhaps a car's lights had created the shadow from a block away, or an owl had flown by the streetlight.

Regardless of what it had been, I reminded myself of the need to get moving. I slipped back into the hall and took three steps to the living room. I bent almost to the floor as I moved swiftly into the room and to Michelle's side. Through the curtains, I could see the patrol car parked where it had been before I went to the back of the house. The silhouette of the lone officer was still inside the car.

I gently placed my hand on Michelle's cheek. She lay there as before, her body slightly cooler now. Gazing at her, I forgot about where I was and the danger surrounding me. "I'm sorry," I told her again, not thinking about the bug.

A sound. Odd. I thought of a hissing snake.

The sibilant noise came from the corner I'd lain against earlier while mourning for Michelle. I looked to it, eight feet away, and saw a dark form huddled there roughly the size of a man. The thing shushed me again, and my heart began to race. Like a phantom, something moved fleetly from the adjacent corner to nearly within arm's reach from across Michelle's body. The thing had *two* green dots where the eyes should have been, instead of only one. I realized it must be the armed men in dark-blue fatigues with night-vision goggles, again. They'd caught me. However, even in the bad lighting, this man's fatigues looked more black than dark-blue, as if that made a difference.

"Shhhh," the one in the corner repeated as the Eagles softly sang *New Kid in Town*.

Chapter 20

The dark figure reached toward my face. I ducked away but found his other hand firmly, yet gently catching the side of my head, and I decided I'd better submit to him. He fumbled with what I thought might be an earpiece in my ear, and I helped him place it. Seconds later, from the earpiece I heard a soft voice.

"Sir," it whispered, "do not speak. I repeat, absolutely, do not make a sound. Nod if you hear me."

I watched wide-eyed and panted with excitement at the other dark shape in the corner. His hands covered his mouth as if he might be the one talking and not wishing his voice to carry into the room around us.

"Do you hear me, sir?"

I nodded slowly.

"Cup your hand over the earpiece, sir."

I did as told.

"Sir, I am Major Lionel Jackson of the United States Air Force Special Operations Command. Lieutenant Carpenter and I are here with a search and rescue team to get you out."

The Air Force Academy was at Colorado Springs. It made sense they were the ones to come here, but why? Why was I so important to the U.S. government?

More whispering came through the earpiece. "Listen carefully, sir. You must do as I tell you and get yourself out of here. That's whatever it takes, everything in your power, and at any cost. If something should go awry, you must do your best to escape on your own. Do not, I repeat, do not under any circumstances fall back into these people's hands. As last resort, sir," he said, his whispering voice lowering, "you must bite into the pill the lieutenant is handing you and then place it under your tongue."

The figure across from me held out his hand in front of my face. Contained in a single bubble pack between his fingers was a small pill. It looked gray in the darkness, but I imagined it was as shiny red as my son's racecar bed.

"Put it in your shirt pocket, sir."

I complied, but I had no intentions of using it.

"Now, sir," the man who called himself a major said. He paused, looking at his wrist. I heard a light, tearing noise as if he'd pulled back a Velcro flap that covered his watch dial. "In exactly six minutes and thirty seconds, our helo will be at the clearing about a hundred meters behind this house. Do you know where that is, sir?"

I nodded again and thought of the clearing. I didn't know whether I would follow whatever orders he had for me even if that area was big enough for a chopper to land, and I was sure it wasn't.

The major continued. "It might be too late. An opposing force is on its way back here now. But you must do everything you can to get to that helo. We will hold off the enemy as long as possible. But sir, do not go within two hundred feet of that clearing until the helo lands. Also, do not wait for us or any part of our team to get on board. We are all expendable. Do you understand, sir?"

I was stunned.

"Sir?"

I nodded once more, wishing he would quit calling me sir, at least in such a precise military fashion. However, I couldn't understand how he or any of his men could be expendable, and I wanted to ask him what was going on, to shout out in frustration.

The major seemed to be looking over my head and out the window. The lieutenant still faced me, and although I could only see green dots, I was sure his eyes were on me.

The major spoke again. "We have little time, sir. I need answers, direct and honest. I must now ask, what is your involvement in the Brainstorm Project? Answer me softly, sir."

I shook my head. I knew nothing of a *Brainstorm Project.* "Never heard of it," I whispered.

"What about Daniel McMaster? Have you seen him? Do you know where he's being held?"

Sunny's husband—I remembered. "I hadn't heard of him until today," I told him. Then, I said something that I'm sure was confusing to the major, "In a dream." I quickly added, "A woman named Sunny said that was her husband's name—and two guys asked me about him this morning."

"So, you haven't seen him? Don't know where he is?"

"No," I said. "Unless he's where they're keeping my son—at Rocky Mountain Biotronics."

Although I couldn't see his face, couldn't hear emotions in his low voice, I was sure the major was disappointed by the way he shook his head and bowed it thoughtfully for a moment. I heard him take a deep breath before saying, "One more thing, sir. No matter what happens, do not give up. Your country, the free world and God himself may be depending on you."

Heartache Tonight came on the CD player.

I finally realized they had the wrong guy. All of this was about someone else. I'd never been involved in anything in which "my country, the free world and God himself" would have to depend upon me. I knew nothing of a project called *Brainstorm*. I'd never been to Stanford. These yahoos and the woman who called herself Sunny had screwed up. I was a freaking dry goods storeowner, for Christ's sake!

Still, it was not a good time to tell them. Sure, I could stand up and call out, *Hey, you've got the wrong guy. Check your records. Take my fingerprints and you'll believe me. Now, let's all quit this silliness and go home. No hard feelings, right? Whadayasay, boys?* That would've only gotten me about twenty pounds of lead added to my ass at this point.

I was beginning to wonder if maybe my first group of pursuers was responsible for the deaths—more accurately the murders. Maybe someone like a sniper with some of those tiny darts as in the movies, someone with some sort of deadly electronic device that not only stops hearts but breaks glass, or somebody with a kind of a biological weapon was responsible for the six deaths, including Michelle's. It could've been something *they* had done to me. But no way had all these people died solely from something I had or was doing. And *they*, whoever *they* were, would pay. On that, there would be no doubt.

I would give total support and trust to my new captors, for now. The entire situation was too mind-boggling for me even to begin to figure out. At least these guys hadn't tried to kill me, up to this point. Once aboard their helicopter, I would explain the situation—that I was the wrong man. Maybe they'd believe me, and I could straighten this all out and save my son. If not, I was sure when I got to where they were taking me, I would be able to talk with the officials and rectify the situation. Then, when I had all the chips and it was my turn to deal, we'd play a little game called payback. I'd have whoever was responsible slapped with criminal charges—murder—so hard, it'd make their helmets spin.

I thought about that crazy woman again, Sunny, she called herself. She was so very attractive. I found her alluring. She had helped me, maybe. Was she tied in somehow to the major? Or were they on opposite sides? Was she alive? There was one way to find out.

"Sunny?" I asked in a low voice.

The major whispered, "She's safe."

They *were* allied with her. She was okay. I was relieved, and my trust in them grew quickly with that news. "Who is this Dan McMaster?"

The young lieutenant glanced back at me and the major. The major shot a look back to the lieutenant.

"Keep watching," he told him, and then he turned to me.

I didn't know what kind of game we were playing, but I

wanted to know at least a few of the players.

"They kidnapped him, like you," the major said. "And we won't leave this place without him or you," he said. "You can be sure of that."

I shook my head. "I wasn't kidnapped. I live here."

"Do you?" the major asked.

Those simple words caused my thoughts to spin again. *Do you?* Of course I did . . . didn't I? I couldn't help but raise my voice and say, "Where the hell did I come from, then?"

The major held his hand out in an attempt to calm me down. "Please, sir, whisper."

"What about the others?" I asked, fishing more than anything.

"We're going to do everything we can," the major said checking his watch. He stood and looked to the street in front, then down the hall toward the back of the house. He motioned for me to stand, also. But when I began to obey, the lieutenant planted his hand on my shoulder and shoved me back down.

In my earpiece a different voice said, "No!"

"What?" Major Jackson whispered.

"The one in the car, he's gone," Lieutenant Carpenter answered. I imagined him much younger from the tone of his voice.

"Shit," Jackson said. "Go!"

The lieutenant stepped over Michelle and hustled to the front door. He stood to one side then the other, looking through the small, diamond-shaped window in the top of it.

"No one," he said.

The night was quiet except for the Eagles softly singing *Hotel California*. I thought I could hear the clock ticking. It sounded louder than before, even though I was farther away from it—but the ticking stopped. The two military officers said nothing as each of them moved about the room.

Major Jackson began pulling me up and then suddenly yanked me toward the hallway. It hadn't been the ticking of a clock I'd heard, but the bolt of an MP5 chambering a round and its safety being released from outside the house. The major's voice came through the earpiece in a yell that made my ear hurt. "Window!"

It was too late. A figure stood opposite the large front window. The plate glass suddenly exploded into shards as silenced bullets broke through. They struck Lieutenant Carpenter's body armor, but also his arms and legs. Carpenter turned to his assailant as he fell, his M-16 spitting out a volley of rounds, its voice loud like a chainsaw. They hit the cop, and so did the charge from the lieutenants grenade launcher fixed underneath his rifle barrel. It shot not a grenade, but what must have been a much softer projectile—I thought immediately, *beanbag*—that hit our attacker in the helmet. The man's protective cover flipped backward into the yard and he fell into the room face first. At the same time, something pelted me like pebbles. The tiny projectiles had bounced around the room and thumped me on the chest, arms and legs, and I happened to catch one of them in my hand. As I ducked, I squeezed the small pellet that had ricocheted off the cop or the wall. It was made from some kind of hard rubber. The lieutenant had fired rubber bullets and a beanbag—nonlethals.

Major Jackson was already at Carpenter's side. Dark streams lined Carpenter's face, and the arms and legs of his dark fatigues glistened from the streetlights now glaring through the vacant window frame.

Outside, several patrol cars screeched to the curb one after another, sirens blaring, like half a dozen cats fighting in a gunnysack.

Jackson turned back to me as I stood hunched over in the doorway. His voice was loud and clear. "Go," he said, "get to the chopper."

He looked to the cop lying about ten feet from him. The cop groaned and his arms began thrashing. Jackson took three quick steps to the man and gave him a sharp tap on the jaw with the butt of his weapon. The cop's arms fell to his sides, and he lay still.

As Jackson hustled back to his comrade's side, I saw the young lieutenant facing me, his goggles and helmet now under one limp arm. His hair was closely cropped, his skull thick and angular. I hadn't actually seen his face, couldn't now because of the shadows, but I imagined it. He was a warrior in the highest tradition. Tough, dedicated and patriotic. He could have marched with Washington, ridden with Lee or Jackson, driven tanks with Patton, charged up bloody hills with Chesty Puller. He was true and blue, and as American as Harley Davidson.

But why was his weapon loaded with nonlethal, rubber bullets and a beanbag?

Lieutenant Carpenter's voice came to my earpiece. "Get out, sir. Don't let me die for nothing."

I couldn't help but pause there as I gazed at his dark form, but what he was saying finally sank in. I turned and ran for the back door. As I did, the lieutenant's voice continued in my ear. It took a higher pitch as he wrestled death and said, "Get out of here, major!"

At the kitchen doorway, I found another colorless figure squatting next to the back door. His hand came out to halt me.

"Stop, sir," he said. "I'll clear your way."

The soldier opened the door carefully and scanned the back yard.

I glanced back and saw the major halfway down the hall dragging the lieutenant's limp body by the shoulder straps beside him. Major Jackson stopped, turned toward the front and lowered his big-barreled weapon. Large projectiles spat from it and burst onto the floor and walls several yards out in front. The foamy-looking covering that the projectiles produced grew to nearly a foot thick.

The soldier at the door tapped me on the shoulder, and when I turned, he was already out in the yard about twenty feet, kneeling and sweeping the trees beyond him with the muzzle of his rifle.

I had to look back again.

The major had made it to the kitchen with his fallen buddy, but light from the front, which seconds ago had illuminated the hallway with a soft glow, was now blocked by several silhouettes. At first, they ran toward us, their weapons spewing bullets.

I ducked as the doorframe next to me splintered.

The shooting stopped as soon as they stepped into the major's foam. They fell into the gooey froth, and it pulled them in farther. It was clear now there were three men, one against the wall and two on the floor, all fighting the sticky-foam, struggling to move like bugs on flypaper as the fast-curing substance hardened.

I turned to the backyard and ran up to the soldier waiting there.

He motioned me on and stood up as I passed.

When I made the tree line on the way to the clearing, I heard those snaps again, so I swung behind a large tree trunk and glanced back.

Half a dozen of our adversaries had come around the side of the house. Fifteen feet behind me, the soldier I'd passed was down on the snowy ground, arms and legs strewn awkwardly, motionless.

I left the path, not wanting to make it easy to be followed, and stomped through the mulched floor of the woods. Bullets snapped over my head and limbs fell around me. I zigzagged, using the small tree trunks to pull myself from side to side. After a hundred feet, the arm of a black field jacket appeared in front of my chest like a crossing gate. The man caught me, and I could only hope he was one of the major's men.

The bullets cracked around me again, and my new protector got between them and me. The only move I could think of was to run to the clearing. It would be the best thing to do for the rescue team and for myself.

But I remembered what the major had said. "Don't go near the clearing until the chopper lands." If the helicopter was on time, I couldn't have been much more than a minute early.

I was twenty-five feet away from the landing zone when I found out why the major had been concerned about me arriving too soon. An explosion lifted me from my feet, and it seemed like the walls of the world itself were falling down around me.

* * *

Tree limbs. Snowflakes dancing dreamily, floating above. Silence—loud silence. I am face up, on my back. I smell—taste cordite. I watch the falling snow. Down the white crystals come, playing in the air, then finally land, cold and sharp, stinging my face.

It took a moment of viewing the pleasant, lazy scene before a crystalline flake crashed into my ear like a wrecking ball, and I snapped to. The pain in my ears was tremendous. They had used detonation cord to knock down the trees. A single wrap of the quarter-inch explosive cord would fell a twelve-inch-thick tree. These trees were mostly less than a foot. All of the trees within fifty feet of the smoke-filled clearing were cut down neatly at about eighteen inches high. Several seconds passed before I realized I was lying in a pile of them, a six-inch trunk against my chest.

A kind of hollow ringing blared in my ears, and when I reached up to touch them I found my earpiece was missing. Soon, the ringing turned into a soft thumping noise, and the wind from a helicopter's rotor blew into my face from overhead. It came in quickly, stopped and hovered within four feet of the ground. Two soldiers dropped from the chopper and ran to each side of me. I thought I was dreaming, because, they looked familiar. They were the two GI Joes I'd met on the sidewalk on my way to work this morning.

"Good to see you alive, sir," the taller one said and the shorter, stocky one nodded to me.

They lifted the fallen tree trunk from my chest. Each man took an arm and whisked me toward the rotorcraft while I hung from them, feet dragging, still in a stupor from the explosion.

When we had made it to within twenty feet, a rush of air shot past me. It rattled my lungs and vibrated the very ground under us. Inside the gun door of the dark-gray Pave Low helicopter, I noticed what had caused the strange sensation. Instead of the typical machinegun, the gunner manned some sort of long-barreled weapon with a diameter of about eight inches. Reverberating charges of air pulsed from it.

At the cargo bay doorway, one of the men inside the helo—I guessed he was the crew chief—stretched out and grabbed my collar. I finally came around and reached for his arm as he hauled me aboard. The guy yanked me in like I was a feather pillow and slung me to the back of the cargo area. Still a little shaky, I stood up and held onto one of the webbed hand loops hanging from the back bulkhead.

Several clanks came from the shell of the helicopter as we took fire from the enemy in the woods. Over the gunner's shoulder I watched as two low-toned whooshes bent light, rippling the air as more of the sound missiles launched at our attackers. No fire spat from the barrel, no visible projectile. Outside, trees quaked and the unseen force slung from the weapon threw several men to the ground. I was in awe.

The taller of the two men who carried me to the helicopter flopped aboard but Major Jackson hadn't shown up yet. We lifted, suddenly, leaving terra firma at a stomach-tossing rate, and I peered over the edge of the doorway to see why the second man hadn't gotten on. He'd been struck by the gunfire and lay still on the ground, pools of darkened snow growing around his body.

Within five seconds, we were hovering outside of the back door of my house, and I was glad we were going back for the major. To the left of the door gunner was a steel-encased box with an open front and a computer screen inside. It appeared to be a part of some sort of infrared heat-sensing device. On it was a red outline of what was likely my house below. Inside the outline were several blurry, red figures. Soon I realized they were the major, the lieutenant who was laying spread eagle and was probably already dead, and their three SWAT-team-like enemies in the hall. In the front room was a prone figure, smaller than the others and a cooler orange and yellow. Michelle. Nearly two-dozen red blobs surrounded the house, their bullets riddling it.

"Get down and cover your ears, sir," the gunner yelled into his microphone. At first, I thought he meant me, but then realized he was speaking to the major.

The gunner fired his acoustic weapon six times in the proximity of the house, and the results were incredible. First, the men in the backyard slammed to the ground as if they'd been thrown. Next, the guys in the front yard got their turn. The front porch collapsed. My garage exploded, and I saw that my car *had* been inside, because the Buick's trunk flipped end-over-end through the air. Propelled by my car's gas-tank detonation, the lug wrench shrieked by the chopper like a Fourth-of-July firework.

"My God!" was all I could think of to say.

One at a time, the police cruisers became fireballs.

I stood directly behind the gunner now, hanging onto a strap on the ceiling. I was within arm's reach of the cockpit, and I could hear the pilot arguing over the radio.

"What, sir?" he yelled, seemingly in response to the major's orders. "No, sir, I can't do that Major Jax. No, sir. I won't do that, sir!"

As bullets whined around us, the man who hauled me in yelled to the pilot, "He said, 'Go!'"

It was only a couple of seconds before the pilot gave in, shook his head and finally responded. The chopper banked radically to the left.

I squeezed the handgrips and couldn't believe we were leaving the major behind. You just don't do that, I thought. Why was I so important?

As we sped away, a fiery stream came up from below. An explosion rocked the helo from outside the open cargo-bay door. A surface-to-air missile had hit our main rotor, directly aft of the right turbine nacelle. The whirlybird we rode pitched and shuddered. It then began to spiral—fluttering like a wounded dove—down to a deadly end.

Chapter 21

From three hundred feet, the helicopter whipped in a terrific helix on a rapid descent. I kept a grip on the hand loops, but the crew chief wasn't as lucky, flung into the darkness from the open side door.

I held on for what I was sure would be a tremendous impact, and time stretched. Another flashback came. I remembered men, faces covered in war paint—camouflage grease paint—sitting on benches along the sides of a helicopter. I remembered standing and facing the lowered cargo ramp on the back of the thing and seeing only a shadowy nightscape hundreds of feet below. I remembered a man standing to the side looking wild-eyed and yelling, "Go!" And I remembered myself running off the end of the ramp and into the dark sky.

The flashback ended when we crashed into the trees. A jarring encounter, the chopper tipped to one side as it fell. The hand loops I held pulled loose, and I tumbled from the opening and into the bough of a large evergreen tree. What was left of the helicopter's rotor blades shattered against the tree limbs around me, and the pieces became deadly projectiles, swishing through the air.

Although I held tight to the branches, my weight was too much for them, and I slipped to the next row with hands full of nothing but evergreen needles. As the chopper ignited into a fireball below, I rolled off of a second limb and fell, spread eagle to the next, felt the one below it swoosh by, landed astride the one after that, somersaulted toward the ground, finally slamming back first on the forest floor in a bone-jarring landing.

A long moment passed before I got my wind back, and I quickly checked myself for injuries, then looked twenty feet away at the helicopter. It lay an unsalvageable steel hulk like some sort of abandoned relic in a junk yard with several small fires burning around it. The door gunner was draped over his acoustic gun, his neck twisted grotesquely. For some reason, I found drawn to a brand name etched on the side of the sound cannon. It said McMaster Nonlethal Solutions, and my thoughts returned to Sunny and her husband Dan.

I looked to the floor and saw the soldier who had boarded the rotorcraft after me lying with his helmet off, a huge gash in the middle of his forehead and his eyes open in a dead stare.

After managing to regain my feet, I stumbled to the cargo bay to check on the pilot and copilot. I climbed in, avoiding the searing flames now flowing out from the ceiling of the cargo bay like an orange waterfall turned upside down. The fumes were thick and noxious, and my only protection against the deadly smoke was my knit shirt, which I stretched up over my nose.

In the black haze, I found the copilot. A large shard of steel had torn through his throat and now stuck out from his chest. Although his upper torso was soaked in deep red, no blood flowed from the horrific wound. He must have died instantly. I turned to the pilot and saw his head moving. He groaned, and I grabbed his arm.

"Let's go," I told him, reaching for his safety harness. "We've got to get you out of here."

He winced in what must have been incredible pain. "No use," he said. "My legs."

It was easy to see what he meant. The control panel of the helicopter had collapsed, pinning the pilot at the knees. I even wondered if his legs were still attached underneath.

"We'll find a way," I said. "We'll get you out. Maybe I can pry the seat back somehow." I placed my hand on the belting across his chest and looked the seat over.

"No good, sir," he said. "Save yourself. This thing is wired to self-destruct. Explosives are placed in a half dozen critical areas, set to detonate ninety seconds after a crash. We wanted to make sure it would clean itself up—the sensitive and top-secret gear—leave as little evidence we've been here as possible, if we failed. We didn't want another Hainan." He grimaced, and his voice came out slowly, exhaustedly. "You don't have much time. Get out." He brought his hand up clutching some kind of folded, laminated paper and slapped it against the back of my forearm. "Take the map and get out."

"No," I said. I'd never left a man behind in combat before, I thought, then wondered where in the hell an idea like that had come.

"Ten seconds, sir," the pilot said as he looked at a digital clock on the dash.

It showed nine, then eight.

"May the Lord give you wings," I said, and I pushed away from him. I leapt from the doorway and sprinted toward the safety of the woods. I stuffed the map into my pants pocket and, as I rounded the large coniferous tree I'd landed in earlier, a ground-shaking explosion came from behind, filling the air with jagged debris.

* * *

Two security guards greeted Xiang in the Biotronics parking garage as he got out of his limousine. He'd spent the past hour on the phone speaking to the Chairman and a number of high-ranking officials. After convincing them he had the situation under control, they had assured him he would get what he wanted—two of their most recent purchases, Boeing 747 passenger jets for evacuation of essential personnel, records and equipment. He would also be relocated in a new, secret facility and be able to resume his research with the condition no word of their project leaked out. They had come so far. They were so close to perfecting their methods, to putting into practice a weapon that was reliable, undetectable, and beyond suspicion.

"Sir," one of the guards said as he stopped in front of

the doctor and stood at attention. "There seems to have been a firefight at Subject 374's residence."

Xiang began a brisk walk toward the stairway as the guards followed one step behind. Yet another complication. "What happened?"

"They had a helicopter, sir. They leveled the house. But we shot them down and wiped out their invasion force."

Xiang stopped before the stairs and smiled at the security guard.

"But there is a problem."

Xiang's jaw muscles tightened involuntarily. "What?"

"The subject has gotten away. He is still in the town, they are sure, but he is loose."

"Damn him." Xiang held his temples. Weller was much more trouble than he was worth. "Cut the security force here in half. Get everyone else to Gold Rush and help Colonel Wu."

The guard nodded and stepped back. "Yes, sir."

"And get a clean-up crew down to the subject's place."

"As you command, sir."

A number of the project's essential scientists—the Alpha personnel—were at home sleeping in that area. As the first guard hustled away, Xiang told the second one, "Get Yumi to send out the reprogramming teams. I want this matter forgotten. Then tell Wu to have the Alpha personnel rounded up and brought to hangar four." Bringing them to the airport early would ensure that part of the evacuation was completed and wouldn't be a worry.

At sunrise tomorrow the remaining citizens of Gold Rush would be nothing more than scattered ashes.

* * *

I didn't remember being struck down by the explosion, but I came to consciousness while being dragged backwards from under my arms. In my blurred vision, the helicopter was now a pile of unrecognizable charred metal over fifty yards away. There were frantic voices in the distance.

I wondered who could be dragging me. None of the crew had lived through the crash and explosion. The only person I could think of was Major Jackson. Could he have survived the shoot-out at the house?

"Major?" I asked, my voice coming out groggily.

There was no response. It became a trying exercise to raise my head, and when I finally did, I saw the straining face of a dark-complexioned man.

We'd gone another fifty yards when the man stopped abruptly, his feet striking what sounded like something metallic, probably a piece of the helicopter, and he tripped. He fell flat on the ground, and I landed with my head on his chest.

"Oh, damn it," he said, panting.

"Who? Who're you?"

"You are alive!" he said in what I thought was a Pakistani or Indian accent. "That is good to know. I am Rajiv Shekhar. We met earlier today . . . although in your current condition . . . I do not fault you for not remembering me." He stood up and took a deep breath. "Can you now kindly stand up for me . . . please?"

I did remember Dr. Shekhar, but I wasn't sure I could stand for him. He held his hand down to assist me. It took several seconds, but I finally managed.

The familiarity of the short, bald man made me smile. I didn't know why. This morning's incident when I met him was the clearest memory I could conjure, for now. What seemed to be a warm and sincere grin spread his lips.

"I am so glad you have lived," he said. "I have been seeing the whole thing. Frightening, very frightening. There are sure to be lawsuits. It is an iron-covered case you have."

I frowned at him. He returned a sort of beaming smile that covered his entire round face.

I asked him, "What did you see?"

"I had come out of my home, two blocks away to see what the police were doing. Half of the neighborhood was there."

"I didn't see anyone but cops."

"Yes, that would be correct. Before you arrived, the police ordered everyone into their homes. They said a man had gone berserk and was trying to kill people. They said he had the plague and was contagious or some such nonsense. They said his name was Robert Weller. That is your name also, is it not?"

"Yeah, that's me. But they had the story all wrong."

"That, I truly believe. You do not have to convince me of that. But everyone else was extremely afraid, and they all hurried behind their doors like scurrying little rodents. I am a more adventurous sort. I found concealment behind some bushes across the street. I saw you come up a few minutes later and hide beside the ambulance."

"You saw when my wife died?"

"Yes, that is, I was seeing her when she fell down. I am sorry to hear she has died."

"Then, why are you helping me?"

"I believe you are a fakir."

I thought he was calling me names. "A . . . fakir?"

"Yes, an incredible fakir. A fakir greater than all fakir's before."

"If fakir means what I think it does, that's not a compliment."

"My friend, from where I come, a fakir is one who performs miracles. I must then trust in you to take care of us and keep us living. I have reason to believe you are not the one who is dangerous. Now, enough of this speaking," he said. "We must get out of Dodge before the posse comes. The fan will soon sling out the cow pies, and I do not wish to be the one standing in front of it."

As he grabbed my arm and pulled me away, I wondered if he might soon drop dead, as had several others who'd touched me. He hadn't this morning. I prayed he would not be stricken, now.

He seemed to know some parts of the puzzle. As we walked briskly through the woods, I asked, "What in the hell is going on?"

"Strange happenings. Very strange."

"What? Please tell me."

"I am not for certain," he said, pushing a branch out of our way. He had small hands, but his grip on my arm was tight, not restraining, but ensuring I wouldn't fall. "I do not wish for you to think of me as a peeping Bob, but I have been conducting my investigations every night for the past month, and I have seen some things that are very strange, indeed. It started with Carmen Campa."

"Carman Campa? Who's that?"

"He was my neighbor. He had moved here from Spain. We both worked at Mount Rainy Biotronics. He resigned from his employment at a medical research center in Madrid. He came here to work, because, according to him, they made him an offer he could not refuse. He told me about some strange occurrences at the Biotronics facility. The next morning, he was gone—his wife and child, everyone. I asked Chief of Police Dailey if he knew where my friend had gone. He looked very sad when he told me that he had been transferred to the San Francisco office. Chief Dailey had no explanation of why my friend had left so suddenly. When I asked my supervisor about his transfer, he said it was true and that was all he knew, and that I should quit asking questions. Ever since that time, perhaps even before, I have felt I am being watched."

"What kind of strange occurrences did your friend speak of?" I asked as he stepped over a fallen tree and then helped me over.

"Things have been moving at an incredible pace at work. All departments have been operating nonstop, seven-eleven, as they say."

"Twenty-four, seven," I corrected.

"Oh, yes. That is it. I seem to always get that one wrong. Anyway, they are experimenting with new concepts in memory to help people with brain damage, Alzheimer's and amnesia. Carman said he had been on the east wing of the facility to deliver some pass cards—that was his job, making pass cards, identification cards and key cards. He had entered the wrong door. Inside was an entire room full of people, all sitting in chairs without life in their eyes, like vegetables, Mr. Potato Heads. He said he recognized several of them as fellow residents of Gold Rush he had not seen for some time. Dr. Xiang came in very quickly and took him away. That was the day before my friend moved without telling me."

"Do you think Mount Rainy Biotronics is using Gold Rush residents for some sort of experiments?"

"I do not know. That is possible."

"Dirty bastards," I said. "My son is in their hospital ward. If they've done anything to him, I'll kill every last one of them."

"Let us not fall to conclusions. We must first determine what is going on exactly. We can go to Biotronics tonight, if you wish. I am to be at work in one hour. You can come with me. Security is strict, so we will devise a plan to get you inside."

"Where are we going now?"

"To my home. You will be safe there."

"No," I said. "I'd be endangering your family. Let's go back to my place."

"My friend, I have seen your place, and it is not very good. Many holes are in the walls there. You would find it to be incredibly drafty."

"But we might have an ally. A man named Major Jackson. I think he might still be alive."

"I will go with you as you wish. You will be my Lone Ranger, and I will be your faithful companion Tonto. But we must have much caution."

I stopped and looked about. I had no idea where we were.

Rajiv said, "It is this way, Kimosabe." He pulled me to the right of where we'd been headed, and we began a slow trot. Within a few minutes, voices came from in front of us and we slowed down. We skirted the clearing where the knocked down trees looked like matchsticks. When we came to my small backyard, I heard a semi truck pull up in the front. Police had blocked the street in both directions and there were two armed men at my back door.

Staying out of sight in the trees, we made our way around to the side of the house as at least a dozen men leapt from the back of the semi trailer and sprinted toward the front door. Some carried gurneys, some carried boxes, some plastic bags. Before long they were coming back outside, carrying loads from the house. I couldn't tell how many bodies were removed in the confusion. I hoped the major's wasn't one of them.

Nothing more would be gained here.

"Let's go," I told Rajiv.

When we turned to go back, bright lights danced up from the direction of the crashed helicopter in the ravine. The high-pitched whine of a revving engine echoed through the woods. My first thought was a motorcycle or four-wheeler. The thing was hard to get a fix on, jostling up and down, from side to side, engine growling angrily as it leapt over rocky terrain and knocked down saplings. It had no lights, but a search light beamed down from the snow-filled night sky and illuminated the surrounding ground, revealing the noisy, rapidly approaching object as some kind of scintillating, blurred mass. Fire shot from the sky like lightning bolts toward the noisy thing on the ground, and I once again heard the beating of a helicopter rotor. It was as if some sort of apocalyptic beast were roaring up the gully.

Chapter 22

The guards at the back of the house raised their weapons as the screaming vehicle raced wildly up the trail. We ducked before it dashed past us, and the attacking helicopter stopped to hover over the backyard. The beast seemed to have some sort of reactive camouflage integrated into it, at times making it nearly invisible. But when the lights hit it just right, it appeared as a shimmering olive drab dune-buggy-like vehicle—a DPV, I recalled from somewhere, sometime. It didn't slow down. The guards pulled two shots then ran in opposite directions. The DPV rammed into the already weakened back wall of the house and knocked out a large portion of it.

When it backed up, I saw a flash of red hair from the driver's side. It was Sunny, hair flowing from under a helmet with night vision goggles. In the back was a huge soldier, manning a fifty-caliber machinegun. He swung the thing around and turned it on the chopper overhead. When the gun spat fire, it knocked out the chopper's searchlight, and the aircraft banked, moving away swiftly.

Sunny stopped the off-road vehicle in the yard and jumped out. Franticly, she ran about the back of the house. The soldier behind the machinegun trained it on several men coming around the side of the house and drove them back with a volley of large caliber rounds.

"Robert!" Sunny cried out. She paced several feet. "Robert! I'm sorry. Please. We're here to help you.

Please, Robert!"

Rajiv and I looked at each other.

"She is an acquaintance?"

"Sort of. She claims we're old friends, but I don't remember her. And she did pull a gun on me."

"She is exceptionally brave."

"Yeah, she is at least that," I said and stood up. "I think we have no choice but to trust her."

"My fate lies in your hands, my fakir." He stood also.

"Sunny," I called out. "Over here."

I hoped the machinegun wouldn't now swing around to me—that Sunny wouldn't pull out her gun and shoot me down. She didn't.

"Oh, my God!" she said, then tossed her helmet into her vehicle. She ran to me, her arms reaching, and hit me like a linebacker. "I'm so glad you're all right."

"Come on, Sunny," a deep voice called from the vehicle. His machinegun reported a dozen more times and several of our adversaries ducked around the corner of my collapsed house.

"We gotta go, Robert," she said. She took my hand and all three of us ran for the DPV. The German shepherd that had confronted me earlier leapt from the side and danced happily.

"Good golly," Rajiv said, running alongside. "We are being rescued by Rat Patrol and Rin Tin Tin!"

"Another friend?" Sunny asked as we got to the DPV.

"He saved my life," I said. I figured Sunny didn't find Rajiv threatening since she did nothing to stop him from coming along.

Rajiv nodded. "My name is Rajiv. I am considered a harmless geek by almost everyone I know, and I hope you will kindly let me join your *Mod Squad*."

"Nice," Sunny said to Rajiv. "You'll have to share with Gunny Sampson."

"I can do that," Rajiv said. "I can do that very fine. Kindly take us from this place now, please."

We hopped into the vehicle and Rajiv hung onto a roll bar above the back next to the big guy. I sat on the passenger's side behind some sort of grenade launcher.

Sunny returned to her place behind the wheel, and the dog poked his head in between us from the back.

"Your . . . car?" I asked.

"Just a little test drive before I buy," she said. "You remember how to operate one of those?" Sunny asked nodding toward the grenade launcher.

The question was ludicrous. I'd never touched one before, yet some sort of instinct took over, and I pulled the cocking lever back to chamber a round and flipped the selector off safety. "Hmm," I said, "I guess I do."

"It's nonlethal. Modified to shoot vortex ring charges, mean little rings of smoke that hurt like hell, but usually aren't lethal."

I smiled at her and nodded as if it were something pleasant she was telling me like a preschool had recently opened down the street, or that bananas were on sale at the local grocery.

As Sunny backed the vehicle around and turned off the headlights, behind us the big guy she'd called Sampson instructed Rajiv on a weapon he'd handed him. I noticed Sampson's fatigues and rank insignia on his collar. The black rank pins indicated he was a Master Gunnery Sergeant in the U.S. Marines.

"This is an anti-traction weapon," he told Rajiv. "Squirts out some of the slickest shit you've ever seen. It's like one of those Super Soaker squirt guns kids have these days. Range is about seventy-five feet. Trigger's right there. Try it."

Just then, three armed men came from around the side of the house.

"Try it, now!" Sampson said, and Rajiv shot the liquid into the faces of the attackers and they quickly went down. They became covered in the oily substance from Rajiv's weapon, preventing them from getting up, or even getting past thinking about it. All three men were on their backs, and no matter how much they tried, they couldn't roll over.

Rajiv grinned widely at Gunny Sampson. "I am finding this to be great fun!"

Two more men busted around the corner, one of them

sliding past the other three and fifteen feet into the yard, like he was a kid on a Slip 'n Slide. The other man managed to stay on one knee. He started to swing his M-16 toward us, but the thing slipped from his grasp and clattered on the ground. He reached for his weapon, but it slid barely out of reach from his fingertips. He began to fall and grabbed for the side of the house, but his hand skidded from the lap siding and he ended up on his back like his companions.

Sunny drove toward the neighbor's yard, our weapons blazing. Two additional armed men came around the other side of the house, and their bullets whined by us as I popped a vortex ring charge at them. A smoke ring shot from the muzzle and grew exponentially as it raced to them-from an inch to probably six feet in diameter. The shock that overtook these attackers knocked them from their feet. They lay writhing in pain as we sped away. After going through two fences, we turned toward the street and came out on the other side of the police roadblock. The big man on the back slung lead into the two patrol cars blocking the road, flattening their tires as we sped away.

We made several turns and drove slower once we were sure of not being followed. Sunny took a back street, and we ended up on a dirt access road leading up a wooded hill. Even though I had been born and raised in Gold Rush, I couldn't remember ever seeing this passage that was now barely visible in the snow-covered ground.

After pulling off the narrow road, we stopped under a clump of tall cypress trees.

"I'll shut this noisy thing off," Sunny said and killed the engine. "It's hell on ears without the muffler."

"We can't sit here too long," the big man said. "They're sure to have infra-red."

I don't know why I blurted it out, except that it dominated my thoughts and I felt the need to get it out into the open. "I killed my wife."

Sunny turned to me. "What?"

"I killed my wife. Just like the others. She fell dead right in front of me. I didn't mean to, but I know I'm somehow responsible."

Sunny grimaced, studying my eyes. "Robert, I'm . . . truly sorry. Very sorry."

I turned away and shook my head, changed the subject. "So, what's the plan?"

"We don't have one," Sunny said. "Not since you wouldn't cooperate."

"So this is my fault," I said.

Sunny's eyes dammed up and tears spilled down her cheeks. "No, Robert, no." Her emotions seemed genuine as she reached over and hugged me. "It's just that we were so close. Our helicopters were right over the ridge."

Now she was in that lovey-dovey mood again. I couldn't help but think this woman had serious bipolar or hormonal problems. "The helicopters?"

"Yes, the ones we came in to rescue you."

"Why?" I asked. "What in the hell is going on?"

The big man turned to me, frustration on his face. "What's going on is, we're rescuing my buddy. And we're not going to leave until he's safe."

"What are you talking about?"

"He means my husband."

"All right, how does your husband fit into all of this?"

"He's been kidnapped like you and we think you know where he is."

"What are you talking about? I have no idea."

"Look, Robert, after all that's happened, can you accept maybe you're missing a little bit of your past. Like there are things you don't remember. I mean, look at how you handled this gun. You said I looked familiar. Can you believe, if for only a little bit, there might be some things in your life you've somehow forgotten?"

"I suppose so," I said. "Like knowing you?"

"Maybe. Let's say we were friends back in college. Let's say you know my husband Daniel McMaster well, and although sometimes you don't act as if you like him much, you're still close."

I frowned, not knowing what to make of all of this. "Go on."

"He's my buddy, too," the big man said.

Sunny looked back at him and smiled. "This is Master Gunnery Sergeant Bernard Sampson. He and Dan were in the Marines together."

"Yeah," Sampson said. "We went through a lot of shit together."

"Kindly excuse me, please," Rajiv said. He reached out and shook Sampson's hand, then Sunny's. "I am Rajiv Shekhar, and I too have been in shit."

Sunny asked, "Where'd you find this guy?"

"He found me," I said. "He knows some things about Biotronics. I think he can help us find out what's been going on around here. But then, maybe you can just tell us, now." I stared at Sunny.

"Okay, Robert. I'll tell you all I can."

"All you can? That's not all you know, though, is it."

"Robert, please. This is what I can tell you. Let's say—"

"Oh, now we're on the 'let's say' kick again."

Sunny ignored me. "You were kidnapped by Mount Rainy Biotronics. My husband and dozens of others, too. I think you can help me find them."

"Now why would Biotronics kidnap me? And when did this kidnapping supposedly happen?"

"Two years ago. You've been gone that long."

"Gone? From where?"

"Your home in California."

"My home is here in Gold Rush."

"No, this is your prison."

"Gold Rush is my prison?"

"Yes, this town is the prison. You're as captive as a bird in a cage. They've erased your memory and given you a new one and—"

"Whoa, whoa, whoa! Hold up a minute," I said, shaking my head. The dog squeezed through from the back, used my thighs for steps to get to the floorboard in front of me and laid his head in my lap. I was alarmed at first, but his head lay still, seeming to mean no harm. I began stroking his neck.

Sampson said to Sunny, "You're going too fast. You're going to lose him."

"We don't have much time," Sunny told him. "We have

to get him at least this far." Sampson nodded. Sunny went on. "I believe many of the residents in this town are also their prisoners."

Rajiv said, "That includes me, also! I have been feeling like this bird you speak of. In Chicago they told me I was to be in the witness protection program after my family and I saw a gang shooting right there in front of us. We had a nice home in Chicago. The FBI knocked on the door one day and the next, I find we are in this place. We found this to be a pleasant home at first. Nevertheless, as time has gone on, I find it to be more like that birdcage every day. I would like to fly back to Chicago, now, please."

"Okay, okay, Raja, we'll get to your problem later," Sunny said.

"That will be fine. But please, kindly do not forget us. My children, and sometimes even my wife—they are especially dear to me."

I said, "What about my wife, my kid? You're not claiming Michelle wasn't my wife, William isn't my son?"

"And if I did?"

"I'd get really pissed, get out of this thing and walk away."

"Let's say, then, what I believe about them doesn't matter right now."

"It does to me."

"What's important to all of us now is getting out of here. I'm not leaving without my husband. Sam and I have the chopper. If you want to leave with us, you'll have to go along with what we say. I promise, it'll be the best for all of us."

"And my son?"

"We'll get him out, too. And Raja's family. You're right. We need to go to Biotronics. I think that's where we'll find answers."

"My son's in their hospital wing."

"Yeah, you told me. If he's there, we'll find him and bring him with us."

"I have a plan of my own," Rajiv said. "I think I can help. Many armed men are surely searching for you. After all that has happened here tonight, the security at Mount Rainy Biotronics will be tighter than a camel's butt at fly time. You will be unable to drive this contraption into the facility, guns flatulently blazing and expect to get to anyplace but down a rocky road to hell. Besides, it does not have a bumper pass."

"You've got a car, then," Sampson said.

"Yes. Yes, I do and although it is an especially fine car, it is still not big enough for our entire band of merry men, woman and canine. It is a Volvo and does not have big guns. But it does have a sticker pass on the front bumper."

"Okay, Rajiv," I asked, "what's your plan?"

"I will leave you here and leap across fences and bushes . . ." He held his thumbs to the sides of his head with his fingers splayed. " . . . like a horny deer until I come to my home and get my car. I will meet you on the road to the Mount Rainy Biotronics parking lot. You will recognize my car as it is small and blue. You stay put in this road-warrior's nightmare we are in now until then. If I were to guess, I would say there will be a roadblock after the last curve before the facility. If you can find a place to wait in hiding before the curve, we will find each other. Without my spare tire, my croquet and bad-mitten sets, there is room for perhaps two people in my trunk."

Sunny asked, "How do you know where the road blocks might be?"

"Biotronics has run many emergency drills in the past. That is always where they block the road. We must be cautious for there might be blockades elsewhere, also." He glanced at his watch. His seemed keeping better time than mine had. "I will watch for you along the road. We must hurry. It is after eleven o'clock. Within thirty minutes, the third shift workers will be driving to work. This entire road will be like a huge jar of traffic jam."

"What happens when we get to Biotronics?" I asked him. "Their security won't let us waltz right in."

"It may surprise you to find out I am not only a neurosurgeon but also what could be called a computer whiz. I can whiz on computers as good as anyone. My friend Carman Campa gave me access codes to all of Biotronics' security programs when he thought something was fishy smelling. I have been careful not to use these codes because access of the high security programs is checked on a regular basis. But since we will soon blow out of this joint, I will get in and get you fixed up, my fakir. Because you are a patient, I am sure your handprints and fingerprints are on file, as are most all of the residents of Gold Rush."

Sunny asked me, "Did he just call you his—"

"Fakir," I interrupted. "It's some kind of Hindu miracle maker."

Sunny frowned and nodded as Rajiv continued, "While you wait in my car in the parking lot, I will copy your prints, photo and other pertinent information to the top-level security files, authorizing you access through any door in the facility. I will also appropriate the proper attire for both you and your lovely companion and bring it back to my car as you wait in the parking lot. Then, you will be able to enter the building and as long as you do not run into someone who is familiar with you, you will be able to snoop and poop on as much as you wish."

I glanced at Sunny and Gunny Sampson. They both nodded. "Good luck," I told Rajiv.

"And may God be with you," he said and got out. He ran, not quite like a deer, but more like a two-year-old with diaper rash.

The dog whined and nuzzled my hand as I watched Rajiv's departure. I realized I'd stopped petting him, and he encouraged me to continue with less than gentle nudges. How could I refuse? The large canine was nearly a hundred pounds, possessed fangs the size of a mountain lion and had his head in my lap. His eyes angled up at me, and he watched me intently.

"What's the deal on the dog? If I don't cooperate, he's going to bite my balls off, right?"

"Don't worry, he minds well." Sunny patted his head. "No snacks before supper, Sarge."

Chapter 23

We pulled onto the road again and drove cautiously without lights. Within a mile, just outside of town, we came to the main road leading to Biotronics. Scouring over the town behind us, helicopter searchlights lit up the snowy sky. Red lights flashed from emergency vehicles. Sirens blared.

It would be only a matter of minutes before one of the choppers came along the road we were on and spotted us. Still without lights, we turned onto the pavement. With only scant light reflected from the white blanketed earth and the hazy, full moon appearing from behind the clouds on occasion to help illuminate our way, Sunny relied on her night-vision goggles and stomped on the gas. The small but potent engine roared, and she slammed it into second gear, the tires chirping, and then third and fourth gear, and we were quickly speeding along at what felt like ninety. She seemed an unlikely driver of such a war machine, but then, I'd found out early on that she was much more than what she appeared.

About a mile from Biotronics, we came to a curve, and over the rise a red glow flashed that we figured came from a police car. Rajiv had been correct about the roadblock. We angled to the side of the road again. There was no way to get to Biotronics except by that road. The facility had been cut into the side of the nearly vertical face of the mountain.

"What now?" I asked as all of us ducked low in the reactive-camouflaged vehicle, apprehensively watching a car pass and head toward the roadblock and Biotronics. I wondered what its occupants might of thought if they'd been able to make out much of our vehicle and the .50 caliber machinegun mounted on top. Hopefully, they thought we were supposed to be there—or a mirage.

Sunny said, "Any ideas, Sam?"

"I say, I drop you off and you get out of sight until Rajiv picks you up. Then I'll go back for the chopper. You push that panic button around your neck when you're ready—or in trouble."

"No," I said. "I go alone."

"Bullshit," Sunny blurted.

"It'll be too dangerous."

Another car went by, and we ducked protectively.

Sampson said, "We don't have much time." He nodded back toward town.

A line of headlights approached from down the road.

Sunny gave me a penetrating look. "What do you think it's been up until now, a game of patty-cakes? I'm going with you."

I knew it would be useless to argue.

Sunny and I got out and Gunny Sampson handed her a backpack and what looked like a ragged blanket roll as he climbed into the driver's seat.

I patted the dog on the head, and he whined and licked my hand. Sunny embraced Sampson, while the big man glared back at me.

"You'd better bring her back in one piece," he said. "And make sure you get my buddy back, too."

I nodded to him.

When Sampson pulled a U-turn, Sunny and I trotted down into some high weeds in the ditch. From there, we would wait for Rajiv.

Sunny untied the blanket roll and shook it out. "This is an active camouflage ghillie," she said, her voice low, as she threw part of it over my head, then ducked under it also. "Like a poncho. We only have the one—I left the one I had in the park when I spotted you."

I realized that she'd placed her head through the opening in the ghillie.

"Cozy," I whispered.

She slipped her head back inside, and what little light came through allowed me to see the outline of her face only six inches away, and I felt her breath on my lips.

"I think we're okay for a while," she said and turned on a small red light. "We should be able to hear Raja's car when it pulls to the shoulder

We sat there for some time, listening to the traffic, staring at each other silently. Her soft, large eyes seemed to explore me from the inside. I wondered what kind of a woman she really was, and felt she was wondering the same thing. The poncho provided warmth on the chill night—but there seemed a warmth in the air outside of what could be measured by thermometer. It was pleasant, sensual. We stared at each other, almost unblinking, and for a long moment, I felt as if we made some sort of connection, psychically, as if I could read this woman's thoughts, or at least her intentions. What I read was complete good will and passion.

We'd been under the ghillie for probably ten minutes, and I felt as though I we might be transcending into something even deeper mentally, when Sunny broke away and raised her head through the opening.

"Here he comes," she said.

I raised the edge of the ghillie and looked down the highway. Rajiv's Volvo slowly came up the road. Several cars passed his as he drove tentatively watching the shoulder and ditch for Sunny and me. I slipped from our concealment and held out my hand toward the pavement when he was close enough to see me, and he steered to the shoulder to pick us up. But the line of cars behind him had grown, and their horns began honking. A car that had started to pass him turned on its red lights. It was a dark-blue Biotronics security jeep. I shrank back under the ghillie and only peeked out.

Rajiv parked directly beside us and the Jeep with two security officers pulled in behind him. The two officers stepped up on both sides of our friend's Volvo. The one on the driver's side asked for Rajiv's driver's license and registration. As the long line of cars heading toward Biotronics continued to drive past, the officer asked why Rajiv had been driving so slowly. Rajiv said something about trying to avoid a horny deer, putting his splayed fingers to the sides of his head like antlers again. The second security officer glanced around them, shining his long black flashlight into the bushes beside the road.

We were well hidden and the constant motion of light and shadows from the passing cars helped to conceal us. Seemingly satisfied he was not in danger of being attacked by a horny deer, the young security officer went to the Volvo's trunk and asked Rajiv to open it. The trunk popped open and the officer checked inside briefly, then closed it. He mentioned to Rajiv driving without a spare tire wasn't wise. After assuring the officers he would drive with the flow of traffic so as to not be a hazard and impede progress, Rajiv was free to go.

I'd hoped the security officers would depart, and we could quickly slip inside Rajiv's trunk, but they didn't. Instead, they motioned for Rajiv to go, then leaned against the front of their jeep and watched the traffic while they lit up a couple of cigarettes. Rajiv had no choice but to leave us behind.

It was at least three minutes before the two security men finally finished their smoke, and drove away. To have any hope of catching up with Rajiv, Sunny and I pushed ahead to make up time, stepping quickly along the weed-filled ditch toward Biotronics.

With the line of cars growing, we found the three guards at the roadblock too busy to notice us, and we slipped by without incident. Rajiv's car was out of sight and the going was slow through the vegetation and snow. Still we had hopes of somehow catching Rajiv before he went through the gate.

After half a mile, we came to Biotronics' lighted parking lot. It was enormous, probably a quarter of a mile square, and surrounded by an electric fence topped with triple-stranded concertina razor wire. We were surprised to easily spot Rajiv's blue Volvo, but it was inside the fence, in the stall nearest the guard shack. His car faced the entrance, and I could make out someone sitting inside. I hoped it was Rajiv, and that he hadn't somehow double-crossed us. Still there was the guard at the gate to deal with.

We got as close as we could without being seen. Cars now lined up four to five deep but passed through quickly. From the ditch, I tried to catch Rajiv's attention by tossing pebbles at his car while Sunny rose up just far enough to see the parking lot and acted as my forward observer. I stayed low to avoid the eyes of any of the people in the cars.

"Add five meters, three to the right," Sunny whispered.

I adjusted and pitched another one.

"Down two meters, one to the left," my spotter said.

I adjusted once more and used a bigger rock with the next toss.

I heard a faint pop this time. Sunny winced. "Good shot. You got his windshield." She smiled. "He's out of the car. Checking the windshield. Looking our way. Now, he's headed for the guard shack." She turned to me. "You think we can trust him?"

I stood up cautiously and watched him.

"Mr. Guard, sir," Rajiv called out much louder than necessary as he approached the armed man.

The guard, a forty-five in the holster at his side, was checking the ID of a driver stopped at the crossing arm. He looked over his shoulder briefly at Rajiv. He handed the driver back his ID, raised the gate to allow the car to pass and then lowered it in front of the next car.

"Mr. Guard, sir, please," Rajiv said again and the guard turned to him.

I slipped from underneath our camouflage ghillie and said, "We have to trust him," I said. "But we can't take the poncho. It's too obvious—attract attention, looking like some kind a chameleon ghost up close. We'll be better off appearing like all of the others."

Sunny nodded, coming out from under the ghillie, and said, "Let's go."

I took her by the arm and we trotted up behind the

closest car in line. Stepping out and walking by the passenger's side nonchalantly, we held hands as we passed.

Rajiv said to the guard, "I have a question about my pass, Mr. Guard." He dug into his pocket.

"Yeah? Make it quick. What is it?" the guard asked with one hand on his hip.

"I do not know, but maybe it is out of date." Rajiv pulled his hand out from his pocket, and with it came over a dozen, loose hundred-dollar bills. They fell to the ground and several tumbled with the light breeze.

"Oh, my," Rajiv said. "It is my entire month's paycheck!"

The guard began chasing some of the bills. Rajiv waved us on from behind his back. We hoped the drivers in the line of waiting cars were too involved with watching the money to notice us, or to care, as we ducked under the gate as if it was something we did every day.

We jogged around to the side of a panel van parked nearby and out of sight, where we waited for Rajiv to come by. He soon scurried past counting his money, and I grabbed him by the shoulder, pulling him back from view. He gasped, but then saw it was only me.

"I think that son of a female jackal kept two-hundred dollars," he said.

I yanked his money from his hands and shoved it into his pants pocket.

"Let's go," I said and headed toward the front door of the main entrance as if we owned the place, hoping no one would think any different.

I scanned the parking lot as we went. A number of people were getting out of their cars and walking toward the entrance. I studied the white walls of the building. Five stories high, dug into the mountain. I couldn't see the peak of Mt. Rainy. We were too close and it was too dark. The building itself must have been nearly a quarter of a mile wide. No windows.

Then I saw them. Cameras. Not hidden but blatantly displayed. One every fifty feet or so had been hung about midway up the side of the building's wall. I looked back into the parking lot. On each light pole was a box. More cameras. How stupid I had been to think it would be that easy. A hardware storeowner might not have known better, but I felt I somehow should have.

I shoved Rajiv. "Get away from us," I said. "It may be too late. Get as far away as you can and don't ask any questions."

Rajiv stopped and stared at me. Sunny, also.

"Get!" I said, as if I were yelling at a stray cat.

Rajiv backed away and hoofed it for the front door. Sunny and I turned the other way.

"What the hell?" Sunny asked. "Have you gone mad?"

"They're watching us. Cameras lining the walls. On the lights."

Sunny's head turned in all directions.

I continued, "If they haven't been, they will be soon. If we're lucky they didn't see Rajiv with us."

"What do we do?"

"I don't know," I said. "I'm guessing they have one hell of a security system in there. There are probably cameras all up and down the hallways and in every room inside. It's useless. We screwed up." I looked at her, eye to eye. "Maybe you should run, too."

"No," she said. "What else could we have done?"

"Nothing."

"There's one way in," Sunny said. She started toward the entrance again.

"Wait a minute, they'll catch us. What's your plan?" I followed her one step behind.

"That's it."

"What's it?" I insisted.

Rajiv went through the revolving door at the entrance fifty yards ahead of us. It appeared he had made it unmolested.

"That's my plan—we walk in. They catch us and we're in."

"Okay," I said, "and the rest of your plan is . . . ?"

"That's it so far."

"What? Are you nuts?" This was the one time I missed Harvey. Even my imaginary nuisance would have surely come up with a better idea.

* * *

A guard scurried out from the doorway of the control room at the Mount Rainy Biotronics installation. "Dr. Xiang, Colonel Wu!" he yelled down the hall to the two men who were walking in his direction. "I think you should see this."

Xiang walked swiftly to the doorway with Wu at his side as the guard stepped back to allow them passage. On the parking lot monitors were Subject 374 and the strange woman.

"They are outside the front door!" Xiang said. "He got this close without me being alerted?"

The attendant bowed. "Sir, with the security alert and our forces stretched, I am doing the job of what would normally take five technicians. I alerted you as soon as I saw them."

"You saw no one with them? Nothing else?"

"No, Doctor."

Wu frowned at the guard as he reached for the microphone and pushed the Security button. "I'll have them killed immediately."

Xiang grabbed his hand. "No. This could be interesting. Ensure your men are in the proper gear and have them bring our guests to me."

Wu smiled. "I hoped you would let me finish him."

"Not so fast," Xiang said. "I do not wish for this to turn into some sort of competition between you two. You are much too valuable. I will get Dr. Yumi and we will meet your men in the interrogation room. I want you to take care of this security breach. You must contain the intruders and ensure they do not interfere with our departure."

Chapter 24

Sunny turned to me with tears in her eyes, but we kept walking. "Yes," she said, "yes, I'm nuts. You already said there was no way in. The thing is, we've got to get in. I don't care about anything else right now. You said your son's in there. I know you're not going to walk away and leave him there. And there're a whole bunch of other innocent people. You've seen what these bastards do. They've been trying to kill us for the past five hours."

I shook my head. We were fifty feet from the door. "I think they wiped out an Air Force Special Ops unit," I added.

Sunny's eyes widened. "Jax—Major Jackson?"

"Yeah, Major Jackson and at least nine others."

"They're dead?"

"I'm afraid so. I'd hoped the major made it, but when we were at the house, I didn't see any sign of him."

"After the first rescue attempt, Jax was the only one on my side."

"First attempt?" I asked.

"Yeah, we knocked on the wrong door several days ago, looking for Dan—this place, Gold Rush. But Jax threw away his career for this rescue mission, even with the slim chance of it working. It's likely we'll all end up in a Federal Prison—or worse—if we survive. There would be no way his superiors and the President, would have gone along with it. They don't even know where we are—yet. He was sure, from the current administration's record, they'd want to bomb everything first—destroy it all—and ask questions second. He put this rescue mission together with Gunny Sampson's financial and logistical backing. And he launched the operation without clearing it—on his own. I know he might not appear like it, but Gunny Sampson is a self-made multimillionaire. He's one-hundred-percent hands on in his business and in his own way, a genius."

I couldn't believe what she was saying. "Bomb everything? Gold Rush? Biotronics?"

Sunny nodded. "But the thing is, they shouldn't worry. Your Dr. Xiang has already started a countdown to do it himself. One way or another, this whole place won't be here past sunrise."

I put my arm across her shoulders and we stopped, ten feet from the three long, concrete steps before the door. Several people walked past us. "I think the guards have orders to shoot us on sight, too," I told her. "Looks like we're dead no matter what happens."

Sunny's eyes glistened in the lights. Dirt smudged her face or maybe it was the nitrates from the gunfire. Still, her beauty hadn't dimmed. I touched her hair. Wild from the abuse, but even now it was soft and florescent.

Sunny said, "Maybe they won't kill us if we make ourselves easy to catch. Once inside, maybe we can make a break for it." I heard a slight sob in her voice. "I don't know."

"If we merely stand here and let them catch us?"

She nodded.

I shrugged. Our situation appeared hopeless. Maybe the guards would show mercy if we offered no resistance. "The major told me not to give myself up." I reached into my shirt pocket and pulled out the red pill the young Lieutenant had handed me. "He told me to bite into this and put it under my tongue if it came down to it. Why am I so important?"

"There's not enough time, Robert."

I put the pill in my mouth, still in the bubble pack and moved it to my cheek with my tongue. Sunny's eyes widened, and she grabbed a hold of my jaw.

I backed away. "No," I said. "Tell me now. The pill is still in the plastic. But tell me what's going on now, or I'm going to bite down."

Sunny blinked at me and then began spilling out like a broken water pipe. "You and Dan have a gift. It's incredibly strong in both of you. We all met at Stanford fifteen years ago. I was a psych student, and you and Dan were right out of the Marines going for physics degrees. We'd volunteered for some ESP experiments the psychology department was doing in cooperation with the Army. We jumped at the chance. And why not? They gave us three psych credits and three-hundred dollars for it. I didn't do so well, but you and Dan—you both exceeded all their expectations. You said you didn't know anything about it, like reading minds or anything, except you always did well at poker—you know, could tell if someone was bluffing." She smiled. "You told me you knew I wanted to go out with you. And I did."

"You're feeding me BS again. I was never at Stanford."

"You were, Robert. I swear."

Several people walked by us and up the steps toward the door.

"Why don't I remember?"

"Biotronics. They hypnotized you, gave you drugs, hydroquanaline or something like it. It erases memories. Then they planted new memories in your head."

"That's ridiculous."

"Is it? What do you remember of your past, Robert? How do those memories appear in your mind? Your first kiss?"

I tried to recall it, and I did. It was with Michelle. But as I reminisced, I thought the memory odd. I remembered it—the view—rectangular, dark around the edges, as if it were being shown to me on a movie screen. I looked at her blankly.

"Did you have a pet when you were a kid? What was his name?"

I couldn't remember that one.

"Come on, Robert," Sunny said. "Every little boy has a pet of some kind. If not a puppy or a cat, they have a lizard or a turtle, or a hamster named *Winky* or something."

There was nothing.

"What about games you played?"

"I got you on this one," I said. "High school football—and baseball. I remember little league baseball."

"How do those memories come to mind? Are they like remembering what happened this morning or this afternoon?"

"Of course not," I said. "That was a long time ago."

"That's not what I mean. How do they appear in your mind?"

I thought about it. In my thoughts, I could see a bunch of boys, one hitting the ball and running bases. I could see another catching it on the ground and throwing it to second. However, again, it all appeared as if it happened from some sort of window or something—a rectangle in the dark, a movie screen.

"How about your wife and son? How do you remember them before today?"

At first, it made me angry for her even to suggest there was something wrong with the memories I had of my family. Nevertheless, I thought about them. The same memories I recalled earlier in the day came to mind. Playing catch with William, somehow in that rectangle again. Michelle walking down the aisle in her wedding dress, in a rectangle surrounded by darkness.

"What are you saying?" I asked.

"Robert, it all boils down to this. The Biotronics people kidnapped you. The Army Captain who was in charge sold out to them after doing the telepathy experiments at SRI—Stanford Research Institute."

I asked, "Vanzandtz?"

Sunny looked at me surprised.

"She must have gotten a promotion," I said. "When I remember her, she was still a lieutenant."

"That's right," Sunny said. "You remember!"

I curbed her enthusiasm. "But that's all I know. It came to me in a dream."

"The CIA, DIA and the U.S. Army, had been

researching psychic powers for twenty years, probably a lot longer. At the same time, the Biotronics people, led by Dr. Xiang, were experimenting with enhancing the telepathic powers of the subjects who exhibit the strongest abilities. Four years ago, Xiang came to some sort of a milestone, an implantable enhancement device. They started gathering up all of the most, let's say, talented subjects discovered over the years. At least three-dozen people who had been involved in those college experiments alone have disappeared. Those are only the ones I could find out about. They've been snatching people. Some, they take away from their families, erase their memories and give them not only new memories but new families. Others are scientists and their families, brought here under the guise of witness protection or some such nonsense, like your little Raja fella."

"Why?"

"I think they're making the people who demonstrated the greatest psychic abilities into some sort of assassins. To use their minds as tactical weapons. To access the minds of others—infiltrate thoughts. To make them psychic warriors."

"That really is nuts."

"You think so? What about all these people who have been dropping dead around you?"

I became short of breath. "Jesus," I said. "How? I mean, why would I?"

"Why did you kill those people? Because your subconscious mind sensed they were there to do you harm. That's a part of your gift. You don't read minds, so to speak. Not like some kind of a swami or something. But you can sense auras or electric fields emitted by other people's brains. You know, brainwaves. How? You also have an incredible ability to project thoughts, also in brainwaves. They implanted an electronic device inside your head—attached it to your brain stem—that enhances your brain's power to do that. The thing on your neck and the one on your shirt collar—they were not only tracking devices but antennae to send and receive signals so your enhancement implant could be turned on and off from an outside source."

It was too incredible. My memory told me I had lived in Gold Rush, Colorado all of my life. I had rarely traveled away, and then only for a week or two. I was a hardware storeowner. I was a simple man. I had a son, a wife—until I killed her tonight.

A commotion came from inside the Biotronics entrance. People ran toward the door. Several men in the now common SWAT gear came out other windowless doors along the side of the building from both directions. They had their helmets on and goggles down.

Sunny saw them, too. "If things go wrong," she said, "give me one last kiss, okay?"

I felt the plastic-wrapped pill with my tongue and thought of what she meant. "Let's meet them halfway," I told her and took the first step in front of the entrance. I didn't care what happened now. William was inside. Planted in my head or not, he was the only one left I cared about. There was too much going on here, much more than Sunny had told me or even knew—more than I could ever imagine.

Sunny came up to my side and took my hand again. We smiled at each other. Not a happy smile, but a thin-lipped, this-might-be-it smile. We raised our hands together, and the guards surrounded us.

Chapter 25

We didn't look at the eight guards who encircled us. Instead, we watched each other's faces.

The guards said nothing, and luckily, their rifles didn't speak either. They searched us, not finding anything on me but the map in my front pocket. The guy who found the map passed it to one of the men standing off to the side. I guessed he might be in charge.

After a brief inspection of the map, he handed it to a tall man at his side, who placed it in one of his many pockets. In Sunny's pocket, they found something that looked like a ring of thin keys. Then I realized it was a set of lock picks. In addition, they found Sunny's little .32 caliber pistol. That guard also gave his find to their leader, and in turn, he passed the gun on to the taller man. Then they found the necklace Sunny wore. I guessed it was the "panic button" Gunny Sampson had mentioned. The guard yanked it from around her neck. After being scrutinized briefly, it ended up in the same tall man's pocket.

Still without speaking, they made it clear with their guns that we were to enter the building. This was what we had hoped, but they took us through an unmarked door twenty feet to the side.

Once inside, we descended a flight of steps down an echoing stairwell. We stopped in front of a door with a sign on it reading *Restricted Area, Authorized Personnel* Only in large, red letters. One of the guards placed his hand on what looked like a red Plexiglas pad angled out from the wall with a backlit palm print on it. The pad turned to green. The lock buzzed and the door opened with a click. They forced us inside, shoving and prodding us like cattle.

They coaxed us down a long, plain-white corridor, until we finally came to an unmarked door. Once again, the leader placed his hand on the red palm-print pad to enter and they forced us inside. After pulling out two metal chairs and placing them in the center of the room, they pushed us into them. A couple of the guards moved behind us, pulled our arms back and restrained us with nylon cable ties.

We waited there with the eight rifles trained on us for what must have been at least twenty minutes. The guards hardly moved, and they kept their helmets and goggles on. I asked one for a cigarette even though I didn't smoke. He didn't budge. Sunny asked for a Margarita with salt on the rim but got no response. When she looked at me and said, "Must be tea-drinkers," the one who appeared in charge showed her the butt of his rifle, making it clear if she said another word, she would regret it.

I was almost thankful to see Dr. Xiang. He came through the door, his blue lab coat flying behind him. The white motorcycle helmet he wore didn't come close to passing for a matching part of his ensemble, and I found myself wanting to chuckle nervously, wondering if he'd just stepped from the movie set of *Space Balls*. In addition, he wore the same copper-tinted goggles their SWAT people wore. An Oriental woman dressed in the same manner followed him in. The whole bunch of them reminded me of some sort of new age, punk-rock group.

"Doctor Xiang," I said, knowing well he had been the one who ordered our deaths, yet hoping acting innocent might buy us time. "Thank God it's you."

I didn't see the rifle butt coming, but I was sure that's what hit me across the side of the face.

Doctor Xiang smiled. "This is where the bad guy tells the good guy all he wants to know," he said. "Then at the last minute, the good guy escapes and saves the day, is that not correct, Mr. Weller?"

It was as if it was too late for the truth to hurt their plan now. I didn't dare answer verbally. I licked the blood from my lip and gave him a narrow-eyed nod.

"Well, Mr. Weller, this is not Hollywood. I am not going to tell you . . . ," he paused theatrically, " . . . shit." He smiled as if he'd just finished a large plateful.

Xiang turned to the woman. "Now we will see firsthand how well our product performs." He motioned to the tallest of the guards, broader shoulders, about my size. It was the guy to whom they'd passed our possessions. "Take off your helmet," Xiang said and I guessed he'd selected this guard at random, possibly didn't even know him.

The young Oriental man looked at Xiang, and through the goggles I could see his eyes widen.

"I said, take it off," Xiang repeated.

The two guards nearest the man turned their rifles on him.

He glanced at both of them and backed up to the door. He looked at the doctor and finally complied, placing his goggles up on his helmet. He leaned his rifle against the wall and then lifted the pot off, and one of the other men took it from him. His gaze raced around the room, but it was plain to see he was avoiding eye contact with me, now.

Doctor Xiang's voice was mild. "Shoot them. Kill them both."

The helmet-less soldier frowned and turned to me. He took his weapon from the wall and raised it. I saw his finger tighten on the trigger, and again I felt the pain shoot through the base of my head. I waited for the bullets, my pain intensifying, but they didn't come.

Instead, the guy's eyes suddenly bugged. He dropped the rifle, stiffened and toppled over into his comrades. They didn't catch him but moved out of the way, and his body slammed onto the floor. My sharp headache subsided.

The doctor's smile grew wide. The woman behind him

seemed horrified, the lines around her eyes growing, her mouth dropping open.

He had used me to kill a man for the sole purpose of demonstration.

"You bastard!" I told Xiang.

Knowing I wouldn't get far, I stood quickly, lowered my shoulder and tried to ram him. He stepped back as one of his men grabbed the restraints around my hands and another placed his foot in my gut, sharply. I fell to my knees.

"Very good," Xiang said, staring at me. "Too bad we can no longer use you. You have become an embarrassment to this project. We cannot have that. We will renew our loyalty to the Chairman by disposing of you." He brought out something small from his lab coat pocket and placed it briefly behind my head. I heard a snap, or more accurately felt a snap that was not painful, rather it gave me an odd sense of relief, a little like a joint adjustment from a chiropractor. But this adjustment was somewhere inside my head. He faced the woman as two men put me back in my metal seat and this time they also secured my hands to the frame of the chair. "His device is turned off, now." He removed his helmet. "He is no longer a danger." He smiled at his female assistant. "Dr. Yumi, if you'd please."

The guards made room for the woman to pass. She stepped around the young soldier's body and brought up a large syringe as she went to Sunny.

Sunny's resistance, her toughness, had worn considerably and her skin was as pale as ivory. I knew what weighed on her the most was that now she wouldn't find her husband. She turned to me, and I could guess what she was about to say. I moved the suicide pill, still in its bubble-wrap, from my cheek to the front of my mouth and prepared to bite into it.

"How 'bout that kiss, now, Robert?" she said, but as soon as she did, the guard nearest her gave her a swift smack on the jaw with the butt of his gun.

Sunny's head went back, agony twisting her face.

I tongued the pill back into my cheek and yelled, "Son-of-a-bitch." I tried to stand again. The nylon cable ties held my arms firm against the metal chair, and although I was able to raise it from the floor, the guards shoved me back down.

The woman doctor with the syringe held her hand up to stop them from assaulting us anymore. "This won't hurt," she said and drove the needle into Sunny's arm. She dispensed nearly half of the clear liquid before withdrawing.

I watched in horror as Sunny's beautiful eyes pled with me. Her body jerked twice, then went limp, and her head fell forward.

"It is much better than a bullet," Dr. Yumi said stepping to me. I glared at her. Through the copper visor, her eyes showed no emotion and her mouth curved into a cold smile.

The needle jabbed into my arm. A warmth rushed from my shoulder into my chest. It grew hot. My muscles contracted. My eyes rolled back. Darkness descended upon me, heavy and suffocating, like a black-velvet stage curtain. It broke away from its traversing rod and collapsed onto me, just another retiring thespian in this, his life's final act. Darkness.

Chapter 26

Heaven or hell?

Lights glaring. Muffled, underwater sounds. Garbled drive-in-speaker voices. Strong odor, antiseptic. Bitterness in my mouth. Aching arms and legs—tingling skin as if covered in acupuncture needles.

Lights focusing. Sounds still distorted.

A clap—no, a slap across my face. No feeling, only the sharp sound. And ringing.

Focusing. The woman with the needle—Yumi. Her face over me.

No white helmet. Her hair long and black. Big, dark eyes and small features. She speaks to me. Whispering. Her lips moving, still sounding like in a pool—a water-filled tank.

Her hand across my face again. Head throbbing, lungs hurting, mouth dry.

Yet another slap. A sputtering. Lights flickering like a machine trying to start.

Something like a lightning bolt flashing across my eyes. A cacophony crashing into my ears like a semi truck.

I gasped, drawing in as much air as my lungs could take and nearly swallowed the suicide pill in the plastic. I coughed it back up and shoved it back into place in my cheek with my tongue.

Yumi gently covered my mouth with one hand and she put one finger to her lips. She glanced at the door momentarily. It didn't move. She turned back to me.

I lay on some sort of table, cold and hard. Along the sides, I felt troughs and when I slowly turned my head, I realized what it was—a stainless-steel examination table, the gutters for draining blood and other body fluids away from a corpse. I looked to my side and saw Sunny staring at me, the semblance of a smile on her face.

"Don't speak," Yumi said, her voice slightly above a whisper. "Just listen for now. I have once again turned on your brainwave projection device—for your protection."

I watched her, still dazed. She wasn't wearing her helmet, so I figured she must trust me and this strange power I had if she'd restarted it. Then, I noticed the tables surrounding us. On them were other sheet-draped bodies. It was a different place than where we met with Dr. Xiang, a morgue, I guessed, with two wide doors on opposite walls. One had a sign on it that said *Furnace*. The other wasn't labeled and probably led to the hallway.

"I wish to make it clear to both of you. I do not like you or what you stand for. Nevertheless, you are the lesser of evils, and with your escape, we will find the path to freedom. It is crucial for you to get away and tell the world of this place. If you do not, we are all doomed. My people. Your people."

She looked at Sunny. "You have a second helicopter?"

Sunny nodded slowly.

Yumi continued. "You have been unconscious for over an hour now. It is imperative you are many miles away from here before sunrise. That gives me two hours to gather the proof. I will make copies of what I cannot take. You must present to the world this proof of what is being done here. Only then will we truly be safe. Do you understand?"

I frowned and shook my head slowly. Real life was beginning to appear like that bad sci-fi movie.

"You will," she said.

I tried to sit up, but fell back to my side. Yumi helped me raise up, and I threw my legs over the edge of the table. They swung there briefly like a couple of sand bags on ropes.

Sunny could only lie there with her hand out to me. I reached as far as I could but was only able to touch her fingertips.

Yumi gave us a visual inspection.

"Why did you come here?" she asked. "You had a much better chance of escaping if you had run when you could."

"My son . . . ," I said, my voice hoarse. I swallowed, and it felt as though razor blades had lodged in my throat.

Yumi went to a stainless-steel sink nearby and drew water into a small paper cup.

"Speak softly, please," she said and handed me the cup. "We do not wish to be overheard."

I took it, gulped a mouthful and looked at Sunny.

" . . . her husband," I said. "They're here."

I handed the cup to Sunny. She reached for it and tried to sit up but couldn't. I slipped from the gurney and nearly fell face first onto the floor but caught myself. The doctor took my arm, and I moved tenuously to Sunny's side. After placing my hand under Sunny's head, I helped her drink.

"We need to call the FBI," I said. "The National Guard."

"You are ignorant of your situation," Yumi said. "Besides, no phones here will reach the outside. They are all controlled."

"We're going to get them out, our people," I said.

Yumi frowned at me. "That may be impossible."

I glanced at Sunny. "Maybe. But we're not leaving until we have them."

Yumi said, "It is time for you to know the truth. However, you must find this truth for yourself, for only then will you believe it."

I repeated the words from the note I'd found that morning, "'Everything you know is lies. Trust not in what you hear or see, but solely in your emotions—for within them is the only real truth.' You left the note in the shower?"

She looked at me coolly. "I am sorry to say that, although emotions are true, they can be deceived." She turned away and went to the door, then opened it a crack. "You would have many discoveries here. But there is not enough time for everything." She peeked outside then closed it again.

Sunny said, "You're the one who smuggled his file out. You're our friend on the inside."

"You have forgotten what I said. I am not your friend."

"What's your story, then?" I asked. I wasn't sure this wasn't another charade of some kind.

Yumi faced me. "I am a member of Falon Gong. We are a peaceful movement against rapid change and unfair treatment of our people."

"Who are your people?" I asked.

She frowned. "The Chinese people, of course."

That made sense. Nearly half of Gold Rush's population was Oriental, mostly Chinese—settled here after the railroads laid rail through the mountains to the West Coast in the late eighteen hundreds. The big railroads had been brutal to the Chinese workers who were the largest part of their work force. They definitely had been treated unfairly, nearly as slaves.

Sunny winced. "Why can't I move?" Her voice was raspy, and her face looked as white as the walls.

"I may have given you too much of the solution for your body weight. You might not find balance for a while." She reached over and felt Sunny's neck for a pulse.

Sunny moaned. "Everything's spinning."

Yumi shrugged. "You will feel groggy for a while, possibly lose consciousness. You must be careful." She examined each of Sunny's eyes as she told me, "The hospital ward is on the west wing of the second floor. That would be where any children are kept—where you will find the answers you seek."

"Yes," I said, recalling visiting my son. "I think I remember." As I thought of it, the screen appeared again in my mind. This memory played out on that screen surrounded by darkness exactly as the others. It was a moment before I realized I'd been gazing in a stupor.

"At the appropriate time," Yumi said, "I will ensure the door is accessible to you. But I am afraid that this is where you will find your emotions have been deceived."

She was talking in riddles that I had no time for solving. "We'll need an ambulance to transport my son to the chopper, and a driver with clearance. Can you arrange that?"

She nodded. "If that is what you wish. You will find them waiting for you in the ambulance garage in the basement by four-thirty. In the vehicle will be documents and video copied from the files of Project Brainstorm for you to present to the world, proof of this terrible project." She faced me with an iron-cold expression of someone who had endured a tortured life. "But do not be surprised if what you discover when you go looking for your people alters your plans." Her countenance changed. She was no longer cool and emotionless. She glared, not at me, but at the world as she spoke, "That discovery will be important for you to better understand the truly terrible things that have been happening here. But no matter what, you must leave this facility by then. After that, it may be impossible to escape."

Earlier, Sunny had told me that Gold Rush would be destroyed. But I wanted to hear Yumi's explanation. "Why the timetable? What does it matter? I heard Xiang say the chairman would close the facility if they didn't find us, but why does that matter now?"

"You do not understand what he meant by 'close the facility'?"

"I guess not."

"In order to close the facility, a twenty kiloton nuclear device is buried under this building."

"That's crazy!"

"In a compartment at the base of the water tower in the middle of town is another, set to go off five seconds after the first. Detonating those devices will 'close the facility'—the project—destroying all evidence of it ever being conducted. Only a handful of us know about this. It is business as usual for those who are not being evacuated. They will all die."

"But if Xiang thinks we're dead, he won't set them off, right?"

"I am afraid it is too late for that. Dr. Xiang and his thugs have been extremely sloppy. Too much has gone wrong. It is only a matter of time before the outside world finds out. Xiang has ordered the essential scientists, key personnel and a number of the Brainstorm subjects to be evacuated to an airfield on the other side of the mountain. Besides his own private jet, two large planes are there. Critical files and equipment are being transported now. They will close shop here and restart the operation at another location. The satellite photos have become too revealing even with the continuous smoke screen."

I thought about the smoke. "The forest fires?"

"No forests are ablaze. Only large smoke pots around the perimeter of the town and facility. The smoke is laced with a special gas that bends light and distorts photographs to eliminate the threat of aerial reconnaissance."

"How can we get to our people? What about the guards, the cameras?"

"Leave that to me, also. In twenty minutes the lights will go out and the emergency lights will come on. Put on one of the guards' uniforms then."

"Won't the lights going out attract attention?"

"This facility has been plagued with power problems. They took too many short cuts building it, putting most of the money into research and building a credible town. It is not uncommon for a rat to cause a blackout that knocks the cameras out. There will be much confusion with the evacuation going on at the same time as a blackout. Nevertheless, we must be careful. Most of the workers have been instructed to carry on as usual. They know nothing of the termination plans, only that we are having a drill. But the guards may search each room. So while you are in this room, you must stay covered up. They will think you are dead, as well you should be."

"And you'll return to tell us when it's safe?"

"As soon as possible. We are supposed to be packing up all of our records. It would look suspicious if I was away from the laboratory long. You must give me some time before going to the children's ward. I will send the guards away from there. You must stay here until I return. Then, go and do what you feel you must, then get out. And no matter what happens, you must leave with the proof of what is happening here and be a safe distance away before sunrise. The world must know."

She stepped up to my side. "Get back on the gurney."

"Wait," I said, "we have a friend here. He could help. Can you arrange for him to go with us?"

She sighed in response. "Possibly," she said. "What is his name?"

I hoped I was saving Rajiv and not betraying him.

"Rajiv Shekhar," I said. "He's a neuroscientist."

"I will try. I cannot promise," she said. "You must escape. You are the important one—part of the proof."

"What about you?" I asked.

"I have been waiting for this day for many years. My life is not important. It is but a small sacrifice, exposing these monsters for what they are and what they are doing to my people. I am willing to make that sacrifice."

She paused, and I thought she was going to smile, but she didn't. I wondered how she could have gotten into such a project.

"Get back onto the table," she ordered again.

"Good luck," I said as she covered Sunny's face with the sheet, and I lay down.

She said nothing in return. I watched her, trying to understand what kind of a person she really was, but I couldn't. She grasped the sheet on my table and pulled it slowly, almost ritualistically, over me, and five seconds later, I heard the door mew as she left.

Although covered, the bright room lights filtered easily through the thin white fabric.

"I can't believe we're still alive," Sunny whispered to me.

"Believe it," I said.

"Do you think we're going to make it?" she asked, and I heard her sheet move.

"And *I can't believe* I'm hearing doubt in your voice," I said and pulled my sheet back.

"I knew there was a good chance we'd get killed," she said. "I knew it'd be nearly impossible, but that didn't matter." She reached out and my hand met hers between the tables. Our fingers entangled.

"You're a hell of a woman. Your husband's a lucky man."

"Robert, I should tell you something about him."

"What? He isn't a part of this, is he? One of the bad guys?"

"No, I don't think so—at least not more than he has to be."

"You said I didn't like him much. Why?"

"You thought he was weak," she said, her voice groggy, slurring as if she was about to lose consciousness. "You thought he wasn't awfully bright, made bad choices. You thought he wasn't good enough for me and my daughter."

"And what do you think?"

"I think he's wonderful. A great father and husband. I couldn't ask for more. And he can take care of himself. Always has. But he needs our help, now." Her voice began to trail off. "You'll understand better what I mean soon."

"Sunny, did we, I mean you and I, uh, see each other after college, I mean up until the kidnapping?"

"Yes."

"Were we . . . intimate?"

She looked at me squinting, then her gaze went to my hand and she acted as if she was trying to focus on it but the grogginess was impairing her vision. She rubbed a place between my thumb and forefinger. She smiled. "Yes."

"My God," I said. I didn't like what I was hearing. "While you were married?"

She said weakly, "Yes," and the word became a sigh as if she had gone to sleep.

I slipped from the table, careful not to fall, placed her arm back across her chest and covered her with the sheet once more. As I got back on my gurney, I glanced at the place on my hand that she was rubbing. I found what appeared to me to be an insignificant dark spot, like a freckle. I had no special memory of it—just a freckle.

Chapter 27

Several minutes passed. I began thinking of William and how we were going to get him out. He was paralyzed. Dr. Xiang had said if we moved him, he could die. Of course, the good doctor also had said the computer chip at the base of my skull was a bump from my fall.

I remembered both occasions. The first was outside of William's hospital room with Michelle. It was one of those memories framed in darkness again, the Doctor leaning close to my face, Michelle in the background with a cast on her arm and bandage across her forehead. "He is exceptionally lucky to be alive," Xiang had said. "We need to be extremely cautious of moving him. The slightest movement in the wrong way could sever what is left of his spinal cord and kill him instantly." I remember Michelle beginning to cry and turning away as Xiang continued, "We have hope, however. Doctors in Bethesda, Maryland have been working on a new treatment to regenerate spinal cord cells. It's still experimental, but I have a friend there, and I'm relatively sure we can get your son admitted within a few months. Certain criteria must be met, and that will take time to compile and diagnose. They must support the prognosis at that time. The only risk to your son is that it might not work. What do you think? Should we try it?" Michelle then turned to the doctor and pleaded, "Yes, doctor. Yes, of course we should. Anything, anything to make my little boy whole again."

The doctor had given me a second warning when he'd told me about my "bump." I recalled it again on that screen in the middle of the dark. "Be sure not to bother the bump," he'd said, smiling warmly. "It could cause complications."

There was no other way to ensure William's safety now but to move him, take him with us.

"Sunny?" I asked.

There was no reply.

"Sunny?"

Still nothing. She was out. Whatever Yumi had given her was too much.

The lights finally died a few minutes later. Within a couple of seconds, the emergency lights came on and an irritating alarm began an intermittent buzz. The sound of running feet came from the hallway. It was like a stampede.

* * *

By the time the big MH-53M Pave Low IV helicopter came barreling up the dry creek bed, its sister ship was but a pile of charred steel below it, barely smoldering. It hovered above the clearing caused by the first helicopter's fiery crash for only a few seconds before a soldier came running out waving his arms.

The chopper touched down quickly, its tires bouncing on the ground. As it settled, the soldier vaulted onto its lowered back ramp. The large helicopter took off again before the man's feet were inside. It banked in the direction of the Mount Rainy Biotronics facility, and its twin turbo engines raced at top speed.

* * *

When the halls quieted, I slipped from the table and tried to wake Sunny. There was no reaction even when I pinched her. I hoped when the time came to get out she'd be more responsive. In the meantime, I was compelled to do more than simply wait for Dr. Yumi. The proof she would give me in copied files and video would be interesting; however, a little firsthand reconnoitering was in order, now.

I wheeled Sunny's gurney to the wall on one side of

the morgue where I hoped she'd be safe, and gently touched her forehead through the sheet before I turned from her.

When I scanned the room of tables, I noticed the sheet on one of them pulled back slightly, revealing the side of a young man's face. It was the guard I had killed at the amusement of Dr. Xiang.

I slung the sheet away and found he was fully clothed, his helmet setting between his feet on the table. Again, I noted he was about my size.

* * *

I paused at the first door I came to, the only one on that side of the hundred-foot hallway, raised my copper-tinted goggles and adjusted my utility belt. Although the young guard had been unarmed when I absconded with his clothing, his uniform afforded me at least a bit of security in my search for the truth, for Will, and for Sunny's husband. And the uniform fit surprisingly well. The only thing close to a weapon I had was intended to do *me* in—the cyanide pill. I couldn't imagine a situation where I'd need the thing now, but to be sure, I took it out of my cheek and placed it in my uniform shirt pocket.

The door was labeled Psychological Enhancement—Viewing Rooms. I guessed that label was for the benefit of those still living in Biotronics' make-believe world.

Harvey was back. My imaginary rabbit yawned and stretched inside my head. The thing was becoming too real. The intrusive bunny smacked his lips as if needing to bring moisture to his dry mouth after a long sleep.

Hey, Superman, Harvey said, *this could be it. This could answer a whole bunch of questions. He yawned again.*

Or give rise to new, even more confusing ones, dumb bunny, I thought. I still pictured him as a big white rabbit. Yet I could see him with a cute little pink nose. And other, more feminine features, maybe. Lazy, drooping ears. Large, bright eyes and long lashes. Full, red lips—kind of like Bugs Bunny's girlfriend. I had to shake my head to get rid of the image before I went too far.

"Geez," I whispered, "leave me alone. You're driving me insane!"

The door was locked, a palm-scanning security pad beside it about chest high. Cautiously, I placed my hand on the red Plexiglas pad and hoped Rajiv had found time to fix my security clearance. I smiled when the lock snapped like a gun hammer. I pushed the door open and stepped inside.

Along one side of the corridor I'd entered were at least a dozen dark rooms in either direction. A dim glow emitted from several of them, and all opened to the connecting hallway I stood in. The place seemed vacant. At least, if anyone was around, they must have been busy with their jobs.

I looked into the first room on my left and found a dozen seats placed in stadium style—three rows of four. The front wall was glass—a huge picture window. In front of the window was a countertop with three cushioned, swiveled office chairs, pushed neatly underneath. On the countertop, three microphones protruded. Three small, color monitors were embedded inside the clear-glass counter and the keyboards were on drawers mounted underneath.

From in front of the window, I looked down one level into a dark space about twelve feet square. Nothing in the room I stood in now was even vaguely familiar, however the room below brought back some sort of remembrance, a fleeting wisp of a memory. That space contained only a simple, metal table and chair and a sort of chrome-framed recliner with black, plastic-covered cushions. An apparatus of some kind attached to a small chrome-plated stand stood between the metal chair and the recliner. A dozen or more brightly colored electronic leads looped from it, their ends, unattached, draped over a chrome bar along the back of the instrument.

Dachau, Harvey said. *Auschwitz. Treblinka.*

"Yeah, a modern day Nazi torture camp," I said before I realized I was talking to myself.

I left the dark room, curiosity and Harvey pushing me toward one emitting light. Peeking around the edge of the closest wall, I discovered a single technician, headphones on, watching intently the monitor in front of him. Past him, through the large picture window, was a room like the one I'd seen a moment before, except this one was occupied. A man in a white, terry-cloth robe sat back in the cushioned chrome recliner.

He watched a movie projected onto the wall in front of him, a set of headphones covering his ears, also. However, it wasn't a movie. It was old TV—*Andy Griffith*. Opie and Andy walking down a dirt road with fishing poles and big smiles.

Harvey began whistling the comedy show's theme song in lieu of the real thing, probably echoing what was being piped into the guy's ears in the *Psychological Enhancement* room below.

I got lost in reminiscing—until I heard a clank behind me. I feared it was the bolt of an M-16 slamming into place against a chambered bullet.

When I turned, I was somewhat relieved to see Dr. Yumi standing in front of the bolted door, even though she was holding a 9mm Makarov like the one Michelle had pulled on me. She was the third woman to have directed a gun barrel at me since sunset. I hoped the weapon was as much for my protection as for hers. Still not a hundred percent sold on her *Falon Gong* story, she had won some of my trust by apparently saving Sunny's life and mine.

With her pistol pointed at me, Yumi said, "What you are doing is extremely dangerous, for both of us."

I pretended not to consider the implication that she might have to shoot me. "Watching TV?"

"The old television and movies in the files before you help demonstrate American family values, stable family relationships with quiet discipline."

"Okay," I said, a little puzzled. "What is this place?" I tipped my head toward the room below.

"Have you ever wondered why you relate so much of the world around you to television, commercials and movies?"

I frowned at her without reply, unsure of where she was going with this question.

She said, "You want it all in one quick, neat little package?"

"Well, yeah, since my son's life and mine are in danger, and I've been thrown around town like I'm some sort of puppet in the hands of a three-year-old."

"You are not going to get it all wrapped up nicely." She shook her head. "It does not come that way."

"Go ahead, I'm a big boy."

"Since you are here now, perhaps seeing for yourself is of benefit, your knowing as much as time allows might help our cause."

Harvey said, *Here comes that "Falon Gong" thing*.

"Shoot . . . ," I said, and then remembered the pistol in her right hand, " . . . uh, let's hear it."

She motioned for me to go out the door. We went down the hall of viewing rooms to the end space, I guessed because it would be the last one anyone might use. Inside was an empty station, and through the large picture window, the room in front of it was dark.

She had me sit at the counter.

"The computer in front of you is in sleep mode. Move the mouse and type in the password *Brainstorm*."

A puzzle piece fit into place. *Brainstorm* was the project name Major Jackson had asked me about. I took off my helmet, sat at the seat in front of the counter and did as she instructed. The computer came alive.

"Now, look for the file *Subject 374*."

Chapter 28

I repeated, "Subject three seventy-four?"

"Yes," Yumi said. "It is your file. You were the three hundred and seventy-fourth subject. The twelfth Robert Weller—however, the first to live. Through hypnotic suggestion, the townspeople knew your name, thinking you were their neighbor, the hardware storeowner, by the brown coat and trousers you wore."

As she went on, I remembered how Mr. Banks had recalled my name by the brown clothing I was wearing. Her comment "the first to live" was bothersome.

"In you," she said, "we have found the most promise. Your potential ranks high across the entire gamut of psychic abilities, from telepathy to telekinesis. Your thought projection skills are incredible, as are your remote viewing capabilities. When Captain Vanzandtz defected to us over ten years ago, it became quite a coup for our Brainstorm project. She brought with her hundreds of names of the people, mostly students, she'd tested over the years and a database of thousands from other Central Intelligence Agency and Defense Intelligence Agency projects including Grill Flame, Sun Streak, Star Gate, Thousand Eyes. Your name topped her list. Added to a list of thousands from around the world, Xiang began gathering them—abducting the more gifted when the opportunity arose.

"Many of the subjects were either too weak or the drugs and mental stress they were subjected to were too strong. Most before you either died or were disposed of. Some were only useful in limited ways. We learned through trial and error the best combination to fit our needs. You would be interested to know Subject 375 was your friend Mike Wu—Colonel Wu. He volunteered, seeking the power our project could unlock. In fact, his implant is a new and improved version. He has a stainless-steel covered, copper plate imbedded in his forehead to help direct his power. You must avoid him at all costs."

I nodded. "Yes, I believe we've already had one of those my-magic-is-better-than-your-magic sort of run-ins at the store."

She continued, "The rest of the subjects—*blanks*, we call them—are here and in various stages of programming. They come from all walks of life. All races and not only Americans. However Xiang had chosen to use mostly super-power nationalities such as English, Russian, French."

When the file Subject 374 appeared in the computer window, it showed four folders. *PhaseOne* contained *Acquire* and *Arrival*. *PhaseTwo* contained *Clean, Program, Personal*, and *Sensory*. *PhaseThree* contained *PracticalApplication*. And *PhaseFour* held *Surveillance*.

"Open *PhaseTwo, Program,*" Yumi instructed.

When I did, a long list of movie files opened.

Yumi told me, "Pick one."

"There are so many."

"Nearly ten thousand hours-worth. During programming the subject is only allowed four hours sleep per day."

The one I selected was labeled *TVCommercialsModern9.avi*. A Dentisol toothpaste commercial began playing. It spoke of "Nothing is better than a clean mouth." Next came a Norelco commercial, then Chevrolet. I fast-forwarded through Downy, La-Z-Boy, Goodyear, Sears, Wal-Mart, Doritos, MacDonald's and countless others.

"Try another folder," Yumi said.

I clicked on *MotionPicturesModern4*. In this file were

subfolders—everything from *MyBigFatGreekWedding*, all three *LordoftheRings*, *Something'sGottaGive*, *TotalRecall*, Scanners, and *ThePassionofChrist*—even The Davinci Code, as well as over a dozen James Bond movies and more. I clicked on one.

The movie *GangsofNewYork* came on.

In MotionPicturesClassic7 I found *Mr.DeedsGoesto-Washington*, *GonewiththeWind*, *TheManchurianCandidate*, *The-SandPebbles*, *Dracula*, and surprise, surprise, *Harvey*.

Yumi said, "Perhaps you've noticed when you see something that seems familiar to you, many times your mind will access the memory of a movie or television commercial? At times the thoughts come to you inappropriately humorous or perhaps the opposite."

I stared at the screen. "Yeah," I said flatly.

"That is because these are all your mind has to associate with reality. This is what you were programmed with."

I scanned the list of folders and subfolders. There was a huge News file with hundreds of subfolders including ones named *Challenger*&Columbia, *PanAmflight103* and *World-TradeCenter*. Another huge file was titled *TV* and its subfolders contained titles like *Soaps*, *Games*, *SitComs*, *Series*, and *Documentaries*. Inside were files called *Survivor*, *GeneralHospital*, *Friends*, *Jeopardy*, *DiscoveryChannel*, and *Croco-dileHunter*.

I tried the *Personal* folder. Inside it was a file called *HomeMovies*, and a subfolder called *SixthBirthday*.avi. The camera shot was of a birthday cake with a crowd of children around it. In the background were a couple of adults I recognized as my parents. I remembered this movie as *my* sixth birthday and I watched it, astonished. On the screen, the children and my parents were looking at the camera, singing *Happy Birthday* to it. However, there was something odd about this movie. A child's hands and arms reached out from the camera toward the table, and I realized the camera must have been on the child's shoulder, or perhaps some sort of a helmet cam, like I'd seen occasionally on televised car races and football games—like I'd probably watched in a room like the one before me.

Yumi said, "Those are no more your parents than they are mine. The memory of your true parents has been washed away."

The thought of it made me grimace.

There were a number of other *Birthday* files. I skipped them and went to the *Wedding.avi* one.

As I suspected, the film was shot from the groom's perspective as if he also wore a helmet cam. Michelle was the bride. She looked slightly younger. Mike Wu wore a tuxedo and stood beside the cameraman. The camera came in real close to Michelle's face for the wedding kiss. Her lips and eyes so close. My eyes began to tear.

I clicked on a different file.

This one was of Will. He wore a Little League Baseball outfit. He stood with a bat over his shoulder. An arm came out from below the camera and pitched a ball to him. He hit it and the camera followed the ball until it bounced and rolled to a tree.

In another file was the view from a walking person, this scene looking familiar. It was of the same route I had taken to work the day before. It also showed the same route from a driver's point of view in what I remembered as our Buick. There was a scene from the viewpoint of a person walking from room to room through our house. Then came the scene from bed. The viewpoint was of a person lying there, looking toward the make-up table where Michelle sat, naked, as she brushed her hair and rubbed on lotion.

"At this point," Yumi said, "an assistant would bring in the lotion and other olfactory prompts to give the memory more depth and realism."

Then came a similar scene of the hardware store. It took time as the viewer inspected a number of different products on the shelves. The viewpoint went to the cash register and went through its operation.

Yumi said, "A narrator accompanies this portion as well as most of the other scenes during actual programming."

I clicked on another file, this one labeled

FootballGame.avi.

The video was shot from seats in a football stadium. It panned around at the people filling the seats. Below, the Denver Broncos played the Oakland Raiders. People were cheering. The camera panned back to the seating and as it came up to the seat next to it, the video jumped as if something had been spliced in. The surroundings were similar, but not quite the same, more like some sort of studio shot scene. Mike Wu looked into the camera smiling big—looking back to the game, cheering the Broncos.

Yumi said, "Go ahead and take a couple of minutes to browse."

I did as she suggested and found video labeled *Sentimentality*—which included ordering of Will's snow skis. There were audio files, one was of my voice repeating, "Doc Xiang is a big man with a big heart. We're lucky to have such a caring doctor, don't you think?" Then, Michelle's voice saying, "Very lucky. Dr. Xiang is a good man and a good friend."

On the last of the *Personal* files labeled *SenatorAvery* was the exact morning show interview I'd watched with Michelle the morning before—Senator Avery discussing his thoughts of running for President and his views on China.

Yumi said, "He was to be your first target."

I shook my head in disbelief.

"We have an entire apartment complex in Washington DC devoted solely to the *Brainstorm* project. Within the next three months, Xiang hopes to have over a dozen psychic assassins such as you there, each with their own targets. Along with them will be several dozen support personnel including new family members. As much of your old information as possible has been either altered or deleted on numerous U.S. government databases including CIA and FBI fingerprint records that we have been able to hack into. Many of the records were easily altered by psychic persuasion of critical government computer information systems employees—basically accosting and hypnotizing them to alter data without realizing it. You were to have been given your new identification complete with social security number, credit cards, birth certificate and even school transcripts—we've been cultivating the many paper personalities for over twenty years."

Now, I'd finally come to the point that I doubted who I thought I was. Up until this, nothing they'd told me made much sense. I chose not to believe most of it, not to consider the possibility it was true. Now, I wondered who I really was, but I wasn't prepared to ask her now. The information Dr. Yumi had already given me was overwhelming. I asked, "What would happen if someone from my past ran into me? How could that be explained?"

"Very rarely would you leave the secure apartment. You would only think you had left after daily hypnosis sessions in which it would be suggested to you that you had visited your son at Bethesda, went to a restaurant, to a shopping center. On the rare occasions it was necessary for you to leave, you would be tasked with your assassination mission. During those times you would be watched, a team of troubleshooters always prepared to, let us say, fix any problem. All you had to do to complete your missions would be to make visual contact with your targets.

"Because of an implanted, hypnotically suggested dislike for the person—for example because of the target being against funding that could mean the difference between having a normal son and a paraplegic one, your subconscious brain would go into a defensive posture. With your telepathic abilities, your subconscious mind would reach out to the target's own brainwaves. The enhancement device we developed works like an automobile coil. It amplifies your brainwaves and helps direct them with greater force to the target. Your brain then tells the target's central nervous system to shut down. It tells the target's brain to stop all involuntarily commands to the heart, lungs and other bodily functions, and the target dies instantly."

"Like the people I've already killed."

"Yes. Exactly. Your subconscious sampled their

thoughts, found them harmful and considered those people threats to your well-being. The only ones safe from you were the ones you weren't threatened by or those who were wearing the copper-lined helmets. The copper protects the wearer from outside electronic fields and signals of all types. That is how the brain functions—through electrical signals. It sends commands in the form of these electrical signals through the body's nervous system to perform all tasks and operations. The brain's constant electrical communication with the body actually causes an electronic field—some people claim to be able to see it as an *aura*. In your case, your brain defends you through its enhanced telepathic powers which are transmitted much in the same way, however, more like through a directed surge of power from that electrical field."

"I'm a murderer."

"No. You defended yourself. All of those who were killed were willing participants in the *Brainstorm* project. None were coerced support personnel or an innocent subject such as yourself."

This gave me but a little solace.

"We have many peoples of many different interests working here. A number are former Soviet KGB agents, like the two men who chased you from your store. They and a number of their colleagues were unneeded when the new Russia emerged, and they were laid off from their cold-war jobs. There are many willing participants besides the Russians, and my fellow Chinese, of course, including North Korean, and North Vietnamese, as well as Pakistani, Iranian, Iraqi, Libyan, Cuban—and yes, even American."

What I was hearing was nearly overwhelming—the scope of this project horrifying.

I selected the file named *PhaseOne*. Inside were two files—*Acquire* and *Arrival*.

In *Acquire*, I found a scene viewed from the open cargo door of a van. There were several men inside, one hunkered in front of the camera with a silenced rifle. The van was parked at the curb, a hotel marquis in clear view, probably a hundred feet away. The sign said *Seoul Hilton*. A man walked out, past the doorman, and began hailing a cab. The man was too far away to be recognized—it could have even been me. But he wore a hat and a suit and tie. I didn't like hats and detested ties—almost never wore one, at least, that's what my programmed mind told me.

The man with the rifle suddenly discharged it, and the guy in the suit grabbed himself at the shoulder.

"That is you," Yumi said.

In the video, four men pushed out of the front door of the hotel like linebackers and bum rushed the man in the suit—me, I conceded for now. *I* kicked the first one in the face, gave an elbow to the gut of the second one and the knife-edge of my hand to the throat of the third guy. The fourth man made the tackle and managed to cover my head with a black cloth hood as I obviously became groggy.

The van lurched forward and pulled up to the front of the hotel. It took four of them a few seconds to wrangle me into the van. They restrained me, still hooded, with nylon ties and duct tape. Two of the men then pulled the guy I'd struck in the throat into their vehicle, and the van sped away as the cargo door closed.

When the video went blank, I tried to shake this craziness from my mind. I was living a nightmare.

I selected a file named *PhaseOneArrival*.

It showed a man through a wire-reinforced, glass pane in a thick door. His face was unclear. He had a light beard and bandaged head, and he sat in the corner wearing a straightjacket. The room inside was white and empty.

"It is you, again" Yumi said.

It could have been me. But it was impossible to be sure without being able to see this man's face clearly.

In the video, three men in blue scrubs rushed into the room, and the disheveled, bound man launched up and rammed his head and shoulders into them. They lifted the man from his feet and bulldogged him to the floor. This video then went blank.

If nothing else, I felt good about the fight I put up.

The *Blank.avi* file had me curious. It was nearly a

gigabyte in size.

As I clicked on it, Yumi said, "This was taken during your recovery after the operation to attach the enhancement device to your brainstem."

I couldn't help but rub the back of my head. I found a small, nearly unnoticeable line of scar tissue where my scalp had been cut and a portion of my skull had been temporarily removed for the operation. The idea of it gave me a sick sort of feeling in my gut.

In the video, the person who was supposed to be me wore a hospital gown, with #374 printed in what was probably Magic Marker on the gown pocket. My head was bandaged still, but this time my nose and chin were taped, also—I guessed from fight injuries. With my eyes half open, I lay in a bed with other occupied beds around me. I was instructed to "get up," by a voice off camera and I sat up. I was told to "stand up," and I did this, also. My next command was to "come to me," and this I did, moving closer to the camera, with halting sluggish steps.

After leaving the room I'd been in for the hallway, I joined a number of others who were walking around the perimeter of the hall. "Follow them," came the command, and I did so without hesitation, joining the others, walking in a large circle, aimlessly, like mental deficients in a psychiatric ward, a scene from *Midnight Express*. "Everyone. Arms out," the man's voice said, and what looked like fifty of these vegetative patients followed the command. These were the "vegetables" Rajiv had mentioned, the Mister Potato Heads.

Yumi said, "Try the *Sensory* file."

I clicked on an .avi file, and what I saw made me cringe.

In the video, it showed a man in a white hospital gown, head bandaged, face bruised, being led from the shadows to a metal chair in front of a projection screen in the middle of a room. His walk was stiff.

"This—" Yumi began.

"I know, it's me," I guessed. I didn't want to believe it, but I was becoming convinced. Still, I looked at the monitor skeptically, not one hundred percent sure. The idea of my mind being made into putty for shaping in any manner some deviant wanted, made me shiver.

The camera came in for a close up as this man—me. I was seated. The subject on this film was a perfect twin if not me, yet I could not remember any of what I watched. The camera focus stayed on the profile, but zoomed out slightly while a video played on the screen. The assistant who brought in this *blank* me laid a box on a nearby table. From it, he withdrew a stuffed bird that looked like a mallard duck. On the video screen, it showed several ducks on a lake bank. He placed the duck in front of me and guided my hands to stroke it. "Duck," he softly said. He then pulled back the wing and used my fingers to fan the feathers. "Feathers," he said, again clearly and softly. He returned his stuffed friend to the box and pulled out an egg. The next scene on the screen showed hens in a hen house. One got up from her nest, revealing an egg. He placed the egg in my hand. "Egg," he said and moved my thumb over the shell.

I went forward in this file to a point where the assistant produced a pair of glasses—my glasses, apparently. He slipped them on me. He said, "These are your glasses. You are blind without them. You must wear them at all times when you are awake, except when bathing. Never leave them."

"Unmagnified glass," Yumi said, "with a transponder inside the frames."

"Uh-huh," I replied. "I'm ahead of you on that one."

Yumi said, "Both the *Sensory* and *Practical* learning portions of the project, although basic, are essential to the successful programming of the subject. We found without them, the subject has no solid ground in reality. That is why it was necessary for you to begin the day as if you had just awakened, then to proceed through a normal day in your new life. This practical experience helped to pull all of the programming we had done over the past two years into what you believed was your reality."

I scanned forward on the file and came to a part where the assistant was paging through a *Time* magazine laid in front of me. To the side were stacks of *Sports Illustrateds*, *Readers' Digests*, *Wall Street Journals*, *New York Times'*, *Denver Posts*, and even *Gold Rush Gazettes*.

I glanced over my shoulder to Yumi. "This is unreal."

"I will give you a quick overview in simple terms about memory. The human memory can be divided into two basic types: implicit and explicit. Implicit memory is of common daily chores such as tying your shoes, walking, swimming and running, using a fork to eat mashed potatoes and a spoon for soup. It also contains identification of traffic signs, types of plants and animals, et cetera. However, no memory of specific people, faces or experiences exists there.

"Those memories are held in the explicit part of the mind. They are like old movie reels. They easily deteriorate, crack and discolor. In a normal mind, they're stored as movie film in a salt mine, sealed and protected so they last longer. These memories have been deteriorated, through a variety of what you might call brainwashing techniques—use of drugs and hypnotism. Your explicit memory has been erased. Such a thorough cleaning was necessary as actually to affect a small part of your implicit memories and that is why those memories were fortified with the sensory portion of your programming.

"At the same time, you may have experienced brief reminiscences of your own true past coming to you as flashbacks. Those pieces of memories that were for some reason not erased by the drugs and hypnotic suggestion were mostly overwritten. If these fragments come to you, they will be like the cracked and distorted film, fuzzy around the edges, yellowed so badly they're barely discernable. They will most likely happen as dreams or separations from reality that you will not find credible due to the stronger memories which have been implanted or programmed over them—replacing them.

"However, some fragments of your true past might have been ingrained too strongly to destroy, due to traumatic experiences you may have had. These memories might flash like lightning through your thoughts.

"For Xiang's purposes, we wanted to make you as much of an average American as we could. That way, you would not rouse suspicion when you were let out among others of your kind. You did not need to think like a terrorist, or a sniper, or a warrior. There would be no reason and no evidence you did the things we would have you do. Nor would there be a way to trace you or your deeds back to us. And with the *Brainstorm* project in place and fully operating, anyone in the way would soon perish and only those who were thought beneficial would be in positions of power."

I selected the file called *Clean*.

It showed a man sitting in a metal chair again. This time, he was completely naked and unconscious.

Harvey said, *Now, this guy is definitely you*.

I frowned, looking closer. Harvey was correct, at least, it did look *like* me.

In the video a man in a blue lab coat jabbed a hypodermic needle into my arm. I rolled my head and slowly my eyes fluttered open. Still in the video, the lights in the room dimmed and Dr. Xiang stepped into view. He held a small flashlight and shined it into my eyes. Dr. Xiang began speaking softly. He gave his hypnotic suggestions. He instructed the terms of allegiance with me, in a familiar, gentle tone. He made me repeat, "True blue, trust them, do," and "We're lucky to have such a caring doctor, don't you think?"

Another file directly following the one I'd just viewed was labeled *UnexpectedInteraction*. This one was oddly out of place, and its contents piqued my curiosity.

Inside the file, it showed me still in a white hospital gown while sitting in a chair. My head was still bandaged, but my face was no longer bruised. At my feet, a small animal skittered around. It stopped by my slipper and sniffed at me. It was a gerbil. Even though in the apparent vegetative state I was in, my eyes shifted downward to the small mammal. The scene cut to a new one of me eating. As I ate in a somber robot fashion like the rest of the blanks, I stuffed a cracker into my pocket.

In the next scene, I was back at the chair, bandage no longer on my shaved head. The gerbil was below me on the floor. I slowly reached for my pocket and pulled out the cracker. Without apparent emotion or facial expression, I broke the cracker into small pieces and dropped it at my feet. The gerbil had a feast.

The progression of the relationship between Mickey Gerbil and me was recorded in six scenes that proceeded. The camera apparently followed our contact throughout my time of programming. In the last scene, my hair had grown out and the rodent was on my thigh, resting back on its haunches while munching on a piece of cracker, and I was smiling.

"This was unusual," Yumi said. "We found this interaction extremely interesting, exceptional. You were the only one who had any sort of mental reaction outside of the programming. That is why the gerbil became an important tool later." Yumi pointed to a file.

I clicked on it. The subfolder *PracticalApplication*, *Initial.avi* seemed blank. After a few seconds, a light came on to a split-screen scene I recognized as my bedroom and master bathroom. The time in the upper right hand corner said 06:00 AM.

In the video, a woman I did not recognize entered the unoccupied bedroom. She wore a blue jumpsuit and carried a linen-filled basket to the foot of the coverless bed. She pulled a sheet from the basket and spread it on the bed. Soon several other people entered the bedroom, one pushing a wheeled coat rod filled with clothes on hangers, one with a hand truck loaded with shoeboxes. One came in with several bags, went to the dresser and began loading the drawers with socks and underwear.

Dr. Yumi then appeared in the doorway, stepped to one side and seemed to be supervising. A woman came in carrying a basket and went to the bathroom, a man following with arms loaded with towels. As they finished in the bathroom, I was surprised to see Chief Dailey pop in. Yumi handed him something very small as he walked by. He went into the bathroom, took a bar of soap from the woman there. As the other two left, Dailey went directly to the shower. He unwrapped the soap, tossed the wrapper into the trash and looked about himself. After a pause, he stepped into the stall and with both hands carefully placed the soap into the shower caddy, then slipped something underneath it that I would have bet was what he'd just gotten from Yumi—the hastily scribed note I'd found under the bar. He went to the linen closet and took something from his pocket that looked like a small pouch. This time, what he held with both hands squirmed wildly. He set the pouch inside on the towels and opened it. Out came a small animal. Due to the distance from the camera, it wasn't obvious, but I was sure it was Mickey.

When Dailey left, Michelle came with another woman who assisted her in undressing. Michelle sat down naked at the make-up table and her assistant used a spray bottle to mist her back. After Michelle's assistant left, two men brought a gurney in, with me on it. They carefully lifted me into place on the bed as Yumi watched. After they departed, Yumi checked her watch, stepped to the bedside, pulled a hypodermic from her lab coat and injected it into my neck. As my head slowly moved from side to side, Yumi stepped away and left through the doorway.

Yumi said, "Those of us who were against the *Brainstorm* project did what we could to give you hints, things that would make you pause for thought. However, we were being watched as well as you were, so any suspicious movements in your home could have been scrutinized.

"Fortunately, while this was being recorded, Dr. Xiang was waiting outside the house and not viewing. The technician in the control room who did have access, was one of my people. Do you remember the new toothpaste tube and toothbrush, the new soap? Normally, we would have left partially used props. We did not spritz the shower, only Michelle's back. We did not scuff the shoes, we did not use laundered clothes, as was the usual case. Chief Dailey even left the gerbil you befriended when your mind should have been completely blank. We found an unusual amount of willpower in you, thoughts and memories too deeply ingrained to destroy. Xiang was excited about your potential."

An alarm went off from the hallway that took our attention from the computer monitor. It reminded me of a submarine dive alarm, and a voice came over the intercom speaker in the viewing room we occupied.

"Security alert!" the voice said in a loud but calm voice. "Security alert! All essential personnel, report to the control center immediately!" The call repeated twice.

"I must go," Yumi said. "And you must return to the morgue and wait."

She removed a cell phone from her lab coat pocket and punched two keys. "This is Yumi, Dr. Xiang." She glanced at me and motioned toward the door with her pistol.

I got up but must have been moving too slowly for her because she waved the gun toward the door three more times, quickly.

"Yes, Doctor," she said over the phone. "I'll be there immediately." She pushed a button and dropped the phone back into her pocket. I slipped the helmet back on, and as I placed my hand on the doorknob, she said, "I must leave now. Essential personnel are evacuating."

I stepped away from the door and motioned for her to go first. "That's good. I'll be left home alone—to do what I need to do."

"Not exactly. Dr. Xiang and his core of scientists and technicians are leaving. That includes me. However, the guards, many of the doctors, assistants, patients and other personnel will be left behind to die when the bombs go off. They have no idea. I would guess at least a thousand people at Biotronics alone. The nuclear device in town will ensure the deaths of over four thousand there."

"My God! How can we stop the nukes?"

"Impossible. The one at this facility is buried in fifty feet of concrete. Dr. Xiang has already remotely started the timer and it is irreversible."

"What can we do?"

"For them, nothing. There is no way to get them all out

in time. The devices are set to go off at sunrise, 05:46 this morning, five seconds apart. You have until then to find safe distance from the blast. Your helicopter is your only answer. I can no longer baby-sit you. You know the situation. You are now on your own."

In the swirl of her lab coat, and without the chance for further protest, Yumi left through the door.

Chapter 29

When I reentered the hallway, I placed my goggles over my eyes and walked guardedly back toward the morgue. I hoped Sunny would be awake, and between us we could figure out what to do about Gold Rush and Biotronics. Twenty feet from the morgue, a voice came from behind me.

"Security."

Harvey said, *Oh, shit!* and I cringed inwardly. The voice sounded like Xiang's. I kept going.

The voice rose. "Security!"

I stopped five feet from my destination.

"Come here!"

I turned slowly, but realized I needed to look the part I was playing or things would unravel very rapidly. I stepped quickly toward Xiang. He waited in front of the elevator next to two cabinets on wheels. Mike Wu stood next to him.

As I approached, I nervously checked my copper-tinted goggles to make sure they were in place. They were. I tried to walk as militarily as possible to him and at five feet away, I stopped and stood at attention.

Dr. Xiang said to Mike Wu, "Take these files to the truck. It's waiting in the tunnel."

Tunnel? Harvey asked. *There's a tunnel?* I wondered where it led.

Dr. Xiang continued, "I'll get Dr. Yumi, and we'll bring the last two." He turned to me. "Help Colonel Wu with these carts."

Colonel Wu, Harvey repeated. *From captain of the high-school debating team to colonel—quite a jump.*

Why would they need a colonel at a newspaper? He'd worked at the *Gold Mine Gazette* since high school. Worked his way up to senior editor. In my reprogrammed mind he was no colonel, and his new title did not create new respect. He'd gotten a two-year degree as I had from Summit County Community College. His associates' degree was in journalism. He'd never been in the military.

The elevator doors opened, Dr. Xiang left down the hall, and I got behind one of the carts. I pushed it onto the elevator behind Mike Wu's lead. I went to the back of the elevator car as the doors closed, and I tried to stay behind Wu. He took out a key and opened a small compartment above the elevator control buttons, which said Authorized Personnel Only. Inside were several additional buttons labeled *Sub Floor 2* through *Sub Floor 5*. He poked *Sub Floor 2*. We were going to a level below the basement of the building.

Wu didn't speak to me, but he looked over his shoulder a couple of times. The second time I noticed he was looking at my name badge, the one that gave the name of the dead security guard.

He watched the elevator doors as we descended, and I could tell he was thinking about me. He knew something was up, I was certain, and I could feel my head getting warm inside my helmet. I felt pressure at the back of my skull, and it pulsed to my temples. A low hum began, and the helmet vibrated.

As the elevator made sub floor two, Mike Wu turned around to face me. His stare was wild and intense. I'd been found out. Moreover, not only was I endangered, but also Sunny and as well, Dr. Yumi for not killing us.

The pressure inside my skull increased to the point of extreme pain, and I began panting. The copper-tinted goggles in front of my eyes started to glow. The hum turned into a roar, the vibrations becoming shakes and even our elevator car shuddered as the door opened. When the ballistic-resistant plastic shell of the helmet cracked, I could take no more. I yanked the helmet off and struck Wu with it in one motion. He caught most of the force when he defensively brought his hands up to his face, but still he fell through the open elevator doorway and onto the floor outside. I shoved the two carts from the elevator, and they toppled onto him, as I jabbed the first floor button.

While the elevator doors closed, Wu was struggling to get out from underneath one of the heavy carts, and he yelled, "I'll get you! You're nothing compared to me. Your ass is mine, Weller!"

Harvey said, *Your magic sucks, ours rules!* and my imaginary ally gave Wu the raspberry.

As the elevator ascended, I fell back against the corner of the car and struggled for breath. Still on the floor of the elevator lay my helmet liner, exposed and separated from the cracked helmet shell. The liner was like some sort of copper fabric—thin, woven copper wire. I deduced the importance of the things. As Yumi had said, the copper stopped whatever kind of energy I exuded, the electrical field. It protected the brain of whoever wore it. In my case, it had contained the energy and turned it into something like a microwave oven on my brain. Between my power and Mike Wu's equal or perhaps greater power, I'd nearly fried my own mind.

I knew Wu would be right behind me, either taking the stairs or another elevator. He'd most likely come with an entourage of security guards.

I decided I'd do my best to avoid Wu and at the same time search for my son and Sunny's husband, Daniel McMaster. Maybe I could somehow outwit Wu, incapacitate him, stop him in some manner at the same time. For now, I would check on Sunny on the first floor, then head directly to the children's ward on floor two.

When the elevator door opened to the first floor, I pushed the number five button. After I stepped off, the elevator doors closed, and it began its ascent to the facility's top floor. A clamor came from the stairway opposite the elevator, but instead of ducking into the morgue, I flattened into a small alcove ten yards down. I didn't dare risk Wu seeing me going back into the morgue—for him to come after me and find Sunny still alive.

* * *

Mike Wu and five security guards busted through the stairway door and stopped in front of the ascending elevator. Mike, at six foot one, was taller than the others, probably all under five foot nine. They jerked their heads in both directions, and I ducked back into the recess enough, I hoped, to observe them unseen. Wu watched the elevator floor lights above the entryway. When he saw the elevator had stopped on the fifth floor, he told three of the men to search the first floor, and he took the other two with him to the stairway, bound for the floors above.

The first door the three security guards rushed into was the lab. Three doors down from it was the morgue and Sunny.

I shoved from the wall of the alcove and raced down the hall, not slowing down to notice if they'd seen me running past the open lab door. Luckily, no one popped out of the lab. I figured they were still checking in cabinets, wall lockers and closets, and under tables where they thought I might be hiding.

I entered the morgue quietly to find Sunny awake, but still on the table. She looked at me groggily, her arms reaching out. I went to her and gave her a brief hug.

"They're coming—three of them, and there'll be more. They're going to kill us this time. I can't stop them, I'm unarmed and they're wearing protective helmets."

Sunny frowned at me. "You can stop them, Superman. There's good reason for your nickname. You were always resourceful. You could figure your way out of anything, solve any puzzle. There's a way—you just have to think."

I remembered how the guy wearing the suit in the *Acquire* video—me—fought the four men. If only I could regain that kind of fighting knowledge, if somehow it would come back as second nature. Yet the men pursuing us now were armed and planned to kill us, not capture us. They could stand back and shoot without having to get close enough for me to have a chance to fight them.

Then, I remembered Sunny's gun. The guard who was wearing the very fatigues I now wore had stashed it in one of his front pockets. When I slipped my hand inside, I was surprised to find the small pistol still there, and I handed it to Sunny. She checked the chamber and magazine.

"Only two rounds left," she said. She looked at me with eyes full of worry. "I need you, Superman. You need to come out of this haze you're in and shine like you used to."

This haze she spoke of was more of a soup-thick fog inside my head. However, I knew it was now totally up to me to keep us alive for the next few minutes, to save Will, to save Sunny's husband, and to save the thousands of innocent people of Gold Rush.

"Robert, listen," Sunny said. "You wanted to hear more of what I know. I'll tell you. I'll tell you about you and Dan." She tried to sit up but fell back down. I helped her, and she sat on the edge of the table, holding her head as I steadied her with one hand. "You two weren't merely experiments for Vanzandtz back in college. You exhibited talent, however uncultivated, in all the tested fields of psychic abilities. You not only showed a high level of telepathic, but also telekinetic power. But what both of you really excelled at was remote viewing. Do you know what that is?"

"We don't have time, now, Sunny," I told her and gently forced her to lie back on the table.

"We don't have time for me not to tell you," she said as I went to the back of the door. "Do you know?"

I watched the knob as Sunny trained her last two bullets on it. "I think so."

"Dan soon became the best remote viewer the U.S. government had. He was so good, the DIA brought him into their Grill Flame project, and he was their top RV. He could do anything, see the future, the past, transcend space and time to distant sites."

I was astonished and unbelieving. "Sunny, I don't believe that nonsense. It's fairy-tale stuff."

"Believe it. It happened."

"How's it going to help us now? Dan isn't here."

"But don't you see? You were just as good as Dan. You can do what he did."

"Okay, say I am. What am I going to do, grab a hold of you and sweep us away to some time in the past or future, so that we don't get killed?"

"It doesn't work that way. Only your consciousness travels—sees. Your body stays here."

"Great, our bodies stay here and get shot full of holes while our consciousnesses fly off to Shangri-La."

"No, I don't know how it can be useful," she said and seemed to consider it. Her eyes lit up. "How about if you go into the future a few seconds, maybe half a minute, and view what will happen?"

"What, watch us die in the future, then relive it in the present? Even if I could, that's ridiculous."

"No, see the future and then prevent it in the present."

"Could Dan do that?"

"I don't know. When he was with Grill Flame, he said he could see the future, but couldn't affect it because he had no physical existence in that dimension. But if we knew the future now, exactly what will happen, we can react to change it. Then, the future that originally appears to you won't happen."

"God, this is crazy!"

"I know it sounds nuts, but what do we have to lose? You can do it, just like Dan did."

"Okay, so how do I do this *remote viewing* stuff?"

"Since you don't remember, this is really going to sound insane to you. Just go along with me, okay—and know it works, that it's been done thousands of times. The U.S. government has spent hundreds of millions developing it."

"Now, you're really making me skeptical."

"Just listen. The CIA called SCANATE—scanning by coordinate. An assistant—me—selects a time and place to view and assigns it two sets of numbers or coordinates. The numbers actually have little importance. They're mostly a point for the viewer's concentration. The viewer then applies his full concentration to those numbers. The talented remote viewer enters a state of total consciousness and concentration and his psyche transcends into a dimension without physical being. It's a place where time and space have no importance. Nothing he sees really exists but are only symbols for information he can view. Dan told me that what most advanced viewers see is what they call the universal matrix, generally appearing as a three dimensional grid of numbers, letters and symbols. They can be thought of as anchors or reference points. He finds the numbers the assistant has assigned to the target scene and is able to access that time and place to view, not physically but more as an audience to what is like a virtual reality movie. Although he can touch, feel, taste, hear and see, he cannot actually move anything, or affect anything in that dimension."

This was all too far out. What had already happened to me over the past eighteen hours had been incredible, and now this—to step completely away from reality, no matter how bizarre it had become, and transcend into a different dimension?

Sunny said, "We're wasting time. Let's try it. Fast forward. The numbers are four, eight, seven, nine and three, five, two, six. Concentrate."

* * *

It is as if some other part of my consciousness has taken control, and my brain is on autopilot. Without willing to, I find my concentration on those numbers and forget about the deadly world around me. The speaking of the numbers seems to have turned a key and unlocked a door to a place I evidently have been many times before. I feel my head spinning, and I know I am somehow putting myself into a kind of trance. I picture the numbers as if they are in front of me, about an inch tall, three dimensional and illuminated. They float in a sort of black, empty plasma. They begin gyrating, as do I. I rotate slowly at first. Then I become part of a whirling vortex, being sucked into a tiny point of light, which seems miles away, and I compare the experience to that of a mouse in a flushing toilet.

"What do you see?" I hear Sunny's voice ask, echoing from somewhere behind the eternal swirling current. It sounds as though she is speaking into a huge steel tank.

Feeling as though I am under nine Gs of pressure, my voice strains. "Nothing. Darkness. I'm in a whirlpool."

The G forces seem to diminish quickly, and I feel only a slight dizziness as I twirl, drawing ever nearer the center. I reach out and grab the gyrating numbers, pulling them protectively into my chest. The luminous figures cling against me like Velcro on felt as I pass through the middle of the vortex. When I come out of it and into total emptiness, a rush unlike any I've ever felt surges through my body. My extremities, the tips of my toes, the ends of my fingers, the top of my head, all tingle as if being misted with tiny ice crystals.

On this end of the vortex is complete peace, quiet. I am floating on what seems to be an invisible cushion of air. In the distance, an object appears, luminous, drifting like a weightless scarf in a gentle breeze. Or no, more as if it is floating in a clear and day-lit sea.

"Beautiful," I say without intending to verbalize.

"What?" comes Sunny's voice, again from another place, not in the same dimension as I.

As the drifting entity nears, I recognized a human form, a woman, angelic, and ethereal.

"An angel," I say. "A woman."

She soon pauses in front of me, and I note her lovely dark hair and the high cheekbones of a Native American Indian. Her garments are airy and near transparent, and the only sort of jewelry she wears is a necklace made of beads. I find familiarity in her eyes, and she smiles and places her hand lightly on mine. I feel a warmth there, but no pressure or weight.

"Robert," Sunny says, "are you okay?"

"Fine, fine," I answer feeling almost annoyed at Sunny's interruption. "I think she wants me to go with her—she wants to take me somewhere."

Sunny's voice is eager. "Go with her, Robert. She'll help you."

I abide and float with her in a euphoric feeling of weightlessness. What seems like long minutes pass as we transcended from the vortex, through a constant aurora borealis of shimmering colors. I cannot yet see it, but I am sure she is leading me to the grid of which Sunny has spoken.

The dark but friendly seraph's lips do not move, but in my mind I hear her mellifluous words, "I am your friend. In this place nothing exists, yet you will find all answers. It is neither a temporal rift, nor a warp in time. Nor is it a dimension. It is nonexistent except in the mind, and your trips to this place will be measured in seconds, although it may seem to you they last for hours. The more often you visit, the easier and quicker it will become. But remember, your ability to come here is a gift from a higher order for a higher purpose. It is for that purpose you will find answers to your questions, understand the thoughts of others, transcend space and time—but only for that purpose, and at the choosing of the higher order."

She lets go of my hand and motions to the universal matrix before me, and it is as Sunny has said. Enormous. I think of it as a huge library where all that ever was and all that ever will be is filed—a tremendous card catalogue for an omniscient library that is organized into a celestial Dewy Decimal System.

"My God!" I exclaim.

"What?" Sunny asks, seeming concerned, perhaps alarmed. "What is it?"

"I see it. I'm there. It's huge! Beautiful. Brilliant light. Like a thousand main streets at Christmas."

The matrix spreads out in three directions to eternity, and I am floating in cosmic nothing at the intersecting corner of the three never-ending planes. The symbols are perhaps six inches in size and nearly three feet apart. But I know this is only as my mind interprets it.

When I glance back at the ethereal spirit, she smiles, and I hear, "Tell my love it was not his fault, that I wait for him eagerly when his time also comes. But before that is to pass, he has much to share with the material world."

For the first time, I notice on her necklace of colorful beads is a small arrowhead—and a name comes to my mind, gently placed there as if laid by God on a cushion of silk. *Moonfeather*. She disappears like a doused light, and still in awe of the lovely entity, I scan about to see where she has gone.

"Robert, you okay?" Sunny's voice says, snapping me out of my wonder, invading the peace of the universal matrix.

I go about the business before me. "Yes, Sunny. I'm starting my search."

As I hunt through the numbers, I find I can use them for handholds and pull myself along through the incredible matrix. Almost without thought, I come to a group of familiar numbers, and I pause considering them.

"I think I found them," I say and pull the clinging numbers from my chest. They correspond to those surrounding me.

Sunny calls out, "Take the—"

I interrupt her, "I know what to do."

When I fling my small numerals at the larger figures, they disintegrate in a brilliant flash of light, creating a vertical pool of a reflective, mercury-like liquid in front of me. Perhaps through some sort of instinct or past experience I cannot remember, I am drawn to the pool, face first. Carefully keeping my hands on the numbers at each side, I push my head into it and discover it is not a pool at all but a sort of atomically thin membrane, a doorway into what I seek.

What I see is terrifying.

Chapter 30

The three men rush into the room, their M-16s blazing. The bullets strike and tear at our bodies. Both Sunny and I fall onto the floor, and blood oozes from our corpses.

I yank my head out of the future and back into the ether's universal matrix, my eyes wide, pulse racing, breathing rapid. The experience has been so real. I have witnessed my own execution. I wonder how soon this reality will come. I have been groping through the grid work of the matrix for what feels like hours, but I wonder if any time has passed at all. I hope not. If I were to go back to my own time, will I find myself already dead? The thought becomes too mind-boggling.

Sunny's voice calls out from the other side, reality, and I am somewhat relieved. "Robert, what's happening? We have to hurry!"

I cautiously edge my face back into the portal to the near future. Again, I see the same scene, the three men bolting into the room. This time, I notice the first man comes through with his gun pointed to the far corner away from Sunny, the second comes through pointing at Sunny and the third turns toward me behind the door. Sunny fires her small pistol, but the bullet strikes the first man's body armor at the shoulder. Again, the bullets riddle our bodies, and we fall to the floor.

This time, I withdraw my head more slowly, thoughtful of what I have seen.

"I'm coming," I tell Sunny, but I need one more look.

For a last time, I peek into the future through the portal's membrane. The first guard comes through, again aiming at the corner. Sunny's bullet strikes him in the shoulder. The second man comes through, pauses briefly in the doorway, then steps in and fires at Sunny. I see that the only exposed part of his body, the only part unprotected and vulnerable to a bullet, is at the man's throat. Still in the future vision, as I rush the man who is shooting Sunny, the third man comes through and fires half a magazine of M-16 rounds into my torso.

Having seen enough, I jerk my head back from the future and grab at the large numbers around me, pulling and pushing. When I reach the outer-space-like void, I swim through the black nothingness toward the vortex, and it comes quickly. I thrust into the ethereal tornado, and there comes a blinding flash.

* * *

I found myself back behind the morgue door, Sunny lying on an autopsy table across the room.

We had mere seconds. I had to decide immediately whether to attempt to take three lives—tell Sunny to shoot the second man in his exposed neck, or go against the odds and try to keep our lives without anyone else loosing theirs.

I yelled, "Shoot level to the doorknob at the hand of the second man!"

She frowned, and I knew she was trying to make sense of what I was saying as the door burst open. In that instant, I hoped she would not question what I had said and simply do it.

The first man came through, his weapon pointed to the empty corner. The second man burst in, and Sunny's gun reported as I went for the third guy's rifle barrel, which was swinging toward me. I shoved the barrel up as he fired the rifle, the bullets striking the suspended ceiling above. With a kick to his armor-cupped groin, then the knife-edge of my right hand to his neck, he fell unconscious and easily surrendered his weapon. The second guard grasped his wounded hand and his rifle fell to the floor, as Sunny kept the small Beretta aimed at him. The first guard didn't have a chance to bring his weapon to bear on us before I placed the muzzle of the automatic rifle I had just acquired against the back of his neck and told him, "Don't."

Now what in the hell could we do with prisoners?

I shoved the guy up against the wall, his face first, and he stood against it spread-eagle.

What I realized when I looked at this man was unnerving. He was taller than I was, taller than Mike Wu, probably six three or so.

As I pulled off his protective helmet, I told Sunny, "These aren't the guys, Sunny. These aren't the guys Mike Wu sent. They must have run into the others and were helping to find us."

I turned to my captive and got up real close and personal to the back of his head. I didn't need the assault rifle I had in my hands to intimidate him, he probably knew that. Still it made me feel more secure.

"What about it, dipshit?" I asked him. "Are the rest right outside?"

He nodded slowly.

Sunny cried out, "Fast forward."

As I look to the door, the doorknob turns.

* * *

I find myself in the eternal vortex of space and time once again, traveling through the ethereal gateway into the universal matrix. This time my trip through is accelerated, supercharged. As my spinning stops, the never-ending grid of symbols and figures appear before me, and I realize I have none of my own coordinating numerals for use in relating to my quest of the immediate future. I make the numbers up in my head, and they materialize in front of my eyes like the ones Sunny had given me before. I grab and pull frantically at the grid to find their match, hopeful, somehow, I can uncover the future and the key to stop what seems inevitable.

I come upon my numbers quickly, drive my face through the reflective portal and begin to view what is to come. Again, a brilliant light flashes unexpectedly.

Suddenly back in the morgue, I'm watching the door

with a sort of ghost-like double vision. The morgue doorknob stops moving in the more opaque view, what I guess is real-time. But the door opens slightly in the ghostly one, which I figure is the future. A voice calls in the present, "Briggs, Carlson, you okay?"

I elbow my prisoner. He knows exactly what I want him to say and the consequences of not obeying.

"Yeah, we're okay," he says. "We got 'em."

I see the door begin to open in the apparition—the future. A head pokes through, and I witness my own see-through, phantom-like arms bring up the M-16 in my hands and shoot at the intruder. Still in the future, they lob a hand grenade through the door, and it cracks onto the floor and explodes in a mighty burst. We are all dead in this blood-splattered and flesh-ripped future, and the double vision ends.

* * *

As the door opened in present time reality, I didn't wait for a head to poke through to shoot. Instead, I pulled my captive from the wall and shoved him toward the face emerging from the doorway. I followed, rushing my prisoner nearly off his feet until we hit the edge of the slightly open door, and I forced him through. I grabbed our other prisoner—the one Sunny shot in the hand—and found a hand grenade hooked at his side. Pulling it free as the other two antagonists rolled out onto the hall floor, I shoved the injured one out the door. After yanking the pin out and tossing the grenade, the only thing I could hear was running feet.

I went to Sunny and leaned over her body on the table protectively. She was groggy, listless. I felt something slip into my pocket. Without taking the time to check, I figured it was her pistol.

"You might need this," she said.

"Brace yourself, Sunny," I said, but her eyes were closed, and she didn't respond. I hugged her tightly.

* * *

The explosion throws the door wide, and I feel myself falling toward the floor in slow motion. Once again, I enter the vortex passageway to the matrix.

I spin rapidly. However, this time in my journey into the ether, Sunny comes with me as I clutch the autopsy table she lays on. We revolve wildly for minutes, hours, or perhaps only milliseconds, until the universal matrix appears before us. And I realize why I have returned.

I climb hand over foot through the symbols making up the matrix's grid, this time looking for answers, not numbers. The whole thing is becoming more familiar to me with each quest. Behind me, I pull Sunny one row of numbers at a time. When I come to a set of figures that are somehow familiar, I stop. The pool-like portal appears in front of me, and I push my face into it immediately.

The world has changed. My vantage point is above what had been Mt. Rainy. In the kind of lunar landscape spreading before me, no visual evidence appears that it had been a mountain at one time, but I know it had been. Now it is merely a crater. I look toward Gold Rush, and it has disappeared, also. The trees and buildings are gone, not even a board or a piece of roofing to be found. It has become nothing more than a barren plateau, now perhaps a day after the nuclear blasts, only long enough for the smoke and dust cloud to dissipate.

I don't like this near future. I pull out from it and struggle forth for a new set of integers, for a glimpse of something that can help. I stop at the next random symbols I feel somehow connected to. This time what I find gives me more hope when I push my face through. I am looking from the end of a cave or tunnel of some kind. The eastern sky glows from a sun that will rise in a matter of minutes. To my left is a small trail that leads away, probably winding between two mountains I see in the distance. I turn to the right and see only more mountains.

Below me is an airfield. Two large passenger planes are loading with cargo and people I am sure are Xiang's essential personnel. The planes look like Boeing 747s. They are completely white with what few markings they have being small and indistinguishable from my distance. A smaller jet is taking off from the airfield, and I zoom inside it to find Dr. Xiang. He looks through the oval window to his side at what he is leaving behind and he smiles.

I want to gaze at this future longer, inspect these jumbo jets on the airfield, but I begin spinning yet again. Sunny slips from my fingers and falls, swirling slowly away, into a cosmic abyss. I grab for the matrix and think I've found a solid hold, but the symbols in my hands and at my feet also begin falling, tumbling away. I grab for more, and they too drop from my grasp. The entire grid work moves around me, plummeting into nothingness. The numerals, letters and symbols cascade like a waterfall, flowing like a landslide. I scamper as if a rat on a burning curtain, until finally, I run out of numerals and fall with them, twirling in a cyclonic storm of symbols.

* * *

I felt the floor of the morgue beneath my back and opened my eyes.

Mike Wu stood over me with a smile on his face.

Sunny's voice said, "Fast forward," and Wu turned to her on the table above me.

* * *

I immediately see the double vision again, and this time without transcending into the matrix.

In the ghost view, Wu looks at Sunny, his stare—the deadly brainwave projection—causing her body to buckle. Her arm falls limply over the side of the table. He faces me and blood immediately comes to my nose, ears and eyes, and as my body quakes a final time, Chief Dailey rushes into the room and gazes in horror at my dead body.

* * *

In the present view, Wu looked toward Sunny. Knowing I had but a fraction of a second to affect the future, I placed my toe squarely to the crotch of Mike Wu's protective-cupped trousers.

With him wearing the shielding jock, my kick didn't hurt him much, but it did divert his glare from Sunny and back to me.

I found the helmet of the security guard I'd captured earlier in my left hand and figured if it had worked as a weapon against Wu before, it might again. I flung it at his face.

He caught the thing, partly with his hands, partly with his chin, and he staggered back. It took him but a second to recover and step up to me again, and his gaze was fearful.

I held my head and tried to combat his psychic energy with mine. The floor trembled. The room, the walls, the ceiling, even the autopsy tables began emitting a low-pitched hum, reverberating throughout and increasing to a cacophony. The metal tables began to jump in a quaking dance. I felt blood trickle from my nose. My vision became blurry. Fluid ran from my ears.

In my bleary vision, I thought I noticed a rivulet of blood spring from Wu's nose, but I knew it would be too little too late. Then, in my peripheral vision, I saw the morgue door open and a figure moved behind Wu. I had delayed Wu long enough for the cavalry to arrive. Wu ducked as if pummeled in the back of the head, then fell. Chief Dailey now stood over us, a Colt .357 revolver in his hand.

"Damn, boy," he said. "I thought you was dead."

He noticed me nervously watching the door.

"Don't worry about the others. I sent 'em away. Told 'em Wu and I would do the cleanup."

He held his hand out and helped me to my feet. I leaned against the table next to Sunny's. I held my head with one hand, my pain subsiding quickly. I looked at Sunny.

"You okay?" I asked before I noticed her eyes were closed. "Sunny."

The chief checked her heartbeat at her throat. Checked her eyes. "Pulse is good. Looks like she's in a deep sleep."

I thought about Dr. Yumi saying she would probably be passing in and out of consciousness for a while, and I hoped that was all it was.

The chief turned to me. "Listen, son. I'm not here to hurt you. You know that, don't you."

I remembered the video made before I woke up in my

bedroom, the chief placing the warning note under the soap. What else could I do but consider him an ally.

"Do I have a choice?" I frowned at him. "I trust you."

"I guess you do or you'd have killed me by now."

I gave him a slight nod, not knowing for sure how my powers worked or how to turn them on or off. "We've got to get everyone out of here, Chief, out of Gold Rush, too."

"I already got the evacuation started in town. My boys are sortin' the marbles. They're gettin' all the civilians packed in cars and lined up on the highway out of here. The abductees are on their way here. I have no idea what's going to happen to them. Maybe Xiang will have a change of heart and take a few of them with him. Otherwise, can't do much until Xiang leaves. If he finds out about the native folks skidaddling, no tellin' what he'd come up with to stop 'em. Even in the best hopes, I can't see how we can save more than a few dozen."

"Civilians and abductees?"

"Yeah. You know, the ones from here and the ones they snatched. If one of Xiang's men radios him about people leaving . . ." He pulled out his walky-talky and frowned at it.

"Here," I said, "let me fix that for you."

I felt an electrical pulse from my cranium, and the radio popped. The chief dropped the thing as smoke streamed out and it sizzled.

He smiled. "Damn, boy!"

"I believe that should have taken care of all the radios that were turned on."

He nodded. "One of these days, you'll have to show me how you did that."

"I hope I get a chance."

He grew serious. "I'll be expected to leave with Dr. Xiang. I'm not sure how, yet but I'll try to get away from him at the last minute and get back to help you folks. I'll get Wu out of here. If he doesn't get back to Dr. Xiang soon, Xiang will come looking for him with a whole mess of security on his coattails. We don't want that. I'll wake up Wu and tell him I found you dead and him unconscious, that this lady, here, was holding a gun.

Figured she'd hit him over the head with it, and I shot her. I'll convince them you're both dead, and that's that. You two get the hell out of here. Yumi says you've got a chopper waiting, so get it called in and get your asses out. We've got less than two hours before the shit really hits the rotor blade. And you've got to be long gone before that happens."

"My son and her husband are still here."

Dailey frowned. "Robert, you ain't got no son."

I didn't like what the chief had said. I felt the tingling at the base of my neck again. The chief grabbed his head as if he was in pain.

"It's the truth, boy," he said, grimacing. "You gotta believe me."

It took me a moment to calm myself. Sunny had been trying to hint to me that Will wasn't real for some time. Now the chief, who was apparently on a different side of the fence than Sunny, was telling me the same thing. Dr. Yumi had played it off, wanted me to find things out on my own. That's why she didn't simply come right out and say it. Nevertheless, the memories were still there, and I wondered if this was yet another game, another trick they subjected me to.

I felt the tension in my skull ease, and the chief seemed to relax some, still rubbing his temple. "Damn, Robert, you really got a way of puttin' a hurt locker on a fella."

"What about you, Chief? Why are you here?"

"You don't know? I figured they woulda filled you in by now."

I shook my head as a moaning came from the floor.

"Shit," Chief Dailey said. "We don't have time."

He hustled over to Wu and grabbed him under the arms. I went to the door, cracked it open and peeked out, glancing both ways in the smoky corridor.

As the chief pulled Wu through the doors and headed toward the elevators, he said, "I was a Marine like you. Went to Cambodia for the *Mayaguez* in '75. I missed the chopper gettin' out, and *they* caught me."

Chapter 31

Instead of answering any of the myriad questions whirlpooling inside my head, the chief had presented me with a big set of new ones. He said he'd been involved in the *Mayaguez* incident in '75. That "they caught" him. What did that have to do with what was going on now? And now, at least a couple of people were trying to convince me I did not have a son. I doubted what they would have me believe. The paternal instinct was too strong inside of me. Sure, the emotions I should have felt when I thought of Will were somewhat flat, but the world I had awakened in this morning was not exactly conducive to warm and fuzzy feelings. A safety margin of less than two hours remained, but I had to find out the truth about William, and still there was Sunny's husband to rescue.

Before I started toward the hallway, I looked back at Sunny. She slept peacefully, undisturbed, and I hoped she would remain that way until my return. I carefully posed her as if she were in her finally resting, her arms folded across her chest. I remembered her medallion necklace/panic button, found it in the pocket it had been put in earlier, and placed it in her hand. Then, before I pulled the thin sheet over her face, I hugged her and kissed her on the cheek. She sighed in her sleep.

"I won't let anything happen to you, Sunny. I promise." I gazed at her, felt a closeness I couldn't remember ever feeling before. "I lo—."

Sunny whispered, "I'm scared," her interruption surprising me. She seemed to have spoken from her subconscious, her eyes still closed, her body limp, her mouth now slack.

"You'll be okay," I said. "I'll be back for you soon."

With no time to waste, I turned away, picked up my former captive's helmet, set it over my head, and found his M-16 on the floor by the door.

After slipping through the door, I considered our nearly defenseless state. More guards could come for us or happen by. I needed a way of slowing them down, interfering with their movements, giving me more time. As I trotted down the hallway, I passed a doorway labeled *Storeroom*, and I stopped. The door was unlocked. Inside were shelves of cleaning and office supplies on one side and foodstuff on the other—the health department wouldn't have liked that.

Harvey asked, *Remember any old recipes from the Anarchist's Cookbook?*

"Hmm." I thought of Sunny. I thought of Major Jackson's search and rescue team. I thought of nonlethal weapons.

I looked about the room and the shelves. Liquid bleach, liquid dish soap, drain cleaner, string and thumb tacks on one side—on the other, gallon cans of honey. In the middle of the floor—four large plastic bags that I guessed were full of trash and garbage.

Hey, Superman, Harvey said, *you thinking what I'm thinking?*

"Uh-huh," I answered aloud.

* * *

Taking less than three minutes to place my *tactical delaying measures*, I took the elevator to the second floor and then jammed its door open. There were sure to be a number of elevators, but this one was the nearest to the morgue—it could buy us a couple of seconds.

I sprinted three hundred feet down the hallway to the children's ward. I'd remembered this part of the hospital from one of those home movies they'd used to program me. After passing through the large double doors, I inspected each of the wardrooms but found only empty beds in them. After about a hundred feet of corridor, I came to a second set of double doors, and I figured if I wasn't already deep within the mountain, I soon would be when I passed through. The Biotronics facility was even larger than it appeared from the outside. Much more of its cold hallways and sterile rooms were hidden underneath the protective mountain, much like the unseen portion of an iceberg floating under the waterline.

These doors were labeled, familiarly, *Restricted Area, Authorized Personnel Only*. Underneath the warning were the words, *Residence A*.

Yumi either hadn't been there or figured I could find a way to get through ordinary locks. The doors were barred and padlocked on my side. The wire-reinforced windows were smoked to the point of being opaque. If there was anyone on the other side of those doors, the only way they could pass through this entryway would be for the doors to be unlocked from this side.

Still curious about what was on the other side, and without keys to enter the doors the more traditional way, I fired a bullet in each of the locks. They were not MasterLocks. Their shanks popped open immediately.

I dropped the bar to the floor and flung the doors open to a long, empty hallway. When I proceeded, I found more rooms on either side. These areas were not empty. The first room was packed with people, probably fifty men, women and children, most Orientals, all huddled, their arms entangled, frightened gazes on their faces as they watched me quickstep by. With no beds or furnishings in the room, I guessed the few blankets on the floor in front of them had been where they had slept. I found the same in each of the next three rooms and figured it would be yet the same for the next six.

I stood in the middle of the hall where as many people could see me as possible through their doorways, and I took off my helmet and sling-armed my rifle over my shoulder. Waving to them, I called out, "Get out. Everyone, get out, now. You have to leave quickly!"

They didn't move, but only stared at me, appearing as

frightened as before.

"Come on, let's go!" I insisted again. Then I ran down the hallway to the other doors and repeated my urgings.

Still, no one moved. "My God, what's wrong with you people?"

Then, a small Oriental man stepped forward from the first doorway. He wore white and red striped pajamas and red slippers as did all of the others. He bowed his head briefly.

"Few of us speak English," he said. "I do, but I cannot ask my people to do as you say. They would be killed."

"They'll die if they don't leave. There's no one to stop you now. Xiang and the others—they've all left."

"You do not deceive us?"

"No. It's the truth. But you must leave immediately. There's a bomb set to go off in less than two hours. It's a very big bomb that will kill everyone within miles of this place."

"It is the truth. I see it in your eyes. But where will we go?"

"Do you know of the tunnel?"

"Yes, we were brought into this place through a tunnel. I know where it is."

"Good." I recalled remote viewing the back side of the mountain. "At the end of the tunnel, a small foot trail leads between two small mountains. If you can make it on the other side of one of the mountains, put it between you and this place, you should be okay. But don't stop there. Don't stop until you've found help, the highway, a way to get very far away. There'll be radioactive fallout, poison in the air that will kill you slowly if you don't get away from it." I was reminded of my tactical delaying measures. "Oh, and when you go down the stairwell stay to the outside—go single file all the way to the basement. You'll see what I'm talking about and understand." I hoped. "Whatever you do, stay on the stairway until you reach the basement—don't go through the doors to the first floor."

He bowed to me again and turned to the nearest doorway. He held his arms out and called to the people in the room in a language I didn't recognize, but I guessed was one of the many dialects of Chinese. He then scurried to the next room and did the same thing again. Soon the occupants stirred and their voices rose, confused and scared. They began rushing from their rooms, and in a few seconds, hundreds filled the corridor.

Someone familiar ran past me, and I could not control the emotions constricting my throat and damming up in my eyes. It was my son, William.

* * *

Xiang had become impatient waiting for Colonel Wu and Chief Dailey. He stood with Dr. Yumi outside his limousine near the entrance of the tunnel that led to the airstrip, after sending a detail of five guards back to the morgue. Their orders were to dispose of Subject 374 and the woman intruder's bodies. To be sure, *all* of the corpses in the morgue were to be incinerated. Then, they were to bring all of the programmed subjects with them in formation and march them down to the waiting planes. Finally, they would report back to Xiang when both jobs were accomplished. Xiang hadn't been pleased with the detail's hesitance with his orders. They knew of the time constraint, and he could sense their fear that they would be left behind to be killed with the others. But they obeyed, sprinting to the stairwell en route to the morgue.

* * *

The detail that was headed for the morgue hit the stairwell all out. They feared for their lives, knowing Dr. Xiang would have them killed if they did not follow his every order, yet knowing if they took too long to accomplish their task, they would be left behind and die.

After making the stairway landing between floors, they found a huge mess before them—trash and garbage completely covering the steps up. Frightened of the consequences of pausing for very long, they did not slow down, but plowed ahead regardless of the clutter.

In a fraction of a second, the five-man detail knew this was no ordinary litter.

In the time it takes a falling body to travel six feet, all five men were prone in the refuse on the steps. They attempted to climb up, slipping back, having to use their hands, finding shredded paper and orange peels stuck to their combat boots and body armor, their weapons covered, their hands now in the gooey mess, pulling up printer paper, used tissues, coffee filters, paper towels, and scraps of cardboard food containers—and thumb tacks—some idiot had scattered thumb tacks! Each man frowned at the muddle they had entered, still pressing farther, progressing slowly, slipping back a step, sometimes two or more, the discarded material sticking to their clothing. Finally, panting and nearly exhausted from battling the quagmire behind them, they made the next floor.

They took a moment to pull some of the garbage and shredded paper from each other's uniforms and equipment—and thumb tacks from their gloved hands—and they saw only more of the same litter on the stairs above. Luckily, the morgue was on the floor they were on now.

But after bursting through the stairwell doorway, they found a different sort of trouble—all slipping face first into a slick pool suddenly before them, too late to notice it was there.

It smelled and looked like liquid dish soap—and they were not surprised to find more thumb tacks. At first, it was just more bother. Then, the smell changed, and they realized that when rushing through the door, a tripwire—a string—had been pulled, and from each side of the doorway, a container had spilled out onto the floor in front of the dish soap. The smell that came to their noses was only irritating at first—then overwhelming, burning their sinuses.

Sprawled onto the tile, the detail's leader grimaced as he struggled tediously with another tack, slick with soap, and finally pulled it from his cheekbone. He glanced back at the plastic containers emptying themselves onto the floor. Drain cleaner and bleach. Their spills ran together in the middle of the doorway creating overpowering fumes.

His eyes widened as he realized the noxious odor was

deadly chlorine gas.

* * *

As they prepared to leave for the airfield in Dr. Xiang's limo, Dr. Yumi had slipped away, explaining to Xiang that she had forgotten her journal—an essential logbook because it was there that she recorded her daily findings and notes on the progress of the *Brainstorm* project. She told him she would catch up—ride with Chief Dailey and Colonel Wu when the limo returned for them, and she hustled away before Xiang could comment—lucky to have left then.

After the limo drove away into the tunnel with Dr. Xiang aboard, Chief Dailey and a groggy Colonel Wu arrived at sub floor two in the elevator. Yumi ducked behind a large support column without Wu seeing her. She waited for an opportunity to dash to the stairwell twenty feet away.

Wu's voice was loud, agitated that Subject 374 and the woman intruder had still been alive even though the injections Dr. Yumi had administered to them were supposedly lethal. He was skeptical even with Chief Dailey's story that, this time, they *were* both dead.

When Wu turned toward the tunnel, Yumi rushed to the stairwell and quietly climbed the steps out of sight. Just past the landing midway to the floor above, she found a strange mess completely covering the steps up—trash and garbage. She used care in transcending, stepping on the few larger pieces of trash she could find. Soon, she found the going much easier along the outside six inches of each step. She remembered the detail running off before she left and then understood that the quagmire had been created for them. The upturned and gooey litter made it obvious they had passed, very arduously, this way.

In a large, open office space used by the research scientists on the third floor, Yumi found Rajiv Shekhar sitting behind a computer desk. He was the only one there when Dr. Yumi came in. All of the others who were supposed to be working at that time had heard rumors of a "bomb threat" and evacuated. It had been Yumi who put out the word—thinking at least those who ran would have a slim chance. Without knowing the size or type of the explosive, some sought the apparent safety of their homes in Gold Rush—at least they would die with their loved ones—while those more likely to survive went to gather their families and flee the area. She hoped they would somehow get past Xiang's guards. None of them knew of the second bomb below the water tower—few would have believed such an incredible story.

Yumi told Rajiv to meet Robert and Sunny at the morgue quickly, that a clean-up team of guards had been assigned the grisly task of burning their bodies, double insurance that no sign of them ever being there would be found. Rajiv's job seemed impossible, even to Yumi—to somehow stop the guards, get them away from Robert and Sunny long enough for his companions to escape. Then, he was to take them to the ambulance parked in the emergency room ambulance garage on the basement level. But if Robert wasn't there, he was to take Sunny to the ambulance and wait there for him.

Rajiv obeyed, but reminded Yumi of the need to get his family out with him. She assured him Chief Dailey was working on the evacuation of the town and there was nothing more Rajiv could do that wouldn't cause delays. The last thing she told him was to avoid the stairwell and take the elevator.

* * *

Rajiv arrived at the morgue to find the detail of five very untidy guards. He understood why they would be covered in garbage and why they all seemed teary eyed. He'd found the elevator not working and had to take the stairway—and slid down the last flight of steps through an incredible amount of sticky trash. After cleaning himself thoroughly, picking off all the messy garbage, he then encountered a terrible odor as he stepped into the hallway—and proceeded to fall on his butt three times on some kind of a slick spill before making it to the morgue. The janitors must have gone on strike.

Two of the guards were at the incinerator, the furnace door open, loading it one by one with the cadavers. An occasional flame licked from the opening causing them to yield to it, stepping back. Two of the other three guards were pushing the emptied tables away and pulling new occupied ones closer to the fiery finale. The last guard, who Rajiv guessed was the leader since he seemed to be doing none of the work, watched from the door.

He gazed at the men, fragments of garbage clinging to their uniforms. "You have not heard?" he asked them.

The guard turned, his rifle pointed at the floor, not seeming threatened by Rajiv. "We have our orders. Dr. Xiang has promised he'd get us out before the bomb goes off. Now, get out of the way." The other four guards continued their task.

"Bomb?" Rajiv asked. "Kindly tell me what bomb, please?"

The guards glanced at each other. "Just get out of here."

"But Dr. Xiang has instructed me to . . . ," Rajiv scanned the tables, looking for his companions, unsure of what he would tell the guards. He feared he was too late, as they seemed nearly finished with their job. He blurted out, "I need a brain."

Again, they glanced at each other. The leader frowned at Rajiv.

"Dr. Xiang has instructed me to come and get two brains for experimentation."

"Only one left," the leader said and pointed to the covered table next to Rajiv. "We're fresh out."

"That is obvious," Rajiv said scanning the guards.

The leader glared at him.

"Come on, Top," one of the other guards told the leader. "Let him have his brain. Let's get out of here. We still have another assignment to do."

"I'm for that—everything and everybody here will soon be vaporized, anyway," the guy called Top said, and the others nodded.

They hustled by Rajiv and out the door.

Rajiv waved at their backs as they sprinted toward the stairwell. They slowed coming up on the liquid detergent on the floor, one slipping as he stepped on an old footprint of the stuff. They moved cautiously to the stair doorway while cupping one hand over their noses and mouths, opened the door and paused, looking up.

The leader said, "It's going to be easier the second time—knowing what we're up against." And they hesitantly went in.

Rajiv searched about the room one more time, his eyes wide and mouth open. Only one table had been left with a body.

"My friend, Robert Weller," he whispered, gaping at the covering. "I hope this is you."

He pulled back the sheet to find Sunny unconscious.

"Oh my," he complained. "It is not my friend." He shook his head. "Lady," he said softly, "Sunny, you must wake up, please." He pushed on her shoulder but nothing happened. He shook her and spoke louder. "Sunny, it is me, the geek. Kindly wake up now, please!" Still, she did not respond.

Rajiv went to the sink and drew half of a small paper cup of water. He returned to Sunny's side. "I am sorry, but you have left me with no other choice," he said.

As Sunny's eyes fluttered open, and she looked to Rajiv, he seemed unable to stop the forward motion of his arm. The water splashed in Sunny's face.

They looked at each other, both shocked.

Sunny blew water from her lips. "What the—"

"I am not your knight in luminous steel, like you may believe," Rajiv said. "I am known to you as the geek Raja. Do you remember?"

"Oh, yeah," Sunny said, her eyes narrowed as she shook her head, "I remember."

"That is good. It is also good you are not cremated."

"At first thought, yeah, that sounds good, too."

"Well, now that the niceties are over, we must run for our lives to the ambulance parked down the hall."

"Where is he?"

Rajiv blinked at her. "If you mean our friend Robert, he is not here. I am hoping he stepped out on important business and did not become ashes. Dr. Yumi said if he was not here, we should wait for him at the ambulance."

"I've done enough waiting," Sunny said and slipped from the table. She stretched her shoulders and arms while holding on to the side. "I need to find Dan." She released the table and found her legs and her balance.

"Please," Rajiv said, "my plan first. Then we can discuss this missing husband of yours."

They went to the door and Rajiv opened it cautiously before passing through with Sunny behind him. "This way," he said and trotted about fifty feet to a set of windowed doors that said *Emergency Room/Ambulance Parking* on it.

After pushing through the wide doors, he looked back.

Sunny was gone.

Chapter 32

"William," I called out to the running boy. "Will, I'm here. It's your dad, son." The emotions brimmed my soul and spilled out from my eyes in hot tears. I became overwhelmed with the joy of seeing William not only on his feet, not only walking, but running. "My God, Will! You can walk again!"

Several yards away, Will found a young Oriental woman and latched onto her arm with both hands. I moved toward him, but the crowd swelled and got in the way. I tried to be respectful to these slight, malnourished people, but it was difficult knowing I need only push through fifteen feet in order to hold my son. They all had lied about William. They all had deceived me, and this was a whole other matter, now. Why would they, my supposed friends and rescuers, trick me in such a way?

By the time I reached William and the woman, we were already through the doors of Residence A. Those leading the crowd of at least five hundred people were now sprinting through the vacant children's ward and to the stairwell midway in the main hall.

I dropped my helmet and grabbed William around his middle as he fled. After pulling him loose from the woman, I lifted him into my arms. He returned a look of horror and panic and began screaming.

"Will, it's me, your daddy," I pled with him. "Buddy, it's me." I looked at his legs and arms flailing about him as he cried. "My God," I said. "Look at you. You can walk and run. My God. It's a miracle." The tears streamed from my cheeks. I didn't understand Will's behavior, but the shock of seeing him as a whole child again, one that could run and play games, ice skate, snow ski, and play baseball, was overpowering.

The next thing I knew, people were slapping and striking me, and tugging at William. I glanced back at them through the tears in my eyes. The Oriental woman William had clung to was one of my assailants, as was an older Oriental woman and man. They were all speaking gibberish to my ears. I was glad when the man who understood English came to my rescue.

"What is happening here?" he asked me. "What do you want with this boy?"

"He's my son," I said. "I'm taking him with me." I pulled him away, which caused the old woman to fall, and I began pushing through the crowd, even though William and the others protested violently in an Far Eastern tongue.

"You are making a terrible mistake," the English speaking man yelled out. "He is not your son."

The old man who had been with the two women stepped in my way, and I glared at him, the pressure building in the back of my head.

"It's you who're making the terrible mistake if you don't get out of my way."

He didn't budge. My temples ached but no shooting pain came, and I watched as this slight man whom I could easily throw against a wall, or strike with such force as to kill him where he stood, remained in my path. He grabbed his chest as the pressure in my head increased. He fell to his knees in agony and gasped for breath.

"Please, you must not hurt these people," the English speaker shouted and made his way through the crowd to grasp my arm.

The pressure in my temple reduced. The old man before me was able to catch his breath.

The English speaker said, "Why do you take this boy, Li, from his mother?"

"His name's William, and I told you. He's my son."

"That is impossible. I saw Li on the day he was born. I know Li's parents. His mother is there," he said and pointed to the woman William had held onto. "And his father was an Australian man named Jason Godfrey. He is dead, now. Dr. Xiang and his men killed him before Li was a month old. You are not the boy's father."

William kept screaming and hitting me. I shook him gently. "William, stop. It's me, Will, your daddy."

The boy quit struggling and stared at me as the tears streamed from his eyes.

"Say something, Will. Speak to me. Say anything."

The English speaker said, "He understands none of your language. He only knows a few of your words that he has been trained to speak like a parrot. They forced him to learn to say these things or to starve."

"Speak to me, then," I insisted. "Speak to me like a parrot."

The English speaker told the boy more gibberish and the boy said, "I want to play catch again, Daddy. And ride my bike." His voice was full of stress and fear, now, but it was what I'd known as Will's voice. He spoke in perfect English. Nevertheless, it was not this young boy's natural tongue, that was obvious from the awkward movement of his lips and jaw. Had they somehow tricked William into thinking he was a Chinese boy?

"Say more," I said. "Tell me your name. Tell me anything."

The boy began crying again.

The English speaker said, "That is all he knows. Please. Let him go back to his mother and grandparents." He pulled the boy from my arms as I gave in to what he was saying as the truth and no longer found the heart to resist. I watched dumbfounded as he helped the old man to his feet, and they went back to the boy's mother and grandmother, all of them in tears.

The crowd pushed through and soon was in the main hallway. I moved in a daze behind them, taking slow, unsteady steps.

To my side, I noticed another set of doors not far from the Residence A entrance. These doors said Residence C and were locked as the others had been. I did my best to overcome the emotional trauma I had just experienced, and I broke these locks the same way, with the bullets of my M-16.

After forcing the doors open I proceeded, finding four rooms. This time, all of the rooms were full of beds, as in a cramped hospital ward. Lying in those beds were men and women of all races. They wore plain white hospital gowns. Some had shaved heads, others bandaged craniums, yet others with normal haircuts. All of them had eyes that were lazy and half-open.

I went to the closest man, a Caucasian of about thirty-five or forty. His blond hair was neatly trimmed. His hands were clean, and his face looked freshly shaven. Yet as the others, he'd been recently abandoned by his caretakers, more accurately his prison guards. I noticed the #386 on the front pocket of his gown. I remembered myself in the film wearing a similar gown with #374 on the pocket. I shook his shoulder to try to get him to look at me, but he lay with his face directed to the ceiling, and his gaze was unflinching.

"Hey," I said. "Look at me."

He slowly rolled his head in my direction. Briefly, as I looked into his eyes, I wondered if I'd seen this man before. Had he been abducted when I had? Had we shared the same cell? Did I know him from before? I raised my eyebrows. This man, whose eyes were empty of emotion or thought, could even be Sunny's husband. I could not find a shred of memory of him.

"Who are you?" I asked.

He didn't respond, his eyes distant, and I wondered if behind them any thought whatsoever went on. I realized then, that these were probably the "vegetables" that Rajiv had spoken of, the Mr. Potato Heads. They were the blanks, the empty memory chips waiting for their programming, exactly like I had been. But what was I to do with so many? There were at least forty. I couldn't carry each one away, somehow transport them out of range of the bombs that would decimate everything within two miles of their epicenters—not even considering what the radiation would do for many miles after that.

I had to try.

I moved back out to the middle of the hallway and yelled, "Get up!"

It worked. They all sat up slowly in their beds, their eyes slightly wider than before, but still droopy enough for someone to think they had gone a couple days without sleep.

"Stand up," I commanded, and they did.

"Come to me," I said, and they began moving slowly toward the doorways.

I walked backward. "Follow me."

They did, their steps short and slow, like mindless zombies.

My platoon of turnips and I proceeded from the C residence out into the children's ward.

Then I saw it. I didn't understand how I'd missed it before. The door opposite Residence C that we just exited. This door was labeled *Residence B* and was not padlocked.

* * *

In the DPV, Gunny Sampson raced into Mount Rainy Biotronics' vacant parking lot as the last of the cars left. The tail end of an incredibly long line of vehicles snaked down the mountain highway to Gold Rush.

As he pulled up to the front entryway of the facility, a large man in a police uniform came running through the doors.

Sampson yanked an M-16 from between the seats and leveled it at the man.

Dailey held his hands up but continued hustling toward Sampson's DPV. He stopped shy of the passenger's side. "You with the rescue team?"

"The question is, who are you with?"

"I'm on your side, damn it! My name's Eldon Dailey, sergeant, U.S. Marine Corps."

"Kinda old for a buck sergeant, aren't you?"

"I made time-in-grade thirty years ago. They call me Chief Dailey here. What's important is now. Your boy is inside with a whole mess of people who need to get the hell outa here."

A helicopter came speeding along the roadway toward Biotronics. Dailey and Sampson watched as it neared. Only seconds passed before the big MH-53M was hovering and then set down. The Gunny and Chief squinted into the rotor wash as Major Jax hustled to them.

Sampson's smile was big, as he shook the major's hand. "Damn, sir, I thought you bought it."

"Not yet, Gunny," Jax said. He studied the man with Sampson. "Who's your friend?"

"Says he's on our side—a Marine buck sergeant, thirty years' time-in-grade."

"Humph," Jax said with a nod. He told the two, "Get in the chopper."

As they obeyed, Sergeant Chambers called to the major from his seat in the cargo bay. He held the SatCom unit, taking over for the fallen Lieutenant Carpenter.

"What is it, Sergeant?" Jax answered.

"Our remote viewer says we've got trouble inside the facility, sir," Chambers said. "The recommendation she gives is drastic."

"All right," Jax said as he climbed aboard, and the helicopter lifted off. He went to the sergeant and looked at the communiqué on the laptop's screen. "Good lord." Jax shook his head and took a deep breath. "Send a message to the President, Sergeant Chambers. It's time we let him in the game. Let's just hope he's on our side."

Chapter 33

My troop of thoughtless bodies stood silently, four wide and ten deep, like rows of corn as I carefully turned the knob of Residence B's door. Forty people—how could I possibly get them all out safely? And what would I find behind this door?

My M-16 leveled and ready, I shoved the thick, insulated door open. Behind it was music, soft, flowing—and voices.

"Dr. Xiang has ordered me to take charge." It was Yumi's voice.

"But he did not tell me," said a male voice as I slipped through the doorway and crouched behind a stack of file boxes on a hand truck.

Yumi was arguing with a small Oriental man only fifteen feet away.

My jaw went slack as I viewed the incredible sight behind them. Filling a room as big as two basketball courts, a formation of dozens of men and women stood in the same kind of white hospital gowns as my veggie platoon—the same vacant look on their faces.

Yumi brought her Makarov pistol out of her pocket and showed the mean end to her opposition. She told him, "Dr. Xiang said if I had any trouble, to use this."

The man said nothing, a shocked expression on his face, and bowed as he stepped backward. He turned from her and scurried past me, opened the door and left without looking back.

Yumi pocketed her handgun and followed him to the doorway as I edged around the boxes so she wouldn't see me. I wondered what she was up to. She looked about the large room as if checking to make sure no one else with any mental capacity was watching. She opened the door and held it while withdrawing her keys.

I stood up, my M-16 pointed at her midsection. "Where are you going?"

Her look was complete surprise. Her eyes widened. "What are you doing? You must leave. Get out, now!"

"I found my son. I realize now everyone was right—I don't have a son. I set loose everyone in Residence A."

"That is good. It is what I was going to do next. But why are you pointing that gun at me?"

"What were you going to do? Lock these people in here?" I glimpsed behind me at the quiet crowd—rows and rows, I couldn't guess how many.

"Yes. They must die."

"What are you talking about? They're innocent, harmless."

"Innocent they may be. Harmless, they certainly are not."

I glanced at them again. All had full heads of hair. Then, I noticed the numbers on the pockets of their white gowns. All the numbers I could see were lower than the one assigned to me, 374. The front row had only double digits. Still, they appeared innocuous, staring out like the others, their eyes lazy, bodies relaxed and unmoving.

Yumi said, "Do not you see? They have all had their implants and completed their programming. They have finished the practical orientation phase you started when you awoke this morning. They are now in a hypnotically induced state of unconsciousness."

"But you said most of those who went before me died, or were killed."

"That is true. You are looking at the numbers? What you do not understand is that once a subject died, his number was used again. There have been nearly seven thousand subjects. The failure rate was one hundred percent until four years ago. Since then, it has been closer to eighty percent. Over six thousand subjects died during our experiments or had to be destroyed. All their bodies were incinerated."

I gaped at her. "Jesus." Xiang's *Brainstorm* project—the Biotronics facility truly was a giant chamber of horrors. I let down my guard and scanned over the crowd. When I turned back to Yumi, I asked, "So who can they hurt?"

"They are armed assassins, just like you," she said, her voice desperate, pleading. "They were to be disbursed to locations throughout the world: Paris, Madrid, London, Rome, Moscow, Buenos Aires, Rio de Janeiro, Warsaw, Tokyo, Mexico City, Prague, Copenhagen, Ottawa, Helsinki, Athens, Jerusalem, Los Angeles, Chicago, New York, Washington D.C.—all of the major cities and capitals of the world. All have been assigned targets, primary and secondary—presidents, heads of state, kings, prime ministers, military leaders and politicians, holy leaders, the Pope. Their support teams are already in place and waiting. The bodies standing before you are no longer mere innocent people. They are psychic warriors—two hundred and eighty-eight of them." She stared at me, her eyes still wide, and I stared back, felt my eyes bugging from the shock of what she was telling me as I lowered the muzzle of my rifle. She said, "Dr. Xiang had sent a security team to bring them to the second plane. I diverted them, said Xiang changed the plans and for them to ensure the building was evacuated from the top down. They listen to me as Xiang has used me many times to pass on orders." She glared out at the large group of emotionless bodies. "They must die, be disintegrated with the facility. Come with me so that I can lock this door, and you can flee to safety."

I'd never imagined the scope of this thing. I couldn't fully grasp what I was hearing. Still, I knew it was wrong—wrong to leave these innocent people. They had been kidnapped, taken away from their families, their lives stolen from them. They had been brainwashed as I had. Even without the vaguest idea how I could save them, I had to try—couldn't just let them die.

I brought the assault rifle's barrel up and aimed it at Yumi. "You go. I'm getting these people out." I shook my head. "If I can't get them out, I'll die with them."

Yumi said, "Then, it is surely what will happen." And she left.

* * *

On the way to his plane, Xiang had a premonition of doom. That, he was not ready for. Setbacks happened, no way around it when dealing with typical human beings. But failure was unacceptable. What he feared most was that somehow Yumi or Wu might have gotten into trouble. He did not want to lose either of his trusted supporters. With that on his mind, he had his driver turn his limousine around. As he entered Biotronics' sub level two from the tunnel, he did not care when the group of Orientals ran panicky past him. Without a plane, they would not escape. Let them run, let them scream, let them pray to their gods—they would die without hope.

As he stepped out of the limo at the tunnel entrance, the last of a large group of the Oriental workers ran by. Xiang was both surprised and relieved to discover Yumi sprinting from around the corner behind them. He smiled broadly, knowing it was quite uncharacteristic of himself. That was why Yumi looked so astonished—even frightened, he decided. He took her by the arm and stared into her eyes. But what he saw, he didn't like. He saw lies and incredible deceit. She had been his right hand, like a daughter to him, yet he saw fear in her eyes. She had no reason to fear him . . . unless she had betrayed him. He must find out the truth.

Yumi immediately became limp and submissive from Xiang's entrancing gaze, as he took a moment to orient himself. He scanned about and saw the nearby shipping and receiving room. After dragging her briskly inside the room, his gaze returned to her, still intense.

"What have you done?" Xiang insisted.

Yumi did not answer, not even under his forceful stare.

Xiang sensed she had deceived him incredibly, that perhaps Subject 374 was still alive and so was the woman—that perhaps they were attempting to escape.

He smiled. Impossible. Them attempting to escape didn't matter. It was too late. And now he would teach Yumi a lesson. She was no longer like a daughter to him.

Xiang slammed the door closed. With a mighty swing of his forearm, he cleared off the top of the nearest desk and threw Yumi onto it. When her body slammed against the desktop, it seemed to bring her out of the trance in which he'd placed her, but he was on top of her in a second. She did not speak, but struggled violently, yet feebly against his strong hands as he made his way to her undergarments, and he discarded them to the side. He could take her easily, control her with his mind and without a struggle. But if she succumbed to his psychic influence, she would not have the same delightful fear in her eyes, the great anticipation of what was to come, as she did now.

He struck her open-handed and put his mouth to hers to taste her blood. It was not enough. He raised up and slapped her again, only to taste her blood once more. Still, she struggled ineffectively. He considered striking her with his fist, his bare knuckles would do considerably more damage. But he realized why she was such an attraction to him. It was that struggle, that defiance he knew he would find when he pressed himself against her. He would give her that—the knowledge that she had resisted. Perhaps it would help her restore her dignity after their first encounter, for he was sure there would be many more—if he decided to keep her alive. If it weren't for her betrayal, he would have thought this to be only a game she played—a little girl's game that all spirited women played. What woman would not wish to be his sexual partner—a man such as him, large, masculine, dominant, brilliant, a leader of peoples?

And now, he suspended his violent foreplay and celebrated victory—Yumi's body relenting as he forced himself inside. And it was good, what Xiang had anticipated it would be . . . until the gun appeared in Yumi's hand and slammed into the side of his temple.

It was all he could do to pry the pistol from her hand before she had a chance to shoot.

* * *

It took a full five minutes to get my new entourage completely out of the huge Residence B room and into the main corridor. I now had a small army of vegetative followers. I was lucky the new regiment took commands and were as easy to direct as the smaller group.

Once we made the stairway, I gave the command to go single file, and we cautiously stepped past the trash on the steps by staying close to the outside wall. In preparing my tactical delaying measures, I'd been careful to leave the outside twelve inches of each step clean of honey and garbage. At the first floor landing, I instructed my silent group to stop by yelling up the stairwell so that all three hundred or so could hear. They did well, halting immediately, and they remained still. I diligently passed through the doorway, closing the door quickly behind me. I didn't want what fumes remained from the cleaning concoction I'd prepared to irritate my quiet mob on the stairway. After skirting the slick dish soap and thumb tacks, I ran the remaining twenty-five feet to the morgue doorway to gather up Sunny and leave this place of hell.

When I shoved open the door, I found all of the stainless-steel tables empty. Sunny and all of the dead bodies were gone. The door to the furnace room was blocked open, and inside, through the inspection window on the incinerator door, all I could see were flames.

Chapter 34

They had come into the morgue while I was gone and cremated all of the bodies on the tables. Before I had left Sunny, I had covered her face as if she were dead. Had they cremated her, also?

I began shaking uncontrollably. I should have left her face exposed, they would have seen she was alive and left her out. If it had been some poor hospital slug's job, an assistant to the assistant of the department, he wouldn't have known Dr. Xiang wanted her and me dead. Then, she might have been taken care of.

Through bleary eyes, I frantically counted the tables to see if one had been removed from the room in hopes my suspicion was incorrect. There were ten tables. There had been ten tables there when I left. None of the tables had been carted out, a living, breathing Sunny as its beautiful payload. I had killed Sunny as surely as I had killed my wife. As surely as I had killed Vanzandtz. As surely as I had been killing all day long. I fell to my knees as nausea came over me, and I vomited straight away onto the crematorium floor. The emotions overwhelmed me, and for the first time that I could remember, I knew they were genuine. I sobbed hard, deep gasps—being responsible for the death of a dear lover striking me hard.

Now, I was completely alone. I had no son. Everyone I knew, or thought I knew, was either dead, had left, or was trying to kill me. I felt the M-16 in my hands and briefly considered ending it all, right there and then.

I stared into the furnace and cried out, "Sunny! Sunny, I'm so sorry!"

Harvey said, *They* need you.

I remembered the *veggies* waiting out in the stairwell and probably lined up halfway down the second floor hallway. They still had a chance, although a slim one. And I knew Sunny would have wanted me to help them, especially if one of them might be her husband. If I could get them to the chopper, we could load as many as would fit, and the rest surely wouldn't protest if they stayed behind to die with me. That was the logical plan, to evacuate as many of these living, breathing, even if non-thinking, human beings as we could.

But when I returned to the hallway, I was suddenly surrounded by five, very unkempt guards, their guns all pointing at me. I suspected they had been some of the security team Yumi diverted from escorting my brainwashed herd. By the trash hanging off each of them and their bloodshot eyes, I was sure they'd been through my little tactical delay measures.

"Hold on, fellas," I said. I dropped my weapon and raised my hands above my head. My only hope was to convince them that they'd been double-crossed by Xiang and Wu and were perhaps unknowingly waiting for their end from a nuclear fireball. "You guys have been duped, you know that, don't you?"

They stood, not saying a word, but glanced at one another through their goggles. I wondered then if they'd already suspected as much.

"Honestly, guys. Dr. Xiang is gone. He left you behind to die, like he did several thousand other folks. You don't have anything to fear from me. You probably passed my little group in the stairwell. We just want to get out of here, just like you."

Again they eyed each other. This time one of them said, "I told you. I told you they were going to blow this place."

"Shut up," said one of the guards in the middle. I figured he must be in charge.

"Come on, Top," the first guy said. "We don't have much time."

"All right," the leader said. "But we're going to kill this

asshole, first." He raised his gun, and I felt like I'd run out of options. They all wore the copper-lined helmets—my psychic gift would be useless.

I yelled out to my zombies in a bottom-of-the-barrel attempt, "Get them."

The few of my night-shirted morons that I could see standing on the other side of the stairwell doorway window stood motionless, but it bought me a second as "Top" glanced back toward my group of blanks.

His head cocked and he grinned. He turned back to me, his rifle barrel aimed at my chest.

* * *

Fast forward, Harvey says.

And I go into *future mode*.

The world is in slow motion. Although my thoughts shift to high gear, I cannot move faster than my adversaries. But I see their movements in advance and know when they will make them.

As the gunman squeezes the trigger, I lurch to one side. Two bullets exit the muzzle of his gun, spinning out with smoke and nitrate debris. My body edges to the side, feeling as cumbersome as a huge aircraft carrier, and the tiny missiles, like torpedoes in the water, come at me. The first will clearly miss. The second bullet becomes a tremendous concern, for I see its green tip and know that the leader's weapon is loaded with armor-piercing rounds. Guessing what I now wore was likely the latest generation of armor, it still wouldn't guarantee against penetration from a zippy little 5.56 X 45 mm round at close range, let alone armor piercing. Ten feet away, I twist my torso, a fast jerk in real time, a snail's crawl in my *fast-forward* vision. And the projectile zips to me, my side twisting back mere centimeters to avoid it, and it strikes me. The bullet enters the body armor, and although the blood is yet to flow, the blazing pain yet to be felt, I know that it has found flesh.

Hoping it has not ruptured a vital organ, I continue the twisting into a spin, getting out of my assailant's aim, then leaping toward the initial gunman.

The entire group begins to bring their guns to bear on

me.

I reach the leader's gun barrel and push it away, just as he lets fly a volley of three rounds.

His back foot leaves the floor. I know it will be directed at my groin. I bring my leading foot up to block it, at the same time I wrench the assault rifle out of his hands. He is off balance, and I shove him into his nearest two accomplices before they can fire at me. I duck and throw my body sideways into the two remaining guards on the other side of him, bowling them over in surprise.

Getting to my feet quickly, I use the first gunman's rifle like a pugil stick, knocking the weapons out of each of the guards' hands. I have to wrestle the last gun from the guard farthest away as he fires, the heat from the muzzle flash burning the side of my face but the bullets passing harmlessly.

Sharp pain from my side finally reaches the receptors in my brain, but I continue my battle. With their weapons knocked from reach, I face the five guards *mano-a-manos* and they rush me. Seeing each fist coming, each arm reaching, each foot rising—each flinch—from my five adversaries, in my mind I have time to prioritize their individual attacks as they surround me. I deal with them coolly: my knuckles into the nose of the first; blocking a kick from the second, then swinging him by the leg into the man beside him; my forearm, avoiding a roundhouse punch, grabbing the arm and pulling the attacker past and into the wall; a punch and a toe to the groin of another.

The leader steps up to me after being blocked away. Anger and frustration fills his face. His words come from his mouth slower than audible, but I can understand. "Let me have him."

The others obey and watch, and I think I'm going to enjoy this.

My adversary throws a right. I block. A left. I block. A right again. I block and slap his cheek. He pauses, face reddening, eyes glaring. He launches a kick. I grab his foot and spin him around. He finds his balance and jabs. I redirect and spin him the opposite direction.

He cuts loose, his fists flailing. Six punches. I block each one. Take him by the back of the helmet and pull his face within inches of mine.

I smile and wink. "Boo-Boo, have we had a ba-ad da-ay?"

Enough being nice—I kick my knee as high and hard as I can against his protected groin. His face is furious until contact—then blank and dumb as my knee raises him from the floor and he falls back. Even with the body armor, it has to hurt.

Now, all the others' eyes are on me, and they have regained their weapons.

The leader raises up, still in intense pain, and one of his men throws his assault rifle to him.

"Son of a bitch!" he says in anger and embarrassment, and takes aim.

No more showing off. Now, it's serious. "Don't try it," I bluff, "or I'll have to kill you." It will take a miracle for me to escape death, now.

And the miracle comes. Before he can squeeze the trigger, a tremor shakes through the entire structure, and it brings me back to real time.

* * *

The guards were stunned when the doorways cracked and the floor buckled, and I realized they thought I was responsible for the earthquake.

"Forget it, Top," the first guy said. "Let's get out of here!" With that, his comrades sprinted through the stair doorway. With the door swung wide, I could see them diving and tumbling as they passed my group, rolling down the steps in the gooey trash. It was obviously easier for them going down than up.

My bluff seemed to work. The leader paused, seeming to have second thoughts, as he sat aiming at me. I was sure in his mind's eye, he was imagining the next bullets he fired somehow redirected and returned to him, me making his gun explode, or causing the floor to open up and swallow him.

As a steel beam broke through the ceiling and landed a few yards beside us, I waved my finger at him.

The anger on his face transformed to terror, and he swiftly got to his feet and dashed away.

The guards' threat banished, nevertheless, I knew we were about to go through hell, as the world around me shook tumultuously.

* * *

"Follow me," I said to my silent army, and I raced by them along the outside of the stairs. When I reached the basement, I trotted through the large double doors of the emergency room/ambulance garage. My group followed slowly, and I was glad of no more stairs to descend.

Try high gear, Harvey said.

"Step quickly," I told them, and to my amazement, they did, yet still not as fast as I would have liked. I was afraid of what might happen if I said run. Would I have a group of dominoes falling all over the place, taking too long to recover? I didn't chance it.

Pieces of the ceiling tile fell as we went. A sign that pointed to our left and said *Ambulance Garage* on it tumbled from the ceiling as we came to a narrower corridor branching off from the main one we were in. Finally, we passed through a last set of double doors and into the parking garage. Before us waited an ambulance loaded with boxes, its front end pointed at a twelve-foot-wide overhead door.

"Stop, here," I told my group and went to the palm pad beside the doorway. However, after placing my hand upon it, the door wouldn't raise.

The earthquake continued. The floor shook. The walls cracked and buckled. I sprinted to the ambulance, got in and found the keys in the ignition. It seemed years since I'd driven a car as the engine started with a roar.

Abruptly, someone sat up in the back like on a springboard.

The person had a familiar accent. "My goodness! We are on the road once more!"

In the rearview mirror, I saw one of the boxes shift to one side and Rajiv's smiling face shown from where it had been.

"But where is the *femme fatale*, Sunny?"

The words are difficult to speak. "She's dead."

Neither of us spoke further for a moment. Then Rajiv said, "I am truly sorry, my friend."

I nodded. "Hold on, Rajiv," I told him, relieved to have found at least one true *friend*.

I slammed the shift lever to drive and stomped the accelerator. The ambulance's tires squealed on the sealed concrete floor, and we busted through the fiberglass doorway and stopped. Ahead of us, a long lighted tunnel lay like a mysterious pathway. Would it lead us to salvation or more hell?

"We are running out of time, my good friend," Rajiv said. "It is now four-forty. We have less than an hour to get our donkeys out of here."

I stuck my head through the window and looked back at my passive mob.

"Follow me!" I yelled out. "Hurry. Run!"

Again, I was surprised when the group of automatons began hurriedly, yet clumsily, into the tunnel entrance and over the smashed door. They tumbled and tripped over one another, but recovered quickly and kept moving.

After driving down a slight incline, a second tunnel met the one we were in, and I guessed it led from the basement. Less than an eighth of a mile farther, we came to the other end of the passageway and saw before us the last of the Orientals who had been held captive inside the facility. The whites of their striped pajamas shone bright in the ambulance headlights. They ran to the left once they got out into the open. I stopped at the tunnel's opening and watched them as they trotted, the five hundred poorly clothed men, women and children in an all-out bid to save themselves, down a snowy, narrow pathway.

Then, I remembered the jumbo jets, and I looked to the brightly lit airfield below us. An eight-foot-wide blacktop lined with boulders, scrub brush and half a foot of snow meandered the quarter of a mile to the airstrip. The big Boeing 747s were being loaded with cargo and personnel, as in my premonition. However, Xiang's jet had yet to take off. And there were three snowplows clearing the field of snow.

* * *

In the Oval Office, Mason considered the alternatives, frantic for a solution. He was now inclined to believe the remote viewers—that incredible changes were to come, biblical in proportions. He was just off the phone with Dr. Ultar, who'd passed on the RV's prediction clearly—within two hours the terrible mechanism would be in place, a sequence of events would begin that could not be stopped. The only alternative was a nuclear response.

Chief of Staff Thurman burst into the Presidential Office. "We've tracked them down, Mr. President. We determined that Major Jackson had requested satellite photos from the U.S. Geological Service and had a SatScan done of the area. And intelligence sources are telling us there's been an unusual amount of EMP activity in that area. It's undeniable. You're not going to believe it. A surgical nuclear strike is imperative."

"Where?"

Jacob Banks pushed through the doorway past Thurman. "God, no, Mr. President. We need to support them!"

"Tell me where they are!"

"There's not much time, Mr. President," Thurman said, as Carl Winston stepped in, Secretary Coates shadowing. "You must make your decision now!"

"Not so fast," Winston said. "Jackson's turned on his transponder so we can pinpoint his *exact* location, and he's asking for help. Say's it's they're only hope."

"Good God!" Mason yelled. "Would somebody please tell me where in the hell they are!"

Chapter 35

From the bushes to our right emerged a dark figure in the predawn light.

It was Dr. Yumi running all out through six inches of snow cover.

"Get out of here," Yumi said. "They are directly behind me. We have been found out!" She was terribly disheveled, blouse torn, lipstick smeared across her face, beautiful hair tousled.

I rolled out of the ambulance as several bullets struck it and the tunnel entrance. I brought my M-16 up and answered with a volley of my own, then yanked Rajiv from the back door as he opened it. The three of us ran toward the safety of the concrete lined tunnel entrance and pressed against one side. Bullets ricocheted through from the direction Yumi had come.

"Stop!" I yelled at my mindless mass as they approached, now only fifty feet away but still inside the tunnel. "Get down!" I commanded and they did. I nodded toward the gunfire and asked Yumi, "Who are they?"

"Wu and eight guards," she said. Her eyes were moist and bloodshot. "While hiding, I heard Xiang give him twenty minutes to kill us and return with proof, or he said he would not let them leave."

"He's quite the motivator. What are we going to do? You got any ideas?" I asked her, the bullets whining and zipping by.

"Die, I would guess," Yumi said.

But then came the now familiar sound of rotor blades. The whoosh of the acoustic cannon filled the air, and the ground shuddered. Another shot of sound, and boulders rolled down the hill from in front of us. In the single remaining ambulance headlight, I could see several men stricken to the ground.

The chopper descended before us, a DPV suspended fifty feet underneath. The chopper placed the vehicle gently about forty yards down the small, blacktop that led to the landing strip. Two men rappelled from the helicopter to the DPV and released its cables. The helicopter then shifted back toward us and landed clear of the tunnel.

"This is it," I said. "This is our only chance!" I stood up and yelled to the blanks behind us, "Get up. Run this way!" And they came like a stampede of kneecapped cattle.

Six of Major Jackson's men jumped off the back ramp of the chopper. Behind them, Gunny Sampson, Sarge, Chief Dailey and Major Jackson, himself. Although I hadn't seen his face without goggles before, I knew it was him, something deep inside was sure of it.

Jackson waved and called out, "Let's go, let's go!" and within ten seconds the entire bunch of us met midway to the helo.

I told my thoughtless horde to stop.

"Good to see you, sir!" Jackson said.

"Likewise, Major Jackson," I said, giving the Major as much of a smile as I could muster.

"Call me Jax," he said, and I nodded to him as three of his men helped a few of the blanks and Rajiv to the chopper and aboard. The other three and Sampson were binding the hands of the security force that had attacked us.

I could not see Wu.

"Be careful," I told Sampson as I watched our disabled enemy. "There's a real bad one still out there."

The major was looking around expectantly. "Where's Sunny?"

Sarge nuzzled my hand and barked twice.

As I patted the dog, my voice cracked with emotions. "She didn't make it."

"Oh, Damn it!" Jax said, and the grimace this hard-core military man displayed surprised me. His lean, tall body swayed from the news. "I'm so, sorry."

I told him, "I know, Jax—about Sunny and me. She told me."

Jax clutched my shoulder in condolence. He shook his head but said nothing.

"I think her husband is among these people." I pointed to the white, night-shirted blanks.

Jax only frowned.

"At least we might be able to save him. But I don't know if any of these people's mental, or psychological states are salvageable."

I couldn't decide what Jax was thinking as he looked at me, keeping his frown.

I nodded. I began to have those flashes of memories again, brief, dark memories of a firefight. Of men dying under fire. Of a helicopter crashing. Of pulling a man out. Of carrying that man on my back, down a hill, through trees to a beach.

Jax looked toward the blanks. "There's no way we can take all these people. We've only the one helicopter. We'll have to pick and choose."

I glanced back at the three-hundred-plus pairs of notion-less eyes. "Let's save who we can," I told him, but I didn't tell him that I would stay behind with the rest.

"Roger that," he said back.

"We've got lots of proof of what's been going on here in that ambulance," I told Jax, pointing to it."

Jax said, "If we leave the DPV, we might be able to lift it."

"Can you give it a try?"

Jax nodded, and grabbed his helicopter's crew chief to instruct him about the ambulance.

As the soldiers pulled the emergency vehicle out farther onto the road so they could attach the lift cables, Yumi trotted back past the entrance of the tunnel and toward the small trail on which the captives had departed.

"Yumi," I called out after her. "Where're you going?"

"Back to my home," she said. "Kill Xiang. Not for me—but for my people." She turned and disappeared into the snow and shadows.

"We've got to get out of here," Jax said. "Our margin of safety is shrinking rapidly."

Dailey stood back, protecting his hat from the rotor wash. A static squawk came from his radio. "Chief, this is Prater."

He smiled at me as Jax gave the chopper pilot the signal to shut off his engines. Dailey said, "Found a couple walky-talkies that were turned off and worked down at the hanger." He then answered the call with the helo's engines winding down. "This is Dailey. Go ahead."

"The bridge is down and it looks like one hell of a rockslide. There's no way in hell we're going to get out of here in cars. We got women and children here. It'll take hours to climb over the rocks and cross the stream."

Dailey looked to me. "That bastard. Xiang got wise to the evacuation. He must have had some of his boys blow the bridge. They'll all die. The entire town."

"Not so fast, Chief," I told him. "Tell Prater to turn around."

"Hold on Prater," he said into the mike staring at me. He shifted his chewing tobacco to the other cheek. "We're working on it."

I turned to Jax and said, "Somewhere in the neighborhood of four thousand innocent people aren't going to make it if we don't do something."

"Even if that's true, there's nothing we can do. It's too late for them—hell, it's probably too late for us."

Chief Dailey stepped up to us. "But he's right. The rest of the POWs, their families, quite a few abductees."

"POWs?" I said, confused.

"I'd guess you folks would call us MIAs," Dailey said.

Jax placed his hand on Dailey's arm and looked at him as if awestruck. "My sweet God. Then it's true? What our remote viewer told us wasn't some sort of red herring?"

"No red herring, major," Dailey said. "Most of the

citizens of Gold Rush are either POWs of Vietnam or Korea—or their descendants. They're over three hundred Americans from the Vietnam War and two dozen from Korea. We've got another two hundred Canadians, Australians, French, English, South Koreans, and South Vietnamese. Besides a couple hundred of Xiang's people, the rest of the folks are my fellow POW's families, mine included. I'd guess you're correct, close to four thousand."

"Ah, Jesus," Jax said. He looked at his watch.

"What about the planes?" I asked, pointing to the two jumbo jetliners on the tarmac.

"No good," Jax answered. "I doubt if they're rigged to hold any more than three-hundred fifty, four hundred each, at most." He faced the horizon to the East. "We have exactly fifty minutes to get as many people as we can over that ridge five miles away." He pointed to a saddle in a mountain crest. "That means this helicopter must, without question, be airborne and heading in that direction in forty-seven minutes."

Chapter 36

With two twenty-kiloton nuclear bombs set to go off in under fifty minutes, we quickly considered possible solutions—ways of getting more than four thousand people five miles to the other side of the ridgeline in time. Suddenly, what I hoped was a viable answer struck me.

I could solve our dilemma if only I could transpose my being, transcend time, and in some manner influence the past. If only I were able to bridge the temporal gap and not only see the past but find a way to segue from my psyche in present time into the past. If that were possible, perhaps I could influence a change to key elements of that past and this present horror we now took part in would not happen, the lives that had already been horrifically altered, and those that had been lost would not have been affected by this madman I knew as Dr. Xiang.

I had influenced others, gotten into other people's heads in present time—even to the extent of killing them, without conscious knowledge of it. I had seen the future. Couldn't I also, then, be able to see the past, find a psyche for temporary residence and influence even the conception of Xiang's life?

I must try.

* * *

Physically, emotionally and mentally drained, I collapse. I feel my body jar as it hits the hard ground, and I enter the swirling portal into the Ether. This time I am nauseated by the spin, and I'm anxious to leave it.

This journey seems truncated as I exit the vortex quickly and float into the eternal home of the universal Matrix. I search for the ethereal angel, but again she isn't present. I wonder if I call out, if the suggestion of calling to the lovely entity comes to my mind, that she might appear once more. Perhaps she holds the answer to our mortal dilemma.

Then too, I consider whether or not there are other angel-like beings within this surreal place that I might summons, perhaps by mistake and not so angelic, but demonic. Could I beckon by error the opposite entity, the demon yin of the angel's yang? And what effect will that cause? I consider another option while peering through the never-ending plasma that is my unconscious' interpretation of Ether: if I examine this place closely, will I see God, will I find His presence, or in the least, can I find evidence of His existence—that this is His domain? Could I then ask Him *why*? Why the suffering, the pain, what is the gist of this thing we call life? What is the real scheme of living in this universe He has made—what is His plan for the human spirit after life? The thought of it makes me shiver—who am I to even toy with the idea of personally approaching God—of confronting the supreme being and asking Him *why*? In the misty distance I see no one, no thing. There is no sound of voice or noise of approach—and I am glad.

I remember my immediate quest and think of the coordinates necessary to locate the place in the Matrix that will facilitate my passage to that time, many years ago. Suddenly, the Matrix becomes a blur of brilliant lights of every color, and I know that I'm traveling at a speed faster than light, yet I feel no motion, and I enter a dark, soundless void. As quickly as I've entered the lightless abyss, I find myself pulled miles and years away from the American town of Gold Rush, and I now hover over a large Chinese city, circa late 1930s.

I know it to be Shanghai, the knowledge of it coming to mind like a whisper. There are tall buildings and streets jammed with people, carts and automobiles. It is a frightening place that I'm sure is full of many dangers.

But I remind myself that this fear is unfounded, because I'm not physically here, and no harm can come to me.

It is a clear night, and there is much disturbance in the streets—sailors of many nationalities drunken and loud, some staggering, some fighting, some singing merrily. And merchants, pimps and prostitutes sell their wares and services like newspaper butchers on the street.

In the harbor are Japanese, American and French navy ships, gunboats and other warships docked alongside the freighters, sampans and junks. And to the east, an eerie scarlet glow lights the horizon in a pulsing wave. I know that none of those on the city streets, the warships or the merchants' boats can see this red luminance, but they all are aware of it. It is a premonition, a knowing of their future I witness. I know it to be the war with Japan looming in this Chinese city's near future that illuminates the horizon so. Many atrocities are to come—the second Sino-Japanese War, the invasion and subsequent massacres of hundreds of thousands in the nearby city of Nanjing, known to those in the West as Nanking.

I descend to a busy street where I pass through the shoulder-to-shoulder crowd—Orientals with coolie hats, English, French and American sailors and Marines, hookers in bright silk kimonos. I move past rickshaws and luxurious Bugattis, bars, flophouses, food and jewelry vendors, and makeshift casinos. The pedestrians speak of cockfights and dogfights, horse races and rat races, and all manners of gambling. They tell of whores and jewelry, bets, and the world back home.

I finally arrive at a hotel—more likely a flophouse brothel. There are many small rooms, the grunts and groans of uninhibited lust coming from them. I am drawn to a particular tenement and, as I enter through its ceiling, I see a young Chinese woman, pretty and innocent. I know she is just that—an innocent twelve or thirteen-year-old, forced into prostitution by a father attempting to support a large family, trying to keep them alive on a miniscule amount of rice and beans. Wearing a worn, padded kimono she whimpers anxiously, sitting in the corner opposite a flattened and soiled feather mattress that lays on the floor.

I quickly become one with her thoughts, understand that the sacrifice she makes for her family weighs heavy on her mind: her life for theirs, her younger sister and three brothers, her father and mother. It is a valiant thing she does for them, yet she wishes she could live an ordinary life, grow to become a woman with a husband and have children, a family of her own. She only wants to live.

The door opens and a tall Caucasian man is ushered in by a squat, aging *mammason*. He is well dressed, wearing a straw-colored suit, his hat in his hand. He pulls from his lapel a small white flower, perhaps a daisy, and hands it to the trembling young girl.

"I have bought you," he says in Mandarin—but I hear it in English. "Not just for the night, but for as long as I am stationed here." She looks up at him and slowly she takes the daisy.

At that moment, I feel what she feels—that this is a better alternative to death, to what she had anticipated. To be this man's mistress will banish her fear of being passed on from one filthy sailor to the next for countless times through each and every night—of contracting an ugly venereal disease that will kill her at a young age, as is the fate of so many other young girls she's heard stories about.

"I am Russian, the Soviet Consul General to Shanghai, and I plan to be here for a very long time. I will be kind to you, visit you often, bring you flowers and furniture. This will be our tenement." He reaches toward her and gently pulls down her tattered robe from each shoulder, and I experience the fright she feels—the shiver, the icy fingers touching and fondling her.

I am pulled away and find myself looking at this young girl through the Russian's eyes. I admire her beauty as the most perfect of paintings, just the right light, the exact hues and softness of the curves of her young body. She is as beautiful to me as he finds her, but I am embarrassed at seeing her this way—yet I cannot turn away. Deeper in his psyche lurks a darkness, a lust for taking over this child's body, controlling it, and being the first to defile her. His lust digresses from humane sensibility to animalistic desire, and it sickens me.

As he loosens his belt and unbuttons his trousers, I go deeper into his psyche and search for what I need to stop this and to stop the horror happening in the time from which I've come. Through his thoughts I rummage, until I find he has a daughter, slightly older than this young girl, at his permanent home in Moscow. With the daughter is his wife who waits for him faithfully and patiently.

If I were to bring this remembrance from the darkness of the back of his mind to the light of his thoughts, he will surely stop his present course. He will become disgusted with himself, turn away from this poor child and let her be—and the Russian-Chinese madman known as Dr. Gao Xiang will not be conceived.

Just as I begin to energize the notion and carry it to where the man can see what he is doing in the light of reason, I am yanked from his conscious to a place unfamiliar to me, an unworldly place of heat and dry swirling winds. I discover a dark and barren landscape before me, rocky and glowing red like the horizon I'd seen earlier, and I know that I will soon be viewing what is to come.

The ground shakes violently, and the heavens explode with brilliant lightning and terrific thunder. A crack in the dark red ground suddenly appears in front of me, and it grows across the terrain. As it widens, I see it is deep, not only feet or meters, but miles, and at the bottom a stream of red lava glows, the liquid rock flowing rapidly, popping and exploding as it surges. The chasm's growth stops and, to most souls, this would seem a formidable barrier, but not for me. I know, should I choose, I can cross this fearsome canyon easily, for it is only in my mind.

I realize it's purpose is not to gobble me up in its fire, but to warn me—cause me to consider my next action, and my choices in *this time* that is not my own. For if I step out over midair and cross this threshold, I will make a choice that I cannot call back, and the malleable future will solidify and be changed forever.

On the other side of the fiery crevasse are numerous tunnels of light, and I peer through them from one end, the beginning, into what will be if I interfere with the past. Another whisper from the dark instructs me that these channels are the variances a mere fraction of a second will make. If I push the reminder of the man's daughter to his thoughts quickly and with force, the first scenario will take place and be permanent. A split second later, and if I include the man's wife, a second version will happen—slower a third—at a different time and with the thought of the man's wife brought to his mind first, a fourth scenario, and so on.

I see in the first tunnel, the man comparing his own daughter to the virgin sex slave he's purchased before him and, repulsed by the thought of what he is about to do, he turns and runs from the doorway and away from the hotel, never to look upon it again. But as I watch through this portal, a different man, drunken and foul, comes through the virgin girl's door. He stands over her, the lust clear in his eyes, then takes the poor child and brutalizes her. The drunk is followed by another and another, and I watch as the hours turn to days. Finally, several weeks pass when I see half a dozen inebriated sailors at her door, and I know that in the next few minutes, she will be gang raped and killed.

In the next tunnel the Russian diplomat flees from the room as before, but slips on a rug at the head of the stairs. As he tumbles down the steps, he breaks his arm. He becomes so angry, when he pulls himself up by a drape nearby, he yanks it from its curtain rod. Frustrated and ashamed, he throws the fabric into a blazing fireplace that heats the bricks used to warm rooms and the foot of beds. The curtain catches fire, as does the oil from a lamp that he's knocked over in the process, and flames suddenly engulf the entranceway to the hotel. In a matter of scant seconds, the blaze spreads through the entire wooden building and dozens of lives, including the young girl's, are lost.

In the third tunnel, the man feels the shame and pain

so deeply, so darkly, that he becomes enraged. He reaches to the girl, and with strong large hands wrapped around her throat, he chokes the young prostituted woman, who is no more than a child, until she collapses to the floor. I know he will then be found out, and the proprietors of the whorehouse, embittered by the girl's death by a foreigner's hand, will run him through with their long knives.

These are terrible things I see, but I wonder if this last scenario would be the kindest for the girl—to get her suffering over with quickly—and if it wouldn't be the most just scenario for the man, justice for his brutality.

But I am given a vision now about my query, and I understand that this man, who would be her murderer, and be killed for it, then would not go back to his wife and child in Moscow when the second Sino-Japanese War starts and the Japanese soldiers invade. He would not become an important commander under Stalin in the Soviet Army, and he would not help defeat the Nazis' Blitzkrieg. Without his leadership, the unit he would have led will fall to the invading forces and allow them to advance only three miles farther to a small village near Kursk. Many more Russian civilians will be slaughtered there. Eight-hundred kilometers away, a traveling merchant, hearing his village has been sacked and fearing for the lives of his family, will speed recklessly from the town of Privolnoye, his truck striking a peasant boy on the side of the road. Young Mikhail Gorbachev will be killed—and the Berlin Wall will not topple so easily, nor as early as November of 1989.

Also linked to this, a young Irishman, a fighter pilot in the British Royal Air Force named Lieutenant James O'Donnell, will be shot down and killed by a German who should have died in the botched advance of the Nazis. The granddaughter named Sunny, who Lieutenant O'Donnell should have had, will never be born.

All of it is baffling.

I decide a different course, to travel forward from this time, to see if there might be a better opportunity to change the future, find what influenced Xiang to become so uncaring of human life and perhaps sway him from his course of darkness and death.

But then, I feel a presence beside me and turn to see the beautiful apparition who welcomed me the first time.

She directs her lovely gaze at me, and I hear her voice inside my head, her lips unmoving. "You have many choices—they are infinite. Few mortals are privileged with such ability—only the wise. For without wisdom, knowing that to alter the past will change destiny itself, the resultant future might be worse than destiny's true course. To make even a small adjustment can create great changes to the future—to destiny. A smile not given to an angry man might lead to the death of an entire race. Kindness given a starving dog could result in a world of complete peace and harmony a century later. You must choose wisely. A hasty act could create a paradox—change the future to where you will never be born. Without your birth, you would not be able to change the past, and your existence and the memory of you will be erased from the universal Matrix—you will never have been."

This notion Moonfeather imparts is unthinkable, confusing, frightening. A simple change in the past, the throwing of a stone, can be devastating to the world two hundred years later.

Chapter 37

I felt someone shaking me, my body being jostled, and when I looked up I saw Jax frowning down on me.

"Are you okay?" he asked.

I was lying on the ground near the tunnel. "Yeah," I said, my thoughts still swirling.

Rajiv suddenly was hovering over me. He checked my eyes and my pulse. "This man leaves consciousness more often than anyone I have ever met or studied. We must have him treated for narcolepsy."

"I'm fine," I told him. "Help me up."

"You're hurt," Jax said as he, Rajiv and Chief Dailey helped me stand.

I followed his gaze and remembered my wound—had not felt pain from it until now as I looked at the dark, blood-soaked spot on my side. I peeled back the body armor and Rajiv stuck his face close to my injury.

After a careful inspection, he said, "It has clotted very nicely. It seems only to be a flesh wound, and I am greatly relieved."

"Me, too," I said as I looked down at the jumbo jets on the airfield.

"You should not twist your body for some time and we must dress this injury soon."

Jax said, "I'll get the Med Kit."

"No time for that, now," I said as the first passenger jet began taxiing behind Xiang's smaller plane. "The 747s. They're our only hope." I broke for the helicopter and the others jogged behind me.

Jax and I reached the open cargo bay at the same time. He said, "Even if we can stop them from taking off now, pack some of these people in, they'll carry maybe four hundred and fifty, five hundred people each, max."

"And leave three thousand behind," I said absently. I met his eyes. "We've got to do that much."

Dailey arrived panting and spoke into his radio, "Prater, turn everybody around. Get 'em headed back to Biotronics. We got us some free airfare and first class seats."

"And what about my troupe?" I asked, motioning to the three-hundred-plus thoughtless followers.

Jax turned to one of his men next to the chopper. "Clark, lead them to the runway."

The young man nodded to the major and ran back to the large group.

I cupped my hands and called out, "Follow him," and I pointed to their new leader.

In a few seconds the entire group began their three-quarter-mile trek down the narrow paved road to the airstrip. I couldn't help but compare them to a cult group of some kind, dressed in white hospital garb following a man in black body armor.

Jax vaulted into the side door of the helicopter and Sarge followed him. "But we still have to get those people to the plane, and the Biotronics side of this tunnel is blocked. Our acoustic cannon made quite a mess of the entire building."

Dailey said, "The tunnel's the only way from town down to that airstrip." He gazed downhill and seemed to have an epiphany. "There's a bulldozer parked beside the main hanger down there. If I can get to it, maybe I'll be able to clear the tunnel."

"Then, if that works," Jax said, "we'll have the solemn task of turning away over three-fourths of them." He held out his hand to assist Dailey, Rajiv and me into the chopper.

"We'll find a way, Jax," I said, not convinced myself.

Dailey asked, "But what about Xiang? Since he's seen

your chopper, he'll be skidaddling pronto."

Jax glanced down at the airstrip. "Looks like they're taxiing to two different, parallel runways. If we try to stop the first jumbo, he'll be gone before we can get to him. We can't knock him down—the acoustic weapon's power supply is depleted, and so's the EMP—wouldn't cook a transistor at two feet." He glanced at the machine gun. "We're even out of live rounds for our fifty caliber."

I said, "Leave Xiang to me."

"No," Jax said. "Absolutely not, sir!"

I turned my back on him, dropped from the doorway and walked briskly toward the desert patrol vehicle.

"Damn it," he said and gave in. He called out, "All right, then. Sanders and Finney are with the DPV. Tell 'em to go with you." I looked over my shoulder and gave him a thumbs up. Jax frowned back, then nodded to the pilot and the big helicopter's engines sparked to life, its huge rotor starting to slowly turn.

"Hang on, son," Chief Dailey said, his heavy footfalls hustling up from behind. "I'll help ya. We'll make short work of Xiang and then you can take me to the dozer."

As Jax and the helicopter lifted, Sarge leapt to the ground from the open doorway. He ran toward the tunnel.

Sampson called out, "Sarge! Get back here, boy."

"No time for that, now," Jax said. "Too many lives in the balance. He can find his own way down to the runway."

The helicopter rose until the heavy cable attached to the ambulance became taut, and they hovered directly above it. Then they took off, slowly at first, but accelerated rapidly with the van swaying underneath. They headed for the airstrip where the first jumbo jet now began its takeoff run.

Dailey and I were sprinting, about halfway to the DPV, when my fast-forward double vision returned. I figured it came to me instinctively, some sort of defensive measure from my subconscious. In the ghost view, I saw Wu step up from behind a bush on one side of the trail. My premonition startled me, and I stopped in my tracks as I continued to view it. Wu gave me one of his intense stares, and with the element of surprise, I had no time to defend myself. I folded to my knees and quickly fell dead.

The future view evaporated from before my eyes and in the present view, I saw the two soldiers who had been guarding the DPV. They lay twisted, and most likely dead, beside it.

Dailey caught up to me and I grabbed his shoulder. "Stay back, Chief," I said, then cautiously proceeded, hoping he'd understand the danger and obey.

A few yards later, I came upon the bush I'd seen in my premonition and focused on it as I approached. I counted on getting the jump on Wu this time, gain the upper hand.

Twenty feet in front of me, he stepped out as I'd expected. He looked surprised that I'd already brought my energy to bear on him, the top of my spine tingling, sharp pains stabbing my temples. I could think of nothing else but to fake him out, to "psych" him.

As he glared at me, his returned force caused a burning from inside of me, and the energy between us increased. I held the heels of my hands out in front of me and advanced toward him. Blood trickled from his nose, then from mine. I gave him a karate yell and pedaled my arms. His eyes widened from my display of BS, and momentarily, I thought I had him.

But the intense heat of his power soon grew overwhelming. The ground around us trembled. We came to within eight feet of each other and stopped. I felt the dominance of power shift to his side and he smiled. His force became too great, as I was driven to one knee.

"Who are you to think you can overpower me?" he said, standing with his hands on his hips like some kind of comic book super villain.

I knew it would be a split second before I would topple over dead. I could not move my lips to even curse him. Then, I thought of Sunny—I didn't know why. I felt not only a great sorrow build inside of me, but also a matching anger. It was Dr. Xiang and Wu's fault Sunny was dead—as well as the hundreds of others who had died and would soon die. I wanted to call him a bastard, wanted to wrap my hands around his neck and watch him die—make him die. But I felt my consciousness dwindling, the earth beneath me seeming to spin as his words echoed inside my head *Who are you to think you can overpower me?*

Then, the last entity in the world I would have ever expected popped into my thoughts—Harvey. But his presence did not distract me this time, he did not harass me with his comments, try to persuade me one way or another. This time Harvey's presence seem to bring with it an incredible energy, refueling and adding to my own. I thought of Sunny again and my anger built with a new resolve. I finally was able to strain out an answer to Wu's question.

"I'm . . . Superman," I blurted, then reached into my pocket, pulled out Sunny's .32 caliber pistol and put her last bullet between his eyes.

The speed and finality of the action stunned even me as Wu fell backward onto the ground with incredible surprise on his face.

I pocketed Sunny's empty pistol. It would be my only souvenir of her. And now for Xiang. I went to the DPV.

"Hot damn," Chief Dailey said, trotting sideways by Wu's body, gaping at him in amazement. "Hot damn, that was slick. You don't mess around, do ya, son?"

I checked Major Jax's two men. They were both dead.

Below us the first 747 turned onto a strip parallel to Xiang's plane, both planes taxiing on the other end of the airfield. Jax's helo was speeding toward the first jumbo jet, as planned. If we could get through the rugged terrain about six hundred yards to our right before Xiang took off, he'd fly directly over us. I fired up the DPV as Dailey swung into the passenger's side, and we shot off through the snow and rough landscape toward the spot Xiang was sure to pass over.

We'd covered considerable ground when Dr. Xiang's jet began its takeoff run, a mile on the opposite end of the strip. It approached, gaining speed. I stopped the DPV about halfway downhill from the tunnel as we came in line with the jet's departure, and I got out.

"Stay here, Chief," I said, and he complied as I jogged away.

Seventy-five feet from our vehicle, I stood in the open and waited. Below, I could see Jax's big rotorcraft landing directly in front of the first 747. He had it and the second jumbo jet pinned in.

About two-thirds of the way down the airstrip, Xiang's smaller jet left the tarmac and gained altitude sharply to avoid the rocky slope we were on.

* * *

As I focus my energy, the double vision returns. I see inside the jet in the phantom view. This time, I realize both visions are real time, the same time but different space. The first, opaque view, is from my own physical eyes. The phantom view is a close up, a peek from inside the cockpit.

But I suddenly find myself embodied inside the plane, standing behind Xiang as he watches the ground over the pilots' shoulders. Time shifts to slow motion again, and no one seems aware of me inside the plane. I look at my hands and forearms and they are translucent, phosphorescent. My body seems to have become pure energy. But looking past Xiang, I see myself on the approaching hillside, and I realize my ability to remote view has transcended another step.

My point of view shifts instantaneously back to the ground to my physical body. My spine, the base of my head tingle again.

Suddenly, back in the plane, I move around Xiang, passing through the copilot's body and seat, and I turn back to glare at Xiang. He jerks his head back and his eyes widen with panic.

"Impossible," he whispers.

I smile at him. "This might hurt," I say, and back out of the cockpit to the nose of the plane, only my glowing, phantomlike head protruding inside through the windscreen.

The pilots' faces contort, and Xiang hunches over in pain between their seats.

My conscience shifts back to the ground, sharp pains

bolt through my temples as the small jet flies nearer, now only two hundred yards away.

Seeing inside the plane again, Xiang's face grimaces incredibly as he stares at me, my ghostly being.

Shifting back to the hillside, the hurt grows stronger, radiates throughout my skull.

In the plane, Xiang's hands claw at his temples from the terrible pain. I move inside the cockpit once again, toward Xiang. He reaches out, grabs for me angrily, and his hand passes through my phantomlike body.

On the hillside, static electricity builds around me as if I am a giant glass rod, and I feel the energy from the very ground I stand on as it courses through my legs. I smell ozone before blood spurts from my nose. The force builds inside my chest and upper body as if my trunk were a huge capacitor, storing an intense power.

Suddenly, violently, the center of my body jolts, releasing a discharge of electricity, flashing like a lightning strike to the jet.

Inside the plane, Xiang screams in anguish, and my self-apparition pops like a bubble, disappearing from the cockpit, and my double vision melds together.

In that instant, I fall limply onto the ground as Xiang's jet torches above me. A hundred yards uphill, it spirals into the mountainside in a conflagration of flames, sparks and streamers.

* * *

I lay, sprawled out on scrub brush, my head foggy, spinning. From behind, I heard the chief's rapid footfalls. The chief came quickly to my side and helped me up. I felt drained, my body limp and uncooperative from exhaustion after such terrific spending of energy.

"You are one bad mutha, ain't you?" he said, leading me by the arm. "Now we gotta get down to the airfield so I can get that dozer."

At the DPV, Dailey got behind the wheel. As my head cleared, he busted the tires loose, and we set off wildly down the slope.

"Chief," I said, "what are hundreds of American POWs—or MIAs—doing here?"

"Don't you get it, boy? This whole town ain't nothin' but a farce. Xiang made this place over thirty-five years ago. Brought all of us to it, all the POWs—many of us MIAs. He had the perfect plan. We'd work for him and not try'n escape. In return, he'd give us a home, a wife, a job and let us raise a family as near to what we had back home as possible, maybe even better in a lot of ways."

"But right under our noses in Gold Rush? And what about everyone else?"

In front of us, a large boulder seemed to emerge from the waning shadows and darkness in the early morning light. Dailey swerved and our vehicle tipped slightly, slammed back onto all fours, then lurched and found purchase. He spat tobacco out the side, his foot back firmly on the accelerator. "Damn, that was close," he said, then continued, "Xiang used a bunch of his own people for hard labor, buildin' and maintainin' and even a few as guinea pigs."

I thought of the people I had found in *Residence A*.

"He used us POWs to help get the town right. He wanted it to have as much of a 'good ol' hometown' feel to it as possible. Hell, he'd brought in big trees and all sorts of plants and animals to make it complete. They used material and products that were standard—stuff you'd expect to see in Gold Rush, Colorado. Built all the cozy cottages, quaint stores, the white picket fences."

We made the tarmac and sped more smoothly toward the hanger where the bulldozer was parked. When we swerved to a stop in front of it, the chief got out, and I slipped in behind the wheel.

"Good luck, Chief," I said.

"Same to ya, boy," he said as he climbed onto the D-9 Cat bulldozer. He started the big diesel engine. "And by the way, that little rodent of yours? Yesterday afternoon, I caught up with the kid they had actin' as your son—Li's his name, I believe. Gave him the little critter. He was as happy as a bloodhound eatin' possum."

I smiled at him and gave him a thumbs up before taking off toward Major Jackson five hundred yards away. I hoped I hadn't smashed my furry friend in Li's pocket when I'd hugged the boy about an hour earlier.

Jax already had the crew and few original passengers of both jets out of the planes and wrangled into a circle off to the side. They'd pulled in a fuel truck and was fueling up the helicopter.

There might have been three dozen of the original crew and passengers lying prone, all but one with their arms extended. That one, a small, rotund Oriental with a bandaged hand, seemed to be unconscious. Major Jax and two of his men guarded the group while the rest of his soldiers were unloading the cargo to make room for more passengers.

I parked within twenty feet of Jax and asked, "How many do you think we can take?"

"I figure, if we clear the baggage compartment, make room in even the unpressurized areas, and load them in there, also, we might cram in as many as eight hundred people in each plane. But we'll have to stay below ten thousand feet so that they'll be able to breath."

"What if we tear out the seats, hell, even the commodes? Make it standing room only."

"Never thought of that. Might be able to nearly double the number. Still, we'll be overloaded. That's a lot of weight."

"Jax, we have no choice. We can't leave anyone behind."

Jax shook his head. "Jesus . . . you're right. We have to try." He looked to the airman next to him. "Get every boarding stairway and loading ramp they have out of the hangers and put them up to all of the passenger and cargo doors on both planes, and get it done." As his man trotted away toward the rest of the group unloading the planes, Jax said, "I'll find the specs on these behemoths, get a quick guesstimate of weight and how much fuel we'll need to get to safety. We'll dump all the fuel we don't need."

We both looked back up the mountain. Dailey had reached the tunnel's entrance.

I asked, "Have you seen Sunny's husband?"

He looked at me from the corner of his eyes. I

wondered what he was thinking. Did he know about the affair Sunny and I'd had? Maybe her husband and I had actually fought over her. Perhaps all of us—Jax, Sunny's husband and I—were all good friends at one time.

"I know already, Jax. Sunny told me that Dan and I didn't get along. But I certainly don't wish him any harm."

"Yeah," he said. "If Dan's here, he'll be fine if we can get the hell out." He looked at his watch. "We've got twenty-five minutes."

Chapter 38

Jax had ordered one of his men to get the spec books out of the cockpit of one of the 747s and to bring them to him. After a quick review of the plane's capacities and load limits, his eyes found the ambulance that was still hooked up by four cables to the chopper. "We're going to have to do something about the van. It's probably three tons loaded like it is."

"Do you have a cargo net we can put the records in?"

"We could do that."

The major signaled to two soldiers to relieve him of the guard duty, and he, Rajiv and I began work on transferring Yumi's absconded records from the ambulance to the cargo net.

As we placed the boxes and bags of incriminating evidence in the net, I noticed a thin bracelet on Jax's right wrist. It had a small arrowhead on it like the one I'd seen on the spirit-like beauty who led me to the universal matrix.

"Moonfeather," I said aloud, almost involuntarily.

Jax turned to me with a frown. "What did you say?"

"Moonfeather," I said. "Someone in a dream had a necklace exactly like your bracelet."

"And her name was Moonfeather?"

"Yeah, she saved our lives."

Jax smiled, the tall man's eyes beginning to water, but we both kept working as we talked.

"Jax, she said something about telling her lover it

wasn't his fault, and she'd be waiting for him when it was his time. But that he had a lot to do in the material world first."

He grinned at me as if he'd just won the lottery as we both carried boxes from the van to the net. "She was my wife." His happiness left and a grim pal replaced it. "Always loved to explore underwater caves. Four years ago, we were down about eighty feet off Waikiki. She was so excited about finding a cave she hadn't explored before. The currents around there shift without notice and an unusually strong one grabbed us out of nowhere. I got hooked up on a rock, ripped my airline open. She was swept away. Out of air, I had no choice but to surface fast. I found help, but by the time we got back, all I could find was her necklace hooked on a rock." He set his box down in the cargo net and raised his arm to gaze at the small arrowhead. "I wear it on my wrist so I can always see it." He dropped his arm. "We never found her body. I got a bad case of the bends, nearly died." He looked up at me and smiled. "You were there."

I stared at him, shocked.

He continued. "You came to my hospital room nearly every day—gave me as much support as you could." He turned to go back to the van for more of the boxed files and records, but then he paused with his back to me. "I can still see her, being pulled backwards into that cave, her arms out to me—begging me for help."

I found honesty in Jax's voice, and for the first time, I really believed it, no doubt—100 percent—that none of what I thought of as my world, as my reality, was true. I wished I could remember this man, Moonfeather, Sunny and her husband. I sensed a great bond between us, and it made me dreadfully sad.

By the time we were finished, lights shone from the tunnel entrance halfway up Mt. Rainy. We had twenty minutes left.

Dailey's bulldozer pulled to the side to let the faster cars by and down the trail toward us. They came quickly in a long stream of headlights that seemed never ending. We were going to get all of these people out, someway. I didn't know how.

Several soldiers began directing traffic, having the cars park to one side. They pointed the citizens of Gold Rush toward the planes, warning them of not taking any personal items with them, there would be no room.

"There they are!" Rajiv yelled. He glanced at me and then looked gleefully at the crowd of people moving toward the planes. He sprinted as best he could toward a group of five who came away from the rest and greeted him with big smiles and cries of joy.

The next sight gave me as much pleasure—Korean War veteran George Washington Banks and his wife, daughter, son-in-law, and granddaughter. Former U.S. Marine Corporal George Washington Banks gave me a toothy grin and a big thumbs-up as they passed. I realized he was one of the Korean War POWs of which Dailey had spoken.

I waved back at Banks as several people rushed by his family to get farther up in line. A couple more boarded the helicopter, and one man stepped by quickly holding his head as if in tremendous pain. He turned his face from me as he got near, and I thought it was odd. But I was distracted when Sampson came up to us.

The gunny gave me a quick smile like there was some sort of friendship between us, now. But for the major, he did not have good news.

"We couldn't get many of the seats out, Jax," he said. "They put those damn things in there good. Stripped them the best we could, though."

"All right, Gunny," Jax said and wiped his eyes. "Pack our passengers in as tight as they can get. This isn't a pleasure trip. Nobody has to be comfortable."

"Who's going to fly the planes, major?" he asked.

We glanced at the 747s sequestered original crew.

"I don't think you should trust them," I told Jax. They still have allegiance to Xiang, even though he is dead."

"You're right," Jax said. "We'll bring them along just in case, but I'll fly the chopper, and Lieutenants Johns and Nelson can fly the big birds. If they can buzz this Jolly

Green around like a dragon fly, those big ol' buses ought to be a piece of cake."

"Yessir," Gunny Sampson said as Jax handed him the spec manuals. He turned and trotted back to the helo pilots who were helping to direct our passengers aboard. A few seconds after he joined them, they turned to gape wide-eyed at the major. He shrugged and gave them a casual salute. They each gave a fainthearted salute back, took the manuals from Sampson and headed for the front of the planes.

"God, Major, these aren't Cadillacs," I said as we trotted toward the cars parking on the field. "It's not a matter of looking at the owner's manuals to find out where the map light and cup holders are."

As I helped a mother and infant out of one car, Jax took the arm of an elderly man and turned to me. "You got any better ideas? As I remember, you used to be a fair pilot. How about you giving it a go?" He smiled at me.

I was a little stunned. I couldn't even remember flying even as a passenger. "No thanks. I can barely remember how to use a stick shift, let alone fly a jumbo jet." I wanted to ask him more about myself, but I was afraid to. I hoped there would be time later—if we lived through this.

"I thought as much. Both of my chopper pilots have had training in flying large passenger jets in the event of hijack situations. They'll do okay."

Sampson had been busy, running about, relaying messages and doing the legwork for Jax. He hustled alongside the major as we helped our civilian charges onto the long boarding steps to one of the planes.

"Major Jax," Sampson said. "Two things. One, our radar has picked up two inbound flights of about four planes each."

"What direction, Gunny?"

"The first group of four are high-fliers from the northeast, the other one is a treetop-hugging flight from the south."

I asked the major, "What's that mean?"

"It's time to get the hell out of here." He said, then

turned to Sampson, "How long?"

"Ten minutes. They'll be converging here in ten minutes, tops."

"Christ, what more do we need?"

"The other thing, sir."

Jax frowned at his senior enlisted man. "What is it?"

"The distress beacon. It lit up for a few seconds. It's gone now. Wasn't on long enough to get a good fix, but it was coming from somewhere in or near the Biotronics facility."

Jax looked at me wide-eyed and then up the side of Mt. Rainey. "Sunny!"

Chapter 39

The major scanned around us as I gazed hopefully back at the mountain. I prayed I would see some sort of sign, a light or a flash of something to indicate Sunny had managed to survive and was coming back down to us.

One of Jax's men trotted up. "It's a miracle, sir! We've about got 'em all on board. And we've calculated the fuel we'll need and dumped all but a hundred mile safety margin. Those people are scared shitless, but they're cooperating. They're sitting two or three per seat, jammed in the aisles, the kitchens and the baggage areas, but somehow we did it—every last soul and even a few puppy dogs. We're guessing right at twenty-one hundred people on each plane."

"Damn, that's too much weight," the major said.

"We've got to try it, Major," I said. "It's all or none."

"This isn't some kinda damn democracy, here!" he said, scowling at me, and this time he didn't call me sir.

I wondered how familiar we were to one another, sure we'd been good friends in my *other life*.

"You always were pig headed," he said. "Your way was always the correct way, for the people, by the people." He turned away briefly and seemed in consideration of his tirade. "Okay, damn it. But if none of us make it off this tarmac, don't blame me."

"Sunny?" I asked.

It took him another second of consideration. "On our way out, we'll swing the helo past Biotronics and see if we can get a visual." He looked at his watch. "Jesus! We have nine minutes before we're attacked from the air and twelve before two nuclear bombs annihilate us."

We ran for the helicopter as the two jumbo jets taxied out onto the field. Jax got into the pilot's seat, and I stood in the open side door. With the blanks and a few extra people jammed in, there had been no room for any of the weaponry the helo had carried into Gold Rush. Those things and any excess were left on the pavement. We were shoulder to shoulder.

We took off, and as I looked out at the mountain, I wondered about Sunny, if she was somehow alive. We would have to take a wide swipe at the mountain in order to gain enough altitude with such a heavy load and to get back up to Biotronics.

I gripped the hatchway tightly as we sped along the mountainside, and again I find myself spinning back into the vortex toward the ether-world.

* * *

When I stop spinning and float out from the whirlpool, I see a dog—Sarge, running through the rubble that had been Biotronics.

"Find her!" I call out. "Find Sunny, Sarge! Come on boy, you can do it."

Suddenly, through the dog's eyes I see the debris before me, under his feet as he sprints across it. Soon, I smell it—the scent of lilacs in the rain, and the dog slows. A woman's body in a green jogging outfit lay before the dog. She is on her back, a piece of concrete across her middle. I am concerned, and I feel the same worry in the canine. But then, in my vision, I see Harvey's face lying there in Sunny's green sweat suit, and I am confused.

The big bunny eyes open. The lips become full and feminine. Long eyelashes, a cute, human nose, and lovely sunset-red hair.

It's me, Superman. It's been me, all along. You translated your own words to my thoughts, pinned the face and the rabbit body to those words. It helped you make sense of the voice in your head. But I've been with you every step of the way. You sought out my psyche over two years ago, and in some less refined way or another, I've been with you ever since—our own kind of *Radar Love.*

I shake my head, still a novice at this telepathy thing, this remote viewing stuff. Now I see Sunny, the real Sunny, lying there, under the concrete with her eyes closed, blood on her lip, her chest rising gently with each shallow, important breath.

Now, the voice I hear is Sunny's. *I need you, Superman. Come to me. I need your help. I need you, Superman. I love you, Superman.*

I witness from Sarge's eyes, the dog licking Sunny's face.

* * *

Abruptly outside of my daydream, someone shoved me from behind, and I was snatched out of my transcendent state. I swung out of the doorway, with only the firm grip of my two hands between the helo and the jagged rocks a hundred feet below. My legs flailed as I looked back toward the doorway of the helo.

Mike Wu stood there, a shiny silver spot on his forehead with a trail of dried blood from between his eyes and down the side of his nose. I remembered the special energy directing plate they'd implanted in the middle of his forehead. It had stopped the bullet. And I recalled the guy who had held his head and turned his face from me when he boarded the helicopter minutes before. Of course, it had been Wu.

I yelled to Jax, "Sunny's on the west end of Biotronics."

He looked at me, and his eyes showed he realized we had one more very deadly problem.

Wu's glare fixed on me, and I felt defenseless as I held onto the doorway. I looked below and saw the file boxes dangling in the cargo net. It was my only chance. As the helicopter swung out to round the ridge and go back to Biotronics, I dropped onto the pendulant net full of boxes and held tight.

Wu tried to catch a good glimpse of me, but could keep eye contact for no longer than a couple of seconds due to the swing of the net. I hoped he wouldn't hurt Jax—of course, that would be foolish since the major was also the pilot. Nevertheless, I wouldn't put anything past this madman. He seemed solely out for revenge. Otherwise, he would have hidden with the group and waited until we were a safe distance away before seeking his retribution.

As the helicopter avoided a tall evergreen, the cargo net swung out again. This time, Wu dropped from the doorway, his body falling toward me, with intentions of grabbing the net thirty feet below.

I ducked as he caught the roping with his right hand, his left grabbing the back of my collar, and he hung on tenaciously.

I felt the tingling at the base of my head again as he held on behind me, and I was sure after all I'd been through, I would be no match for him.

The pains shot to my temples, and the heat became intense. I looked back at his forceful stare and realized he didn't appear affected by me in the slightest. Again, my nose bled and eyes became bleary. Pressure built under my skull.

* * *

I fast-forward again, to find a way to stop him, the near-future image blinking like a shorting light. A hundred yards ahead is the tree that will knock us from the net and down to our deaths on the jagged rocks below.

* * *

I hoped Wu had a firm hold because, if he didn't, what I was about to do would kill us both before any tree.

I let go of the net, relying solely on Wu's right hand's grip of the roping and of my collar. We turned out, and before he could release me to let me fall to my death, I grabbed his arm. We faced the treetop of the ancient redwood. He let go of my collar, but as he did, I caught his belt and pulled myself up behind him, then put him in a leg lock so that he couldn't turn around. As he tried to pry loose from my legs and elbowed my thighs and knees fiercely with his free arm, I clutched the net with one hand and dug into my front shirt pocket with the other. He was screaming at me now, cursing in what I guessed was a Chinese dialect, making my next step easy. After finding the suicide pill, I quickly pulled it out, forced it between his angry lips, and gave him a quick but awkward uppercut.

It is the thought that counts, I remembered, because this action didn't matter when we hit the tree. As I released Wu and scrambled across the webbing hand over hand away, the old redwood knocked the net out so violently the helicopter stammered. I held fast, but Wu was stricken free. It was like he'd been slammed by a giant flyswatter. He fell, his limbs splayed and motionless, eyes rolled back in their sockets, slowly tumbling head over ass one hundred feet to a rocky end.

When I looked back up to the chopper, Gunny Sampson was peering out the side doorway, the crew chief's helmet on his head. He gave me one of those man-that-was-close headshakes and then glanced over his shoulder. Looking back down at me, he stuck out his hand and four fingers. I knew we had four minutes to make it to safety.

Now, I looked for Sunny as we flew toward the pile of debris that used to be Mount Rainy Biotronics. We would only have time for one pass, and I wondered what I'd do if I didn't find her. Would I leap to my death and join her? Why not? She was the only thing I cared about, now.

We passed over the west side of Biotronics, where I was sure she had been. However, I saw neither Sunny nor Sarge. I felt the helo swing back in the opposite direction and realized Jax had determined we could risk no more time.

As I contemplated my end, I thought I saw something running through the trees near the road back to Gold Rush. It might have only been a deer, but I waved at Sampson. Finally getting his attention, I pointed to where I had seen movement.

He glanced over his shoulder toward Jax again, and the helo immediately followed my signal. Soon, below us were a German shepherd dog and a cut and bruised but beautiful redhead in a green running suit. My eyes moistened with joy, and briefly I put aside the fact that it might be too late. Soon we would be together, rejoined—that was the important thing.

Sunny waved at the chopper as she and Sarge ran to an opening in the trees. Jax brought the helicopter in fast, but close enough for the dog to leap to me. With both feet and one arm hooked into the netting, I helped the large animal find a halfway secure footing on top of the boxes. Then I reached out for Sunny as she ran alongside. She grabbed my shoulder and the chopper rose quickly to avoid more trees. Still holding to me with one arm, she found footholds and looped her other arm into the net.

The smile Sunny gave me was worth the risk. It was worth eternity, worth my life and death. We held onto one another as tightly as if we melded into a single body.

As we slowly ascended toward the low point of the crest's saddle, I looked over my shoulder to the ground and saw the large rocks we'd passed over only a moment before when Wu fell. About two hundred feet below, his body lay spread-eagle on a large, flat rock. It was obvious he'd landed on his head, his blood in a crimson splatter. Five feet from his corpse was a small, cupped object shining in the first rays of morning light—the steel plate they'd implanted in his forehead.

"You're hurt!" Sunny said. She was staring at my side with concern.

"Rajiv said it's only a flesh wound."

She seemed reassured as our eyes locked, exploring each other's thoughts. With our faces only inches apart, we drew nearer and kissed briefly, however, passionately.

But a violent turbulence interrupted our reverie, and caused the dog to lose his balance and nearly fall. We were suddenly watching the tail ends of four fighter planes from their jet wash. I wasn't sure what type of jets they were. But I *was* sure what types they were not—they were not American fighter jets, at least not like any I'd ever seen. I noted their parallel, twin-vertical stabilizers similar to our F-14 and 15s. They sped past at nearly Mach speed, and with vapor trails curving from their wingtips, they banked at the other end of the airfield over two miles away. As the second jumbo jet cleared the runway and began to follow the first, another group of four of the fighter jets came up from the left—too far away to discern their markings.

"SU-27 Flankers," I realized aloud—the ones Jax said were coming. "What the hell are they doing here?" Were they from Cuba? Could a Russian aircraft carrier get anywhere near close enough to launch a flight this deep into the U.S.? How could they expect to survive, or was this some sort of kamikaze suicide mission? Had the world been turned completely upside down in my two-year stupor, and the Russians or the Communists taken over our land? Or had I returned from one of my trips to the ether into some sort of parallel universe in which the United States no longer existed?

Whatever the answer, I knew as soon as any of the fighter planes were pointing back in our direction, we'd be shot down, and so would the 747s loaded with over four thousand people.

The huge jumbo jets looked like cumbersome dirigibles compared to the supersonic Flankers. They seemed to inch away from the airstrip as the fighter jets zoomed past. Obviously, the new pilots of the big passenger jets were pushing their unfamiliar aircraft to their limits to avoid the smaller fighters, but they wouldn't stand a chance.

Sunny looked up to Sampson who was still leaning from the cargo doorway of the helicopter. She yelled, "The DHILs," her lips exaggerating every syllable.

Sampson still looked back, obviously not understanding this code or whatever it was that Sunny was speaking. He certainly couldn't hear her words over the noisy helicopter motors, had to rely solely on reading her lips.

She repeated, slower, even more exaggerated, "DHIL."

He got it. Sampson gave a quick nod and turned back inside. I guessed he was conferring with Jax or giving instructions to one of the other men.

Seconds later, I noticed some kind of aircraft coming in from the opposite direction of the Flankers. At about two hundred yards away, it crossed our earlier path. It was an odd sort of plane, all black and triangular shaped. Probably going near Mach speed, it suddenly accelerated even faster, now the rapid pulsing of its engines—a sort of loud sputtering explosion—overwhelmed even our helicopter's roar. This new plane streaked away, flying past the Flankers, over the next mountain ridge and disappearing before the SU-27s had time to even think about it. The contrail it left was as strange as the plane, looking like a white rope full of knots.

Sunny must have seen me staring at the thing's contrail signature.

"Donuts on a rope," she said, as I turned to her smiling face. "The Aurora."

The name sounded familiar. A concept plane—a top secret futuristic military aircraft that can fly seven times the speed of sound by virtue of a pulse-detonation wave engine. I was confused of why, and I was sure the Flanker pilots would be also, but not for long.

Suddenly, the dawn sky filled with white streaks and in the next instant several of the SU-27s fired their countermeasures and jockeyed to avoid destruction from the incoming missiles. When I looked to the horizon in the opposite direction I couldn't yet see where the rockets had come from.

A couple of seconds later Sunny tugged on my arm.

Her eyes were wide, staring back toward the landing field. "They're lined up on us."

When I turned to see, white bursts came from two of the Flanker fighters and four air-to-air missiles shrieked toward us. The helo that carried us was much slower than even the jumbo jets, and its over-loaded cargo hampered it even more. Jax put the big whirlybird into a steep bank and tried to climb even faster.

As the missiles came, mere seconds away from detonation, chaff flares shot from both sides of our chopper—three dozen bright, smoky streamers—and the enemy missiles discharged as they flew through the countermeasures.

Sunny and I hid our faces from the explosions that jostled us harshly, but nothing could be done about Sarge. The fierce shockwave knocked him from the top of the cargo and he fell. As he tumbled past, Sunny and I each freed an arm, and in desperation we caught him by a front and hind leg. The heavy animal hung precariously for a brief time until, with great effort, we achieved better grips.

When a dozen F/A-22 Raptor stealth fighters streaked in, three flights of four, I found new confidence. I had no doubt they were our own made-*mostly*-in-the-good-'ol-U.S.A aircraft. But I'd had no idea there were that many of these next generation fighter planes in existence, and that they were even beyond prototype. I had been gone a long time.

They fired four more of their missiles that darted toward their targets. The SU-27s dispersed in short order and in unison, avoiding the incoming missiles.

The Flankers returned missiles to the Raptors. Some of their rockets came so close to the Raptors, a couple appeared to even go through the fast moving fighter planes. But none hit their targets, and the missiles either disappeared from sight or exploded on a mountain ridge. When they fired their missiles again, the results were similar, except two that seemed to pass through the F/A-22s struck an SU-27 coming up from the other side, destroying it in a huge fireball. The Flanker flying on the downed aircraft's wing returned fire, one of its missiles also harmlessly penetrating an F/A-22 Raptor, but striking another SU-27. I couldn't understand what I was seeing. It didn't make sense—the Flankers seemed to be shooting at each other, downing their own comrades.

And Sunny was cheering.

The damaged Flanker lost one wing to its comrade's exploding missile, and it spiraled down, its two pilots ejecting out to apparent safety.

"They're confused!" Sunny yelled to me. "They don't understand why they don't see the Raptors on their radar screens—why they can't get a weapon's lock—why their missiles are all missing. I'll bet their scared shitless!" She laughed.

The Flanker pilots weren't the only ones confused.

With the SU-27s in utter disarray, the two jumbo jets were just making the mountain ridge two miles to our left. That ridge would help protect them from nuclear destruction.

Four of the F/A-22s cruised nearby apparently guarding their exit, and the last of the SU-27 Flankers streaked over a far mountain ridge, driven from the area. I imagined the Flankers would be regrouping. But then, after what they'd just been through, we might not have to deal with them again.

After reaching the other side of the protective ridge, the jumbo jets dove out of sight, and the last flight of four F/A-22 Raptors banked sharply and disappeared from view. I felt incredible relief that the thousands of Gold Rush residents had overcome the impossible and made it this far.

But our air show wasn't over. From the direction the Raptors had come, a flight of four World War II vintage P-51 mustangs buzzed in, painted black and yellow like bumble bees. Behind them were four P-40 Warhawks, Flying Tigers complete with shark's mouth paint job. As soon as they disappeared over the mountain ridge, three World War I era SPAD biplanes droned into view, headed in the same direction. I had to shake my head in disbelief.

The next plane that appeared was the kicker—a single biplane, simple in design making me think of the Wright's Model A.

We seemed to be directly in its flight path, and as it neared, I was concerned it would fly too close. But it kept coming. Now, I could see two people in the open aircraft. They sat side-by-side, wearing the old leather pilot's caps and goggles.

"What are they doing?" I yelled out above the helicopter's roar.

Sunny turned to see them, and her only reaction was a smile that I took as one a proud mother would give her child.

Surely Jax would divert the helicopter before we met the small plane. But our helicopter stayed its course.

Gripping the dog tightly and realizing a midair collision was imminent, I stared at the slowly approaching antique biplane.

I gritted my teeth, seeing the pilots.

They were both smiling.

The small biplane loomed before us.

I could read their names on the front of their aviator's hats. *Wilbur* one said. The other *Orville*. They still smiled like crazed Japanese *baka* pilots—kamikazes.

Collision imminent, I braced myself protectively against Sunny.

Bright lights from the ground—perhaps three spaced a considerable distance apart—blinded me.

The Wright Brothers' classic plane passed through us, and the intense lights were gone.

There was no impact, no turbulence, not even additional prop wash from the small craft's push prop.

I turned to watch it edge away. In a few seconds, it dimmed and disappeared—not flying out of range of sight, or behind the mountains. It just vanished.

Sunny was still smiling, straining to help hold Sarge. "I pieced it together pretty quickly," she said and turned to me. "Didn't have time to edit that last part out. But it worked. Holographic aviation models."

I looked at her perplexed.

"The DHID. It's a large-scale, dynamic hologram illumination device. I designed it. What you just saw was its first practical field testing."

The F/A-22s were mere holograms—the Aurora, the Wright plane? Impressive, it was, but I had little time to be impressed. My hold on Sarge grew weaker, and I wouldn't be able to manage it much longer even with Sunny's help. We each had one arm still hooked in the cargo net and the other around the shepherd. The dog didn't struggle and was obediently calm, but he was a big dog. I hoped we would clear the danger and find a safe place to put down soon.

I turned to find our last hurdle directly in front of us. We approached the ridge much too low. I suspected the crest's altitude was near, if not over, the helicopter's ceiling with such a heavy payload. If there were more time, we could set down, get into the helicopter and leave the cargo net full of valuable records. But we would be lucky to make the ridge in time as it was.

The chopper's rotor accelerated to its maximum and the twin-engine turbos rapped loud and tight. We climbed, steadily, but so terribly slow, I set my jaw as if that would help. We neared the ridgeline—two hundred yards, a hundred and fifty.

Gunny Sampson stuck his head out, looked up at the ridge, then back at us. He seemed to be listening over his shoulder. He looked down at us, made a hooking motion with his arm and then held it to his chest, signaling for us to hold on.

Sampson showed us ten fingers. Then nine. Then eight. He counted down the time to the first nuclear bomb's detonation. At seven, Sampson gave a quick salute and ducked back inside. Sunny and I embraced and held onto Sarge like we were about to ride a roller coaster to Hell.

I counted down the first explosion in my head as I looked into Sunny's eyes, remembering that there would be yet a second detonation five seconds following it.

Five.

We weren't going to make it, fifty yards from the ridge, the helicopter seeming sluggish, now, at its limit and barely creeping higher.

Four.

"I love you," I told her.

Three.

She yelled back, "And I love you. Forever."

Two.

We kissed.

One.

I held Sunny close and watched over her shoulder as the bomb buried deep within Mount Rainy exploded five miles away. The entire Biotronics facility pushed out from the mountain, mostly in one piece for a fraction of a second. A forceful conflagration followed, fire and smoke engulfing and pulverizing to dust and ashes anything that had been recognizable, launching fiery debris miles into the air. Then the shockwave came, like a thousand-mile-an-hour freight train of destruction, it rolled down from the leveled mountainside toward the town before me. The ground buckled in huge waves, racing toward us. Buildings and homes tossed, crumbled. I knew we had only a couple of seconds before the second explosion annihilated us also—it was less than two miles away and above ground. Although that blast was imminent, I feared the tsunami of earth that shoved toward us from the first one, now streaking up the hillside below, toppling large trees and tossing boulders into the air under our feet. Then, it hit.

The shockwave struck us with an incredible gust of hot wind, and the helicopter flew wildly, nearly out of control, being pushed up toward the rocky crest.

Somehow, we topped the rim, our cargo net scraping against the rocks, sending us into a tumultuous spin.

Seemingly gaining some control after cresting, Jax forced the helicopter into a severe dive over the backside of the ridge, and I felt it in my stomach.

Chapter 40

The light is blinding.

The shockwave of the closer, above ground bomb follows much quicker and hits us as if we've struck a concrete embankment.

I lose Sunny and Sarge in the dust cloud and only know I'm falling. Evergreen limbs lash at me time and time again, and I land on a mattress of pine needles. The wind is incredible, burning hot, yellow with pungent smoke and ash, and dark with dust.

* * *

A moment passed before I realized a body lay across me, and I prayed it was a living one.

"Sunny," I called out, the sound of a hundred tornadoes engulfing us.

"I'm here, Dan," she yelled. "I'm right here. I'm okay, sweetheart."

I was sure she was delusional, and I was disappointed the first name she called was her husband's.

As the wind calmed and the air cleared enough for us to see the eighteen inches separating our faces, I said, "Sunny, it's me, Robert."

I noticed her sweatshirt torn at the right shoulder, and I inspected her skin for an injury.

She smiled at me. "Danny," she said and touched my face. "We made it."

She hadn't heard me. "Sunny, I'm Robert."

I noticed the mole on her right shoulder. It was the mole missing from Michelle's shoulder. It was the sexy mole I wanted to see there, the one Harvey—Sunny—had pointed out wasn't on Michelle's skin.

Her face straightened. She looked seriously into my eyes. "Sweetheart. Don't you know? There is no Robert Weller. You're Daniel McMaster. You're my husband."

I blinked in surprise, trying to piece it all together, and we kissed, but as we did, I couldn't help but analyze and question what she was telling me.

When we pulled back, I asked, "Why didn't you tell me before?"

"Danny, would you have believed me? Or would you've thought I was nuts and pushed me away?"

"I don't know." For only the second time since this morning, I knew what I was being told was the truth.

"I wasn't sure at first," she said. "Everyone thought you were some kind of brainwashed duplicate or clone that only looked a little like you. Then, when I saw you in the park I knew it. That little nose job and the hair die they gave you couldn't fool me—they even added pigment to your eyes to change them to brown."

I touched my hair and then felt the bridge of my nose.

"I knew for sure in the morgue when I saw the dark spot between your thumb and forefinger. It was such a small detail, they had no reason to duplicate it. But I knew it was from pencil lead. You'd told me about the third-grade bully that stabbed you with a pencil when you were defending a little girl classmate. You've had the graphite scar ever since. Even after I saw the proof, it was easy to pretend Robert and Dan were two different people. You were always so critical of yourself. But that doesn't matter, now. We made it through the tough part. Now we've got to get home."

But I didn't know where home was.

The radioactivity was worrisome. I glanced around at the dust. The blast had dissipated the snow cover that had been there only a minute before. "Radiation in the dust," I told her. "We're being poisoned."

"We were several miles from the blast," she said as if she knew what she was talking about. "The fallout yet to come will probably be worse than what's in the air now.

They have potassium iodide treatments now, and new drugs made from turtle's blood." She smiled. "Maybe we can be guinea pigs."

"Turtle's blood?" I shook my head and patted her knee, a great relief beginning to set in. "Sounds like a slow remedy. Think we can talk them into using greyhound blood instead?"

She kept her smile and put her arm on my shoulder.

Whether we'd be affected permanently or even fatally by the radiation would depend upon how much we'd inhaled and were now inhaling. After tearing a sleeve from the opposite arm of my now already tattered, dark-blue fatigue shirt, I ripped it into two strips and fashioned makeshift dust masks out of the two pieces. We quickly put them to our faces and helped each other tie them around our heads.

In the meantime, Sarge came trotting up, whining and wagging his tail anxiously, and we both greeted him with enthusiasm, joyful he was alive.

"He's yours," Sunny said.

I could have guessed. I hugged the dog. Sunny began to tear her right sleeve off the rest of the way, and I helped her. We made a scarf over Sarge's muzzle, and I was a little surprised he didn't seem to mind playing our version of nuclear-fallout dress-up.

"What now?" Sunny asked, stroking the dog's neck.

I remembered the map the dying helicopter pilot had given me, the one that was taken away from me at Biotronics. I was wearing the fatigues of the guy who had stuffed the map into his pocket. I unsnapped one of the side thigh pockets and reached inside. The map was still there. I pulled it out, and unfolded the laminated paper.

Sunny asked, "Where's Jax?"

"Jax was piloting the chopper. I hope they made it okay. I don't want to find their wreckage."

"That wind was so bad," Sunny said.

I nodded back, translating the frown that accompanied her words—that Jax and everyone in the helicopter might have run out of luck.

"Where do we go?" she asked.

I kept the large topographical chart folded in quarters for convenience and ran my finger over it. None of the places looked familiar on this section. The names were all wrong. I tried to sound out a couple, but I couldn't to my satisfaction. Then, Sunny pointed to a hand-drawn circle near the middle of the map and the hand-printed words Gold Rush.

"There," she said.

I searched near her finger, trying to find Summitview, but couldn't, not even penciled in. Couldn't find Denver, or Colorado Springs, or Estes Park.

"What the hell's going on?" I asked glaring at the map. "This isn't Colorado!"

Sunny gazed at me, dumbfounded. "Oh, Danny, I'm sorry. I took for granted you knew by now."

The sound of the helicopter drawing near uplifted my heart. The chopper's rotor kicked up dust once again as I found on the map a machine-printed name that looked, sounded familiar. I'd heard it somewhere, but never associated with Colorado. I read it aloud, "Qinghai Province."

I thought of the POWs, Dr. Yumi and the Falon Gong, and the Flanker fighter jets.

Sunny was smiling at something downhill, and I turned to find out what it was. Through the dust, a man emerged wearing a flight helmet and a big smile. It was Jax. An image formed quickly in my mind. This one wasn't framed by some sort of viewing screen, and I immediately realized it was a scrap of actual memory. I remembered this same smiling face without the helmet, Jax wearing a tux, handing me a ring, huge flowers all around. I recalled taking the ring and turning to the woman to my left—Sunny, smiling big, sublimely warm eyes. I remembered the feeling inside my chest—how I compared it then to the first time I stepped from a jet at 20,000 feet for a HALO parachute jump. The memory made me smile.

I looked down at the map and unfolded it completely.

A word was printed at the top in large letters.

CHINA.

Chapter 41

My mind numbed.

When Jax stepped up, he said, "Looks like we lost most of your records of proof."

I scanned about us, and in the slowly clearing air, I saw the broken cargo net draped halfway over a small twisted pine tree. A few sheets of paper were stuck to it, and some danced in the dust around us. Several busted video cassettes lay scattered at the base of the tree along with empty cardboard file boxes. Two of Jax's men were picking up what they could quickly gather.

I pointed to my temple. "It's all up here."

Sunny, pulled her scarf down and said to Jax, her face beaming, "It's him, Jax, Dan!"

He returned her smile, and his eyes met mine. "I know. Known it since Sarge greeted him at the chopper, and then *he* started telling *me* what had to be done." He chuckled as did I.

Two more flights of four jet fighters streaked in overhead, as Jax and Sampson helped Sunny, Sarge and me to the helicopter.

Sunny and I looked at Jax questioningly. He relieved us both when he said, "They're ours. F/A-18 Super Hornets from the Abraham Lincoln in the Bay of Bengal. They're going to escort us out."

Several explosions came from the distance, and again I looked at Jax for an answer to my unspoken question.

"Cruise missiles armed with electromagnetic charges. They're making sure we did a good job of knocking out all the radar on the way in. We're pretty popular now. Got lots of friends in high places. President Mason is on our side. We've an AWACs monitoring our egress, a C-130 Black Talon meeting us halfway and flying point to the border, and there's a KC-135 on standby to refuel us when we cross."

"But China, Jax. They've got lots of defenses—and offenses. How can we possibly make it through? We're liable to start war."

"Just be concerned with getting out of here, now. Let the big boys worry about the war business. The Navy's been sending in all kinds of decoys—unmanned drones with big radar signatures. They've been hammering the Chinese communications and defensive radar network with EM charges on cruise missiles for the past ten minutes. We're hoping we can keep them confused long enough to slip away."

It wasn't a minute later, and we were sitting in the side doorway of Jax's crowded whirlybird. Sunny clung to me. Her head pressed to my chest as we lifted off. Dust was everywhere, pine needles in the air. We squinted to protect our eyes. Bitter smoke saturated the sky.

Sunny raised her face to my ear and said over the roar of the engines, "We have a daughter, Lilly. You call her Lill."

I turned to her, but had no words to answer. A daughter, not a son. Lill, not Will. I had felt a paternal void in my chest since discovering I had no son. The cavity suddenly filled with a warmth and brightness I could not describe. I pulled down my makeshift dust scarf and smiled. Sunny did the same, and our noses touched. We kissed.

* * *

As she rests her head back on my shoulder, my vision blurs.

The motion of the world around me speeds up, and I know I'm entering my subconsciously evoked remote-viewing mode again. My viewpoint leaves the helicopter and races, hugging the treetops, at what feels like gravity-escape velocity. The trees and landscape blur and the sun that has just risen sets and rises again. News reports flash before me like paper in the wind.

In my mind, I reach out and grab one, and it says:

September 27

War with China Narrowly Averted—
Temporarily

Washington (AP)—President Mason announced today that a daring rescue was made deep in the heart of communist China, confirming rumors and conjecture circulating over the past twenty-four hours. He made strong accusations against the Chinese government and rebutted that country's allegations that the U.S., in support of the Falon Gong movement to overthrow the Communist regime, had "penetrated China's sovereign airspace to commit acts of war by attacking radar positions, shooting down aircraft and killing thousands of Chinese citizens . . . ."

The report tears away from my hands, and I immediately grab another.

September 28

American Commandos Return After Daring Rescue

Bangkok (UPI)—U.S. special forces troops returned here to Korat Royal Thailand Air Force Base from a military rescue mission deep inside China only two days ago, according to a U.S. Air Force spokesman today. Accompanying them were two jumbo passenger jets packed with over four thousand hostages previously held by the Chinese. Coordinating the mission was former U.S. Marine Force Recon Gunnery Sergeant Bernard Sampson, who is now an executive with Thai Air Travel . . . .

I found the next news leader interesting and I realized how a people's leadership can distort the truth to their own liking.

China Tests Defensive Non-Nuclear Weapon

Beijing (CNA)—President Sun Yung Jung of The People's Republic of China announced today the testing of two experimental, non-nuclear, fuel-air bombs as part of this country's strategic defense system. This report puts to rest the United States' unfounded claims that nuclear devices had been used to cover up a paranormal training camp . . . .

September 29

Most Members of Rescue Team from Local Base

Hurlburt Field, Florida—Air Force Special Operations Command (ASFOC) based here in the Florida panhandle confirmed today that the majority of the rescue team that played an important role in returning with over four thousand hostages were stationed at Hurlburt . . . .

Chinese Psychic Assassination Cell Discovered in Capitol

Washington (AP)—Hundreds of FBI and DC police raided the Biotronics apartments in Silver Spring early this morning after evidence of the harboring of illegal aliens with counterfeit passports and fake IDs was uncovered due to the daring raid into China three days ago . . . .

Missing McMaster Research Executive Rescued in China

San Bernardino (AP)—Daniel McMaster, founder and president of a locally based nonlethal weapons research company, McMaster Nonlethal Solutions, was one of several hundred American hostages rescued from China. According to some reports, much of the nonlethal weaponry used in the mission was developed by McMaster's company including acoustic cannons, radar jamming units and electromagnetic pulse devices that helped knock out critical radar and sensitive detection systems, which are a part of China's defense and early detection network . . . .

Colorado Ghost Town Model For Chinese Psychic Warrior Training Camp

Denver (AP)—Reports now surfacing indicate the Chinese prison camp, which had become home to thousands of hostages over a period of more than three decades, was modeled after the small Colorado ghost town of Gold Rush . . . .

Local Man Heroic Leader of Rescue Operation

Honolulu (AP)—Major Lionel Jackson, the son of a local pineapple grower, has been confirmed to have lead the daring and successful rescue of thousands of imprisoned people, many of them American citizens or born thereof . . . .

Psychic Assassins Unleashed on the World

London (UPI)—China's incredible plot to kill political and military leaders of the Free World through the use of Psychic Warriors, was only the beginning, according to . . . .

World Outraged Over Chinese Plot

New York (UPI)—The United Nations today approved a statement condemning the Chinese government for its role in the shocking plot to send out psychic assassins to murder key world leaders in order to gain world domination . . . .

I wasn't surprised to find the Chinese's propaganda machine again distorting the truth in the next headline.

October 8

U.S. Lies to World

Beijing (CNA)—Our honorable Chairman Yin expressed outrage today over the feeble attempt made by American military to conduct a raid and assist members of the outlawed Falon Gong movement. American claims of rescuing hostages held by the People's Republic of China are untrue. Chairman Yin confirmed that on September 18 American aircraft, led by their latest technology fighter planes, entered our sovereign airspace, but were turned away easily. In the brief but decisive encounter, eleven of the American warplanes were shot down without a single loss of the Peoples . . . .

After this last paper, the press reports quit coming, until, from some distance, what looks like another newspaper spins toward me. The thing approaches, twirling faster and faster, until it finally slaps into my face. I peel it off in the gusty air stream. It's the front page of the *New York Times* dated three weeks from today, it says:

October 18
CHINA DECLARES WAR!

The newspaper rips from my hands immediately and disappears. I am floating from a vantage point several thousand feet above the ground. Missiles launch from below. ICBMs. Multiple warhead, ten and twenty-*megaton* hydrogen bombs are aloft. These weapons are not merely city killers—their blast radius' alone could be up to a hundred miles. I pray this view is of some sort of movie again—a Cold-War-era film about nuclear war with the Soviets, *Dr. Strangelove* perhaps—but I know better.

The rockets swoosh by close enough for me to see the Chinese flags on their nosecones. Then from above the horizon to the north come more missiles, these are heading in, just reentering the atmosphere. The newcomers proudly display American Flags.

In the incredible conflagrations that follow, the ground quakes and the air itself shudders in a hellish ferment. The Earth's mantle blazes.

Time passes quickly, and from my viewpoint I scan over the scorched ground and the charred remains of cities—Beijing, LA, Chicago, New York, Washington DC. I follow a huge yellow cloud glowing in a nuclear midnight as it engulfs the cities of London, Madrid, Paris, Berlin, Moscow and Tokyo.

* * *

My view altered abruptly, like the changing of television channels, and I felt Sunny shaking my arm. I was back in the present, inside the chopper. Sunny gazed at me, worry filling her face.

"Are you okay, Dan?" she yelled over the noisy helicopter. She smiled, hopefully.

My eyes were moist with emotion. I didn't smile back, knowing the world faced nuclear devastation in three weeks, and I realized what must be done to stop it, what I must tell the President. We clung to each other.

The rest of the flight to the Thailand border was for the most part uneventful as we hugged the treetops all the way. The electromagnetic pulse devices Jax's team used to slip into China had fried all the electronics in their path—every radar, missile guidance system and toaster. The few SAMs that popped up spiraled away from lack of guidance or fell short because of the distance from which they were launched.

At the Thai border, our fighter escort had a confrontation, and we lost one of the Super Hornets and its brave young pilot as three Flankers were downed. Everyone else made it out okay.

Gunny Sampson's Thai wife met us at the airport gate. A beautiful woman with long black hair, her smile was warm and genuine. She wore a rich, floral-ceremonial kimono, and she kept her hands to her back. I reached out to greet her with a handshake, thinking that although I couldn't remember this woman, we'd been good friends in the past, and she would be used to this Western custom. Instead of only her hand, she pulled from behind her a little blonde friend wearing a kimono matching hers. I knew in my heart immediately it was my daughter Lilly.

Epilogue

It is early evening of the eighteenth of October. I've been trying to get used to being Daniel McMaster after leaving Robert Weller in China three weeks ago. I'm sitting with Sunny and my daughter Lill on a sofa in the cabin of our new sailing yacht that I have christened *The Chairman*. It's evening, and the porthole shades are drawn. Sarge sits on a rug in front of us and a Chinese/American dictionary is laying open on the nearby lamp stand. We're anchored in a small northern California cove, and the only light inside our comfortable sailboat is from the television set before us. We're watching *CNN Headline News*.

With my arms around my girls, I'm content but not satisfied. Memories of my past life haven't been restored. I get flashes of the real thing but never much more than a few seconds worth. I've been able to remote view and revisit some of the events from my past. However, I see those times as a spectator, never as a player, and I'm sure the emotions aren't the same.

I consider my friends from the Chinese's Gold Rush. Rajiv has been given back his old position as chief neurosurgeon at the Mayo Clinic in Chicago. Chief Dailey and his Chinese wife and children have been given new identifications. He's been promoted to the rank of Sergeant Major, time-in-grade so to speak, and is working in a top-secret department at the Pentagon. Mr. Banks and his family are cooperating with the gag request from the Executive Office and have new identities and homes in the DC area, also. It was a big surprise to find out his son was the U.S. Secretary of Defense—his American wife had passed away years ago. I was privileged to witness the son and father's private and tearful reunion. Secretary Banks seemed overwhelmed but ecstatic about suddenly having a step mother, half-sister and niece—and of course, about his father being alive.

But most of the remaining 4,000 citizens of the Chinese town of Gold Rush are living at a secret and remote U.S. facility in Thailand. They're slowly being reprogrammed and repatriated. It could be as many as three years before they're able to be repatriated into the U.S. and their other home countries.

As for us, becoming reacquainted with who I am will have to be postponed because of a phone call fifteen minutes ago. I've yet to tell Sunny or Lill. The caller was Jax. He said it wasn't over. According to evidence found in the few records we'd brought back from China, there are as many as fourteen psychic assassins and their handlers—sleeper cells—already in place in the U.S. and around the world. We will start "somehow rounding them up" first thing tomorrow.

On the TV, the anchorwoman summarizes the President's afternoon press conference, and how, amazingly, the relations between China and the Free World—especially the U.S.—have improved greatly. China has inexplicably warmed up to the West, has shown a willingness to agree with disarmament treaties and make concessions on human rights. Some speculate the President has some sort of secret bargaining chip he's using to sway them toward Western ideology.

I think of my implanted enhancement device and wonder if it still works after being subjected to the powerful electromagnetic pulses from the two 20-kiloton nuclear bombs. I hope I'm never tested, that I never have to find out.

A Dentisol toothpaste commercial comes on saying, "Nothing is fresher than a Dentisol fresh mouth," and I smile.

* * *

It is early morning on the other side of the world. In a luxurious bedroom in Beijing, the Chairman of the Chinese Communist Party sleeps fitfully. His wife is slumbering peacefully beside him.

Chairman Yin has complained to his physicians of bouts with insomnia, severe headaches and chest pressure. None of the prescribed medications, natural healing herbs, or even acupuncture has helped.

Now he is dreaming, his eyes racing from side to side in REM sleep. In his dreams comes a mild voice. It speaks in Chinese like a whisper in the dark. *I'm watching you—I'm always watching you!*

The Chairman sits up abruptly, startled awake, wide-eyed and panting, beads of perspiration on his face.

For the fifth night in a row, a grinning face appears following the Chairman's nightmares—Daniel McMaster's face. The image laughs.

On this same morning before sunrise, bodyguards find Chinese Premier Sin Jou hiding in his closet. The only thing they can make out from the Premier's irrational babblings is that he is sure his mansion is haunted.

Across town, President Sun Yung Jung has decided to take up residence with the forty-eight man security detail assigned to him. He seems to have become hooked on amphetamines, only napping occasionally in the middle of the barracks with never less than twenty-four members of his special security unit standing guard around him.

* * *

In the cabin of our sailboat, I change the channels. In calm water, the satellite TV works well, and *Old TV* is on—*Andy of Mayberry*. I chuckle as Opie baits a fishhook with a worm. The humor is bittersweet, and I'm sure Lill and Sunny don't understand when they look up at me. I pull my girls close and hug them, and I think about . . . *you*.

Have you ever had one of those dreams that seems too real to be *only* a dream? When you lie awake at night, do you ever wonder if you're dreaming—if your reality is your dreams and your dreams have somehow become your reality? When you wake up tomorrow morning, think

about what I'm asking you—question, just for a second, if the person lying beside you is really your mate? Are those memories of yours real or are they scripted video implanted into your psyche? And what about those déjà vu moments that make you pause?

Be careful my friend. Watch for the little inconsistencies, those moments that make you wonder if you're living on a stage according to someone else's program. If somebody's guiding you along—behind the scenes, pulling your strings—according to *their* wishes.

Never forget this: all that you know is lies—merely what *they* want you to know. Trust solely in your emotions—only within emotions will you find the real truth.

Be ready. They will come for you soon.

The End?

If you enjoyed *Brainstorm* and have any comments or questions, please share them with the author:
Gordon A. Kessler:
Gordon@GordonKessler.com

Gordon is a member of the Indie Writers Alliance:
www.IndieWritersAlliance.com
Writers who dare to be independent!

Please check out Gordon A. Kessler's other thrillers:
Jezebel and *Dead Reckoning*
His book on fiction writing *Novel Writing Made Simple*
And his short stories: "Jack Knight" (nostalgia/coming of age) and "Toothpick for Two" (humor)

Connect with me online:
Facebook: http://facebook.com/GordonKessler
https://www.smashwords.com/profile/view/readersmatrix

www.ingramcontent.com/pod-product-compliance
Lightning Source LLC
Chambersburg PA
CBHW030822310726
48980CB00006B/588/J

* 9 7 8 0 9 8 3 1 9 0 5 2 3 *